"Bevard is a remarkable talent." - Brian Keene, author of *The Rising* and *Island of the Dead*

"The single creepiest book I've read this year... a slow descent into madness... freezes the blood." - Ben Young, author of *Stuck* and *Home*

"Hardcore horror in the best sense of the term." - *Hellnotes*

JUNKMAN

CHRISTOPHER BEVARD

Junkman
Copyright © 2025 Christopher Bevard. All rights reserved.

4 Horsemen
Publications, Inc.

Published By: 4 Horsemen Publications, Inc.

4 Horsemen Publications, Inc.
PO Box 419
Sylva, NC 28779
4horsemenpublications.com
info@4horsemenpublications.com

Cover & Typesetting by Autumn Skye
Edited by Joseph Mistretta

All rights to the work within are reserved to the author and publisher. No part of this publication may be reproduced, stored in a retrieval system, or transmitted in any form or by any means, electronic, mechanical, photocopying, recording, scanning, or otherwise, except as permitted under Section 107 or 108 of the 1976 International Copyright Act, without prior written permission except in brief quotations embodied in critical articles and reviews. Please contact either the Publisher or Author to gain permission.

All characters, organizations, and events portrayed in this novel are either products of the author's imagination or are used fictitiously. No generative artificial intelligence was used in the creation of this book or its cover.

All brands, quotes, and cited work respectfully belongs to the original rights holders and bear no affiliation to the authors or publisher.

Library of Congress Control Number: 2025948385

Paperback ISBN-13: 979-8-8232-1030-0
Hardcover ISBN-13: 979-8-8232-1031-7
Ebook ISBN-13: 979-8-8232-1032-4

This is a work of fiction. Any resemblance to persons living or dead, places, or situations is purely coincidental.

CONTENTS

I: SCARECROW

Chapter 1 1
Chapter 2 12
Chapter 3 18
Chapter 4 21
Chapter 5 25
Chapter 6 30
Chapter 7 35
Chapter 8 38
Chapter 9 44
Chapter 10 56
Chapter 11 68
Chapter 12 72
Chapter 13 78
Chapter 14 82
Chapter 15 88
Chapter 16 94
Chapter 17 98

Chapter 18 107
Chapter 19 110
Chapter 20. 114
Chapter 21 118
Chapter 22. 129
Chapter 23. 137
Chapter 24. 140
Chapter 25 143
Chapter 26 148
Chapter 27 151
Chapter 28. 157
Chapter 29 165

II: THE TROPHY

Chapter 30. 172
Chapter 31 185
Chapter 32. 188
Chapter 33. 200
Chapter 34. 213
Chapter 35. 225
Chapter 36 233
Chapter 37. 238
Chapter 38 251
Chapter 39. 255
Chapter 40. 265
Chapter 41 275
Chapter 42. 278

III: TRICKS

Chapter 43. 284
Chapter 44. 286
Chapter 45. 290
Chapter 46 302

Chapter 47 313
Chapter 48 317
Chapter 49 322
Chapter 50 324
Chapter 51 329
Chapter 52 345
Chapter 53 353
Chapter 54 358
Chapter 55 360
Chapter 56 362
Chapter 57 367
Chapter 58 369
Chapter 59 372
Chapter 60 375
Chapter 61 377
Chapter 62 380

Book Club Questions 385

I: SCARECROW

1

Uncle Tony used to tell them that Grandpa kept a devil in the attic. It lived in a wardrobe, Tony explained, but it didn't mind being closed up because it could still play tricks on them whenever it wanted.

Of course, Mark knew it was bullshit; Uncle Tony loved telling stories to freak people out. When Mark was eleven and Ann was still six, he overheard Tony and Grandpa Brunner (Brute for short, his Marine nickname that continued with him into old age like an anchor) laughing about it in the kitchen. Nevertheless, Tony's delivery was convincing and—even with the benefit of the truth—a little frightening; Ann bought it fully. On half a dozen occasions, she asked Tony what it looked like, and their uncle just smiled—wickedly at first, but then softening a little, a way of letting her in on the con—and said that he'd never actually laid eyes on it. Ann would cast a slow, cautious eye toward the pull-chain over their heads when they went to their bedrooms at night, the little cord dangling out of the ceiling that gave entry to the attic, and, apparently, the presence of absolute, unerring evil.

By the time Mark was a teenager and Ann was in junior high, Brute's house was no longer a place of potentially illicit wonder; rather, it was just a modest, increasingly dated Colonial home built in the early 1950s where they'd sit in front of the TV and share shallow platitudes with the old man, as he was never very conversational; he was pleasant, but not that interested in deep philosophical dives with his adolescent grandchildren. Still, to a teenaged Mark, he seemed to be a troubled, contemplative man, one who spent perhaps too much time in his own head cultivating nostalgia or regret, a wan little smile creeping into his face when they'd talk about their late Grandma Lynn or something that happened when their mother Audrey and Tony were kids.

Regardless, Mark and Ann tried to make visiting Brute a regular part of their routine throughout high school and even into college when Mark was at WIU, just forty or so miles away. They'd go over with their parents—sometimes just the two of them once Mark had a car—and they'd have a simple dinner, maybe soup and sandwiches, sometimes spaghetti, followed by a cup of coffee and a little TV. Every now and again on those nights, as Mark was clearing the table or making coffee, he would see Ann standing at the landing where the steps made a sharp, ninety-degree turn to the right, staring at that corner of the ceiling.

"I heard something up there," she'd say with a kind of detached concern in her voice, as though it wasn't really hers to deal with, but something someone should be aware of.

CHAPTER 1

"Squirrels, Annie," he'd say. "Remember, Mom and Dad said they had to lend Grandpa three grand last year to fix his roof?"

Her brow would furrow a bit. "Squirrels wouldn't live long stuck in an attic, would they?"

"They wouldn't be stuck. They've probably chewed their way out, right through the wood." And then he'd make little gnawing sounds, imitating a buck-toothed squirrel chomping through wood. When she was younger, it made her laugh, though Ann grew serious in her later teen years, and it became harder and harder to bring her joy, for whatever unknown reason.

"Maybe," she'd say, and eventually, she'd rejoin them in the living room, where any one of a variety of nighttime cop dramas was playing, *Hunter* or *Magnum PI* or some one-named, sleazily attractive guy who drove a hot car and collected a new blonde each week after solving oddly convoluted crimes. How could Ann possibly still cling to that silly story designed to keep them from going up and mucking around with Brute's antiques from the war (his clothes and his rusty gun with the notches in it which they knew about because of course they'd snuck up there anyway), not to mention the old trunks full of clothes, jackets, musty-smelling dresses, holiday cards, and decorations, all of it?

Mark remembered the last time they'd been up there; it was around the same time that their mother had tried to set up half of the attic as a little art studio for the two of them, though once Brute saw what she was doing, the devil story came into play.

"I don't want them up there, Audrey," Mark had heard Brute telling their mother one afternoon when

JUNKMAN

Ann came down covered in finger paint. "They got no business being around the things that I keep up there."

"What on earth does that mean, Dad? What are you keeping up there? You dealing coke now? Hiding bodies for the Galesburg mob?" She'd chuckled and shrugged it off, but Brute had only given her a troubled look in response, and she dismantled most of their makeshift art studio anyway, repurposing it in Ann's room instead: a simple wooden easel and desk chair, a little telephone stand for some paints and brushes.

And there they still stood, thirty-one years later.

Mark stared at the easel, coated in dust, propped in the corner of what had been Ann's room for that time when they'd lived with Brute. The telephone stand was still there, too, albeit devoid of paint. The child's presence that had once filled that room was gone, and now it was just more stuff that had aged along with everything else. It had been seven weeks since Brute's funeral, and Mark was nearly finished moving his things from his scant little studio apartment in Knox Village—Galesburg's enclave of affordable, shoebox apartments designed for students at the local college—to the three-bedroom, two-bath house on the edge of Day Street where Alfred and Lynnette Brunner had lived out almost sixty years of marriage.

The attic turned out to be just an attic, and an uncomfortable one to boot, nothing like the musty playground he and Ann had taken it for as children. An unreasonably low ceiling with wooden beams offering splinters if you leaned against them, boxes filled with old photos, school papers, and winter coats. There was the aforementioned chifforobe where the devil supposedly lived—a seven-foot slab of oak with ornately carved doors and a two-inch-thick sliding bar to hold it shut, along with some worn-out dining chairs.

Might as well give up the ghost, Mark thought with a smile, sliding the wooden bolt and opening the doors to the antique closet. The doors creaked with mild resistance, and inside, there was nothing but a grocery sack of old holiday cards that Lynn had saved for whatever reason. Nothing hung on the heavy brass hooks inside the doors or from the iron bar mounted across the top. No devils, no demons. *Ann would be so disappointed.*

As far as the rest of the attic went, there were tubs of holiday trinkets and table linens, a few scrapbooks that needed a good dusting and were probably coming apart at the seams from their cheap, aged glue, boxes of old books and *Good Housekeeping* magazines, a handful each of *Popular Mechanics* and *Playboy*, plus a couple of suits in plastic dry-cleaning bags that Brute hadn't worn in probably twenty years judging from the rod of a cardboard standing wardrobe that looked like a single tap would collapse the whole thing. The suits could go on the Goodwill pile. One of them, Mark even recognized: a dark blue, pinstriped Calvin Klein that Brute had worn to Mark and Madeline's wedding ten years before.

"The secret to a good marriage," Brute had extolled at their reception with a heavy arm over Mark's shoulder, "is agreeing with her, making sure she doesn't ever wanna leave you, and keeping a copy of some boob mag hidden somewhere she won't find." He'd given Mark a playful jab in the ribs, and Grandma Lynn had responded with a roll of her eyes and a playful shake of her head; Brute wasn't usually that crude, but he'd had a few glasses of scotch, and Mark could tell that it was in good fun. Brute, whose name was actually Alfred, had married their grandmother Lynn when they had both been nineteen. Lynn passed when Mark and Ann were kids—eleven and six, respectively—after suffering through two years of breast cancer that hadn't been content until it wrought havoc on her entire body. What little Mark remembered from that period was spotty; there were a lot of closed doors, hushed conversations, drunken sloppiness from their uncle, crying jags from their mother that appeared seemingly out of nowhere.

The sum of their grandparents' marriage—and of that quiet, dark time in Grandma Lynn's illness—was contained in the modest house where Mark now sat, in his late Grandpa's easy chair in the living room, nursing a Heineken and staring at the few boxes of things he'd brought over.

Brute had left everything to their mother, fully excluding their uncle Tony, which made sense given what had happened. And after their mother's recent move to Marigold Assisted Living, it was, by writ of a family lawyer, left to Mark and Ann to deal with their grandfather's estate however they saw fit. Audrey wasn't likely to leave Marigold, however cold that sounded, and otherwise, Brute's place would just fall to ruin.

Mark's initial thought was to devote as much time as he could to cleaning the place out, to have it over and done with. Brute hadn't been a hoarder, not exactly, but he'd hated to arbitrarily throw things away, and the more time Mark spent at the house, the more he thought that stretching the process out might actually

CHAPTER 1

be nice, a change of scenery from his drab apartment to a place that was relatable and occupied mostly happy space in his mind. So when his apartment lease came up for renewal in August, Mark suddenly thought, why not? He'd save money by moving into Brute's place, and with Ann still working in South America, it would just be him. He liked the idea of having a house as opposed to an apartment, and it would be satisfying to have a space that was fully his own instead of the three rooms he'd called home since his divorce. And even on his bus driver's salary, he'd be able to put some good money away if he didn't have to worry about rent, finally get back to school, and finish his degree. He told their mother he'd take care of it, that he'd go through Brute's things and then see about selling the house in good time.

Mark tossed his empty beer bottle in the kitchen trash and got another from the fridge. Getting acclimated to living at the old house Brute had occupied for nearly five decades felt a little like being a child again, though, if he was being honest with himself, it wasn't necessarily a feeling that brought Mark much degree of comfort so far. It was largely a trip down memory lane—both the high rises and slums of that particular street—and it felt a bit like being homeless, since he didn't have any of his things really organized as yet. It was mostly a series of boxes in the living room and some clothes hung in the main bedroom next to Brute's flannels and t-shirts, all of them smelling a little like Old Spice and the musty confines of the bedroom.

Maybe the first order of business was getting some of those clothes out of there and cleaning out the closets; that was an easy place to start. Brute had been bigger than Mark by a long shot—broader in the shoulders and heavier, too—so there was no point in keeping the clothes, for the most part. He thought maybe his mother might like to keep a couple of Brute's signature flannels, but other than that, the lot of it could go to Goodwill or the curb. A little over an hour later, the closet was largely dealt with.

    Mark went downstairs to the kitchen, cracked a beer, and pushed the screen door open, the scent of grass and someone burning leaves in the near distance offering a pleasant sense-memory on so many levels. How could anyone live anywhere but the Midwest? He stepped from the slab patio to the yard and took a deep breath before pausing.

    There was a shape at the mouth of the tree clearing, and sure enough, Mark recognized the crossed planks of the scarecrow's mount, though it looked somehow wrong. When he was six or seven (Ann was too little to play with him much at that point), Brute had taken him out to the edge of their property line to the dense thicket of trees and brush that wound a crooked path separating the neighborhood from the cornfields and farmland on the other side, where the city gave the land back to the country. It wasn't too deep, all things considered, probably an acre or so, equivalent perhaps to half a city block. But to Mark, it felt mystical, like Hundred Acre Wood or Sherwood Forest, his own magic kingdom that held innumerable secrets waiting for him to uncover. The thicket had a couple of access points where the grass was thick, but the branches and thorny areas weren't. Brute had marked the entrance point to the little patch of woods with a scarecrow he'd made of tall strips of wood—broken planks from a pallet

CHAPTER 1

of some kind—and a pair of hastily stuffed old clothes, just worn-out dungarees and a thick, blue flannel shirt.

For a head, Brute had tied an old Halloween mask to the to the top of the shirt, a hairy-faced thing with long teeth and empty eye sockets that looked like it had come from the back of a comic book; knowing Uncle Tony, Mark thought, that's probably exactly where it came from, as the thing was cracked and peeling apart, age having melted the latex together in some spots, giving the face of the thing an uneven, incorrect shape. Mark remembered his mother joking that it looked like a coffee bean with teeth or a mole rat, whatever that was, and Mark found it cool if vaguely unsettling, the way it just slumped on its post. Every time they'd come to Grandma and Grandpa Brunner's house, Mark would take the first available opportunity to run all the way to the back of their yard and greet the thing. Once, Brute had even stuck a watermelon up there as a joke when they arrived to visit.

Mark walked across the backyard now, sipping his beer, squinting as the scarecrow grew more fully into his view. Instead of a mask or a wig or a melon or some other goofy adornment, the wooden frame now wore what looked like a papier-mâché effigy of a person, albeit incomplete. The cross leaned, age and weather having strained the relatively thin pieces of ply board that held the thing upright. Mark set his beer on the grass, put a hand behind the thing mounted on the wooden X, and straightened its position in the damp earth.

It was crude, grotesque even, as though someone had tried to make a body cast of what was likely a woman but stopped halfway through. Rough features had been either drawn or hewn into the face with some sort of tool, giving it a vaguely unsettling, puppet-like quality. There was a thin, carefully tapered nose, and lips that erred more on the side of feminine, careful lines coming together with shaky delicacy, a slit cut across the middle of the lips. One eye had been carefully but clumsily drawn in, the aforementioned oval and black marker denotation, and the other side had been slit out and peeled open a bit, as though it had been intended that one see from the inside. The childish ambiguity of the features made it lean toward androgyny: the wide eyes, the pert, red-lined mouth. It was complete past the shoulders, almost fully to the torso—even the head fully formed and encased. Mark realized that it was probably big enough to fit him—though the right arm ended at the elbow, and the left arm went down to part of a hand, just a few fingers, before it was rendered incomplete. The chest was lumpy, suggestive of where breasts would be, and the body suit, this strange, paper-crafted carapace, was stained and pocked with what looked like mold or dirt. Maybe paint. In some places, it looked like small pieces of fabric or construction paper had been mixed into the layers of papier-mâché that had to be two inches thick, and the back was open, as though it had been cast from someone lying down. It looked like a Halloween project someone had started and abandoned.

It was vaguely familiar to Mark, as though he'd read a name to which he couldn't connect a face. But why out here? Where had it even come from? Why would Brute have put this here?

Beyond where he stood, just past a low-hanging branch that looked like an arm draped over the path flanked by the massive trees, there was still a little

CHAPTER 1

weather-beaten scrap of police crime-scene tape stuck to the base of the trunk, three years out now, a little plastic part of the ecology.

Mark picked up his beer and then, on a whim, reached into his pocket and took out his phone, snapping a picture of the thing and messaging it to Ann.

[Mark: Family treasures. Aren't we lucky? Hahaha!]

She might not get it right away. The service where she was in South America was god-awful, but she'd get a laugh when she eventually did. The clouds overhead began to give way, rain pattering the yard and the trees, beating a rhythmic pattern into the woods before him, so Mark headed back to the house. He stood at the kitchen window, staring out at the thing and finishing his beer.

Just before the rain picked up, he dashed back out, slid the thing off the aged wooden cross, and brought it inside, leaving it on the floor of the garage, though he wasn't sure what compelled him to save it. Maybe it was the thought of having to weed out the wheat from the chaff when it came to the contents of the house, the summation of Brute and Lynn's lives in his hands and his hands alone, for all intents and purposes, with his mother probably never getting out of Marigold and Ann halfway across the world. It was up to him to be the arbiter of their family's historical record in terms of things, stuff, objects. The body cast had shaken something loose in his mind, far back, something he couldn't quite grab a hold of as yet, and it felt somehow wrong to let it drown in the late summer rain on a broken, lonely cross.

2

The room smelled like burned coffee; the pot had been left on the burner a little too long with no water in it, and Mark pulled the plug from the wall. He took a deep breath. Behind him, Audrey chuckled vacantly at something on TV. He scribbled "PLEASE UNPLUG AFTER USE" on a Post-It note branded with the Marigold Assisted Living logo and stuck it to the bottom of the four-cup machine.

On most days, his mother was okay, but on others, it was like a different person had switched rooms—switched bodies—with her: a dark, brooding version of his mother emerging from somewhere deep inside her brain to pull the switches. He and Ann had taken to categorizing the good days as Bulls-Eyes—their favorite candy as kids—and bad days as Circus Peanuts, after those horrible spongy candies. "How was Mom today? Total circus peanuts."

Audrey looked up slowly and frowned.

"You don't look happy, Mark," she said simply.

CHAPTER 2

"I'm great, Mom. Everything's great. How are you feeling?"

"You don't look happy," she said, staring at the television with childish wonderment. "Do you work here?"

"No, Mom, it's me. It's Mark." He sat down in the chair next to her and did his best to ignore its stiff back and wobbly leg, the vinyl padding underneath having poked through on one side. He wondered if it had belonged to someone who had passed away; secondhand furniture in the place felt that much more depressing. "Are you eating?"

"The food here isn't too bad," she said thoughtfully. "But I'm not usually hungry." She patted his hand; she had a broken fingernail that was on the verge of a painful tear. He'd talk to the staff about it on his way out. "Could you get me a Tylenol?"

The bathroom made Mark think of a hospital, all iron support bars and flat colors, though his mother had added a little clear vase filled with purple and yellow potpourri and a picture of him and Ann when they were kids. The medicine cabinet consisted of an open series of shelves without a mirror. "A security measure," he'd been told when he'd brought his mother there a year ago, "we don't want someone falling and breaking the glass." The shelves were sparse: a tube of Bengay, Benadryl tablets, and generic Tylenol. He took the Tylenol bottle and popped it open, shaking a couple into his palm, then a couple more. His head had started to ache just before he'd left the house, a dull, creeping pain right behind his eyes.

"Here you go, Mom," he said, handing her the pills and a paper cup of water. He gathered a bunch of wilted, dead flowers from the vase near her bed and chucked them in the trash. "Does your head hurt?

"Could you get me some Tylenol, Mark?"

"I did," he said, and showed them to her. "Hold out your hand, Mom. Here." She took them and swallowed them with the water.

"Halloween soon," she said suddenly and turned her whole body, the way she had since arthritis had all but paralyzed her neck as an individual working part of her. She stared out the window at the little decorated trees that dotted Marigold's front lawn and netted strings of orange and purple lights accented with the kind of cutesy, grinning pumpkins and black cats you'd see in a grade-school classroom. "They have lights out there. On the trees. We used to drive around and look at Christmas lights when you were little. Do you remember that?"

"Remember how the Holmes family used to do it, the whole farm done up with characters and lights?" Mark said. He watched the recollection disappear from her face until finally she stared at nothing.

"I went to the grocery store this morning," she said brightly, then hesitated. "It might have been last night, actually. I might have gone last night."

Circus. Peanuts.

"Mom, you haven't been to the grocery store. You've been here. Can I get you anything from the grocery store?"

"Some graham crackers," she nodded. "Oh, and some sardines. I told Ruth across the hall that I liked to eat sardines and crackers, and she told me that fish carried plague, and that the plague would get inside me if I ate them."

CHAPTER 2

"I don't think I'd put much stock in anything Ruth has to say, Mom," he smiled. "Half the time, Ruth doesn't know that her name is Ruth."

She flashed a conspiratorial grin, then leaned in, and whispered, "She stole magazines from that old man's room down the hall. Arthur, I think? She took a bunch of magazines."

"Does Arthur know?" Mark whispered, playing along.

"I don't think so!" she snickered. It came out high and girly; it made Mark's chest hurt for the part of his mother that was still in there under the dreamy gauze of terminal illness. "Your dad came by yesterday."

He sighed and sat down on the edge of her bed. The worse she got, the more often his father visited her, and though he wanted to humor her, he couldn't find it in himself to play along with some of the phantoms. "Mom, Dad's long gone. Remember all the pretty flowers they sent him? All the people who came to the funeral?"

"It was a nice funeral," she agreed, entering the conversation all at once, like someone who'd just arrived. "Don't you get me anything for Christmas. I don't want you spending your money on me. Get the good stuff for the trick-or-treaters. We always had a lot of trick-or-treaters."

"Full-sized bars only at Chez Brute, Mom, gotcha." He patted her shoulder, and she leaned her head against his arm. "Anything good on TV?"

"I worry about you on your own," she sighed. "You and Ann, always such loners."

"I'm 42, and I'm not alone, Mom. Remember, I'm seeing Cory Blevin? Do you remember her from high school?"

"Cory Blevin, she was a pretty brunette girl, wasn't she? Lived over on Hawkinson Street?"

He smiled; it felt good that she remembered Cory, though it didn't really matter. "That's her, yeah."

"You should bring her to visit, honey," she smiled, though she looked more sad than anything else.

"Maybe this weekend, Mom," he said. "Maybe we can come and have dinner with you?"

Audrey didn't answer; her eyes landed on Mariska Hargitay as the actress hugged an alley wall in search of a perp.

"I have to go, Mom. I'll be by in a couple of days."

"Take care of yourself. Bring Annie by next week–" Her words disintegrated; Mark could see in her face that she was searching for something. It wasn't the first time she'd forgotten his name, but it wasn't something he saw himself ever getting used to.

"Bye." He leaned over to hug her, but she didn't budge to return the gesture; her body was rigid as she stared at the television. "Goodbye, Mom."

"Is Lori here?" Before he could reply that he didn't even know a Lori, she phased out again, to use Ann's phrase, staring blankly at the wall just over his shoulder for a few minutes before starting to doze.

"Do you mean Ann, Mom? Or Cory? Did you mean Cory?"

But she'd fully withdrawn into her catacombs of fuzzy memories and dull catatonia. The bouts were getting longer, though the instances were no more frequent. He'd talked to the doctors to try to determine what might cause them, but they insisted it was likely the Alzheimer's getting worse. They'd need to keep an eye on it, Ann said, but that was easy to say from hundreds of miles away. He was the one who had to go home and measure that time with increasing worry, though after everything he'd been through as a result of Tony's conviction, he saw the opportunity for caregiving on multiple fronts as a kind of welcome penance, despite the surreal nature of it at times.

He pulled the blanket up around his mother's shoulders, kissed her on top of her head—her thinning red hair only adding to the picture of her fragility—and quietly closed the door.

3

There was little to keep him awake, and most nights, Tony went to sleep early for lack of anything else to do. It was a bit like getting drunk and falling asleep on the couch, only he couldn't get drunk, and there was no couch. Just his shitty cot, a wool blanket so thin he could practically see through it, and a pillow that felt like a bag of cotton balls wrapped in gauze.

He stared at the ceiling, the sound of his cellmate's snoring offering something like comfort.

Three nights in a row, he'd woken up with the idea of the thing in his head again.

That's how it felt: an idea, an impression. Not a presence, nothing like that. It wasn't like being haunted or some comic-book silliness. It was like having something inside you with its own thoughts, its own will, its own desires. It just so happened that the longer it had been inside him, the more those thoughts, wills, and desires became his, too. Funny how that had played out. A shame that he hadn't been smarter about it. If he hadn't chased the high of having that thing inside him, he might not have done what he did to Dara. He might still be *out*. He might still be at home, which he'd have to himself now that the old man was dead and gone these few months.

God, the things he could do if he were at home.

Tony absently reached for his cock, growing hard as he thought about Dara. Her daughter, that teenaged body just aching for a man; he could tell even though she'd barely stopped crying the whole time he … hell, the boy, too. There had been so much blood.

He had to piss, and he snorted with disgust as it threw off his flow. Tony got up, stood at the toilet to relieve himself, and glanced over at the bunk above his, where Eightball had been sleeping, snoring peacefully, just a few seconds ago. Eightball was gone.

Now, in his place and propped against the cell wall, sat a thin young woman, her ribs visible through her skin, barely covered by a peach-colored camisole. Tony recognized her, but he couldn't place a name, not for certain. She slumped forward with bony, pockmarked arms draped limply in her lap. Her eyes cast down toward where he lay, and her face frozen in a rictus smile, swollen tongue teasing at her lips. A long string of viscous spit hung from her lip, which was split as though she'd been hit hard, and it dripped to the floor with a soft *splat*. Where her legs should have dangled from the edge of the bunk, there were only sludgy, black stumps that barely made it to her knees before tapering off like dark blobs of candle wax. Her eyes were empty holes, and the exercise shorts she wore were wet in the crotch.

He grinned back at her. *So much blood.*

JUNKMAN

Tony returned to his bunk and lay back as his hand settled into a steady rhythm, closing his eyes against the lonely, echoing sounds of the cell block.

4

M ark sipped a can of Old Style as he stood between the thick hedges under the front window, scrubbing the glass and siding with a horsehair brush, pausing every few strokes to dip it in a bucket of hot water and Clorox.

"THE JUNKMAN COMETH," the graffiti said, stretching tall in red spray paint with a skull and crossbones.

Stepping back into the yard to give his shoulder a break, Mark squinted in the fading evening light. It was coming off, little by little. This was the sixth time in the three years since Tony's incarceration that he'd had to scrub the work of scumbag vandals from his grandfather's house, and he knew that Brute had done it a few times, too. Little towns loved their boogeyman stories, and Tony had driven his deep under Galesburg's skin, never to be removed. He'd even garnered the nickname smeared there in foot-high white paint. It wasn't catchy, but it didn't need to be; his crimes had spoken for themselves, and they'd taken place two weeks before

Halloween, which made them automatically a part of local holiday lore.

Mark looked at his watch, glad that he'd decided to knock off a little early and let Gunnar Samuelson take the rest of his shift. It was already ten after six. On a normal day over the last two weeks at Brute's house, he came home from work around 5:30, made something basic for dinner, then spent a few hours going through boxes from the basement or the downstairs closets, separating things into new boxes for packing away, donating to Goodwill, or throwing away altogether. Pictures, newspaper clippings, and anything paper went into a pile to get scanned so there would be a digital copy of everything, and then, when Ann got home at Christmas, they could determine who would get what.

An old white t-shirt sat in the bucket of steamy water; Mark finished his beer, set the can down on the porch, then dunked the cloth, saturating it as he wiped the soapy foam from the windows. The sun, tired of watching such a depressing exercise, slowly eased its way behind the field out back, and soon, Mark worked away at the painted message in near darkness.

Brute had dealt with more than a fair share of voyeurs and true crime enthusiasts in the time following Tony's trial and incarceration. Usually, it was just drive-by gawkers who would snap a few pictures of the house for whatever purpose and drive away, sometimes honking in morbid celebration at seeing the former home of the man they—and the rest of the free world—knew as the "Junkman Killer." A few times, they'd actually come to the door, and one ballsy college student had actually asked if he could get some pictures of the house's interior for his blog. Brute had shut the door in the guy's face without a word—kinder, Mark thought, than he would have been.

Other times, it was graffiti from local punks without anything better to do, and the house was an easy target, given its unfortunate infamy. More than anger—which was certainly his reaction while Brute had been alive, on the old man's behalf—now Mark just felt pity for such behavior. It was symptomatic of how Galesburg had fallen from its solid, middle-class place of blue-collar jobs and a downtown community that catered to Knox College following the departure of all three factories in town. Outsourcing the thousands of manufacturing jobs had burned the town's bright Midwestern candle into a mess of dirty wax, and what followed was a tidal wave of unemployment, drug abuse, and petty crime. It was no Detroit, not by a long shot, but it wasn't a place Mark thought he'd really want to raise a family, which was part of where things had gone sideways with Maddie, though the thought of leaving his mother at Marigold filled him with too much guilt to consider moving, starting over. The empty storefronts downtown and gradual economic depression had driven a kind of melancholy under the skin of everyone who'd known it as a thriving, all-American town from the '50s all the way to the '80s.

Mark stepped back, squinted to make sure that a ghost of the spray-painted message couldn't be seen, and dumped the water out in the bushes, carrying the bucket back to the garage.

He couldn't let himself get hung up on nostalgia. After all, memories always evolved beyond reality, and he was certain that, no matter what might have been before, there was a future for the town as there likely was for every place that saw economic upheaval. People came and people went, families moved and shifted, but there were always others to move in and take those places. Plus, he had Cory now, which was more than he could have hoped for just a few months ago. He'd done a reasonable job of putting his and his family's past behind him; there was no reason to stop now.

Things were definitely looking up.

5

Saturday came in on gray skies and even cooler temperatures than they usually had in the fall, and Mark sat down in the living room with a microwaved bowl of canned ravioli for lunch and watched a bit of an old Godzilla movie on TV. Svengoolie mugged along with a rubber chicken, and Mark smiled; the old Svengoolie shows had always made him want to move to Berwyn when he was a kid, even though he didn't even know where that was. With all the lights on and the overcast weather, the house felt pretty cozy, and it was the first time he really felt comfortable there, as though it was *his*, that he wasn't just visiting or wearing out a welcome.

Grandma Lynn had clearly been the organizer of the house, as numerous boxes in the closets bore the same careful handwriting in blue marker. Mark started with the first of six broad shoeboxes, separating photos out into those he recognized and those he didn't. The latter outnumbered the former by leaps and bounds; there were endless shots of family events, friends, parties, holidays, and portraiture in which Mark knew few, if any, of the people caught on film. Their family wasn't close in the sense that family gatherings brought relatives far and wide; those who were near—a couple of aunts, a cousin or two—came together when they could, and beyond that, it was largely Christmas cards and the occasional phone call that kept everyone connected. It was a congenial kind of disconnection. That's how Tony had always put it.

Tony. *Speak of the devil, and he shall appear,* Mark thought as he stared down at a Polaroid with bent edges. A banner in the background of the photo wished a happy 1981 to all, and in the foreground, his uncle wore a salad bowl on his head like a space helmet, a bottle of PBR in his hand, food stains on his shirt. *I hope you enjoyed it,* Mark thought. Tony's life sentence meant that he would die in prison, which, given what got him there, was a good thing. Next was a rumpled, square, black-and-white photo of his mother and Tony sitting side by side on respective swings, looking back over their shoulders at the camera and grinning, surely no older than seventeen or eighteen.

Mark was struck by how much Ann looked like their mom and, for a moment, he felt a pang of guilt that he was going through all these things without her there. Should he wait? Should he just bide his time in the house, filled with Brute's things, and wait the three months until Ann got home? *But what would be the point of that?* he thought. After all, it wasn't like she was somehow more qualified to know what was important and what wasn't.

Like that papier-mâché thing in the garage, he thought, and chuckled out loud as he went to the kitchen for a beer. *Keen eye for rarified objects, dude, keen eye.* He started back toward the living room, but then he stopped, turning back toward the garage door and opening it. The body cast sat on the concrete floor, looking even more absurd—pathetic, almost—than it had when it was banished to the yard in the rain.

Why did it remind him of something? He knelt down in front of it, again studying the comically shitty features that were partially drawn, partially cut. They were unsettling in their silliness, calling to mind some of the horror movies he and Ann used to watch when they were kids; the cheap, sleazy quality to the special effects actually made them more scary, in a weird way.

Mark picked it up. A mirror hung over the worktable in the garage; Mark raised the thing up and sniffed it, getting a vague whiff of old glue and something rotten, an earthy smell; how long had it been outside? It smelled musty, almost, which made no sense, since it had at least been in the fresh air for a few weeks, had to have been since Brute must have been the one to put it there, and he'd been gone for months. There was something else, too, a vague scent that reminded Mark of jasmine. He stood in front of the mirror, and without thinking, he slipped the thing carefully over his head, guiding his arm down into the stiff paper tube and pushing the thing against his body with his free hand, situating it on his shoulders so it was firmly in place, fitting the mask portion fully over his head.

It was a little big for him, so someone of broader shoulder and build had worn it; there was definitely a bit of give in the chest that made him think that this had been fitted to a heavier woman's frame. But it did fit, and the crudely scribbled features took on a more purposeful quality as he stood in front of the mirror, with only part of his shirt, most of his left arm, and his body from the waist down visible outside of the body cast. He took a step forward and leaned a little toward the table; the thing held to his body. He chuckled, but it came out as a muffled grunt; the little holes cut for nostrils and the slit mouth did a pretty good job, but they weren't perfect. It actually did remind him of the Halloween costumes from when he was a kid—the plastic masks and flimsy rubber bands, the way the thin plastic dug into your skin around your eyes and mouth. The crudity was both ridiculous and vaguely off-putting. *If you went trick-or-treating in this thing*, he thought, *someone would call the police before you could even knock on a single door.*

Mark took his phone out of his pocket and snapped a quick selfie, then texted it to Cory.

[Mark: What do you think? Date night?]

Within a few seconds, her response came back.

[Cory: Gross, what the hell is that thing? Are you drunk, lol?]

There was another smell, something like oil, like burning motor oil, mixed with that cloying jasmine sweetness, just for a second. Then it was gone, but it lingered in Mark's mouth like he'd tasted something bad. He eased his arm out of the shell, then lifted it off his body and head, setting it back down on the floor.

CHAPTER 5

"You're an acquired taste, apparently," he said, smirking at his own joke, clicking off the light as he went back into the house.

6

Salads weren't normally a part of his standard cooking regimen, but Cory loved salad with dinner, and after checking the recipe on his phone, Mark decided he had everything he needed after bagging a bunch of radicchio. The purple lettuce had a strong, bitter aroma, though he figured she knew what she was talking about, so he carefully knotted the plastic bag and tossed it into the cart along with the rest of what they needed for the veggie lasagna she'd wanted to try. More than anything, he was thrilled to be shopping for dinner—*their* dinner. He felt a pure, simple warmth at his pleasantly mundane routine with Cory. There was no pretension, no need to be anyone other than himself, nothing to do but just enjoy the time together. This is what normal feels like, he thought sometimes when they were together at the movies, out at Pizza House, talking on the phone about their days. After everything with Tony's trial and conviction, his mother's dementia and getting her set up at Marigold, and then Brute's death, he'd felt like anything good was, for whatever reason, being held just out of his reach. When he and Cory had reconnected, it was like saying *fuck you* to the universe and all the bullshit that had besieged his life, and doing it with a big smile.

Mark found the shortest checkout lane and parked his cart behind a tired-looking middle-aged woman with a little boy who was chattering at his mother about some superhero movie. She gave him placid smiles every now and again, offering "uh-huh" or "oh, wow" as her part of the conversation when it seemed appropriate. They exchanged glances, and Mark smiled at her. She returned it and rolled her eyes with a chuckle.

The checker was taking her sweet time, and before long, a line had formed behind him, another four shoppers deep, and he glanced around, checking his list again. Should he grab another bottle of wine? He'd lose his place in line, but then again, they were all long, so it's not like he was going anywhere soon, and he remembered that Cory really liked one specific pinot gri—

He felt a light tap on his back, and he turned to see an elderly, frail-looking Asian woman with glasses and hair pulled into a tight, wiry bun staring up at him. Behind her was another Asian woman—her daughter, perhaps, maybe even a granddaughter—who looked at her quizzically.

"No," the old woman hissed at him, staring for a few seconds before hiding her face, dissolving into tears as she held her liver-spotted hands to her face like a child facing a monster. "No, no, no, no..."

"Grandma," the other woman said, offering Mark a worried, apologetic look. "Grandma, we're at the store, please—"

"Hungry," the old woman said, tapping her fingernail against her stomach, speaking louder now. "No, no, no..."

"What, ma'am?" Mark replied, forcing a smile to try to defuse the awkwardness of the situation.

"You see it!" she shouted, as though he'd confirmed something by simply responding to her. She began rattling off a series of urgent phrases at her granddaughter in their native tongue, and again, the younger of the two stared at Mark in a silent apology as other shoppers began to watch the bizarre situation unfold, pausing in aisles and craning their necks from other lines. One woman took out her cell phone and began to record. Great, he thought, *I'm going to go viral for getting yelled at by someone's grandma.*

"I am so sorry," the young woman replied as the old lady continued babbling between them. "She has spells, she—" The woman paused, listening to what the older woman had to say for a moment. The line moved a little ahead of Mark. "Have you—okay, I'm sorry, but she's asking, have you been to Japan recently?"

"No," Mark chuckled. "Not recently, not ever. Why?"

"There's no telling. She asks this all the time when we go places." The granddaughter shrugged and shook her head at the old woman, who looked incredulous, turning back to Mark and narrowing her eyes. What had sounded like anger before now sounded like fear as she spoke again, this time in careful English. "Grandma, *please.*"

The old woman pursed her lips and set her jaw; she sighed in frustration, then shook her head as a few tears leaked down her cheeks. "So hungry. Always hungry." She looked back at her granddaughter, her thin, bony shoulders almost showing through her faded green sweater.

"Sir?" The checker, a youngish guy with glasses and a puzzled, toothy smile, motioned Mark forward as the exchange between two generations continued to argue behind him in Japanese. Mark stared at them. The old woman continued her rant, quieter now, and it struck him that she didn't seem out of her head; her tone and words were careful, measured, despite her granddaughter's attempt to pass off the rant as that of a dotty old woman. Whatever she was saying, it was serious, and she meant it.

"How we doing today?" smiled the checker, giving each item a once-over as he scanned them through. "Got big dinner plans, I see?"

"What?" Mark turned back. "Oh, yeah, yeah. Big dinner plans."

"Lookin' good, lookin' good," the checker replied, whizzing the groceries over the scanner as though he had the greatest job in the world. "Garlic, got some good salad dressing here, some good ol' radicchio. Ra-deech! That's what I like to call it, radeech. Sounds more fun, right?"

"Yeah," Mark said absently. The old woman was fixed on him again, staring into his face, studying him as one would a photograph. "Sure, I guess." He auto-piloted his way through paying with his debit card, saying no to coupons, using a discount code, up-charging for charity.

"Good deal," the checker said, winding the receipt into Mark's bag. "Enjoy your radeech, my friend. Happy Sunday!"

JUNKMAN

"Happy Sunday," Mark muttered, matching the old woman's troubled stare as he pushed his cart through the automatic doors into the chilly afternoon.

7

Four rings, and it went to voicemail.

"Hey, just wanted to say what's up, kid," Tony said blandly in his dull, cigarette-ravaged monotone. "Hope you're doing alright. Stay safe." A long pause. "Talk to you soon."

He hung up the phone and sighed, leaning his forehead against the wall, feeling the cool slate against his skin. Time to go back to his cell, and fuck, he'd really hoped to talk to Mark. Last time he'd called Audrey at the facility and caught her on a good day, she'd said Mark was staying at Brute's place, getting it ready to sell.

What did that mean, Tony thought, *getting it ready to sell?* Getting what ready? Paint? New wallpaper? Performing some fucking cleansing ritual? He'd seen some dumbass home renovation show in the common room one night where a woman had been burning herbs, waving this smoking stick around the room to get rid of "negative energy." Jesus. The things people were willing to believe to feel safe.

The cell door closed behind him, and Tony was back in his closet of space; Eightball lay in the upper bunk reading a book about UFOs. A few sketches were taped to the wall of his own bunk; Tony lay down with a groan and stared at one where he'd tried to sketch a version of a photo he had of him and Audrey at Christmas one year. He absently ran a comb through his thick, dark beard; he'd let it go and looked like your stereotypical biker now, one of his brothers in the Highway Ravagers. There were a few inside, but no one he'd gotten close to yet. It didn't matter, really; he was there for the long haul, and it wasn't like he had the means, opportunity, or even inclination to stage a prison break or some shit.

The sketches helped get him outside a little—outside of his head. There was one of his mother, Lynn, another attempted facsimile of a photo he'd seen of her when she was young. There were some iterations of the overpass near Abington where the train tracks hooked north, just a pretty spot he'd always enjoyed stopping and looking at. Another of a girl he'd known from Chancellor back in the band days, a groupie, for lack of any other term. Danielle something. Whittaker? Danielle Whittaker sounded right. Strawberry blonde, a little curvy, hell of an ass. They'd had some good rides on his bike during the off-tour times in, what, '76? '77? Christ, the years had gone by so fast it felt like time had eaten its tail up to its fucking neck.

Next to the sketch of Danielle was a sketch of Dara.

They'd had some good times, too, despite some weird history; she got around. He knew that when they took up together. But there were some good times, at first. The first time he raped her that night when everything changed, it had been so hard to focus: the sound from the back of his brain like a motor running, her daughter sobbing, her boy screaming and hollering, Dara herself crying, telling him, "not inside me, not inside me." It had taken him a few to realize what she even meant, that she didn't want him to cum inside her, as if that was what had mattered, as if he *wasn't* going to kill her. Maybe some pathetic part of her still believed in that moment that she was going to leave that bed. Regardless, it was forgotten once he was spent, and the thing began to take what it wanted.

It must have been a terrible thing for a mother to witness, he considered, sitting back on his bunk and folding his arms against his chest. It made him feel good to think of how Dara's daughter's body had felt against his. How, when he'd licked her skin, he tasted the sourness of fear in her sweat. When he concentrated hard enough, he could almost feel that sensation again, and it made him feel out of his body. It made him feel like he still had the costume on, though that was impossible; he'd burned it up in the car just before the police found him, he'd watched it burn, and the things that came out of it, all of those horrors, Jesus Christ, that had been the worst part of the whole night, watching it release what it had collected as the fire ate his car from tits to tail.

It made him think of his niece, Ann, of the wardrobe in the attic. He felt a surge of something electric deep inside.

Tony slid down in his bunk, his head coming to rest against his pillow as he closed his eyes and thought of being in the old place.

Mark. Lucky little fucker.

"You know I had to fight off a crazy woman to get this bunch of radeech." Mark grinned at Cory as he ran the veggies under water, scrubbing them clean and lining them up on a cutting board.

Cory chuckled with surprise as she began chopping the spinach. Mark noticed that she'd had her nails done before coming over, a deep, ruby red. "Well, I hope you didn't do too much damage."

"She'll live. No, for real, there was this senile old lady at the grocery store cursing me in Japanese and losing her shit."

"Bitch better back off. Age ain't nothing but a number, right?"

"I think you're safe. She wasn't my type." He gave her a playful hip check as she began sautéing the greens, stirring them around the skillet with a spatula and somehow looking sexy in the process.

Cory shook her head. "I hope I don't turn into that."

"An elderly Japanese woman?"

CHAPTER 8

She full-on snorted with laughter this time, which spurred Mark into laughter as well. "No, senile. Dotty. Not myself, like that."

"No one stays the same." He thought of Brute, the last visits, how different the old man had been. Weak and sleeping all the time, drifting from memory to fantasy and back to some version of reality, something that had been crafted out of those drifts. Mark had never heard Brute talk as much about the war and his time in the Pacific as he did during those last few months.

He dried his hands and came up behind her, carefully slipping his arms around her waist as she tended the vegetables. She leaned back into him, and he felt her sigh contentedly, the soft weight of her holding him in a kind of thrall the likes of which he hadn't felt since the first time they'd done this.

Mark and Cory had been seeing each other, off and on, for about four months, a reprisal—a reset, really—of their failed attempt at a relationship back in their mid-twenties, and it was so far, so good. She was divorced, having finally cut loose her meth-head, criminal husband, Adrian, several years back. The dramatic arc of that relationship—the abuse, the unpredictable behavior—had put Cory in therapy and left her wanting something blissfully normal, and their date nights tended to be low-key affairs, which was fine with Mark. It was difficult for him to put his feelings in order when he was with her, doing literally anything—driving somewhere, talking across the table at dinner, watching a movie on the couch—because the high school version of himself could barely reconcile that Corene Blevin was leaning against him, periodically leaning in for a few minutes of passionate kissing and a few sips of wine before resuming their movie. Cory Blevin. The first girl he'd ever had real feelings for, and she was still the same. Time had had a graceful way with her, and the abuse she'd suffered at the hands of her ex-husband hadn't in any way that Mark could see diminished her capacity for seeing good in people and pursuing happiness; there was no bitterness there. He knew beyond doubt that he'd always loved her, though they hadn't exchanged that as yet. It was okay. He could wait.

Tonight, they ate lasagna and salad in contented silence, snuggling together on the couch, watching TV. Cory's legs crossed over his. Her feet were always cold; she wore thick, wool knee socks with a leopard print that reached toward her shorts.

"What are you thinking about?" Cory said, responding to his long silence, sitting cross-legged on the couch with a bowl of popcorn in her lap, thick, auburn hair pulled up into a loose ponytail. The talk show that followed *The Walking Dead* was wrapping up, and the host was gifting an audience member with a hat worn by a character who had been killed off in that night's episode. "Something Hardwick said there seemed to have really resonated with you."

Mark laughed. "I was just thinking about where we'd go if we were in a zombie apocalypse, for safety."

"Well." She munched popcorn thoughtfully and finally nodded. "So, you can drive a bus, and we could deck it out with boards and spikes like in the *Dawn of the Dead* remake? And from there, it's just finding a good place to hole up and wait it out. Probably someplace with a tower."

"A tower," he grinned. "Sure, tons of houses around here have towers. We should be fine."

"No, idiot," she laughed, gripping his knee and giving him a playful shake. "Like, a guard tower. I mean, they did have a prison in season three. That was about as good as security gets, right? We could always go and hole up wi—" She paused and gave him a sheepish smile. "We'd find somewhere."

"What?" he said. "With my uncle, is that what you were gonna say? Infiltrate the prison and wait out the zombies with Uncle Tony?"

She rolled her eyes sheepishly. "I mean, he can ride a motorcycle. Between a bus and a motorcycle, we'd have transit pretty well bagged."

"Except for a monster truck," he said. "Then we'd really be on the road to rebuilding civilization."

"Nope, they flip. Bad plan. You wouldn't be able to off-road for too long before that thing would flip."

"Monster trucks flip?"

"They can. Adrian was into that stuff. I got dragged to a bunch of Knox County Fair monster truck exhibitions. Trust me. When it comes to all that crap, I know my stuff."

"Man, you get more surprising every day," he smiled, and he could tell that she was watching his reaction to her changing the subject. "You can talk about him, you know. It's really okay. It's been three years."

"I know. I guess, I just didn't really … okay, I didn't know." She slid in closer to him, and he could smell her raspberry shampoo. "Do you think about it? What he did, I mean? Or how he was before?"

"I don't really know how he was before." He put his arm around her and affectionately ran his fingers up and down her shoulder. "I mean, yeah, I have good memories, stuff he and I would do when Ann and I were kids. I know how he was with us. But, I mean, did we really know him, if he did what he did? I mean, no, that came out wrong. He did what he did. There's no question there, but how could he ... be someone that I knew to be cool or trusted at all? If he did that?"

Cory munched popcorn and sat back against the couch, freeing her hair from the ponytail. "Do you remember the Swallow Kid?"

Mark frowned. "Is that a movie?"

"No, when we were in junior high, that's what they called him afterward. This kid ... I don't remember his name. He came home from school one day and stabbed the neighbor lady to death. Said that the swallows in her birdhouses told him to do it."

Mark stacked their plates and wadded up his napkin. "Jesus, no, I don't remember that."

"Well, it happened." Cory shrugged. "We went to school with him. My older sister used to do odd jobs and errands for his parents. His dad was on disability from Maytag. They were pretty poor. But he was a nice enough kid until he took scissors to the neighbor. And after he did it, his mother, she used to write letters to the editor of the *Register-Mail* talking about what a good kid he was, how he deserved a second chance, all that." She curled her body into him, and he slipped his arms around her. "I'm just saying that everyone is someone to somebody. Even people who do horrible things. Those people ... still belong to someone. If that makes sense."

Mark sipped his wine and laced his fingers into hers. "Doesn't mean we should accept it. What they did."

CHAPTER 8

She turned her head to look up at him, kissed him on the chin, and laid her head against his chest. "What choice do we have?"

9

"Hey, just wanted to say what's up, kid," Tony said in his voicemail message, the sound of other inmates shouting in the background. "Hope you're doing alright. Stay safe. Talk to you soon." Mark hadn't noticed the voicemail until Cory had gone home for the night, which was just as well.

Sitting at his kitchen table and enjoying a late night glass of Jameson's, drifting on a light drunk, Mark thought about Tony. How he'd idolized him as a child, how his uncle had seemed like some sort of wizard, a rebel of the highest order.

Mark wondered at the nature of loss. How did we lose people? How did people fall out of our lives, drift from our transom, lose touch with what made them the people we knew? Did we decide to change, decide that we wanted to see our lives evolve, or did it happen like a mutation in a lab, cells twisting and realigning to become something new? Something beautiful, perhaps—or something horrible?

CHAPTER 9

Mark thought of his daughter, then pushed the thought out of his head. The words still felt foreign in his head, never mind on his tongue. Too late to make amends there, though Mark thought of her often, the impulsive night of young lust that led to his becoming a father in his mid-twenties. How, why, had he let that happen? Shame? Embarrassment? Probably. The things we did when we were young, reckless decisions mired forever in regret. He wondered if her mother felt the same.

God, he'd wanted everything for her, even from a distance. The guilt, the unimaginable guilt at never having told Maddie he had a kid. He'd never been able to shake it; it held on like a tentacle wrapped around his ankle. One low thought led to another: how the fuck had he ended up a bus driver in his hometown? Nothing else, no other history?

And how the *fuck* had his uncle gone from a good-natured pothead rocker to being the infamous fucking Junkman Killer?

A high school dropout who'd gone on tour as a drummer for a stoner rock band called Cataclysm back in the '70s, Tony seemed to Mark, at least in his younger years, like the model of escaping a small town for more exciting pastures, though within five years his band was defunct, he had a minor cocaine habit that he had trouble supporting working as a line cook at the Holiday Inn's restaurant in Knoxville, and he was all but living in his car until he moved back in with Brute, staying there in his childhood bedroom and working a steady job for the Galesburg Department of Sanitation for a few years before he'd done what he did. Even before the unspeakably horrific act that had landed him in maximum security, Tony was a good example of how to burn your life down, though Mark couldn't help but remember his uncle's goofy, happy-go-lucky attitude in his younger days and feel sad, almost guilty, though he certainly couldn't have changed what happened, could he?

"We all make choices," Brute had said quietly after court on the afternoon of Tony's sentencing, sitting in the living room and thoughtfully plugging away on a Budweiser. "We make choices we have to live with, Mark, and Tony's going to have to live with his. He's my son, he's your uncle, but he should. He should live with it." That was the only time Brute commented on Tony's sentencing to life in prison, but Mark remembered the old man's face as he'd said it. Resolute. The hint of tears at the corners of his eyes that defiantly, angrily, refused to fall. That was that.

There had been rumors, when Mark was in high school, of Tony's taste for young women. Very young women. His mother never acknowledged it. Ann wouldn't talk about it, and it wasn't something Mark even wanted to bring up to Brute. He remembered seeing Tony outside Corner Connection on one particular Saturday night during Mark's junior year, chatting up a girl in Mark's homeroom. She was fifteen, a budding punk with purple hair that he knew a little from seeing her on the strip from time to time, smoking cigarettes out at the brickyards with some seniors and a few dropouts who had made careers of selling pot and buying beer for some of the high schoolers who were so inclined toward the same path. Guys always paid cash; girls had the option of paying in other ways. Tony had been there at the brickyards one night, too, buying drugs from a guy Mark knew had dropped out the previous year. It was strange, Mark thought, the things that occurred to us outside of a momentary perspective, how at the time it was something that just came and went, lost in the detritus of high school angst and teenage existentialism.

What was her name? He remembered the bookshelf upstairs in Ann's old room, his old high school yearbooks lined up there. Mark dashed up the stairs, slid out his sophomore edition, and flipped through the pages. There she was, though her purple hair was muted by the black-and-white photo: Regina Marling. Marling, that's it. *God*, he thought. *I am getting old.* He paged through the yearbook for a few minutes, sitting on the edge of the aging twin bed, the occasional picture sparking a grin or a chuckle that echoed through the upstairs hallway.

The soft moan of a board somewhere in the house shook Mark from his flashbacks. He replaced the yearbook, got up, and paused in the doorway of the bedroom.

"Hello?" he called into the house. But of course, no one answered. He was alone. Outside, he could hear some kids chattering with laughter as they sped down the street on bikes. Just the house settling. He closed the door and headed back downstairs.

Mark wondered if perhaps Brute—and the rest of his family, himself included—would have had an easier time with things if Tony's crime hadn't been multiple counts of rape and murder. Drugs would have been a stupid way to go down, or a series of DUIs, even theft: any of those would have been stupid but ... approachable, in terms of wrapping one's head around the nuts and bolts of the crime. But not what had really transpired, never that. That was nothing that any sane man could come to terms with, and Mark sometimes wondered how, exactly, Tony *did* live with it.

Tony had broken into the home of a woman he'd been dating named Dara Ensinger, a forty-year-old single mom, while she and her two children—fourteen-year-old Lily and eleven-year-old Dustin—had been away on a camping trip. He'd spent three days living in their house, eating their food, sleeping in their beds, even feeding an aquarium full of fish before the Ensingers returned, at which time he attacked them, bound them, raped and dismembered the daughter in front of her mother and younger brother, tortured the boy to death, and then kept Dara captive in her home for nearly a week of rape and torture before finally disemboweling and decapitating her as well. He'd wrapped up the remains of all three in bedsheets, then stowed them in a rowboat that he set adrift in the middle of Lake Storey, where some unfortunate fishermen discovered the remains after less than a day on the water, the result of some gulls that had picked open the bloody sheets and found an easy meal amongst the carnage. Tony had wrapped up one of the knives he'd used for the crime in the sheets by mistake; a history of petty crime and some drug arrests had made his fingerprints easy to trace, and the Galesburg Police Department had him in custody just four hours after the gruesome discovery. He'd also set his car on fire, for reasons unknown to the police.

The following days, weeks, and months were a unique kind of nightmare for the Devold family, and Mark remembered well the nights when his mother would call him to just sit in silence on the phone,

CHAPTER 9

occasionally murmuring some nugget from the depths of her memory. "I remember when Tony and I went camping for the first time. I was eight. He taught me to fish." And then, silence, until she said something else along the same lines or, on some nights, just hung up. Their lives became a slow-moving conveyor belt of loosely connected thoughts and recollections, and when Bill Auster called Mark to the station to talk about Tony, just after his uncle had been convicted, Mark agreed with the detective that it would have been a bad idea to call Audrey.

"I don't want to put that kind of strain on a mother," Auster had said, sitting down with Mark in the interrogation room, which, for a few moments, put him on edge until another detective poked his head in and said, "who's this?," only for Auster to wave him off. "Someone I know who might be able to help," Auster had said, and he wasn't that far off: Mark and Bill Auster had been in school together, had even run track together freshman year before diverging as so many high-school friendships do.

"Mark, I'll be honest," Auster had started. "I don't... I've never dealt with something quite like this. I'm not fishing, I'm not... well, okay, I am ... looking at this as a detective, but I'm also..."

He got up, at that point, poured a cup of coffee from a thermos he'd brought into the interview room with him, and held it out to Mark, who declined. Auster lit a cigarette and thoughtfully drew on it, sipping his coffee. "I'm also just, as a person, you know, trying to wrap my head around what drives someone to do ... this. What your uncle did."

Mark shrugged, trying to read anything ulterior into Auster's demeanor and coming up with zilch. The guy looked like he hadn't slept in a week, the gray lines under his eyes sagging into shadow as the detective lowered his head and sipped his coffee, puffed his cigarette. "I wish I had anything to say that was meaningful here, Bill. I have no idea. My uncle Tony was—"

"—a mess," Auster finished, nodding as he spoke, stamping out his cigarette in an ashtray. "But come on, man, a messed up life doesn't always equal this. This fucking—did you see the pictures?"

"No," Mark said, holding his hands out in front of him, "and I don't—"

Auster ignored him, picking up a file folder that had been lying there, opening it, and slipping out a series of glossy 8X10 photos, slapping them down on the table between them. Mark's line of sight caught just enough, bits and pieces, and he turned his head.

"I don't want to see these, Bill. Come on," Mark said with disgust. Auster said nothing, forcing a silence between them that guided Mark's gaze back to the table.

When Mark and Ann were kids, they'd begged a babysitter to see one of the big horror movies on video at the time; he couldn't remember the name. Their babysitter's boyfriend worked at a local video store, and in an attempt to be cool in the eyes of her charges, she'd let them watch it. Mark vividly remembered the sickening revulsion he'd felt, the fascination mixed with absolute horror, at a scene depicting a body that had been chainsawed to pieces, the individual segments twitching with death spasms and dripping with gore.

This was so much worse that he could barely comprehend it.

CHAPTER 9

The seven pictures presented a scene that seemed to stretch across a bedroom that opened into a large living and dining area in a ranch-style home. Normal furnishings—framed pictures, end tables, easy chairs, a queen-size bed, a loveseat—were so splattered with blood that it was hard to even fathom what it had looked like in a normal state. Two arms that had been carved from a torso at the shoulder, sporting gnarled bits of bloody flesh around the shock-whiteness of bone, lay on the carpet pointing out in a V-shape, as though raised in victory. Between them lay the head of a teenage girl—Lily Ensinger—facing away from the arms in an impossible configuration. Her lips were slightly parted, and the tip of her tongue was visible between blood-smeared lips. Her eyes had hemorrhaged, giving a pair of formerly emerald-green irises a cloudy, zombified look. Dara herself lay naked and splayed on a queen-size bed, arms tied to the headboard, ragged bites taken out of her face, and a hole so big you could see the box springs of the bed through it had been chopped into her chest with some sort of large blade. The thought that any human being could do what had been done here to another human being—much less his uncle—made Mark feel hopeless, in a way, that sickening feeling giving way to a vacant sickness deeper inside him.

"Bill," Mark said evenly, refusing to make eye contact with those pictures again, Jesus Christ, that poor girl, that poor fucking girl, "I'm telling you, I have no idea. Tony was always a bit wild, he drank a lot, did some drugs, ran with a rough crowd, but this is nothing like any of that."

"I remember your uncle. I rode with you guys to see Van Halen that one time, remember, freshman year?"

Bill noted. "I just meant, insofar as that he was loud, rowdy, that kind of thing. I remember he used to get arrested a bunch when my old man was a captain here. Tony's name came up, is what I'm saying. But you know, since this whole thing happened, the things he's said, they just... they don't make a lot of sense. And he just sat there like the goddamn Mona Lisa."

"What did he say?" Mark's eye flitted to the table; Dara gaped up at him with an open mouth full of blood-stained teeth.

"Well, when we arrested him, he said that 'all that unhappiness had to go somewhere.'"

"What does that mean?" Mark said.

"You tell me, partner." Bill drifted off, looked elsewhere, then shook his head, lighting a cigarette. "Then at one point during our interview, he said that Dara and those kids had to die because 'the Jacko told him they'd be fun to play with later.'"

"He said that, in those words? What the hell does that mean?"

Bill nodded thoughtfully, his gaze landing on the pictures. "Mark, your uncle's gonna rot in jail, that's the plain fact, and I think we can both feel good about that, looking at these." He stamped out his cigarette and sat back in his chair, crossing a leg over his knees. He wore a pair of black loafers that were just about rubbed through all the way on the soles. "But, there's crazy crazy, and there's what I'd call mission crazy, like ... reasonable crazy, I guess."

"Wouldn't that be an oxymoron?" Mark said.

Bill grinned, flashing his nicotine-stained smile at Mark. "Mission crazy is when I just ... I just know that someone isn't totally batshit, you know? That there was something reasonable going on in their heads when they did whatever the hell they did, that they had a ... a mission they felt like they had to complete, you know? Your uncle's a lot of things, Mark. But I don't think he's crazy crazy."

"Then why...?" Mark trailed off, looking down at the pictures. "I mean, how else do you explain what he did to these people?"

"That's what I was hoping you could help me with," Bill sighed. "But, I guess not. I guess not. You know, your uncle carries a picture of you and your little sister in his wallet. When we picked him up and went through his things, after we arrested him, we saw that. He loves you two. I guess. I don't know how someone who does this squares the idea of love, exactly, but I believe he does."

"I guess he does," Mark said. He stared up at Bill, whose gaze narrowed just a hair, just enough for Mark to notice. They studied each other for that brief moment, and then Bill stood up, opened the door, and asked if Mark would be so kind as to let him know if he thought of anything else that could help. Mark said he would, and five minutes later, he was on his way home.

"The Jacko said they'd be fun to play with later."

What the hell did that mean? And who the hell was Jacko? Probably one of Tony's biker buddies, or a dealer, or who-knew-who-the-fuck, honestly; the rogue's gallery that comprised Tony's friend circle went pretty low. It made Mark somehow more uncomfortable that he agreed with Auster; there was something at the heart of why Tony had done what he did. Surely there was. Surely whatever dark motive, whatever sickening, degenerate inspiration Tony had for such grisly killing, that was better, right, than no motive at all?

Mark had visited Tony twice since his uncle's conviction. Both times, they sat there on opposite sides of the glass, the phone receiver pressed to their ears, and Tony had offered little more than weak platitudes. Take care of your mother; make sure Brute takes his pills. The kind of superficial crap you said to people you barely knew.

"What the hell happened, man?" Mark finally said toward the end of the second and final visit to the prison. "Who's Jacko, Tony?"

Tony had stared at Mark through the glass like he wasn't even there, as though everything his uncle had given up, all the things that were part of life on the outside, were right there, just out of his reach. The expression on his grizzled, unshaven face was that of total and absolute resignation. "It's gonna get old being in here, that's for damn sure," he said. Then he shook his head and snorted, almost a chuckle. "You kids used to stand out there in Brute's yard during thunderstorms and look up at the rain coming down like turkeys drowning themselves, you know that? Jesus. I worried for you kids. Annie knew about being safe, but you, Marky, you just … never understood how bad the world was sometimes."

"What do you mean?" He took a vague offense at Tony's offhand comment. "What do you mean, 'Ann knew about being safe'?"

"Time's up," the guard standing near Tony's shoulder said, and Tony nodded without looking at him.

CHAPTER 9

"She knew what the world was," Tony said, his words drifting as he hung up the receiver, still talking. "You spent too much time in your own head."

10

The week went by quickly and consisted of little more than Mark running his regular bus route, picking up some super-sized bags of Halloween candy, and taking three carloads of clothes to Goodwill. A scheduling error at work left him with an extra day off, so when Friday morning arrived, he had a three-day weekend on his hands. He'd intended to see if Cory wanted to get out of town, maybe even just to the Quad Cities for a night in a nice hotel, change of scenery, but she was chaperoning the Homecoming dance at the high school on Saturday, so they'd have to settle for a weekend in.

And as it happened, he spent Friday morning on his knees.

Mark sucked sour bile back onto his tongue as he lurched and vomited again, hard, splattering the inside of the toilet with everything he had. Jesus, what had he eaten? Cory wasn't sick, so it wasn't something they'd shared. And he didn't get sick from drinking; he'd never gotten sick from drinking. Forty-five minutes on the floor of the bathroom, and he was finally able to stand up, wobbling a little, and steady himself. He made his way to the kitchen and managed to keep a glass of water down, which felt like progress. He yawned. It had started at one in the morning and hadn't stopped until... fuck. It was 9:30 already.

And now he was hungry, which made even less sense. Ravenously hungry, all at once, the endless waves of nausea suddenly overwritten with pangs that felt like he hadn't eaten in days. He wolfed down two bananas and three pieces of plain white bread, then sat down in front of the TV, where some schmaltzy show on the Food Network was showing a studio audience how to pickle vegetables. With Cory indisposed, he had the rest of the day, plus Saturday, to himself. He'd promised Mom he'd stop by Marigold over the weekend at some point, maybe bring lunch or something, and outside of that, his time was wide open.

He wanted a beer. His stomach felt normal again, so Mark popped the top on a Heineken and walked out onto Brute's back porch, where only a few ivory streaks across the sky betrayed the blue. It was a clear, calm, comfortable day. He sat on the stoop and watched as a rabbit, followed by several baby rabbits, darted from the brush back near where the hole in the thicket led into the dense, wooded area. They darted through the tall grass, skirting the broken cross where the scarecrow thing had been leaning precariously into a thorny bush. The rabbits disappeared into the neighborhood. Mark needed to get someone out to cut the grass; from what he could see, Brute didn't have a lawnmower, which made no sense, but Mark figured, maybe he'd been in the habit of letting neighbor kids do it. It was a big yard, and it'd be worth twenty bucks to get it off of his to-do list.

He finished his beer and dropped the bottle into the trash can at the side of the house where he'd started depositing all manner of porch sweepings, random trash from the garage, and the basement. Pieces of old cardboard, rotting newspapers, boxes of toys that had once belonged to him and Ann and had since been victims of basement flooding, all in the trash. Progress. He'd watch Sportscenter with another beer; then he'd start working on the attic. It was barely noon. He had all day.

There was a thump behind him, and Mark turned to see that the body cast had fallen over on its back. He set it up again, and it leaned to the right from the weight of its one complete arm. There was a black smudge across the side of its head on the right side as well; it must have gotten scuffed when it fell over, though the garage floor was clean. Mark steadied it upright and stared at it. It reminded him of something that might have been used in an old monster movie, and it was, after all, October. Maybe he could do something with it, he thought, make a decoration out of it. He picked it up, its one complete arm dangling at its side, and slipped it on again.

It went on easier now that he knew how to get his arm into the rigid sleeve without pulling on it. He stared into the mirror again. It wasn't Frankenstein, but it would be something entertaining, though Mark had no idea how many trick-or-treaters to expect. He turned and walked carefully into the house, still getting used to the bulk of the thing, snapping the light off in the garage and closing the door. He caught a glimpse of himself in the glass of a kitchen cabinet and started, then laughed out loud.

He stood straight, adjusting his posture to see how it sat on his body. It fit over his shoulders and around his head almost perfectly, as though it had been molded to him, but he knew that couldn't have been the case. Still, it felt different now, somehow. Tighter. Maybe more relaxed, a little less stiff since he'd tried it on once already? A grocery store flier had been used for a five-inch-or-so patch on the shoulder; he ran his fingers over the surface of the rigid papier-mâché. It was so ugly that Mark found it oddly compelling, like those weird little dogs with the bug eyes and wiry hair, Brussel something. He *did* remember the thing now, from when he was a kid, but damned if he could recall why it was actually there. He supposed it could have been something that Ann brought home from school, or maybe his mother had run across it at a yard sale; she was forever coming home with bargains in name only, some useless gadget or unnecessary acquisition that she'd bought only because it was cheap. *This, he thought, would certainly have fallen into that category.* Mark opened the fridge with his good arm, the other remaining stiffly at his side, and took out another beer, popping the top and raising it to his mouth before realizing that the slitted mouth wasn't exactly big enough to accommodate drinking or eating.

The odor hit his nostrils suddenly, and Mark started to cough, the way horseradish took your breath away, and he gasped from behind the layers of paper. His chest was pounding, and he could have sworn that he felt his blood moving through his veins, everything under his skin taking on a sensitivity the likes of which he'd never felt. *Breathe*, he thought, *breathe, breathe, breathe*, then—

   —then, just as he was reaching up to pull the thing from his head and shoulders, his breath came back to him in a rush like pulling from an oxygen tank, and he felt light, dizzy, but in the best way, oh my god, the rush that hit him all at once, a tingling feeling that spread over his skin like a balm, warm; he felt like he was on his tenth beer but without the accompanying alcohol fog, his mind so open that the roof was coming off the house, the sky was coming close, he was suspended in the air like a bird drifting in flight, watching the world move, every breath a deep, sparkling orgasm in his lungs. Mark clenched and unclenched his fists; then he hit the floor, though there was no pain, just the awareness of impact with the concrete. His hands and arms were numb.

"What the *fuck*?" Mark groaned, sitting on his knees there in the kitchen, that burned smell lingering in his nostrils, then that perfumed aroma, jasmine and oil and something else; something musky, animal. This was wrong, had to be. He was sick. First, the vomiting, now this inexplicable, nauseated euphoria. Had he been bitten by something while cleaning out the basement and yard, a spider of some kind? Food poisoning? Some sort of bug, or maybe a case of bad beer? He sniffed the open bottle—it smelled normal—and tossed it in the trash can, just in case. Steadying himself against the dizziness that had settled in his bones, Mark slipped off the costume and set it on one of the dining chairs in the kitchen.

   Mark took another beer from the fridge and popped the top. The dizziness subsided as he stood there, letting the cool air hit his face and bring the heat under his skin to some kind of normalcy, before sipping. Jesus. He'd have another beer or two, then see if he had any Theraflu or DayQuil or something. The sun ducked behind clouds outside, and the kitchen light dulled in acquiescence to the gray sky.

Propped up in a chair that way, the thing looked awkwardly like a man, ready for dinner, waiting for his family to join him.

By 4:30, his buzz had crossed over and Mark was riding a good, hard drunk. He'd lost his balance walking outside to get the mail, and he realized that he was nearly seeing double. Goddamn it. It got away from him too quickly. That was his problem, had always been his problem with drinking. Tony was the one who had taught him to pace himself; his uncle had let him have free access to beer for his last two years of high school, and by the time Mark's friends were able to legally drink and attacked their newfound freedom with something near zealotry, he was already used to that pleasant, disconnected feeling that a good buzz brought. But today? Today, it was a primal, bone-deep feeling that he could only equate to the way steroids must have felt. He was shaking, but he felt good, strong. Borderline euphoric, for reasons he couldn't fathom.

Mark flipped through the mail—all junk—tossed it into the trash can, and opened the fridge. He had three Heinekens left, not nearly enough to last him the rest of the night. Maintaining the high was the hard part, as any dedicated addict was likely to say, so he drank two big glasses of water before getting in the car. There was a Casey's Gas and Grill just four blocks away, and the odds of his getting pulled over or having something happen were really slim to none. He fumbled the keys into the ignition and turned it over. He met his own stare in the rearview mirror as he backed out of the garage. *I'm actually fine*, he thought. *Now that I'm thinking about it, I'm actually okay, I'm not really drunk.*

He heard Ann's voice, somewhere deep in his brain, asking if he was sure about that. He sighed. Ann was always so grim.

He took the four blocks slowly, probably slower than he needed to, but hey, he was being careful—that was the name of the game. Not getting cocky or reckless, he did have a buzz—that was fair and true. He couldn't kid himself on that front, but again, he knew when he was okay. Why would he lie to himself? He mashed the brakes a little too hard at a four-way stop. Why didn't he just walk?

Mark parked around the side of the building so the cashier wouldn't see him driving. No one knew how to mind their own business anymore, he thought; if he drove away after being seen, it'd be on Facebook and trending within an hour. He went inside and bought two twelve-packs of Heineken and a pack of unfiltered Camels. Sometimes, in the middle of a good drunk, he liked a couple of cigarettes, and tonight was one of those times, a celebration, of his finding his home, a real home where he *felt* at home, of Cory, of, hell, of everything. Everything good.

Outside, it had started raining, and he pushed open the glass doors to see a woman standing near the corner of the building, arms folded tightly against her chest, a cutoff t-shirt not providing much coverage against the storm. She was barefoot, and her long, dark hair was a wet mess. He gave her a polite smile as he walked past her, watching his steps. Jesus, he really should have walked—

"Hey." She was calling to him as he stuck his key in the driver's side from around the side of the building as Mark put the keys in the ignition. "Hey, listen, are you—would you mind giving me a ride?"

Mark set the beer in the back seat and glanced around. There were no cops, no other cars, really, as the storm was getting worse, pelting the car to a marching rhythm. "Where, um, where you headed?"

"Just up the street, to Powell," she pointed, "but I'm gonna drown out here if I wait for my boyfriend. Please? I'll give you ten bucks."

"No, that's—" He glanced around again. "No, sure, get in. You'll get soaked." Surely, he was sober enough to get her the additional three blocks to Powell and then back around to his place. A third of a mile, maybe. Maybe a little more. Not far.

"God, thank you," she said, scrunching her shoulders as she dashed for the passenger side, as though retreating into herself would keep her dry. She slid into the seat, wringing out her brown hair before closing the door. "Thank you, seriously, this came up fast."

"Yeah, no worries." Mark realized that he was taking deep breaths, trying to level off. He felt hot, and his head was fuzzy, for sure. God, he should have walked, but then he'd be stuck there, too, and what then? Drink on the curb like a wino? No, he was smart to drive. That was the better of the two choices. "Just the corner, down there, Powell and Fremont?"

"That's fine, yeah, his house is just two down, I can run from there." She smiled. "God loves a Good Samaritan, you know?"

"Does he, now?" Mark said, chuckling more at the random oddity of her thought than the actual sentiment. "I mean, that's good, I guess. Your boyfriend okay with a stranger dropping you off?" No other headlights, just the tacka-tacka-tacka of the rain, the steady, white flickers of the center line slipping past as he maintained a careful speed.

She grinned, not looking at him, her eyes fixed on the road. "Oh, I think so. Better that than a stranger sleeping in your bed, right?"

"Yeah, I guess, depends on the stranger, though," he smiled, and she laughed. He was okay. Fuck, he was *fine*. He was actually more sober than he thought, now that he was back behind the wheel. Yes, sir, this was just fine. He noticed the beer on the back seat and realized that it was only just before five. Total win. He had the rest of the night to tackle the attic, and then—well, no, maybe not anything involving a ladder, he considered. Maybe he'd watch TV a bit, have something to eat, another couple of beers, then he could—

"Better than having a stranger put a cigarette out on your tongue, right?" It was a question, but it came out as flatly as a statement. The sky is blue. The world is round. Better than having a stranger put a cigarette out on your tongue, right—

"Excuse me?" Mark said, and he felt heat at the base of his neck, rising, spreading along his throat, he was already easing the car to the curb where she'd said to drop her off, "did you—"

CHAPTER 10

The woman moaned, clutching at her chest before crying out. Mark watched as she sunk her fingers into the flesh above her breasts and pulled, tearing out a ragged hunk of meat, spraying the dashboard of his car with blood, and then he recognized her, Dara Ensinger, the pictures at the police station had been nearly unrecognizable, and her head lolled forward as through she was just an empty shell devoid of bones or structure, a thick, gloppy torrent of bloody slime running out of her mouth and all over the emergency brake, blood mixed with that pasty, Elmer's smell he remembered from grade school—

Ann used to use that glue, he thought dumbly, *Ann used*—his shirt was soaked, and Mark looked around as a sudden pounding right behind his forehead made him wince. The rain hammered the windshield as he swallowed hard. He was sitting in his driveway. He looked in the rearview mirror; the two twelve-packs of beer sat on the passenger side seat.

Had he fallen asleep? But how had he made it home? He remembered seeing Dara in the car, but there was nothing to indicate that she'd been there. The car was clean. What had she said about Tony putting cigarettes out on her *tongue*? Holy Christ. Holy, holy, holy Christ. Was that true? Maybe he'd heard it somewhere, in court, maybe. Mark laid his head back against the seat. His mouth was dry, and he didn't feel like having any more beer. He took deep breaths, counting the beats between thunderclaps and lightning strikes. It was just before seven. He'd somehow lost two hours in the car.

He got out, looked up into the sky as the rain pelted his face, and closed his eyes. His stomach felt sick again, his head ached, he felt like he had the flu, and it was different, somehow, than just being drunk. He put his hands to his face and took deep breaths. His palms smelled like sweat and glue.

Glue.

He turned and looked over his shoulder, surveying the car again. The dashboard and console were clean, though the seat was getting wet from the rain coming in. Mark walked carefully toward the porch, ignoring the twelve-packs of beer in the seat, when he noticed movement in the backyard.

The figure was shambling toward the tree line, and while the top half looked like Dara, her curly dark hair and t-shirt, it looked like her bottom half was dissolving in the rain, the curve of her hips and thin legs beginning to break down into amorphous masses of runny flesh as she half ran, half crawled toward the grove. Her face was dissolving out from the middle, features collapsing into each other like melting wax.

"Hey!" Mark shouted, and her upper half turned around as the bottom half kept moving, flailing, a bloody, fleshy mass that seemed to be coming apart as though she'd suffered some horrible deformity at birth. But, no, no, no, he thought, *this is a dream*, and he was nearly there, reaching for her, and then her eyelids were peeling back, her lips curling away from her mouth, as though she was being turned inside out. The thing collapsed to the wet grass with a yawping howl, no longer pretending to be human, but still wearing a version of Dara Ensinger's face. The thing clutched and scrabbled into the brush, and its sound died out as the storm picked up around him.

Mark's legs left him as he lay down in the mud and let the cold rain soak his shirt, his hair. He saw

CHAPTER 10

a flash in his head of something, not quite a memory, but not quite a dream, and then he succumbed to unconsciousness.

11

Cory stared at the ceiling.
At its peak, her anxiety that Adrian would suddenly reappear in their lives kept her from sleeping entirely. It wasn't that she'd toss and turn, none of the insomniac clichés. Rather, she'd simply lie there, staring at the ceiling, replaying the worst of times in her head like some hellish highlight reel of what not to allow in a relationship. Yes, they'd been young. Yes, they'd made some impulsive decisions. Yes, she'd gotten pregnant because they were careless, though Geo was the joy of her life, and she couldn't imagine where she'd be without her daughter. But those arguments were little comfort to her now; now, she was forty-three and decidedly not young; now, she lived with the specter of abuse hanging over her shoulder like some evil imp that picked at her, teased her, tortured her brain.

The voicemail that afternoon from Erica, one of the math teachers at GHS, had made Cory's stomach feel like a ball of acid.

CHAPTER 11

"I felt like I should tell you, Cory," Erica said, a soft, ominous tone to her voice. "I saw him ... at the Point House Tap out past 41, one of those little towns? We stopped for gas on the way home from visiting Kylie at school in Macomb, and I saw him through the window, sitting at the bar. I'm sorry, honey, but I felt like I should tell you."

So Adrian was back in the area after two years of zero contact. Cory had heard he was in jail for a while, but no one seemed to know for sure. Georgia had offered to look it up online, but Cory said no, it didn't matter. She didn't want to know where he was. That was part of the point. She wouldn't let him back in. That was part of what kept her awake. Her scars had faded—one on her neck and two on her lower back—and Georgia didn't remember much; Cory believed her, mainly because Georgia didn't seem to betray any concern beyond just the fact that the thought of Adrian upset her mother.

If he came back, Cory would do whatever she had to do to keep them safe. She wondered if she had it in her to kill, should the need arise. She'd thought about it before. *If that bedroom door eased open right now, and I saw his shadow in the doorway, that black shape looming for a moment before coming in, what would I do?* She could reach the phone, certainly, and she had her mace. She hadn't felt comfortable with a gun in the house; a couple of her support group friends had suggested it, and she'd even gone so far as to go to a store, hold one, see how it felt, but it didn't work. It didn't give her comfort; it gave her more anxiety, the thought of having to be ready to use it. No, she had her mace, and she had friends to call, stay with, if need be.

Getting out altogether felt like the more reasonable option.

She'd never really imagined leaving Galesburg. Not because she loved it—she was indifferent—but because the opportunity, a real opportunity with real consequences and upward mobility, had never really presented itself. But now, knowing that Adrian was still out there somewhere nearby, doing whatever he was doing, having finally left her alone for a few years. It was inevitable, wasn't it? That he'd try to come around? Maybe under the pretense of wanting to see Georgia, or maybe more directly in just wanting to see what he could get out of her, Cory was ashamed to admit to herself that she'd let it happen early in their relationship when things got tumultuous. Money, sex, a crash pad; it was hard to tell with him, and it didn't really matter.

She'd filled out the paperwork for a leave of absence in the spring, if it came to that, and the deadline for processing it through the district office was approaching. She'd need to have it submitted by the middle of November, and she'd been sitting on it since May, when she'd ironically started wondering about a change of scenery. But then she'd had to go to the DMV one morning, and who should be there but Mark Devold? Ten minutes of conversation, numbers exchanged, and suddenly, their attempts at finding a relationship seemed to be working after a false start in their teenage years and another later in their twenties, just before she met Adrian. Maybe Mark wasn't the one who got away. It wasn't as dramatic as all that, but Cory had always wondered, and it turned out that he'd felt the same. So there was that, and now there was this, the knowledge that Adrian was back.

CHAPTER 11

Cory stared at the ceiling, and the overhead fan above her stared silently back, the five points calling to mind a star.

Can I get a wish? she thought. *Can you tell me what the hell to do here?*

Somewhere outside, a dog barked, and a truck rumbled by. Then it was silence, with five more hours until the sun rose.

12

Mark woke up on the couch in front of some late-night talk show he'd never heard of as a rubber-faced host mugged through his monologue.

Someone was breathing in the room.

Gradually, his eyes adjusted to the pre-dawn blues, slivers of light creeping around the curtains. Had he brought someone home? Jesus, what the fuck, the woman at the gas station, was she there?

That wasn't just a woman; that was Dara.

Surely not. Mark closed his eyes, pulling together the random images he had from the night before into his head like fireflies in a palm. He listened.

Someone breathed—carefully, evenly. Steady, heavy breathing.

"Who's there?" he said, sitting up suddenly, the pain in his head announcing his hangover like a bomb going off. Looking around, he saw that there was no one in the room. The costume, for whatever reason, sat awkwardly propped upright in the rocking chair near the windows, and while he didn't remember putting it there, he knew that he must have.

The sound of breathing was gone.

"What the fuck?" he muttered. At some point in the night following his rainy encounter with whatever he'd seen in the yard, he must have come inside and fallen asleep on the couch in his wet clothes. The cushions squished with mud and rainwater that had a decidedly moldy smell to it. His head was a little heavy with sleep, but for as hungover as he knew he should have been, he felt oddly okay, strong even. His muscles weren't sore at all, and sore muscles were normally a telltale sign of having tied one on too tightly the night before.

The clock said 8:40 in the morning. He had three missed texts from Cory, the first saying good morning and how she missed him and how lucky he was to be off work, the second asking if he wanted to have dinner and finally meet her daughter Georgia one night that week, and the third indicating how chaperoning the Homecoming dance was going to make her feel old beyond words. He took a deep breath, stood, stretched, and found his way to the kitchen for water.

Mark drank three glasses of water and found his new pack of cigarettes on the kitchen counter; had he come into the kitchen, or had he gone straight to the couch? Christ, he couldn't remember. Blackout drunks were terrifying, and for as often as he had a few too many, he rarely had so much that he lost time that way, though...

God loves a Good Samaritan
DARA

...that didn't much matter now, after the fact. He certainly didn't feel like drinking anytime soon, so maybe he'd actually make good use of the weekend. Mark stepped onto the back porch and shook one of the Camels from the open pack, leaning against the door frame with a sigh. A couple of rabbits were chasing each other through the yard, skidding on their heels as they sprinted in silent, broad circles.

Watching the rabbits, Mark suddenly noticed the prints leading from the porch all the way back past the cross where the costume had been hung. Boot prints, it looked like, and at a glance, he thought they were probably the ones he wore for cleaning the basement, though he couldn't swear to it. They were relatively fresh, partially filled in with rainwater, so they'd had to have been made at some point during the previous night.

Dara?

It couldn't have been, he considered grimly; whatever or whomever that was, it hadn't had any legs by the time it reached the back, scrabbling and clawing its way toward the grove. Mark winced at the thought of her face peeling away from her head like a snake shedding its skin...

He'd been drunk, and he'd hallucinated. That was all it was. That was all it could have been, of course.

Had he gone back out there after he woke up on the porch?

Mark slipped his sneakers on and tied them tight, then followed the muddy tracks carefully back toward the brambles—the wooded area that ran parallel to the cornfield beyond. The tracks continued, though they became harder to discern on the spongy, wet ground, particularly as vines and weeds grew up in rough, wild patches, bullying the pathway out of existence after only ten feet or so. Mark kneeled on his haunches and listened.

For what? he thought to himself, but still, he waited, quietly. He steadied himself by planting a palm on the wet, cold ground. There was nothing to hear, really, just the occasional rustle of an animal, the rusty brown-orange of autumn foliage, the trees beginning to exchange their lush, heavy branches for skeletal arms that bobbed a little in the morning breeze.

"Jesus." He laughed out loud with relief. "Jesus, man. Get it together." He wiped his hands on his jeans, leaving thick, dark streaks of mud, but that was okay. He would do a load of laundry. It was okay, not a big deal at all. He needed something in his stomach, and he was pretty sure there were still some eggs in the fridge; he could make eggs and some toast and watch TV for a bit before diving back into sorting things in the guest bedrooms. His day was back on track. Making his way back toward the house, he saw what he'd missed on his way in.

A t-shirt, snarled and torn on a branch, fluttered a little in the morning air, rusty smears here and there, the Aerosmith logo on the front still clearly visible through the dirt, grime, and what looked to be dried blood. A wide, ragged hole was torn right in the middle of the shirt.

The Jacko said they'd be fun to play with later.

Mark reached for it, then hesitated.

What was this?

Was someone out there with him? From the look of it, it was a woman's tee, the band's logo faded, one of those shirts that was made to look naturally weathered by time.

JUNKMAN

It was a dream, Mark argued with himself, the night before had been a dream, and maybe this is what triggered it, maybe he'd seen this out here, or somewhere in the neighborhood, in a trash bin or something, maybe a kid or an animal had gotten ahold of it, dragged it out here.

Bullshit.

Careful not to get his fingerprints on it, Mark found a stick with enough weight to support the shirt and fished it from the stubborn grip of the branches. He carried it inside, closed the back door, and draped the shirt across the kitchen counter. Mark stood there, arms folded, wondering what to do. Part of him thought he should call Auster. If it was, in fact, Lily Ensinger's shirt, then the police should have it, a*lready* had it at some point; it was in the pictures Bill had shown him, so it was part of the crime-scene evidence, wasn't it? Of course it was. Had someone planted it there?

He felt a hungover hopelessness drift across his thoughts, that chemical sadness that sometimes followed a hard drunk. A short while ago, when he'd woken up, he felt good, but now, all he felt was paranoia. What sense would it have made for someone to put it there? His uncle was in prison, end of story. Lily Ensinger was dead, and Tony was locked up for the rest of his life. A sad end to a sad chapter all around, but an end, most assuredly.

Mark took a plastic grocery bag from the cabinet under the sink, stuffed the shirt inside, then tied the bag tightly and opened the basement door. At the bottom of the stairs was a plastic trash barrel filled with random junk and the sawdust sweepings from Brute's woodworking shop; Mark tossed the bag, watching it arc through the air and land on top of the mess in the barrel. It was nothing. It was Aerosmith, for fuck's sake. They were as beloved as any rock band in history. There were ten million of their shirts out there, and it's not like it was some vintage shirt; he'd seen it at Target, for Christ's sake. It was probably some teenagers screwing around in the field back there, trying to find a safe place to fuck, and some girl had forgotten or lost her shirt.

He opened the fridge, pushing the distraction of the footprints and shirt to the back of his head. Eggs. Eggs, toast, and the bedrooms. That was his weekend. He'd spend it sober, nursing this little nag of a hangover, and he'd make some real headway.

13

Student volunteers were teeming through the hallways, excitedly chattering about the dance that night, who was going with who, the latest gossip from end-to-end. Cory sat at her desk, eating some leftover pasta from a Tupperware bowl. The morning had been hanging streamers and mirror balls, scattering the floor and tables with glitter, checking the sound system. It was fun, and the periodic flashes of nostalgia Cory had for her high-school days spent in that same gym had helped her to put the angst of the last day or two behind her for a few hours.

Her phone rang in her hand as she'd started texting Mark, and it was an unknown number, which she'd been getting a lot of. She'd been ignoring them, but now, a flower of heat opened in her stomach; she immediately lost her appetite. She answered, and he spoke before she even had a chance to say hello.

"Took you long enough." Adrian's voice sent an inky cloud of dread, and sickness rolled through her. *FUCK.* "Where you at, girl?"

CHAPTER 13

"None of your business." She finally managed to even her voice enough to speak. She couldn't give him the satisfaction of knowing that she'd been dreading this, fearing it, though she hated admitting that to herself. She went to the window and looked out, wondering if he was sitting in a car somewhere on Henderson, just fucking with her. He'd been known to do stalkery shit like that. She dropped her voice low, closing her classroom door and moving back toward the desk, as though he might somehow see her from the doorway. "And why are you calling me?"

"Just to talk," he said nonchalantly, then chuckled, and it was *that*, that carefree fucking laugh that gaslit you, made you feel like you were the one blowing things out of proportion, that any judgment of or disagreement with him meant that you were the difficult one, that was what settled in Cory's blood and made her want to scream. "I was outside of Nashville for a while. But, uh, I'm back in town."

"You're in Galesburg?" *God, god, god, no.* She heard the people in her support group telling her not to give in to what-ifs, but that was bullshit, and in an instant, two years of empowerment and coping strategies went straight out the fucking window like a bucket of dirty water; was he at the house, near the house? Had he seen Geo? Called her? Anything? Was he watching one of them now? "What the hell are you doing back here, Adrian?"

"Eh, you know," he said, then the chuckle. "Had to call up some favors and pay a few visits. Thought I'd, uh, maybe see what you were up to. Thought I'd come by tonight."

"Like hell you will," she hissed into the phone, louder than she'd intended, and she saw a couple of students passing by outside the door glance toward the frosted glass. "You will not go to the house, Adrian, and you goddamn sure will not talk to Geo. We have nothing for you. You have nothing for us. Nothing. Do you understand me?"

There was a long pause, and Cory thought she could hear the sound of liquid swigging. He was sitting somewhere at 11:30 in the morning, having a beer, maybe playing pool, Christ, maybe just down the street at the Clarabelle Tipper, sipping a Miller, talking to the other laid-off career drunks, scheming god-knew-what.

"I hear you," he said.

"Do you underst—"

"I understand that I have a right to see my daughter even if my ex-wife says I can't," he said, that same even tone. "Who's gonna stop me? You? Your fuckin' bus driver boyfriend?"

How does he know I'm seeing Mark? Fuck, fuck, fuck. Cory felt her face flush, her neck getting hot. "Listen to me, Adrian. Geo isn't... she's not even home. She's on a school thing until next week."

He snorted. "She take off on her school thing in the last three hours? That sure looked a lot like her heading out of Starbucks with a fancy coffee this morning. The shit you two blow money on. Sit here and tell me you can't help me out. Bitch, I'll burn that house to the goddamn ground just to spite you. You understand that, right?"

His voice grew thinner as Cory tuned him out, her brain moving into process mode, that was what they said in group, that you had to have a plan, that you

CHAPTER 13

couldn't get upset and say things weren't fair, you couldn't throw a tantrum, you had to get ready to take action, to do what you had to do to keep you and your kids safe—

"I hear you," she said, and he chuckled with a kind of satisfaction, the kind of respect you show when the other team scores a well-earned point. She'd called his bluff for now, but she knew what he was capable of.

"Okay, okay," he said, his voice softening. "Let's not go this hard, girl. I want to see Geo. And I want to see you, too, okay? It's been a while. I know we aren't exactly on track, right? I get that. Shit, I didn't get a fucking head injury, okay? But I want to see you, both of you. If not tonight, then tomorrow, or the next night, okay?" Another pause. She could hear what sounded like a jukebox in the background throwing down some shit-kicker country; her memories and fear and disgust were a tangible taste in her mouth now, her throat growing so dry that she felt like she might not be able to speak. "I'm not going away until I do, Corene."

For now, she had to buy time. Cory swallowed hard.

"Call me on Thursday," she said, "and we'll work something out."

Something almost like hope crawled over the chuckle this time. "Alright, then. Thursday. It's a fucking date." The line was dead, and Cory sank into her chair, letting the phone slip from her fingers and into her purse.

14

2:00. It had been a productive Sunday afternoon, with three plastic totes worth of old cards, photos, school papers, and magazines mostly headed for the trash bin outside, freeing up one of the bedroom closets, the one that had been Ann's room during the time when they'd lived with Brute. Some findings were poignant, most notably a series of Ann's crayon drawings shortly after their father died. Stephen Devold had died in a plane crash outside Mobile, Alabama, a tragic, isolated case of a pilot with too much confidence behind the controls of a small craft in a storm. Mark was seven at the time, and Ann was two, so while she hadn't been fully aware of what had happened, they'd grown closer then, forging a kind of emotional reliance upon the two that was hard to shake, a sense of loss, almost, when the other wasn't around. Ann had always had the soul of a wanderer, so it was little surprise when she'd decided to study abroad; with her grades, scholarships were easy to come by, and there was nothing for her in Galesburg. She had studied anthropology, of all things, and Mark didn't guess there'd be any significant discoveries in that field awaiting her at home.

She'd texted him the night before, though he'd missed it during his incident on the porch. It was a picture of something that looked like a big wooden tray with a strange face carved into one end.

[Ann: Probably a box of these somewhere in Grandpa B's house, right? Hahaha!]

[Mark: Not yet, but I'll keep ya posted. Miss you. Love you. Mom okay. Things are fine here.]

[Ann: Send me pics, net here is crap, gives me something to look forward to - headed to a dig site later today and out of comm for almost a week. Stay safe, bro].

In response, he sent a picture of an old girdle ("Saving this for you!"), three Polaroid photos of what appeared to be a black lab squatting in a yard to poop ("What the hell was Grandma Lynn wanting to preserve here?"), and a picture that Ann must have drawn in grade school of the two of them in what looked like a canoe, rowing through water that was, in places, on fire ("School counselor much? Good God, sis").

The last pic he sent was the one of him wearing the costume, followed by the caption, "you probably made this monstrosity, correct?" He chuckled as he plugged his phone in to charge in the bathroom, then lugged a box of trash into the garage to await the curb.

His hangover was gone, essentially, and while he felt a little like when you come off the tail end of a cold, stirring up dust had made him thirsty, so he grabbed a Heineken from the fridge and drank deep. It tasted good, but a few plugs were enough; there was something about it that made his mouth feel dry, and he didn't like the feeling. He poured it down the drain, had another glass of water, and headed back upstairs.

The bedroom that had been his when they'd stayed with Brute was largely as he'd left it. Since he moved back into the house, he'd been sleeping in Brute's bed, as it was relatively new and had a queen-size mattress; this one was a twin with a quilt neatly tucked under the pillows, ready for whomever might need it. Mark guessed it hadn't been slept in since he'd been probably fifteen or sixteen, and until that point, it had been littered with the detritus of a teenage boy's interests, circa 1990. Had Brute cleaned the room completely in the years since he'd last been there? Because if not...

Mark kneeled and reached under the bed, his hand brushing a dust ball as he found the edge of a shoebox and slid it out. There was a stack of comic books maybe three inches thick, some DC, a few Marvel, but mostly independent science fiction and fantasy comics from the early '80s, stuff he'd forgotten about for years, but now, holy shit, how could he have forgotten? There'd been a comic store in downtown Galesburg for just a few years during his time in junior high, but it was enough time to amass a small horde of treasures on the comic front. *Alien Encounters*, *Death Rattle*, *Mr. Monster* ... the list went on, and Mark chuckled out loud.

For the brief time in which he'd been obsessed with comic books, they'd meant the world to him. He wiped his dusty hands on his pants, and with a grin, began flipping through the stack and marveling at the covers again—lurid, colorful explosions depicting alien

CHAPTER 14

women with absurdly huge tits, bloody horrors of all kinds returning from the grave, even one story that had stuck in his preteen brain about an alien masquerading as a woman to seduce a group of astronauts that ended with a guy getting his dick eaten off. He remembered how worried he was of his mother catching him with such a thing. Not that she would have gone ridiculous on him, she was pretty understanding and wasn't going to lose sleep over a comic, but it would have been awkward, as a twelve-year-old kid discovering sex for the first time, to have your mom bracing you about a story involving a killer vagina.

He sat down on the bed, leaning back against the headboard, paging through a few issues as the sun poked out from behind some clouds, bathing the room in a warm series of sunbeams that slid across the bedspread and over the floor, drawing a long shadow over the doorway. Mark felt something rigid in the middle of one issue, maybe a bookmark, a piece of paper or cardboard, and he slipped it out.

Three Polaroids. They were dark, all shot from head on, the photographer's focal point being the spread thighs of a woman, the slightest hint of dark brown pubic hair topping the slick, pink flesh there. In one, a hand reached down to spread the labia, the way you'd see in dirty magazine centerfolds, but there was something very different about the sight of homemade photos depicting that same thing. Something almost upsettingly vulnerable, and he was almost ashamed to realize that he'd felt a stir. His skin felt hot; who was this? Whose pictures were these? And why were they in his comic books from junior high? Surely they'd been hidden there because it was a safe place because they wouldn't have been seen by anyone but ... him? He set the pile of comics on the bedside table and held the Polaroids gingerly. There was nothing identifiable in them, nothing that suggested who the model was or who had taken the photos. He knew they couldn't be his, but that was little comfort, given how odd and jarring the discovery was.

There was one more, but it was nothing he could really discern. It looked vaguely like a shirtless man taking his own picture—a guerrilla selfie, holding the Polaroid up to a mirror—and the glare looked like a giant, white burn in the middle of the photo, partially obscuring what looked like something protruding from the man's stomach.

A face?

It was blurry, and the picture cut off the photographer's head. Around the subject was a faint, gray aura, a trick of the light, most likely, and something near the edge of the picture had blurred as it moved, from what he could see. Nothing in the photo made sense: not the subject, not the photographer, and not the uncertainties of what he saw at the edges of the photo—the things that looked like eyes glimmering throughout the background, like wild animals in the darkness.

Mark tucked them into his back pocket; the idea of throwing them in the trash felt irresponsible. Not that he thought he could actually figure it all out, but something was very wrong in their being there, and to throw them in the trash where someone else could find them ... that seemed wrong, somehow. He turned them over and looked for a date, anything identifiable, before tucking them in an envelope and slipping them into a junk drawer under the kitchen sink. He supposed it had to have been Tony, but finding them in his old comics, in his grandparents' home, something about that seemed almost corrupt—

A banging on the back door behind him made him physically jump, and he almost dropped the pictures. Mark glanced over his shoulder; Cory's smiling face was at the window, laughing at his reaction. He stuffed the pictures in the envelope and back into the drawer.

"Didn't mean to startle you, big guy," she said, slipping her arms around his waist as he opened the door. Something in her smile was sad, though Mark couldn't pin down why, exactly. "Whatcha doin'?"

"Oh, nothing, just—going through stuff upstairs," he said absently, glancing behind him to make sure the drawer was closed.

Cory looked up at him and swallowed hard. That's when he noticed that her eyes were bloodshot from crying. "Can we talk?"

15

After they drove out to Abingdon and ate chicken nachos at an off-the-path sports bar called Kilowatz (Cory's choice, as she wanted to go off their standard grid of places in town), after she had told him the details of Adrian's past-abuse and his phone call that afternoon, after she'd fallen asleep on his couch while they watched a bad sci-fi movie on HBO, after she'd woken up, after they'd kissed more deeply and passionately than any other time before, and after she'd gotten home, texted him that her doors were locked and that she was okay and that she'd talk to him tomorrow, Mark sat on his back porch and stared into the woods, sipping a beer. He'd asked her to stay at his place, his worry metastasizing as she told him about Adrian, but she didn't want to disrupt Georgia. She was thinking of a way to deal with it, she'd said, and she needed him to trust her. Which he did, but this went beyond that, in Mark's mind. The guy might not be more than your garden-variety scumbag with a periodic penchant for intimidating violence, but that was enough, Mark had told her, and he'd wanted to call Auster, but Cory asked him specifically not to do that.

Mark texted her to say I love you and to come over if she needed to, then set his phone down on the concrete step, and squinted into the darkness.

There was something moving in the brush near the edge of the field.

The moonlight shifted a little, and Mark could see what looked like an approximation of a face peering at him from just a couple of feet off the ground, as though someone sat crouched, watching him. An approximation, because in spite of what should have been enough light, the face looked somehow incomplete, as if the features were in the process of forming, a time-lapse composition of flesh.

Adrian?

Mark sat still for a few moments, trying not to stare at what was definitely a face now, though from where he sat, it was impossible to see who it was. The more he squinted into the near darkness, the more it looked like female features, petite bone structure and a small mouth. Mark stood, and still, he could only see the face, the vaguest suggestion of a body behind it. He stepped into the yard. His strange voyeur sat unmoving.

"Come out. I can see you." Mark glanced back at the house. The back door was unlocked, and there was a baseball bat just in the garage, but he doubted he had time to get it and be back before whoever this was took off. Probably whoever the little shits were who kept spray-painting crap on the house. Or was it something more than that? Were they casing the house? Was it someone who knew that Brute had died?

(better than having a cigarette put out—)

Mark drained his beer and flipped the bottle over, holding it by the neck. At the very least, it was something. The face didn't move, and now he wondered if it was a trick of the light as he stepped carefully through the yard. His movements threw tall, sweeping shadows over the yard and the house; if someone was trying to remain unseen, now was their chance to run as he closed the distance little by little. He stepped up his pace, the face unchanged, the lips drawn into an O as though the person was yawning, the eyes now too big, the closer he got, perfect rings with nothing in the middle, but that wasn't possible, and the howling mouth on a face with no other features, like skin that had been burned smooth with ruined tissue, and a choking, gurgling sound from the bushes, from the face, shoulders and hands, now, clutching a tree, and Mark raised the bottle—

He cried out, stepping backward as the thing came fully into view. The thing was slight, maybe two or three feet long, like a giant, fleshy slug pocked with dark bruise-like spots, and the hands that clutched the tree were made from flesh that looked like it had been burned into smooth, rippling scars. The face was a misshapen blob of loosely organized human features, though somehow, Mark could tell that it was a woman. What few patches of hair stuck out of the thing were dark with purple streaks. Christ, had there been an accident nearby, a car fire or an explosion?

"I'll get help," Mark gasped, and the creature groaned, a hollow, deathly sound tagged at the end by that same gurgling noise he'd heard from the porch. He turned and ran for the house, hands shaking as he took out

CHAPTER 15

his phone, punched in Auster's number, and stared into the backyard.

The dark hair, the purple streak.

Regina Marling.

Auster shined a flashlight across the cornfield, a beam of light distorting the shadows of the stalks into stick figures, dancing and frantic.

"You're sure?" he said, looking at Mark with something like concern and skepticism.

"Abso-fucking-lutely," Mark said, arms folded against the chill that had kicked up, the temperature dropping by the hour as a cold front surged into the Midwest. "She—it—was right there."

"What was her name, again?"

"Regina Marling, but that was then. Maybe her name is different now." Mark shook his head and stuffed his hands into his pockets. The way Auster watched him, carefully and without breaking eye contact, made him nervous for no reason.

"We can check the database," Auster said, waving it off as he shone his light across the ground near where Mark had seen the woman-thing. "And what was wrong with her?"

"She was ... there was something wrong with her skin. I think she was burned. I don't know." Mark pretended to search for the words; he had them, but they were too unreal to make sense of, especially to a cop. "She looked *injured*, I guess. There was ... head trauma."

"What kind of head trauma? She was bleeding?"

He knew that being honest was best, even if it made him sound insane. Mark sighed. "No, her face looked like it had been rearranged, beaten or something. Like a Mr. Potato Head or something, the face was all wrong, the way it was, set up, I guess?"

"Beaten and burned." Auster made a clicking sound with his tongue, clipped the flashlight to his belt, and took out a piece of gum, chewing it thoughtfully. "Okay, well, there's nothing here now, so I mean, good that you called, and if you see anything else, you'll let us know, right?"

"Yeah, sure, of course," Mark said, defeated. "Listen, when you were interviewing my uncle, did—"

"Hold the phone," Auster said, peering into the brush and squinting. He waved another officer over, and together, they crept toward the property line where the cornfield and the trees met. Hanging from a branch was a bracelet, something cheap, imitation gold. "You see this before? You recognize it at all?"

"No," Mark said. Auster took out a pair of rubber gloves, slipped them on and snapped them tight around his wrists, and picked the piece of costume jewelry from the limbs.

"Let's bag this," Auster called to another officer. "Regina Marling, you say?"

"Yeah," Mark said.

"Run that name," Auster said to the same cop who had now opened the evidence bag. Auster dropped the bracelet inside and slipped off his gloves. He turned back to Mark, studying him. "You sure that doesn't look familiar?"

Mark's gaze was steady; he wasn't going to be called crazy. He wasn't crazy. He'd seen what he'd seen. "I'd tell you if it did, Bill."

"Lieutenant Auster, please."

"Yes, fine. Lieutenant. I'd tell you if it did. Look, whoever it was out here, they scared the shit out of me."

"Well, I'll let you know what we find out," Auster said. "In the meantime, just lock your door and let us know if anything weird goes down, alright?"

"Yeah," Mark said, nodding. "By the way, do you—any of you—know an Adrian Thompson?"

"If we're talking about the same guy, he held up a bunch of gas stations, car washes, did some time for meth distribution. He was a few years behind us in school, I think. Punk piece of trash. Why?"

"He might be stalking my girlfriend. She's his ex. I thought it was him, out here, until I saw the—" *Thing, it was a thing, not a person* "—the girl."

"Wait, Cory Blevin married that guy?"

"Yeah." Mark rubbed his eyes. "I wasn't supposed to tell you that. She didn't want me to say anything, but I'm a little concerned, to be honest. Guy sounds like a real piece of shit, and apparently he's back in town."

"Understandable," Auster returned. "I can't offer you much if he hasn't done anything, Mark, but let's stay synced up on that one, okay?" Auster's radio squawked with static-drenched chatter. "Gotta go, Mark. I'll be in touch."

"Thanks." Auster strode across the yard toward the other side of the house, and Mark stood there, staring into the darkness, until he heard the cars pull out of the driveway, their headlights sliding over the field, out of sight.

16

Ann wondered at the nature of guilt.
She crouched on the edge of a sturdy, green cot under the cover of her tent, and outside, the afternoon sun was merciless; it had been impossible to get anything substantive done for the past few days. She bit at her thumbnail absently, something she hadn't done since she was a kid, then stopped, disgusted with herself. Her nails and cuticles were filthy, fingers rough from the careful chemical cleaning she'd had to do to the snuff tablet they'd found that afternoon. It lay on the ground in front of her with a thick plastic tarp underneath. It was a little cooler in the shade and cover of the thick canvas, a battery-powered portable fan facing her, causing the ends of her sweat-drenched blonde hair to flutter a little. She sipped water from a plastic bottle and stared down at the wood carving, a roughly two-foot, smooth wooden plank topped with a carefully carved effigy in the shape of a strange, glowering animal with big eyes and claws that had served as a surface for grinding herbs to make hallucinogens. Roughly

sixth century B.C., from what they'd been able to determine so far.

Making their own drugs in the sixth century. Christ. Ann thought of home, the meth explosion across Knox County and the shit she'd seen her uncle go through, countless friends from high school. *Nothing's changed.*

Ann looked at her texts. The picture Mark sent, wearing that body cast thing. Ann rubbed her eyes; they felt dry, they'd felt dry every damn day since they'd been at the site in Tiahuanaco. What the hell was he doing? Didn't he realize? Didn't he remember?

Why would he? Mark was five years older, so he was just outside her circle as they'd grown up. They'd been close as kids, but once Mark hit his teenage years, their time together was more cursory. Never bad, just more distant, formal. Did he know what had happened to her? Her, Tony, all of it? Any of it?

Getting out of Galesburg, the way she'd gone about it, had always sat heavy on her bones. She knew that it had hurt Mark as well as their mother, and if she could go back... but that was a pointless conversation to have with oneself.

Changing things would have brought its own issues, new ones. She'd dabbled in religion, a couple of mission trips with the Episcopal church in Peoria, and while it didn't give her the insight she wanted, it drew into sharp focus the extent to which travel could force a kind of disconnect. Out of sight, out of mind. Mark was fine, and their mother ... well, their mother was their mother, and her years of alcoholism had taken the toll they'd always assumed it would. If anything, she was probably better off at Marigold, and Mark had always been a dutiful son; any attention he paid to Audrey wouldn't be out of guilt or obligation, it would be out of love. Mark always scoffed when Ann told him he was the better child, but it was true, wasn't it? A good child, a responsible child, wouldn't have let what happened happen, even if she was a kid, even if she didn't know better. Didn't she know better?

She stared at the costume in the picture, the cock-eyed way it hung on her brother's lanky frame. Jesus. Jesus, she did not need to see that.

"Hey." Silvio's voice caused her to start. "Whoa, sorry to scare you."

"No, I'm good," she said, tossing her phone on the cot next to her. "What's up?"

He tapped his sunburned knuckles against the metal frame of the tent. "I just wanted to let you know we were gonna knock off a bit early, some clouds rolling in a couple miles off. They got a lot done, but nothing quite like that yet." He pointed at the wooden tablet lying on its plastic blanket. "Maybe have a fire tonight if it gets cool enough?"

"I'm going to stay in tonight, make some notes on this," Ann replied.

"Always the workhorse," he smiled, nodding. "Sounds good. Let me know if you need some company."

"Thanks, Sil." Next to her, her phone lit up with another text. She glanced over.

[Mark: You probably made this monstrosity, right?]

He didn't know. He didn't remember.

"Hey, Sil," she started, taking a deep breath as she realized how tightly she was clutching her phone. "So, um... look, I—may need to go."

CHAPTER 16

"Go?" Silvio smiled, as though awaiting a punchline. "Go where?"

"Home."

"Back to the states, you mean?" His bushy eyebrows furrowed. "Why, what's happening?"

Ann stared at her phone, then looked up, and gave him an apologetic smile. "I don't know." She shook her head. "It's my brother."

"It'd be a hell of a loss to this team, Ann, you know that," Sil sighed. "Is he sick or something?"

Ann got up and crossed the tent to a card table filled with water bottles, a few plates and glasses, random liquor bottles, a six-pack of Coke she'd paid way too much for at a village a few miles south of their site. She unscrewed the cap on a bottle of Beefeater, poured a finger, and took a bigger-than-usual sip, staring down at the tablet.

"Something," she answered finally.

17

Mark let the bag of trash thump to the ground next to the plastic can (which itself was almost overflowing), leaving cleaner closets, a tidier basement, and a yard free of sticks and storm debris as a tradeoff. Brute's clothes that had been too worn to donate in good conscience—the old man could wear out some armpits on a polo shirt, that was for damn sure—had gone in a bag, as had the innumerable pieces of scrap wood from the basement and garage where Brute had done his woodworking, though Mark had left the Aerosmith shirt in the basement for safekeeping. He hadn't been able to sleep the night before after Auster left, after he'd seen ... whatever it was he'd seen. He'd tried, even gotten into bed and stared at the ceiling for a while, but he'd gotten up around two, made some coffee, and started cleaning, determined to channel his anxious energy into something productive. He'd picked up the back yard—as much an excuse for watching that area behind the house for activity as anything else—then swept and taken a Shop-Vac to the basement, the hallways, the garage.

For a moment, he'd considered stuffing that papier-mâché piece of shit in the bag as well, but he thought better of it. Why, he had no idea. It was simply a thought that had entered his head as he looked at it: *let it stay*. He rubbed his eyes and felt what he thought was a raindrop. Godforsaken goddamn weather anyway. Normally, he'd find it impossible to feel good when it was gray and cold every fucking day, but he couldn't lie to himself: he felt good. Weirdly good, deep down, as though he'd hit on the perfect combination of diet, exercise, and sleep, but he hadn't been focused much on any of those things. He hadn't been sleeping, waking at every little sound and creaking settle the house had to offer throughout a given night, and his diet was the same as it had ever been. He'd been drinking more, actually, and yet ... something felt good, deep down. Something in his bones. His soul.

Someone went by on a motorcycle, revving and preening as the engine chuffed and growled. Down the street, Mark could see the garbage truck four or five houses away. Just in time. He walked back to the porch where he'd left his Coke and stood under the awning, the sky dull as dusk though it was just ten in the morning.

The hydraulic brakes of the garbage truck lurched it to a stop in front of his curb, and a guy got off either side, quickly dumping the cans and bags into the metal jaws of the vehicle. One of the men paused as he dragged the cans back to where they'd been sitting a moment before, then smacked the side of the truck with his palm. He tugged at the bill of his cap that reigned in patches of thin red hair that poked out at various intervals around its bill, studied Mark for a few seconds, then started up the yard toward the porch.

"Morning," Mark said. "Did I do something wrong? With the cans?"

"Mark Devold?" The guy tipped his cap back a little. His face was deeply scarred down both sides, ridges that had distorted the shape of his face, and one eye drooped a little in the socket, as though it was set about a half-inch too low. His lips had been burned to thin strips that barely accentuated his unusually petite mouth. "Charlie. I don't—I don't know if you remember—"

"Jesus, Charlie?" Mark said, trying hard not to stare at the aged wounds, "Charlie Barrow?"

"Yeah." Charlie smiled, and the burn scars immediately turned it into a sneer, both pathetic and welcoming, a real sense of gratitude coming through in it that made Mark feel suddenly, deeply sad. "Long time, man. When did you move in over here?"

"It has been," Mark agreed. "Few weeks ago. My grandpa passed, and my mom's out at Marigold, so I'm just getting things squared away around here."

"Sorry to hear that. You still driving for the city?"

"Yeah, yeah, I am. It's alright. You are, too, I guess?"

Charlie shrugged thin, bony shoulders slumping under his jumpsuit uniform. "Yeah, getting by. I—um, I don't know, man, if this is awkward, I—you know I worked with your uncle."

"I imagine you did, yeah," Mark said.

"I'm sorry as hell for all that," Charlie said. "Sorry that you had to go through something like that, your family, I just—goddamn. Rough shit."

CHAPTER 17

"It was." Mark changed the subject. "So, where you living these days?"

Charlie shrugged again. "Still out at the farm."

"Are you really?" Mark said. He tried his hardest to keep the surprise from his voice, but he knew he'd failed when Charlie gave him a hangdog nod.

"Easy, you know? Don't have to do much, nothing I have to pay for." When Charlie tried another smile, it distorted his face that much more, pinched the whole thing into thin folds of scarred flesh.

"I can see that, sure, that's a smart move, actually," Mark replied quickly, trying not to overcompensate for whatever shame he'd inadvertently thrown Charlie's way. *Still living at his old place? But how was that possible, was it even still intact? Was it even still technically a house?*

The driver of Charlie's truck blared the horn once—a high-pitched, irritated *whonk*—and Charlie glanced over his shoulder.

"Hey, I gotta roll," Charlie said, and wiped his hand on his pants before extending it to shake. "Maybe get a beer sometime?"

"Absolutely," Mark said, shaking his old friend's hand. "Stop on by, give a call, whatever."

"Cool, let me give you my number." Charlie rattled it off, and Mark punched it into his phone. "And anyway, I know where you live." Charlie grinned again, this time a little more confidently, and Mark found himself glancing away as the gesture drew the scar lines tight against Charlie's face, his eyes all but disappearing in the process as he turned and made his way back across the yard, his lanky frame swallowed by the passenger side of the truck as it pulled away from the curb to continue its rounds.

Charlie Barrow. Jesus, Mark had forgotten about Charlie and the fire. It was as though a window had broken somewhere in the house of his brain. Through that window was the memory, his first in so long, of Charlie and the horrific tragedy that had occurred when they were what, eleven, twelve—?

"Hey, you." He hadn't even noticed Cory starting up the driveway.

"Hey," he said, smiling, pushing the thought of Charlie's scarred face out of his mind, along with the memory of the fire beyond the fields that extended for a mile behind Brute's house, licking the sky like something that had crawled out of Hell, all those years ago. "Shouldn't you be in class?"

"Lunch break from setting up the gym for Homecoming and a mercy mission," she said, following him into the house. "Mike French's car battery died, and I wondered if you had any jumper cables I could take over to the high school?"

"And here I thought you loved me for more than just my car services," he said, and rolled his eyes dramatically.

"Mmm, I don't know, your services are pretty good," she nodded and winked. "I'm here for your jumper cables and whatever you have to drink that isn't alcohol." She opened the fridge and held up a bottle of Arizona tea. "May I?"

"It's yours, m'lady," he said. "Let me grab the cables out of my car." He opened the door to the garage, which ran a good ten degrees hotter than the house, for some reason, and stepped inside, noticing as he did that the costume had fallen over on its back. He chuckled at the comically dramatic sight of the thing flipped over, arm splayed out to the side. It called to mind Bugs Bunny pretending to drink poison or something, going through an exaggerated series of movements before fainting away into some pose like this.

"What is that thing still doing here?" Cory said, stepping into the garage as Mark dug through his trunk for the cables. "Couldn't bear to part with such an artifact?"

"Ha! Go ahead, try it on. It'll be a sexy new look." *Those legs, the flawless thighs of a young woman spread wide, maybe early twenties—*

"Oh, yeah?" She said, a smile creeping across her face. "We'll see about that." She kneeled down, picked it up, and started to slip it over her shoulders.

"No," Mark said suddenly, handing her the jumper cables, "come on, I was kidding, don't put that—it was outside, in the rain, it probably stinks like—"

"Jasmine," she said, her voice hollow from inside the thing. "It smells like perfume."

"I think it smells like mold and oil," he countered.

"That, too, a little," Cory agreed, easing the costume's shoulders fully over hers, and it slumped heavily on her smaller frame; she was almost six inches shorter than Mark, and the one intact arm on the thing looked massive on her, like a kid's homemade robot costume from the '60s. It tilted a little to one side, giving her the impression of a permanently cocked head looking back at him, Cory's shadowy eyes behind the strange glue-and-paper visage. "There. How do I look?"

"Ravishing," he laughed. "I particularly like your left arm being so much bigger than the other. it's like you lifted weights with one hand for a few months. Trendy."

"Come to meeeee," Cory Frankenstein-moaned with a chuckle, stepping toward him, and then she paused, as though she was unsure of her footing. She froze.

"Can you not see your feet?" Mark asked. "You're good. Just step to the right. I'll guide you to the bedroom." He laughed again until he saw that she still wasn't moving. "Cory? You okay?"

"Yeah," she said, sounding surprised and straightening her body up all at once. "Yeah, no, I'm fine. It just ... felt heavier for a second than I thought it would. God, that smell." She started to slip it off, losing her grip as though her hands had stopped working, and Mark caught the front, easing it up and off her head and shoulders. "What a weird-ass art project that is."

"If you can even call it that," Mark said, setting it back on the garage floor, sitting up. He took a second to prop it correctly against the wall so it wouldn't slide flat on its back again and put his arm over her shoulders. She seemed winded, shaky, but then took a deep breath and steadied herself. "You good, player? You need a rubdown before the next round?"

Cory smiled, and she looked up at him, her eyes misty with tears. "I'm good. Yeah." She looked around as though emerging from a trance, and she laughed as he held up the jumper cables. "And yes, that's why I was here. I remember now."

"You really okay?" he said with a frown, and she responded by hugging him tightly. "The tears say no, but your face says yes. Boyfriend is confused."

"Yes, yes, yes," she laughed, giving him a squeeze with her arms around his waist. "Totally okay, totally, totally."

CHAPTER 17

Mark hesitated, both wanting and not wanting to mention the elephant in the room. "And no word from him?"

Cory's expression didn't change. "None."

Mark tapped the garage door opener, letting sunlight fill the concrete space. "You sure you're okay?"

"I'm great." Cory leaned in and kissed him quickly. "Later, gator." He watched her dash down the driveway and waved as her Range Rover slipped out of sight down the street.

Mark closed the garage door and headed back into the kitchen. There was a heavy silence, oppressive, and in an instant, he felt compelled to take the pictures from the drawer.

Studying them again, there was a birthmark on the woman's thigh, about halfway up on the right side, a little tan discoloration that looked like an X. Mark sighed. Frustrated, he switched the light off, put the pictures back in the drawer, and left the noonday sun to itself. There was an urgent, hot sensation that spiraled down his spine, an electric feeling that made him stretch. Mark felt as though he'd just taken a hit of oxygen.

The intermittent pain he'd felt in his lower back from driving the bus over the last few years was suddenly, inexplicably gone.

Bracing his hands on the edge of the counter, he leaned backward in a stretch that would have caused him to cry out in pain under any normal circumstances. But now ... nothing. It was gone. Jesus. Three doctors, two chiropractors, and an acupuncturist over eight years couldn't figure out what was happening to his back, and now it was just gone?

Not gone, per se; it had been replaced with a tingling numbness. Mark closed his eyes and took deep breaths, a sensation of euphoria sizzling from his spine down his arms, straight to his fingertips. He'd never done heroin or anything like that, but this was the only thing he could imagine it felt like, without the sleepiness. An unspeakably delicious high, something that felt so good it almost made you sick. It was as though he'd discovered some buried secret, something hidden in a fucking pyramid, that no one was supposed to know about.

What the fuck? What is this? Was this a trick of some kind, his body just fucking with him? Was he sick? Like, really sick, the way people who were freezing to death felt warm right before they turned into popsicles?

The sound of his phone ringing shook him from the sudden, inexplicable spasms passing through him. He swallowed hard, took a deep breath, and answered. "Mark Devold."

"Mr. Devold, this is Sandra Flamm from Marigold Assisted Living. How soon can you get here?"

18

Mark stood at the entrance to the dining room, complete with cheap, orange carpet and ten or eleven tables to accommodate four or five diners apiece. It was the assisted living version of a mess hall.

"How long has she been like this?" he asked the orderly, next to whom stood Sandra Flamm, facility director of operations.

"We're not sure," Flamm replied with a vague note of concern. "We don't lock the dining hall, since there's nothing dangerous in here, as a rule. She ate lunch with Ruth and a couple of other residents, then went back to her room as usual. One of the nurses played cards with her until about 1:00, after lunch. Marvin found her like this about twenty minutes ago. We tried to approach her to get her back to her room, but she started throwing silverware at us, knives and forks. We got the blanket around her, but she wouldn't budge and started sobbing. We thought it best to call you."

"I appreciate that," Mark murmured, slowly making his way into the room. His mother stood at the far end of the room near the kitchen doors, her arms raised into the air and reaching toward nothing, slack-jawed and staring blankly. A rumpled microfiber blanket lay at her feet. As Mark approached, he realized that her breathing was heavy, her droopy bosom heaving with laborious effort. Her mouth was full of what looked like pink mush, and as he approached, he realized that it was chunks of raw chicken. Audrey stood, frozen, taking deep, measured breaths. "Mom?"

She didn't move, arms up, eyes fixed on empty space. A piece of the raw meat slipped from her lips and hit the floor near her bare feet with a wet splat. Mark took a deep breath, doing his best to ignore a wave of nausea. "Mom, what's wrong?"

Audrey's eyes shifted to look at him, the only part of her that acknowledged his presence, and he put a hand on her shoulder.

"Spit it out, Mom," he coaxed. "You're gonna get sick. Spit it out; it's okay." He could feel Marvin the orderly moving behind him, carefully inserting himself into the situation. Her head tilted forward a little, as though it were on an invisible string, and the meat fell from her mouth onto the floor. She began to hawk spit, strings of drool hanging from her lips, and her arms fell limply to her sides.

"It's Thanksgiving," she muttered.

"No, Mom, it's not," Mark said, putting his arm over her shoulder and guiding her to a chair. "This isn't cooked. This will make you sick. Did you eat lunch?" He glanced up at the orderly with insistent annoyance, and the orderly nodded back. Audrey didn't speak as she slumped into the chair, fingers playing at her mouth as though she had a hair on her tongue. Mark took

CHAPTER 18

her hand away as one might chastise a child, and she looked up at him, her green eyes bloodshot. "Have you been sleeping, Mom?"

"Mice." Her lips barely moved as she spoke.

"You have mice?"

"We do not have mice, I can assure you," Dr. Flamm said quietly behind him.

"Mice," Audrey repeated. "At night, making noise. Hard to sleep." Her eyelids drooped, and her body went a bit slack as Mark held her in the chair.

The three of them wheeled her back to her room, where Mark tucked her into bed. She lay there as he talked to her, telling her random stories about Ann, things he was finding as he cleaned Brute's house, whatever came into his head, filling her room with the sound of his voice. It was as though his one-sided conversation with her was a tether somehow keeping gravity in the room, and without it, the elements of his mother's deterioration would begin to float aimlessly, crowding each other, crowding him, until there was nothing else and the room was filled with nothing but doubt, uncertainty, pain.

When she was asleep and steady in her rhythmic, shallow breathing, he turned out the light and left the room, locking the door, and only when he was done sobbing in his car for the duration of three, maybe four songs on the radio, did he pull away and head home.

19

Mark wondered at the nature of structure.
In his lap lay an envelope full of clippings from local and national newspapers—even one from *USA Today*—covering Tony's arrest and trial; Brute had apparently collected all he could. The headlines for such an event couldn't be anything short of salacious: "LIFE IN PRISON: Junkman Trial Concludes," "Galesburg's 'Junkman Killer' Dodges Death Penalty," "Monster Among Us: Midwest Sanitation Worker Charged With Horrific Slayings." The list went on. Did collecting them bring the old man some sense of order, as though he'd been able to neatly categorize the events of his son's criminality and imprisonment? Clip the stories, tuck them away, and move on? Was there comfort in such organization? A sense of safety?

Safety.

Mark sat back against Brute's beloved recliner, sighing deeply, feeling the humid warmth of his breath from inside the costume. It felt heavy on his body at first, uncomfortable, but the longer he wore it, the more natural it felt. He took shorter, more deliberate breaths. He could feel the moisture of his exhalations, a sharpening of his senses. The TV looked like a movie edited from its original form through the slits in the mask, a ribbon of action with the top and bottom cut off.

It was storming outside, but the house was sturdy. The windows barely rattled; the roof muffled the sound of the thrashing rain and wind.

He felt safe there.

The thought settled into his brain like sugar dissolving in water. He felt safe in Brute's house, in a way that, being honest, he hadn't felt since he was a kid. Not when he was on his own out of college and desperately trying to find a job, not when he was married and obsessing over every bill, every dollar spent so that he and Maddie could build a future, not even after the divorce when he knew his time, his life, was his and his alone. There were still stressors, outside elements that could encroach on any sense of stability, and those felt ... gone now. Distant.

Mark took a deep breath and felt his hands shake. Every time he breathed deeply, he experienced a rushing high that was wholly new. An edging orgasm, that slow build without the tip over the cliff, teetering on the edge of euphoria. All the time.

Not *all* the time, he considered.

When he wore the costume.

That's ridiculous.

Still, days of inexplicable sickness after trying it on, which had given way now to... to...

To whatever this feeling is, he thought, sliding the body cast up over his head and setting it on the ground near his feet, sipping his beer. The mouth slit wasn't big enough for a bottle spout, unfortunately.

Mark pulled at his Heineken, letting *The Sons of Katie Elder*—one of Brute's favorites—play out in front of him on the dated flat-screen. After a while, he leaned back in the chair, closed his eyes, and took deep breaths as he thought about Cory. Her face, her laugh. Then he thought about Ann, the best Christmas they ever had, the year they got a Super Nintendo and played the new Zelda together for months afterward. Then he thought of nothing, focusing on just his breathing, the darkness behind his eyes. Deep, measured breaths until he was unaware of how long he had been drifting.

Then, he reached down, picked up the cast, and slipped it back on.

The difference was immediate. His lungs felt like a tornado was suddenly surging through them, and for a moment, he could have sworn the movie went from black-and-white to color. He tried to measure his breathing as he had a moment before, but it wasn't the same. It was more jagged, angular in some way. Shaky.

When the phone rang, his hand trembled so violently that he could hardly lift it.

Hey, he heard himself say in the room. He was sitting and looking at himself sitting looking at himself, sitting looking at himself sitting looking at himself—

Yes, he heard himself say. *Sorry, I didn't hear the doorbell. Give me a sec.*

Cory. Outside.

Mark caught a look at himself in the mirror across the room, costume and all. For a moment, he looked taller, wider, his figure distorted like a funhouse reflection. And for just a fleeting second, his face wasn't his

CHAPTER 19

own: it was a leathery visage that looked like tanned skin stretched into a Halloween mask.

He was still blinking what felt like sleep from his eyes when he opened the door to greet her.

20

Pacing. Back and forth.

Latitude and longitude. The landing.

The island is unoccupied.

Hiding in dark, muddy trenches dug by hand.

Water and a thick, humid stillness.

Sucking air, can't breathe.

Waiting. Insects in his ear, nipping and buzzing.

The wretched, steaming smell of feces, somewhere nearby.

Dying of hunger. Going to die from hunger. Hungry, hungry, hungry.

CHAPTER 20

A sharp, thin pain, a pinpoint, then a slit, then the white-hot sensation of flesh pulling away from bone, his eyes red with blood, screaming, a hot, salt-sweaty hand over his mouth—

Light.

A kiss. The quick, innocent peck of a child's affection.

Black.

A woman, dying from something eating her insides.

An ivory canvas floating in space.

The unknown vista of death.

No.

A ceiling.

A child, smiling. Crying.

Shhh.

Please don't go.

The smell of glue.

Tricks.

Get what we want through tricks. It's good to feel, to be hungry, to live. To play tricks.

JUNKMAN

To take faces.

Hungry.

Jesus Christ, Cory moaned, *you are so fucking good at that, baby, please don't stop, please, please, Mark, your tongue, please—*

Mark looked up at Cory, her thighs clenching against the sides of his head, the taste of her on his lips, coating his tongue as he slipped it inside, out, swirled, inside again, and fuck, he was so hungry—

"Trick or treat!" they screamed in unison, and Mrs. Chalmers grinned widely, her two front teeth stained a dark yellow. She wore a makeshift Wonder Woman costume that consisted mostly of a homemade headpiece, a jumpsuit that tied around her waist, and a pair of red workout pants. She gave it a shot, Mark thought. Someone in their group snickered, and he felt bad for her.

"Cool costume, Mrs. Chalmers!" he shouted.

"Thank you!" she smiled.

Something touched his shoulder, something sharp and sudden, stinging. More than one sharp thing. Behind him, he could feel something wrong. A shadow.

Claws, he thought. Fingernails?

Trick or treat.

There was nothing there. Nothing but his friends, nothing but—

CHAPTER 20

―*fuck, fuck, fuck, yes, God, Mark, yes, I―*

Cory screeched with a sudden, jarring wail, and Mark jerked upright from where his face had been planted between her thighs.

"What was that?" she gasped breathlessly.

"What?" he said. *Breathe, breathe, breathe, blood, blood, blood, someone screaming―*

"―bite," she said, surprise creeping into her voice. "Don't bite."

"God, sorry, I'm sorry," he said. He forced a smile. "Jesus, I'm sorry, baby." His teeth felt like they didn't fit his mouth. He swallowed hard, and suddenly, he was fine again.

(Trick or treat―)

"It's okay," she cooed as he lowered his face again, his lips back on her as she closed his eyes, her staccato moans and movements taking him out, out, out from―

21

Cory rolled over and held up a thin, tightly rolled joint. "Never let it be said that chaperoning a high school dance has no rewards. Just say no, kids." She lit it, dragged, and handed it to Mark, who did the same and passed it back.

"Thanks, Galesburg high-schoolers, for carrying our torch," Mark said, raising a fist in mock salute. He lay back against the pillow, resisting the pull of post-sex dozing, and Cory rolled onto her stomach, sprawled across him as they shared her confiscated prize. She kissed him on his chest.

"Two truths and a lie," she said. "You first."

"Uh-oh, here we go," Mark said. "Let's see." He mulled it over for a second, then nodded. "I ... went to Jamaica on vacation once and got bad jet lag. I met Chris Cornell from Soundgarden at a truck stop in Davenport when we were in high school. I've never been on a train."

Cory held her smoke, then let it go in a languid cloud that slipped slowly from her lips, curling and twisting over their heads. She tapped his shoulder with her fingernail. "Soundgarden."

"Nope," he smiled. "I did meet Cornell, at that Denny's by the interstate in Davenport, Badmotorfinger tour."

"What the hell, I didn't know that!" She grinned. "I met Jim Nabors one time at a concert my grandparents took me to at a casino, but that's all I have on that front."

They continued passing the joint, and Mark gave her ass a squeeze. "Your turn."

"Okay." Cory lay back, and Mark rolled over on his side, fingers exploring her skin, the ghost of stretch marks along her stomach, the soft curve of her breasts. She began counting on her fingers. "I've never eaten a tamale. I thought I saw my cousin's ghost at my aunt's house once after he died in a car wreck." She paused. "I almost died in childbirth, when I was having Georgia."

"Whoa." He thought it over. "I'm hoping that last one is the lie."

"Nope." She shook her head, holding smoke, and then sliding up to blow it into his parted lips. "First one. Who the hell hasn't eaten a tamale?"

"Wait, you almost died having Georgia?"

"Yeah," she said. "I never told you that?"

"Hell, no," he said. "What happened?"

"She was a partial breech, and they had to get creative," she said, making a grimace that indicated he didn't want to know details. "I started bleeding, and they couldn't control it for a minute or so. I was drugged, so I was numb, but yeah. I was within a few minutes of dying."

"Jesus, Cory," he said, pulling her toward him, running his fingers down the silky length of her ash blonde hair and tucking it behind her ear. "I didn't—Jesus. I didn't know."

"It's okay," she shrugged. "I don't think about it much."

"Enough to include it in two truths and a lie, though."

"Yeah." She considered this, her brow furrowing. "Yeah, I mean, I guess I did think about it ... earlier this afternoon."

"How come?"

She stared down at the covers, as though reading something there. "I don't know." She continued to stare at her lap for a moment before sitting up and sliding up against the headboard. "Your turn again."

"Alright, let's make this a good one," he said. "Okay. We toured Chicago in a helicopter when I was a kid. We had to—" Mark stopped short, watching Cory's face as she dissolved into sudden, silent tears, shaking a little as she wept. "Baby, hey, it's okay, don't—what's—"

She smiled through the tears, reaching up and affectionately stroking the side of his head. "It's okay, not bad. Not bad tears." She sighed deeply. "I love you."

There was a moment of silence between them, a pregnant, burgeoning pause, and he felt the words in his mouth as he spoke, as though it was a physical thing to savor. "I love you, too. Not sad tears?"

She leaned in and quickly kissed him, pressing her warm, moist lips to his and tasting him with the tip of her tongue. She sat up, crossing her legs Indian-style. "I'm not sad, Mark, it's not that. I just ... earlier today... When I stopped by, I just had this ... this moment, I don't know how to describe it."

"Okay, try anyway."

She laughed. "It's like ... all of the worry I had over Adrian, and what an asshole he's been, how he's tried to make my life hell, poison Georgia against me, all of it. All the fear that was just rotting inside me, feels better. It feels gone. Like it's just been ... taken out of me." She paused and shook her head, a look of amazement creeping over her features, her eyes sparkling with lingering tears. "All the horrible shit he did is just gone. It's like... imagine a tumor, and then imagine that it just becomes a, a paper-doll version of the tumor. It's there, but it has nothing inside it. But he's back here, in town, and I know I should be worried, or terrified, but I'm not, and I... I don't know why, or what I should feel instead."

"Happy?" Mark kissed a trail down her neck, then turned her toward him to taste her lips again. "For a well-deserved change?"

"I'll take that." She grinned, her body melting into him again, reaching for him, feeling him getting hard.

When they were done the second time, they lay there in a comfortable silence for what felt like hours before Mark felt Cory drift off, her body snuggled up against his, arm across his chest, her nails playing lazy patterns on his shoulder.

Should he have told her? About his daughter? But that was a past life, certainly nothing that so much mattered now, or so he tried to tell himself. It was nights like this when the darkness of that thought felt like a living, claustrophobic thing, and the guilt, god almighty, the guilt settled over him like a second skin.

I'm sorry, kid.

God, I am so, so, so goddamn sorry.

Mark stared into the darkness of the bedroom, letting the slow, soft rhythm of Cory's breathing guide him into sleep.

JUNKMAN

Mark woke up suddenly: a sound.

There had been a sound from downstairs. He'd heard it as clearly as hearing someone speak his name. Cory was gone, her side of the covers pulled back in a rumpled mess.

Jacko. That was the last thing he remembered from his dream: the old woman from the grocery store, but they'd been in a boat, standing side-by-side in a little wooden skiff, his arm over her shoulder, staring at an island in the near distance, the lazy drifting and fluttering of palm trees dotting his line of vision.

What the fuck did that mean?

He groaned; waking so abruptly gave him a head rush, and he lay back on the pillow. "Cory?"

No response. She was probably getting some water or something, or she was in the bathroom. He waited for the sound of a flush, of a faucet, the refrigerator sucking shut, but there was only silence. Did she leave? Had the sound he'd heard been the door? But why would she have left?

Jesus, did she find the Polaroids?

"Cory?" He felt a hot pain rise into his chest, getting out of bed in his underwear and making his way carefully through the dark. He didn't like the sound of his voice echoing through the hallway, as though he was somehow disturbing the night's peace in an irrevocable, dreadful way, tearing the contented stillness open.

She wasn't upstairs; Mark made his way silently down the staircase to the first floor, toward a soft, white glow coming from the kitchen. She was getting a drink. *Settle down, what kind of—*

The kitchen was empty, the fridge closed, the back door still chain-locked. The door to the garage was slightly ajar, and the light was on. "Cory, are you in there?" Mark paused, listening, before stepping into the garage and peering into the dark. "Cory, babe, are you in here?" There was nothing unusual, nothing out of place, no reason to feel uncomfortable with anything. She was nowhere to be seen. In a low whisper, he called into the garage. "Cory?"

Then he noticed that the costume was gone.

"Cory?" he hissed into the bright garage.

When no response came, he stood motionless in the doorway, listening for anything that would tell him where she was. Where did the costume go? Did she take it? Where would she go, and why would she leave? Did he say something, do something she—

The motion light over the back porch popped on, soaking everything in a harsh, white light. Mark's stomach seized a little, and he tried to smile, chuckle off the anxiety he felt at her being gone when he'd woken up, the worry that had metastasized in his stomach like a tumor (*a paper-doll tumor*) so quickly that he felt sick.

Slowly, Mark stepped barefoot into the backyard, greeted by the sound of crickets and the light breeze rustling through the cornfield. Mark saw the shape near the grove now, almost blending into the trees, if not for the gray pajama shirt that Cory had worn to bed being barely visible. The concrete of the patio slab was cold on his feet as he called again. "Cory!"

The shape didn't move, and he felt his legs weakly willing him to motion, to run across the yard toward it, toward her.

Cory was standing in front of the broken scarecrow's cross, her arms out at her side, standing stock still, as though she, herself, was crucified to thin air, her body grotesquely dwarfed and hidden by the papier-mâché cast, her feet bare and muddy, her pajama shirt pulled down past her waist like a nightgown. Mark reached out to touch her arm.

"Cory," he said softly. Surely she was sleeping, she had to be sleeping, *please*—

Cory moaned a little from beneath the mask, and Mark gave her arm a squeeze, though still she held them out at her sides, frozen in place.

"Cory, Jesus, *wake up.*" Mark chastised himself as he lifted the thing from her shoulders and head. *Don't sound angry. Don't be angry. You're not angry, you're afraid, but what's to be afraid of? Why would she*—

Cory's eyes were closed, as though she was deep in sleep, and she had dark smears around her mouth. Mud, Mark realized, smears of mud. Her lips parted a little as she moaned again, talking in her sleep, and Mark could see that she had lumps of mud in her mouth, coating her tongue, her teeth. Mark looked down at where they stood, saw her handprints still clearly there, as though she'd been on her hands and knees there, where the soft ground fully turned to wet, sticky mud. Had she eaten it? Eaten a handful of mud? What in hell?

Mark set the costume on the ground next to them and put an arm around Cory's waist so she wouldn't fall, gripping her shoulder and shaking her, maybe too hard, but he didn't care, this was unsettling, it made no sense, and he glanced up toward the house, half expecting to see himself staring down, a waking dream. Slowly, he led her back toward the house. "Wake up, babe. Wake up, what happened? What the hell are you doing?"

Cory's eyes opened lazily, though she looked as though she'd slip back under with each flutter of her lids. "Mark," she murmured. "He's in the house."

Mark stared at her, trying to determine whether or not she was actually awake. He felt his heart beating faster as he led her into the kitchen and pulled a chair out from the table, easing her into it. Was someone there? Had someone broken in? Fucking Adrian? "Who is?"

"He's here." The words barely slid from her lips as she started to tip forward, and he held her up, an arm around her waist, cupping her shoulder. "He's here. He likes babies. He wants to do bad things to babies, Mark."

"Who is here, Cory?" His face was inches from hers, and he tried desperately to keep his voice even. "Who? Is it Adrian?"

"Mmmm," she murmured, head lolling against his shoulder. "Doctor. The doctor was here, and he wants..."

"Okay, babe, it's okay," Mark said, nodding, a pang of relief striking his bowels and making him feel like he might piss himself, fight-or-flight digging its claws into him. She was asleep, there was no doubt of that, and she slumped backward into the dining chair while he tore paper towels from a roll and soaked them in warm water. "It's okay, Cory, just wake up, okay? Just wake up."

He kneeled in front of her, her knees and calves smeared with mud and grass, and began cleaning her, carefully swabbing the warm cloth over her skin, getting another swatch of wet paper towel, repeating the process until all that remained was her mouth. He felt a mild wave of embarrassment, a self-consciousness, as he wiped the chunks of mud and drying clay from the corners of her lips, as though he were a parent with an unruly child. Two hours before, he'd been inside her, made love to her, and now she was this vacant creature that somehow, for some reason, made him uncomfortable, as though something else inhabited her, that perhaps what was inside her before—the laughing, sweet, passionate Cory he'd been with—perhaps *that* was the imposter that had finally relented to its true form. He pulled out another chair from the table and sat next to her as she drifted in and out; if he didn't know better, he'd have thought she was drugged.

"Cory," he said after a few minutes, leaning in to lace his fingers through hers, stroking the back of her hand. "Cory, baby, wake up. Please? Can you wake up for me?" As he spoke, he saw her twitch in her sleep; was this what sleepwalking looked like, really? Because if so, all those parents out there with sleepwalking children who saw it as nothing more than a nuisance or just "one of those things" deserved medals: this shit was terrifying. "Cory. It's Mark, you're asleep. Right? You're asleep."

Her eyelids slid open, and she looked around the room slowly before landing on him and fixing her gaze. The glassy quality of her stare gave way to a gradual awareness, and she sat up a little in the chair. "Mark?"

"Fuck, thank God," he said with a self-deprecating chuckle. "Yeah, babe, do you—remember what we were doing here?"

"No." She sat up the rest of the way in the chair and looked around with sudden, animal suspicion. "You were calling my name, and I got up to come down here and see what you wanted."

Mark felt the hair on his arms tingle in the darkness of the kitchen, the outside motion light having winked shut. "No, I didn't. I was in bed. I woke up, and you were gone."

"I was dreaming," she said, nodding, as if this thought was just dawning on her. "Did I sleepwalk down here?"

"I guess so," he said. "I don't know what sleepwalking looks like. But it... you were in the yard and all muddy and I think you... ate some." He shook his head and chuckled again. "It sounds fucking ridiculous when I say it like that."

She sat forward in the chair and rubbed her eyes. "I ate mud?"

"Y-yeah," he said. "And you were talking in your sleep about someone being in the house."

"I told you, I heard you down here calling to me."

"Not me," he said. "You mentioned a doctor."

She sat back against the chair and sighed deeply. She looked around the room and finally shook her head. "Well, there was someone here. Someone calling me from the kitchen. And when I got to the kitchen, they were calling me from the yard."

"Who was? What did they say?"

"It was a man. He had a voice like yours, but older, maybe, now that I think about it. He had a beard, greasy brown hair. He wore a heavy plaid shirt and a pair of dark corduroy pants, work boots, and he ... said he— wanted to take my picture. But his eyes were missing, like if you were wearing someone's face as one of those old plastic Halloween masks."

They sat there then in silence, as it began to rain in heavy, noisy sheets outside, pulling the night underwater. Mark pulled a chair close to hers and sat down, and Cory leaned into him with her head on his shoulder.

He didn't tell her that she'd just described his uncle Tony, wearing the clothes he'd had on the day he was arrested for the Ensinger murders.

22

The next morning was benign, an exchange of I-love-you's and coffee, some toast for Cory before she was off to pick up Georgia for school (she'd asked her daughter to spend a couple of nights at a friend's house, given the uncertain situation with Adrian's whereabouts) and square the work week. All was seemingly normal, Mark thought, the strange events of the night before seemingly out of mind, and they would have faded completely had Cory not hugged him tightly at the door, kissed him deeply, and said, "Hey, after last night, be sure to lock your doors, okay?"

"You seemed to find your way outside in spite of that, Houdini," he said, but neither of them smiled at the comment. They kissed in the driveway for a few minutes before she left and agreed to have dinner later that week. To Mark's surprise, Cory offered to bring Georgia along for the ride. He hadn't yet met Cory's daughter, and he knew what a big step that was for her, and him as well.

JUNKMAN

Mark went back inside and dropped two frozen waffles in the toaster, sipping coffee and looking out the window at the backyard, the grass that needed mowing, the overgrown patches of sorrel and morning glory beginning to tangle at the entrance to the grove just past the scarecrow's cross. Soon, the leaves would change—potentially within the week, even—and start to scatter to the earth, leaving the trees skeletal and naked. Nagging at Mark was what he'd left out when telling Cory about her behavior. He hadn't mentioned the costume, how she'd been wearing it when she'd sleepwalked.

Why? He had no answer, regardless of how many times he'd asked the question. After she'd gone, he went back out there, the thing still sitting in the mud, dotted and smeared with dirt from the rain. He'd picked it up, hosed it off, and taken it back into the garage, where he left it to sit on the floor again, though as he looked at it, slumping against the wall where the paper and glue had started to wear and fray on one side, he wondered why he was even keeping it. Why not throw it on the curb with the rest of the junk he'd found in the house and felt no need to keep?

He sat down on the concrete step leading down into the garage and sipped his coffee. He'd woken up worried about Ann, all the way in South America helping to excavate old buildings and temples and who-knows-what. It was perfect for her. She'd always been that way, even digging holes and burying toys in the yard for him to find—that was an annoying phase—but still, it made him worry. Maybe he'd had another dream after he and Cory had returned to bed.

CHAPTER 22

About Tony... and Cory. Or Ann. Or all of them. He couldn't remember now. Christ, he was tired.

The cast was starting to smell; maybe the rain or the mud or some combination, but he'd washed it off, and it was still starting to take on a fetid, musty odor, just a hint of it, behind that jasmine smell and the stink of old oil. It occurred to him that the smells felt layered, as though you smelled one, then another, then another: an onion of sorts, even beyond the actual strata of paper and glue.

"Get over it," he muttered to himself, setting his coffee cup on the step and standing to pick up the costume. He set it on the hood of his car and stood in front of it, as though he expected it to move, two actors getting ready to run a scene.

Mark dug in the tool drawer behind him, finding a nearly clean cloth (Brute was obsessive about washing his car, and he always had supplies for doing so in his garage work area) to wipe the thing down. He held the thing in place by the head, wiping it off, bathing it, almost lingering on certain spots that seemed worse than others. After a few moments, he settled into circular motions that overlapped, the way one might wash a car, until the residual mud and dirt were gone, revealing that yellowy, stained-paper look from the dried glue.

There, he thought. *Now you're a little more presentable.*

The thing slumped a little in its uneven posture. Mark stepped back and studied it. Someone had put work into the thing, that was for sure. And how, exactly, would one create such a thing? By covering someone in papier-mâché? And how, exactly, would one do *that*?

JUNKMAN

Mark sighed and tossed the rag on the tool bench, then went inside, and got a bottle of water from the fridge. Without thinking, he opened the utility drawer.

The ivory thighs spread open, the hands reaching down to spread open the labia, the glistening lips...

He slid the drawer shut, ignoring the vague, involuntary ache in his pants.

(don't bite)

The pictures were Tony's handiwork, had to be. Even before he'd become an actual criminal, Tony was nothing if not a pure hedonist. He'd gone through a consistent litany of loose or pretty rough women when Mark and Ann had been young, and his penchant for recreational drugs and alcohol was well known to say the least. It wasn't a stretch to assume that his uncle liked his porn—the kinkier the better—which was fine, on its own, and gave the Polaroids some context, certainly. Tony had stayed with Brute periodically for the couple of years leading up to the Ensinger murders, now that he thought of it, and Tony must have found some of Mark's comic books, used the pictures as a bookmark or something. He could think of a half a dozen times since his childhood when Tony had to live with Brute for a while due to one thing or another—gambling away his paychecks, losing jobs, getting a DUI, and needing rides to look for new jobs. One of his barflies had probably let him take some pictures at one point. That wasn't really tough to envision.

And maybe this thing, for whatever reason, had been Tony's brainchild, too, though that was a little further off in terms of context and purpose. His uncle hadn't been an artist, and this was definitely a weird one, even as art projects went. Still and all, he figured Tony was somehow to blame.

Mark returned to the garage, to the frayed, yellowing costume sitting on the hood of the car. He stuck his hand inside to pick it up, and his fingers touched something that wasn't the same texture as the rest. He lifted it, trying to see inside it, but the muted light of the garage made it tough to clearly see; was it dried mud? Probably, though it looked lighter. Dried blood? Mark raised it up, slipping it over his shoulder, trying to angle the thing so he could see. Mud. Probably left over from Cory's late-night sleepwalk. He slipped his arm inside it for leverage, then scraped off the remaining little clod of dried, gray clay. He caught a glimpse of himself in the mirror that hung on Brute's tool cabinet. Half on like that, it looked like he was shedding his skin. Mark eased his shoulder into it, the costume conforming easily to his body.

He stared at himself in the mirror.

"Who made you?" he muttered, his voice muffled. "And what were you supposed to be?" He raised his arm, and it looked like a robot learning to use its limbs, a stiff, silly-looking movement. He let his arms hang at his sides. It made him think of the Marvel guy with the metal arm, only he got the wrong end of the lottery and ended up with one made out of glue, ads for milk, and notebook paper.

The sensation started then, with a violent urgency, in Mark's legs; he felt like he'd just stepped off a boat, wobbly, nervous sea legs, and he reached out and touched the tool cabinet to balance himself. That jasmine smell again, and the oil, and something else, something unmistakably like the coppery smell of blood, and he was shaking, now, his arms and his legs; was he having a seizure? He'd never had one before, never felt anything like this before, this was like *nothing*, Christ, he felt his stomach fold into itself, a pang of unimaginable, inescapable fear as he stared in the mirror waiting, surely, for someone to appear behind him in the garage, there to hurt him, kill him, destroy him, but why, it was Tuesday morning, sunny outside, everything was—

—Mark saw the creature before it saw him.

The thing sat on haunches near the back of the car with its back to him, and the wet sounds of chewing, a sickening smacking of lips and grunts, almost drowned out the sound of Mark's heart pounding in his head. It was a naked man, though certain aspects of the bone structure and contours of the body didn't look quite right, not quite fully human. The man's hair was brown and stringy, and he turned to look at Mark, suddenly. His eyes and mouth were sallow, sunken, discolored, a dull yellow-brown, the flesh pulled tight to the bone as if starvation had set in. It was eating something, though Mark saw only a wet mess of blood and sinew splattered across the concrete floor.

Mark felt the sudden urge to vomit at the overwhelming stench of hot oil, jasmine, and roadkill. He half-ran, half-stumbled backward, and caught the concrete edge of the step as the man paused. It—for it was surely an *it*. *It couldn't have been a real man*, he thought—pivoted at the waist to face him, and Mark reached behind him for anything to use as a weapon, coming up with a piece of the broken mirror that lay on Brute's tool bench. He slashed at the thing, waving the glass like a knife, and the man began to scream at the top of his lungs, voice cracking as he reached up with trembling fingers and dug into his forehead, tearing back a layer of flesh that began weeping blood immediately.

This isn't happening, Mark thought, gasping for breath as he held the glass shard out in front of him. The man's screaming broke into laughter as he continued pulling his face from the bone, revealing not the bare muscle and tissue Mark expected, but another layer of flesh. There was a wet splat as the man's face—a yawning, staring mask of torn skin—hit the concrete near Mark's feet.

The little man's body now wore Cory's face, and she grinned up at him insanely, the voice and hysterical laughter shifting to hers now as Mark felt the wind go out of his lungs, as though something had kicked him in the chest, hard. He sank to his knees, palms flat on the concrete floor, the pools of blood continuing to seep in every direction.

He was alone in the garage.

There was no man, no Cory-thing, no blood. Only his mangled shirt sleeve from where he'd stabbed himself in the arm with the broken piece of mirror.

He groaned out loud, a primal, ridiculous sound that almost inspired him to laugh if the blood running down his arm hadn't caught his attention. Jesus, he'd really cut himself, his shirt sleeve saturated and dripping. What the fuck was that? He dropped the shard on the garage floor next to where the costume had fallen near the front passenger tire of his car, leaning on its face, the back right shoulder of the thing dotted with blood from his wound. Goddamn, it would need stitches—no doubt, no fucking question.

JUNKMAN

Mark snatched his car keys from the kitchen counter and locked the door behind him. The hospital was only five minutes away; hopefully, he wouldn't make a mess of his car in that much time. He stepped over the costume, unlocked the driver's side, and threw himself into the seat, starting the engine as he punched the button and sent the garage door rumbling open behind him; gripping the wheel sent a shooting a hot lance of pain into his left shoulder from the wound in his arm. He backed out fast, too fast, jerking in his seat as he switched gears, leaving the garage door open, the costume lying face-down on the floor in a small pool of Mark's blood.

23

Cory counted the pills left in the little amber bottle. *Lucky thirteen*, she thought, replacing it in the cabinet.

It was a given that she wasn't to stop taking the pills outright; her anxiety had been getting better, certainly had seen a diminishing since Mark came into her life, but even still, feeling this ... different, this alive, vibrant, sexy, changed, that was all new. And it wasn't the pills, couldn't have been, unless the side effects of Ativan included inexplicable happiness and lowered blood pressure. Imagine that at the end of one of those commercials, she considered with a smile. People would be standing in line at their doctor's office for days.

But there *had* been an inexplicable change in the way she felt, body and soul. It was as though the fear of Adrian coming back—that paralyzing fear that she would see his car outside the high school, that she'd get a call from Georgia saying that he was at the house, the thought of having her life invaded again that way— was a fog in her brain, and someone, something, had turned on a fan, forcing it to dissipate into nothing more than memory. All of those primal nerves that had wrapped themselves around her like live wires over the last two years were suddenly dormant, and she barely knew how to feel. There was an urge to cry alongside an urge to just climb onto the roof of her house and scream in triumph.

There was also an urge to go. To turn in that paperwork, not to run, but to go, just get in her car, to pull Georgia out of school, pack their things into the trunk, and drive away from Galesburg forever, to shed the bad vibes and to safety tuck the good ones into her heart as sweet memories. Plenty of time to start over, and Georgia had become more self-reliant, if anything, in the last few years, dependent upon little outside of herself. They had a good relationship, strengthened by hardship and the terror that Adrian had wrought in their lives, but she had no doubt that Georgia would be able to leave for college in another year without any of the melodramatic trappings that went along with leaving one's high school years behind; she'd be the one visiting Georgia wherever she was, she thought, not Georgia coming home to Galesburg at any opportunity.

But, she thought, *not yet*. She could turn that thought over in her head for a while now that she was free of the psychic pain that Adrian had wrought. There was Mark to think of. Cory smiled to herself, pinning her hair up and pouring coffee into her travel mug before heading out the door for work. She loved him, and she was glad she'd told him so. She loved how he made her feel safe and appreciated. He was good in bed. He was kind. He was thoughtful. He was attentive to her, though he clearly spent a good deal of time in his own head—she could see that from watching him in normal moments.

CHAPTER 23

She could see him quietly working through the things that had happened to his family: his uncle, the Ensinger murders, his grandfather's death, his mother's health. There was a middle-aged sort of melancholy that he seemed to carry like a loaded backpack at times, though she felt like that went away when they were together, for the most part. That made her happy, too.

Cory got in her car and backed out of the driveway, one of her neighbors giving a cursory wave as he draped fake cobwebs across the bushes, a pile of inflatable Halloween decorations waiting for assembly in his driveway. She waved, catching a glimpse of herself in the rearview mirror as she turned on the radio and filled the car with Blue Oyster Cult singing about Godzilla. Seeing herself in the mirror also made her happy, in an unexpected sort of way. Maybe after her meeting, she and Georgia could go get Pizza House, then maybe go walk around Target or JoAnn Fabrics. Just a normal, stress-free girl's night. They needed it.

God, she felt good.

24

The nurse pulled the gauze tight, yanking his arm a little, and Mark grimaced.

"Sorry," she said, the flatness of her voice suggesting otherwise. She clipped the little plastic grips into place over the brown cloth and sighed. "So, like the doctor said, you'll want to change your dressing every five or six hours just to keep the wound clean. Only eight stitches, nothing too bad, but you don't want an infection."

"No, I definitely don't," he said. "But changing my clothes every five or six hours seems excessive." She stared at him blankly, and his weak smile at his own joke faded. "Got it. Five to six hours."

"What did you say happened again?" The nurse slid her glasses down the wide bridge of her nose a little, scrutinizing the prescription for Oxy that she prepared to hand over.

Probably thinks I did this just to get a scrip, he thought. "Accident, in my garage. Washing my car. Wasn't paying attention."

CHAPTER 24

"Bet you will now," she said, and finally, a tight, almost smug smile as she nodded and walked away. There was someone who'd made the wrong choice when deciding whether or not she wanted laugh lines, he thought, and wadded up the prescription into his pocket. He didn't want opioids, didn't want any fucking part of them.

Accident, in my garage.

Like hell it was.

Now, as Mark pulled back into his driveway, the front door was shut normally, and there were no signs of any forced entry as he entered the still-open garage. The interior door leading to the kitchen was closed, as was the door leading to the backyard.

And sitting on Brute's workbench was the costume.

Perfectly upright, directly in front of him as he turned off the car. There were still smears of blood on the floor of the garage, and the spatters along the fraying, glued edges of the thing confirmed his memory of it lying on the ground when he'd pulled away. Someone had set the thing back up on the worktable.

Someone is fucking with me, he thought. That was undeniable now. There could be no other explanation. Again, his mind went to Adrian, though he had no real reason to assume that it was Cory's ex. And besides, what was to be gained from it? Intimidation? That was a pointless exercise for someone who probably needed to stay clear of the cops.

Yeah, that's probably it, a sarcastic voice in his head intoned. *Cory's crazy ex-husband probably came by, saw the blood and the open doors, set the costume back up on the shelf, and locked the house up tight for you. Or it was the naked guy in the garage who tore his face off. Take your pick, idiot.*

He was right; that didn't make sense either. Nothing did, frankly. Nothing about the night before with Cory or the day so far made a lick of sense. He didn't look at the thing as he went into the kitchen, hitting the garage door button and hearing the metal hinges roll into life. Mark dug the prescription out of his pocket and tossed it on the counter. If he started on Oxy, he'd have to have someone take his shift at work, and he preferred to not do that; the cut was deep, but not *that* deep. Better to suffer the bit of pain and just take Advil or something; he was scheduled to be on at six for the late shift. He had three hours. He'd take a nap, take a shower, redress his stitches, and clear his head with what would likely prove to be an uneventful night of driving.

25

There were no lights on in the house. Actually, no, there was one: the kitchen light facing the backyard was on, from what Adrian could see as a faint glow on the concrete of the driveway. Why she left that one on—as though it actually suggested someone being home—made no fucking sense. But then again, neither did she. He finished his cigarette and tossed it out the window onto the street. He rolled up the windows and got out, pulling his coat tight against him. The wind was wicked, an early winter rolling in for sure, barely forty degrees this close to Halloween, for fuck's sake.

Where the hell were they on a weeknight? Probably at the store, shopping, doing something. Spending some mom and daughter time. Adrian pulled up the hood of his sweatshirt and dashed up the driveway, ducking past the motion lights. The neighbor's curtains were open to the kitchen, and he could be seen. He didn't want to be seen.

He tried the back doorknob, and it was locked, so he took out the skinny metal tools his buddy Skimmer had given him before Adrian had left Memphis to come back home. "Case you end up needing a few of someone else's bucks," Skimmer had said without a trace of humor. Adrian wiggled the thin, metal reed around in the keyhole, and after a few seconds, he felt the bolt pop.

He let the door drift open a few inches; then he listened. No TV, no music, no voices. Adrian stepped carefully into the kitchen and closed the door behind him. He didn't mess with the lights, but he opened the fridge, took out a can of Sprite, and popped it open, drinking deeply before stepping into the living room.

"Cory?" he called. "Georgia?" Nothing. Where the fuck were they? It didn't matter; he'd stay if he wanted to, and it wouldn't be hard to get his old life back. Cory had never been good at shutting him down, and with Georgia around, she'd probably be especially anxious at the idea of conflict.

The occasional car went by outside, and each time, he waited to see if it would turn in. He walked slowly from room to room, sticking his head in, getting the lay of the land. Georgia's room was unusually sparse; he'd expected all the pink-furniture clichés one could think of, but instead, it was tidy and dark with a laptop computer open on her desk. He didn't know what teenage girls were interested in, but he was definitely interested in teenage girls. So, as far as Adrian was concerned, waking up the keyboard was research.

Georgia had a series of open tabs on Firefox. One was for a cloud sharing service, a bunch of folders that looked like school stuff. There were a couple of tabs for makeup websites—Sephora and Lush—and, in stark contrast, one tab that presented a prison database for looking up inmates. The last two were from different local news sites about a triple murder that had taken place about three years earlier, right there in town, some guy who'd gone off and killed a woman and her two teenage kids; he remembered hearing about it at the time. Facebook was open, and Georgia had a text chat going with a friend.

Dinner w ur mom and her bf this week, right, the first one said, to which Georgia had replied, *yeah - his uncle's the Junkman Killer, crazy shit, that lady and her kids, kinda flippin' weird.*

What the fuck? Adrian thought. He opened the desk drawers. There were a few loose bills, a couple of twenties and fives that he took and shoved in his pocket.

Continuing his tour of the house, he took his time in Cory's room and going through the closet, her nightstand, where he found three paperbacks, a vibrator, and an old iPhone, among other things. He took out the vibrator and held it up. It wasn't very big, and he spat on it before returning it to the drawer. *Bitch.*

Adrian went back into the kitchen and made a sandwich out of some odds and ends in the fridge, then sat down on the couch, and ate slowly in the dark. He needed to think. He had a few options. He could wait, surprise them when they came home like this, like an intruder, and risk getting the cops called right off the bat. Or he could leave, come back when they were home (or just Cory, he suspected Georgia was the one who wouldn't take any bullshit) and sweet-talk his way in.

He could always do what Skimmer had suggested, but that was ... problematic, at best. He wasn't looking to spend any more time in jail. Skimmer had spent some time in minimum security, and while he was there, he'd gotten a few leads from the outside—odd jobs, a couple of shitty bouncer gigs that hadn't amounted to that much. But there were apparently some guys who came through the Quad Cities on a semi-regular basis on their way west, and they paid pretty well for girls. The thought of turning Georgia over to someone like that wasn't something he was totally comfortable with yet, but then again, he thought, when the hell had she ever reached out to him? What difference did it really make? Plus, it would destroy Cory. She'd be easy to bring back into the fold, especially if she thought that Georgia had just gone missing. He'd have no trouble convincing her that he could help, and she'd take it. This Mark guy would be out of the picture, Adrian would have a little over ten grand in his pocket for passing Georgia off to the guys who would eventually have her junked out in a matter of days and traffic her in another part of the country—if not another country altogether—so there'd be no chance of her being found.

When he considered the long view, it was actually a reasonable option.

Adrian went back into the kitchen, washed his dish, and put it away. He'd think about it. In the meantime, maybe it would be best to leave, to play Cory's bullshit game, make her think she had things under control. On the fridge was a Post-It note that said *Mark*, followed by an address, a house on Day Street.

That was the stuff, Adrian thought as he unclipped the note, folding it and sticking it in his pocket. He'd give Skimmer a call, see if the offer was still on the table, and in the meantime, first things first: he'd pay

CHAPTER 25

a visit to this Mark guy and see what he could see on that front. It'd be a hell of a lot easier if that son of a bitch was a nonissue.

A few minutes later, Adrian started his car, lit a cigarette, cracked his window, and headed for Day Street.

First things first.

26

Cory wondered at the nature of trauma.

The Cottage Hospital Angel Brigade met at Galesburg High School every Tuesday night at 7:30. It was one of the only local safe havens for victims of spousal abuse—both male and female—in the area, and Cory had attended for six years before bumping into the role of personal mentor, the equivalent of an AA sponsor, when Adrian had skipped town. Mona Ramirez, a forty-three-year-old mother of four who had been coming to group for about three months, sat at her left and occasionally reached over to grab Cory's hand to give her fingers a squeeze. Mona's husband had started doing toilet-brewed crank in jail, had graduated to making his own when he got out, and regularly sent Mona—along with one of her children, upon occasion—to the Cottage ER. Cory felt a personal responsibility for Mona, in a way, as she'd found her sobbing in one of the remote hallways of GHS, about to stop before even starting, on her way back to her car before Cory convinced her to come in, sit, have some coffee, and listen.

CHAPTER 26

So here they were, months later. Mona was still with her scumbag husband; Cory hadn't been able to head that off, not yet, but each week—with any luck—brought her closer. Now, they sat and listened to a woman from Bushnell whose husband drove trucks and made meth during his time at home talk about sleeping in her car behind gas stations to get away from the bastard when he had deadlines to meet. "These motherfuckers on the road ain't gonna settle for watching a fuckin' movie with your wife; they need product," he'd told her before knocking out one of her teeth and returning to the immobile RV in their driveway to craft his wares.

Cory had Adrian to thank.

This thought occurred to her without vitriol, without anger. She had Adrian to thank for her being here, and, subsequently, for meeting these women who had given her such strength, even a laugh here and there in their lighter moments. Without him, she never would have had to be here, to spill her guts about how he'd beaten her and left her for dead in a hospital parking lot during her pregnancy with Georgia, how he'd done it again when their daughter was only three years old, his in-and-out arrivals throughout the years, the acceptance and shame that had finally culminated in denial, fear, friends sleeping over, a local cop she'd dated threatening him at a local bar, all the forces she could muster rallying to drag him, kicking and screaming, out of their lives.

And now, here she was.

Mona gripped Cory's left hand tightly, almost too hard, as Debbie from Bushnell growled through sobs about how she'd found her peace and left her husband to his drugs and the road. Cory didn't hear the words, just looked at the circle of women clapping and giving it up for Debbie, and she joined in, smiling at Mona.

Mark. She had Mark. So many choices that could have been headed off by just recognizing love and trust where it appeared along the highway of her life experience. God, he was amazing. He was sweet. He was smart, but not full of himself. He trusted her. He respected her.

He loved her.

Cory clapped harder, the thought of Adrian drifting through her transom and spurring her to clap more furiously.

No, her hands said, the applause and Mona's hopeful smile overwhelming her.

NO.

27

The giant wipers thumped like batons against the windshield of the bus, back and forth in a grating rhythm. Mark watched the darkness wrap itself over the top of downtown Galesburg like a plastic dome; it was only 9:00, but it felt like it was the middle of the night on the moon. Mark adjusted his cap and ran a hand through his hair. He yawned.

An elderly man took his time fiddling with a worn, black umbrella before stepping off onto the curb, and a middle-aged woman led two children off behind him, the kids wielding small umbrellas—one adorned with Batman and the other with Hello, Kitty—while the woman simply pulled a hood over her head and took the brunt of the storm. The doors whooshed shut again, and Mark pulled the bus from the curb, heading toward the garage. It was his last stop of the shift, and in spite of the lack of sleep, he was eager to dig back into the boxes he'd found in the basement, myriad antique tools of Brute's—or maybe even *his* father's—that had been left to rust. From the look of them, they'd been down there for decades, and if he could clean them up, they might still be worth a good chunk of change for a collector that went in for that sort of thing.

The bus was empty, and he glanced in the rearview to make sure no one had left anything obvious behind. There was nothing visible; he'd do a seat check when he got in. The rain came down harder, and after just a few seconds, he couldn't see anything beyond the virtual tide of white rain that seemed to envelop the bus. Mark eased the metal ark to the side of the road, turned on his hazards, and decided to wait it out for at least a few minutes. He stretched in the seat, locking his arms behind his head, realizing suddenly the sciatica that had played at his back and legs for weeks prior was gone. He leaned forward in the seat and stretched again. No pain, as though it had never been there at all.

Maybe all the activity helped, he thought. *Moving boxes, working in the yard. Working it off.* Mark's eyes passed over the rearview mirror again.

Someone was sitting at the back of the bus.

Mark paused, feeling a tingle in his back as he adjusted himself in the seat. He squinted into the rearview, hesitant to turn around.

The figure sat slumped forward in the last seat on the left, as though whomever it was had fallen asleep during the journey, and the figure appeared— Mark couldn't tell if it was a man or woman—to be clutching the seat in front of them with one hand, as if to stay upright.

"This is the end of the route," he called, his voice coming out less authoritative than he'd hoped. "You need to leave the bus. I'm sorry."

CHAPTER 27

The figure didn't move. The lights in the bus had a depressing whiteness about them, a stark quality that seemed unreasonably cheerful given the rage and darkness of the storm outside. Mark got out of his seat. He stood there at the front of the bus, watching for a moment. Still, the figure didn't budge; not even the vague machination of breath seemed to pass through it. *Christ, my luck that some old timer dies on my bus, at the end of the route.* He'd heard of it happening, but it was a bullet he'd always hoped to dodge.

Mark took a few tentative steps forward, measuring his footfalls, even though he felt a little silly trying to, what, sneak up on a sleeping passenger? He was seven or eight steps down the aisle of seats when the figure jerked, suddenly, violently, to one side, as though it had woken suddenly, but then, it held its position again. Someone was having an attack of some kind, a seizure or a convulsion or something; Mark considered grabbing the first aid kit from under the driver's seat, but instead, he moved with renewed confidence down the aisle.

"Listen, do you need me to call someone, an ambulance, or the police, do you—" He stopped short, just two or three feet from the thing.

It was the costume. Its one partial hand taped to the top of the seat in front of it to crudely anchor it in place, but since there was nothing but a torso and part of a leg, it had slid out of place. There *had* been a person sitting there, he was sure of it: someone with hair, a full body, not this childish mockery of someone, the crisscrossed mouth pert with the promise of a secret, the flat, marker eyes gazing up at the ceiling of the bus. Mark stepped backward, as though the thing were preparing to advance, and then he was turning and running back to the driver's seat. The road kit had flares, and he fumbled in the glove box for one of them. Turning and dashing back, it was a person sitting there. That paper-and-tape carapace, sheathing the upper half of his body. It was a man. A man wearing a jumpsuit, a blue jumpsuit with a patch on the left breast pocket, and there were little pieces of red hair sticking through the ear holes that had been cut into the layers of glue and newsprint. The human form underneath the thing shuddered a little, spasmed as Mark drew near and lit the flare, holding it out as both a torch and a weapon.

How would someone have gotten this from my fucking house? he thought as he opened the back door of the bus, the emergency exit, and hopped out the back into the rain, the door flapping open like the torn skin of a fresh wound. Mark tossed the flare inside, near where the thing sat—*maybe it'll keep it from getting up,* he thought stupidly, but that was insane—

The thing shifted toward the aisle as Mark slammed the emergency exit door and ran to the front of the bus, unable to get inside, watching as the thing stiffly walked down the aisle toward the front of the bus, as though the person underneath that cartoonish shell was trying to walk under an immense weight. Mark saw the paper sheath of the thing's hand reach out and grip the worn vinyl, lurching suddenly into the seat nearest the front, its paper face pressed to the glass, leering out at him, and its human hand now held the flare, guiding it toward that shiny, paper face, pushing it into the flesh of its chin as one might push candles into the frosted surface of a cake.

CHAPTER 27

There was a dull red glow from behind the layers there, and the head that wore the mask began to writhe and twitch; Mark could see flesh there now, real flesh beginning to char and melt into bloody soup, dripping onto the papier-mâché hand that held the flare like melting wax, and the soppy, steaming blood that chased it. *Like a jack-o'-lantern lighting itself*, Mark thought dumbly, and he began to pound the bus doors harder and scream for help. Running to the rear of the bus, Mark threw the emergency door back open and heaved himself inside with a groan that came out as a weak cry, for the fire extinguisher mounted near the back window—

The flare lay on the floor of the bus, sparking and sputtering itself out of existence.

The bus was empty.

Mark stood there for a moment, waiting, waiting for the figure to emerge from behind one of the seats, from a hiding place on the floor somewhere, but it was still and quiet save for the rain that pelted the metal tube just a bit less than before, the sound of the storm leveling off as Mark slowly made his way down the aisle back toward the driver's seat. There was nothing, no one.

His phone vibrated in the cup holder near the massive steering wheel, and he took it out to see a text from his supervisor and sort-of friend, Maurice.

[Maurice: The fuck are you, afraid of a little rain, come on—drive that motherfucker, I need to get out of here. Janie made pot roast, and it's getting cold]

Mark sat down in the seat and realized that he'd been holding his breath, his chest aching for a moment as he began to take in air again. He turned in his seat and lurched the bus into gear; the wipers began thrashing their familiar rhythm once again, and all was quiet. He pulled away from the curb, driving the rest of the way to the garage without once looking in the rearview mirror.

By the time he checked in, clocked out, and grabbed something to eat, it'd be 10:00, which wasn't too late, he hoped. There had been an attempted break-in down the street a week or so after Brute had passed, and between that and the vandals who kept spray painting things, Mark had made a habit of leaving a light on at night when he was gone. He realized, as the painkillers for his arm started to wear off, that he'd forgotten to leave lights on in the house before he'd left that afternoon.

No matter, he thought. Criminals or no criminals, he was tired, and his arm was sore. He looked at the clock on the dashboard and back again, nervously, at the rearview as he neared the bus garage. 9:14. Forty-five minutes or so, and he could collapse onto the couch with some Advil and a beer. He needed to sleep.

28

There were lights on in the house.

It was 9:22, and what looked like a living room light and a kitchen light offered a soft glow through the curtains, illuminating the shadow of someone moving, slowly, past the windows. Adrian had seen a picture of this Mark guy, and it didn't look like him; this was a bigger, bulkier shadow that suggested someone older, someone with a bit of a slouch.

Probably has a retard brother or something that he's taking care of, Adrian thought. He took out a brown vial and tapped a line of powder onto the back of his hand, snorting deeply, watching the house for a bit in the warmth of his car. The rain was coming down relentlessly, and it was cold as hell, unusually cold even for October. He didn't see a car in the driveway, but there could have been something in the garage for all he knew. He'd see if the garage was unlocked, and from there, he'd find something flammable, maybe do a quick walkthrough to see if there was anything worth taking. Then he'd get it lit, duck over to the Quad Cities for a few nights. Once Cory was convinced he'd gone again, he'd come back for Georgia, get her to Skimmer, and collect his money. The only thing he regretted was that he wouldn't be able to tell Cory that their smart-ass daughter was sold off to some biker gang in Indiana. Fuck, the look on her face would be worth just about anything.

Adrian got out, pulled his sweatshirt hood over his head, and ran across the yard, around the back of the place. There was a back-porch light that offered little help in the dark, and a broad, thick patch of woods ran along most of the cornfield he'd seen from the road; beyond it was nothing but absolute blackness. The thick tree coverage between the backyard and the cornfield would be good in a pinch if someone came home.

He tried the back door, and surprisingly, the knob turned in his hand. *Unlocked? What a fucking moron.* He found himself standing in a dated kitchen that had to go back to at least the mid-60s from the look of the tile. Fake wood paneling on the walls, dated fixtures and appliances with the exception of a newish microwave. There was a door off to the side that had to be the garage and a door next to the refrigerator that was probably a pantry or the basement.

Adrian waited to hear signs of movement. He felt in his sweatshirt for the gun he'd brought, just a .38, but it was enough to do what needed to be done if the occasion called for it. The jury was out on that. He crept into the open doorway between the kitchen and the hallway that separated it from the living room, where a staircase led to the second floor.

The light in the living room that had previously been on was now off.

CHAPTER 28

Must be on a timer, he thought. The heavy, mustard-yellow curtains moved a little from the heat blasting out of a vent on the floor; that was what he'd likely seen in the window. But there had been a figure, a person's outline, hadn't there? He wasn't so high that he couldn't see the difference between curtains and some dude who had to be over six feet tall.

Regardless, he'd still have to be quick about it, just in case he wasn't alone. Maybe whoever it was had gone upstairs, so if he gave the downstairs a quick once-over, that'd be enough. Adrian carefully slid open the drawers on a couple of end tables in the living room, but there wasn't anything worth taking. On his way back to the kitchen, he tried the glass doors of a china cabinet, but it was locked, and that was too risky, way too much potential for noise.

Adrian went through the kitchen drawers one by one, hoping for a money clip or a cash-stash somewhere. Three drawers and nothing, but on the fourth, he had to stifle a chuckle.

There were Polaroids, just a few, and amateur stuff, but damn, they were worth keeping. He squinted in the darkness at the images of female thighs spread, waiting, exposed. It wasn't Cory, he could tell that, so there was no telling. Maybe this Mark prick had some revenge-porn thing going with a side piece. Whatever. Adrian tucked the pictures into his sweatshirt pocket and carefully moved across the kitchen to the garage, opening the door and easing it shut again.

Anything would work: gas, turpentine, some combo of cleaning solutions. Just something to get a good blaze going, and an old house like this would go up like fucking matchsticks, no question. He spied a workbench on the other side of the car, and as he rounded the bumper, he stopped abruptly.

What the fuck was he looking at? Adrian took a step toward the thing, which looked like some ugly-ass prop from a children's play, yellowed, aging tape, and a shiny glaze of glue coating the thing. Without really knowing why, he picked it up.

It was a costume, wasn't it? He raised it up and set it on his shoulders, where it eased into place, though he had to slip his arm into the casing that was made of papier-mâché, from what he could tell. He could see a little through the peeled-back slits that served as eyes, but breathing was a bit of a problem. The nose wasn't much more than a mushy little wad with two tiny holes in it, and there was a bigger slit for the mouth; it reminded him of that mask in the Tarantino movie, with Bruce Willis and the black guy getting fucked in the basement. That was what it called to his mind. Was it a sex thing? Jesus, he thought, this Mark guy might be weirder than he thought—than Cory thinks, he considered, and for a moment, Adrian almost felt something like concern. He paused, listening for sounds from inside, the weight of the thing settling onto him, almost like...

(it's wearing me)

...when you have a suit tailored to you, that comfortable situating of high-quality clothing. Though this thing was as far to the other side of that as you could get. Adrian took a deep breath, reaching into his pocket without thinking, taking out the Polaroids, and holding them up in front of the thing's face. The spread thighs and wet pussy were barely visible through the slits in the mask.

CHAPTER 28

I hope he hurt her, he thought suddenly, but he hadn't thought it, not really. The consideration just appeared in his head, apart from him, somehow. Adrian took a deep breath, feeling a heat in his lungs, a dry, almost painful warmth in his chest. He was flushed.

He stuffed the pictures back in his pocket and pulled the thing off, setting it back down on the boxes. Weird shit. He shoved the thing aside so he had room to kneel near the workbench, checking a series of paint cans lined up on the floor. Paint would do it. He tried the lids; two were open, which was all he needed. He went to stand up, lost his balance in the near dark, and fell backward into the stack of boxes built up behind him.

Motherfuck! He wanted to shout, and he almost did, but he caught himself and froze, waiting to hear any sign of movement from the house. Fuck, man, he needed to get out there as soon as he could. Maybe he'd just shake shit up a little, make a mess, put a little fear into them, and come back another night to do what he'd been planning. He'd dump the paint all over the car, light it up, open the kitchen door so the fire could ventilate into the house, and get the hell out. Maybe even watch from that little spot behind the house near the field.

On his knees now, Adrian felt in his pocket for the folding knife he kept, wedging it into the lid of the can and prying, laying his other hand on top to keep it from flipping off and making more noise. It finally gave, and the acrid smell of paint hit his nostrils. He picked up the can, stood up, and turned, noting that the stack of boxes was now strewn all the way across the garage floor. That made no sense, but that wasn't the issue.

That weird costume prop was gone, too. But that wasn't the issue, either.

The issue was that someone stood in the opposite corner of the garage.

Fuck, Adrian thought, *here we go.* He wasn't sure how someone had gotten in, but it didn't matter. He'd have to do what he had to do now, and damn whatever followed, he'd see it through and out. The only way out is through. Isn't that what his buddies at Met Correctional had said? The only way out is through. So fucking be it.

"Hey," he said with a wicked grin. "Look, I'm just... I'm going, okay? I'm getting out of here." The shape didn't move, and it was big, fucking hell, broad-shouldered and tall, slouching at one side, one arm longer, somehow, than the other. *This was the guy in the window.* In the dark of the garage, Adrian couldn't make out features. Christ, he couldn't even make out male or female, really. It was just a shadow from where he stood, and from where *it* stood, he couldn't get to the kitchen door. Fuck it. He'd go over the hood of the car, and he'd start the whole fucking thing burning. Fuck this guy, or whoever the hell it was. The figure stood in that peculiar slouch, not moving, not speaking.

Adrian hopped up on the hood of the car and carefully slid across while keeping the paint steady, and now he stood just a few feet in front of the figure, the door leading out back right behind him, the door to the kitchen at his left. He had to choose: bail out entirely, or get back into the house and see what damage he could do first?

Fuck this guy.

"Hey, asshole," Adrian sneered, taking a step closer and flinging the can of paint across the room at the figure. There was a flash of hot pink. *Who the fuck paints a room pink*, he thought, and then the figure was splattered from the chest down with the viscous mess. Still, it didn't move, didn't even flinch. His fingers wrapped around the knife handle in his pocket; fine, then, it was going to go this way. He'd have to cut this son of a bitch to make a point.

Adrian drew his knife and stepped forward before realizing that, Jesus Christ, this wasn't a man, he wasn't looking at a man, it was that fucking ugly costume thing on the boxes, only it had been on the other side of the room, no question. No fucking question.

The thing lurched forward, and the jerky, sudden movement caught Adrian off guard, causing him to stumble backward and fall against the concrete steps leading back to the kitchen. A tingling feeling surged up and down his arms, his legs, down the nape of his neck, all the way down his back, a sudden stirring in his cock, as though he'd just seen a beautiful woman. A hot, urgent feeling inside him that, after a moment or so, exploded into pain. Adrian looked down and watched his stomach open up as though he'd been slit with a razor; it took a moment for Adrian to realize that he'd cut himself open. *What the fuck, why had—*

He dropped the bloody knife as he lost feeling in his fingers, his legs, and he was on the ground, on his hands and knees and crawling toward the door to the kitchen as the shadow behind him grew.

Someone was wearing it, that was it. He could see legs, clearly, taking careful, deliberate steps toward him, though the more he stared at it, the less tangible its form was; no, he was pretty sure that the legs were just masses of flesh globbed together like putty, like someone whose legs were horribly deformed—burned, maybe. Adrian looked for anything in reach that he could use as a weapon, cursing as he loosened his belt and tried to work the heavy copper buckle free. He fumbled with it until it came loose, skittering across the concrete floor, lost to him. A searing pain in the tendons behind his left kneecap attacked him, and he knew now that he couldn't walk if he wanted to.

Sshh, the thing said through the lipless slit of its mouth, and then the blow to his head, something stinging; heavy, metal. *A hammer?* Adrian thought dumbly, blood running into eyes, unable to feel his own weight now as he recognized the futility of his trying to get in the house. The thing loomed over him, and now it had a face: it was Cory, but it was like someone had carved a shitty Halloween mask of his ex-wife into a piece of thin leather, splintered and cracking apart.

Not leather; it was flesh. A piece of dried, old flesh into which, somehow, Cory's face had been molded. Adrian had a flash of being twelve years old, an episode of *Tales From the Darkside* on TV, a Halloween story about a man plagued by a monstrous troll that wouldn't leave his house. *What a fucking joke*, he thought, but his thoughts were coming apart, and he didn't have much left. *This isn't a guy inside this thing. This is something else.*

"Bitch," he managed to sputter, and the thing reached for him. The smell of old glue and rotten blood overcame Adrian's senses as the thing pushed its papier-mâché fingers against his face, into his mouth.

29

Charlie Barrow had been a gawky, red-headed country kid with buck teeth that Mark used to pal around with in junior high, and he'd been funny, a class clown, likely to make up for his deficiencies as a student. Not a dumb kid, but not a bright one in a book-smart way. They'd had fun together for a few years collecting and trading Garbage Pail Kids, nicking the occasional candy bar from the 7-11 near Mark's house, riding their bikes on the trails out around Lake Storey.

When they were in seventh grade, Charlie's father, Nicholas—a beast of a man who repaired farm equipment for a living—had, in a fit of drunken rage, held a lit flare against Charlie's face, burning away a chunk of the boy's right cheek. Charlie had passed out from the pain and ended up losing a third of his teeth due to the extensive burns on his gums, as well as a good half of his face, and while he survived, it destroyed his body and ruined his mind. It also burned half of their house down out on Pickett Road, just past the field behind Brute's house and about a half mile south.

JUNKMAN

As far as Mark knew, that experience had turned Charlie into a veritable recluse, at first living with relatives in Bushnell for a while, then bound to a disability check and an inability to really function in society, though apparently Charlie had found his way back to something like a life through his job at Knox County Sanitation. Charlie's dad had died in prison, not after what happened with his son (for which he did do some time after Charlie's mother had divorced him and cut ties entirely) but after a bar fight at Stetson's in Monmouth in which he'd stabbed a guy in the neck with a broken beer bottle following an argument. That sent him up for murder, where he presumably spent the rest of his days being as much a piece of shit on the inside as he had been on the outside.

Mark hadn't thought of Charlie Barrow in decades, until the previous morning when Charlie hopped off the garbage truck and forced Mark to remember the intricacies of Charlie's injuries.

It was Charlie he'd seen on the bus. The face on the thing, the white-hot glow of the flare in its mouth, melting away its features in a mess of blood and dissolving flesh that dripped from under the mask. It had been Charlie, for just a few seconds, the way Mark's head had played the scene out in nightmares for years after the incident.

From where Mark now stood in the living room, he could almost see out past the drive-in to the Barrow farm looming on the horizon a few miles south of town. But otherwise... God, when was the last time the Barrow family had even crossed his mind, come up in conversation ... anything? Decades, for all he could recall. But that face ... pressed against the bus window.

What was happening to him? First was the ropy creature that had looked like Dara Ensinger, and then something that looked like Regina Marling, no question. The thing in the garage that he'd hallucinated, and of course he did, because that couldn't have been real, nothing like that could be real, and then the Charlie thing on the bus. Mark had seen the flesh dripping onto the vinyl seats, how it sizzled against the green material like lumps of candle wax. The thought made him sick. But he'd seen it.

Mark's mind ran through all possible options. A gas leak? Was he blacking out? A brain tumor? He checked the number of beers in his fridge. He couldn't remember how many were supposed to be there, but it's not like he was drinking before work; he hadn't been drinking that afternoon with the thing in the garage. And his back door had been opened when he got home from work, though a sweep of the house indicated nothing out of place or beyond the ordinary. Had he forgotten to lock it?

Mark poured himself a couple of fingers of Jack; his arm throbbed through the painkillers he'd decided to go ahead and pick up on his way home from work. It was almost midnight. He was off until Thursday; maybe he needed a little Oxy high after all. He sat down in Brute's old recliner, tipped it back, and turned the TV up a little just to fill the house with the sound of voices. Artificial company.

The house had started to feel lonely late at night. The walls, the hallways, the staircases: all oddly cold, vacant. The house had been built in 1951, and it had the two-story charm of any home built around that time on the blueprint of the post-war American Dream.

Of course, as a child, it felt inviting and cozy, as if each room, each part of each room, had been carefully curated by his grandparents to feel warm with their presence. And it had felt that way again, at times, since he'd moved in. But that was slipping away, day by day, for reasons Mark couldn't explain. His body felt good; he felt younger, stronger than ever. But his thoughts had taken on the quality of a lucid dream over the past few days, hallucinations aside, though they were concerning enough.

But was it really just those last few days? Maybe not. Perhaps the satisfaction of being with Cory had sent a part of him into a honeymoon phase; maybe that's what had been carrying his days since he moved into the old place, but his feelings for Cory weren't fading, not by a long shot. If anything, they were getting stronger, and now he was about to meet her daughter.

Her daughter.

Fuck, don't go there. Not tonight. Thoughts of his daughter were never far from his mind, and with them, the deep well of regret and guilt that had driven him to near-isolation before finally reconnecting with Cory. Mark picked up the remote to switch the channels from some late-night news program. There was a piece of tape wrapped around the remote, upon which Brute had written "POWER" next to the power button. Mark sighed and sipped his whiskey.

It was sad to think of the old man and how he'd slowly failed during the last few years of his life. And his last few visits to Brute... they'd been strange, hadn't they? Or had that just been Mark's inside knowledge that Brute's last days were upon him, and had he just projected the melancholy that accompanies such knowledge onto Brute's behavior?

He considered this as a rerun of *SVU* filled the screen, but no. No, they *had* been odd, some of those last visits. Three of them, in particular. The first one had been the previous Thanksgiving, and the other two earlier this past spring, just before the old man's passing.

The previous November, Mark and Audrey had gone to Brute's house for a low-key Thanksgiving dinner. Not the full shebang with all the trimmings, but a scaled-down version so they could enjoy some turkey and dressing, along with Brute's favorite side dish: wild rice with pickle relish, which Mark had always found odd if not foul. A holdover from the war, Brute had always joked, that he'd developed a taste for and just wouldn't leave him, no matter how weird it seemed. Brute had been the only person Mark had ever known who would smear a little jelly on pizza crust if it was available. The old man's taste buds were impaired.

Mark and his mother—who herself was starting to slip at the time, much to his dismay—roasted a turkey breast, made Brute's wild rice monstrosity along with some packaged mashed potatoes and gravy, Stove Top, and some canned green beans. It was modest, Mark considered, but it felt like a win for the three of them to be able to enjoy what he knew at the time was likely to be one final Thanksgiving together. (If he was being honest, he resented the fact that Ann hadn't found time to come. She'd been in Mexico and had insisted that she'd try to make it after Mark told her it would likely be Brute's last Thanksgiving. "You don't know that," she'd shot back, but he'd been right.)

Late that night, Mark had gone downstairs for a glass of water and found Brute at the kitchen table, sitting alone in the quiet with a bottle of Jack Daniel's. Every now and again—usually on a holiday—a little whiskey and nostalgia would get the old man talking. "Wanna have a drink with me, kid?" Brute had asked, and Mark, relishing the moments he got like this with the old man, to hear some old stories and shoot the shit together, said yes despite it being nearly three in the morning. Mark sat down, and Brute poured.

That was the night when Brute finally told Mark about the worst thing he had done in the war.

II: THE TROPHY

30

The particulars kept the old man up at night, on occasion. Drafted at eighteen to fight in the Pacific, witness to things he still didn't like to talk about over there with the Japanese, back home to marry Mark's Grandma Lynn pretty much the second the war ended, Brute grew up quickly to be a loving but brooding, silent man who was forever changed by what he'd seen over the course of two weeks in September, 1944.

Brute had been part of the 1st Marine Division, which, along with the 81st, had been tasked with taking the southwest island of Peleliu and staking out an encampment to be used against Japanese forces moving through the region. "I remember the smell of the water," he'd said, "as we were getting up to the beach. Salty, rank, like something dead in the surf fighting against the fresh air and everything ... good. We should have known."

When they hit the beach, they realized that U.S. intelligence had gotten it wrong: the Japanese already occupied Peleliu to lay in a protracted, relentless ambush against the incoming American troops. What should have taken days took weeks, the worst of it concentrated around a series of tight paths that allowed for measured ambushes by the Asian-led forces and led to the death of nearly everyone in Brute's division, including a nineteen-year-old from Philly named Mixon 'Hop' Hopewell, who had a girl back home named Carol (*spitting image of* Veronica Lake in The Glass Key, *Brute had noted with a wink*) and had shared a love of Brute's favorite radio programs. At night, they occupied dug-out foxholes in pairs so one could sleep and the other could keep watch, and there were close calls, the worst of which was a Japanese soldier who very nearly discovered Brute and Hop's hiding place.

"If the moonlight hadn't shifted, I wouldn't have seen his shadow." Brute swirled the amber liquid around in his glass and sipped before continuing. "And we wouldn't be here. But I did, and I held my knife, always, all night long. Clutched that son of a bitch like a lifeline, and it was. That was the end of that. Guy was coming back and forth down this little path, patrolling, I think. But their food had run out, or he couldn't get to any without blowing his cover. He started ... I don't know. Losing it. He started calling out, babbling, laughing to himself. We were dug down in a hole on the other side of this little ridge, and you'd see him saunter down the path, then go back, over and over. Seemed like he was a lookout or something, but I think starvation was driving him batty. Anyway, he finally made the mistake of coming too far down the path, and he went off into the brush, just a little above the ridge from where we were. I managed to get in behind him. Thank the lord no one came by until after we were done."

"Done doing what?" Mark asked.

"Cutting the bastard's face off," Brute replied without missing a beat, reaching up to scratch the gray scruff of his beard.

"Jesus Christ, Grandpa."

"Yeah." There was nothing akin to pride in the old man's voice, though it didn't sound entirely like shame. "You never heard such black magic bullshit that what came out of that mouth while I cut him. Swear to Christ, he was calling on the devil for a way out. Cursing me. But we did what we had to. They were evil. Christ, the things they did to prove a point, they made you give it right back if you wanted to get out of there."

"What do you mean, black magic?"

"Eh, nothing much, really," Brute mused. "A situation like that, Mark, you just ... things work differently, in your head. You start grabbing onto anything that'll keep you going. Feel like your heart's gonna burst from adrenalin, that your head is just gonna split open." He paused and carefully slathered apple jelly onto a corner of his toast. "This little bastard, once we had him down, he—"

The old man chuckled as if he was reconsidering the telling, but Mark waited.

"His teeth were chattering, like it was cold, he was so revved up. He kept hissing at us, amanojaku, amanojaku. Over and over again. *Amanojaku.*"

"What's that mean, anyway?" Mark went to the fridge and began assembling two small plates of leftovers from dinner, tidy portions of turkey, stuffing, and rice.

"Damned if I know," Brute shrugged. "That's what I mean, guys start blathering, saying things that don't make sense, praying, calling out for their mothers. One of the guys in our group, when he went down—he got hit in the side of the head, and it took a while for him to go—he kept saying that dinner was late, apologizing to his parents for being late to dinner. That kind of thing." He scratched his unshaven chin. "Hop had my back the whole way in. Even when a few Japs blew their cover and tried to be shit-stupid about their gains. We took 'em as we could. We were quick with a knife—had to be. All we had when you can't afford to make any noise." He shook his head, sipped his whiskey, and somehow found a smile, raising his glass. "Good friends."

"Good friends," Mark said, shaking his head as he lost the thought that was to follow it, watching instead as clouds drifted in front of the gibbous moon, his grandpa's silhouette holding ground against the muted light as they ate their late-night snack in thoughtful silence.

By February, the emphysema had gotten worse, and Brute had been on heavy antibiotics that compromised his ability to stay awake for any length of time, as well as the clarity of whatever thought happened to pop into his head. As a result, conversations with him quickly turned into a series of non sequiturs, and it was hard to keep up with anything he said before he inevitably drifted off to sleep.

"Here we go, good sir," Mark grinned on one particular Saturday morning, setting two cups of coffee down on the table in front of them. A recording of *The Price Is Right* was reaching its climax with a contentious Showcase Showdown chattering at low volume, and Brute's eyes were heavy, grayish rings dragging him toward sleep. Ann was in Thailand at the time, attending a human rights summit. Having his sister that far away made Galesburg feel all the more insignificant in the grand scheme of things, a tiny little pebble in a sea of exotic coral, and while he was happy for her, he felt a certain stubborn pride at sitting there with Brute and quietly burning out the day in the old house. "Can I get you anything else?"

"All good here," Brute said, and his voice was upbeat through a thin smile despite the wear and exhaustion creeping through. "Thanks, Tony."

"Mark, Grandpa."

"Jesus, yes, Mark. Sorry about that. Pink elephants on parade." He raised his cup and took a sip, giving the OK sign with his thumb and forefinger. "Just right. You been over to the new store yet?"

"Which?" Mark sipped and watched a bleached-blonde housewife in a tracksuit win twenty-two thousand dollars. She leaped into Drew Carey's arms as the credits started rolling.

"Danny's Fresh?"

"Oh, the new grocery store, you mean?" Mark shook his head. That had opened around Christmas, but he figured the passage of time to be a moving target insofar as Brute's psyche and schedule were concerned. "No, not quite yet."

Brute tapped the arm of the recliner with his finger. "You remember your grandma?"

"Of course, Grandpa, yeah. Why?"

"Went over to England once for a trip to see a friend of hers from back in school. And we went into this grocery store that had squid in a can, you believe that? Who in the hell they think is gonna eat a canned squid?"

CHAPTER 30

He chuckled with laughter, and the shredding rasp in his throat and lungs said it all. "You see that they're doing a reunion? The guys that are left from '44? Got the thing from the VFW in the mail the other day." He sat back against the recliner and yawned. "Haven't seen Mix or Hop in forever."

"Didn't Mix and Hop both die a few years back, Brute?"

"Oh." The wrinkles gathered around the old man's eyes, and he squinted as though trying to see through an impenetrable fog. "Yeah. Yeah. I forgot that." The old man smiled tightly, and it looked to Mark like the old man seemed pained by something. "Hop saved my bacon more than once. Brought home a cunny blade."

"What?"

"Cunny blade," Brute said, sipping his coffee and nodding. "I thought of it the other morning, when I woke up, had a dream or something, I guess. We brought it home. From the island. One of those big curved knives, the big ones?" He held his liver-spotted hands out about a foot.

"Like a machete?"

"Yeah," Brute nodded, leaning his head back against the folded quilt that hung over the back of the recliner like a pillow. "Fred Loving used to call it a cunny blade; he used to hunt. He'd truss a deer, start at the, you know, the genital region? Used to use one of those to cut open the carcass."

"So you brought a machete back from the war?"

"Yeah, and other stuff," Brute said, his voice starting to fade toward unconsciousness. "Someone used it, too, for something rough. I don't know why I took it. Think about it honestly." His voice was barely a whisper now.

"I don't know why we brought that stuff home. That bastard's face."

"What?" Mark said. "Who do you mean, Grandpa? And how'd you get stuff like that back to the States? Didn't they like, check you guys for contraband or anything?"

"Ways to get stuff back, you knew the right people," the old man muttered, eyelids fluttering as he settled into sleep, mouth slightly agape, snoring a little as his half-drunk coffee steamed and the local news started on TV.

Mark got up carefully, pulled the sliding pocket doors shut to close the living room off from the rest of the house, and went into the kitchen. He dumped the coffee grounds in the trash, wiped down the counters, washed out the pot, and left it as he found it; then he heated up a can of Dinty Moore beef stew—a Brute lunch specialty—and ate it on the back porch, staring off into the field at the coming spring. The days were getting longer, finally, and twilight had some extra time to wait before it encroached on the day.

He knew that Brute would die soon. It was as inevitable now as it had been when Grandma Lynn had started to decline. He knew full and damn well that when cancer decided to go sideways, it went sideways on a motorcycle shooting Roman candles out of its ass, and no one could tell it otherwise. Mark knew that. But it still seemed impossible, at that moment, and for that, Mark was grateful. Brute was still too much himself to imagine the old man succumbing to the physical inevitability of disease. Not yet.

Mark finished his lunch, then got up, and went inside, heading upstairs to use the bathroom and do some

CHAPTER 30

laundry. Passing through the long afternoon shadow lying in the hallway, he looked up. The string that triggered the attic door hatch dangled in front of him.

That bastard's face. Mark remembered their conversation from Thanksgiving, like a pebble dislodged and wedged into his brain, in which Brute had mentioned cutting an enemy soldier's face off.

Surely the old man didn't mean that he'd brought *that* home. No fucking way that was the case.

Mark pulled the string and eased the hatch down slowly, carefully, taking the thin wooden steps with care as they softly whimpered under his weight.

The attic was nothing remotely interesting as an adult, but as a kid, it had been a forbidden space, surely filled with wonder, a doorway into another planet's worth of artifacts from his mom's and uncle's childhoods. And while it shared almost all the square footage of the house itself—serving as a third floor of sorts—it wasn't the kind of place where you could have a cool bedroom with a sloped, loft ceiling or a cozy office tucked away in the most remote corner of the house. At its lowest point, it was barely big enough to stand up in, and Mark found himself hunched over as he crawled through the hatch. Near the edge, where he'd climbed up, was a broken wooden cradle. The rockers both cracked—shipwrecked, leaning to one side and packed full of more stuff. The cradle held a decades-old paper bag, the kind with handles, and it was folded over on itself to close it tightly.

The scent of something stale and something like lavender came from inside it, and Mark couldn't resist looking inside, coughing immediately as dust rose from a dried bouquet of some kind that had been wrapped in a white dish towel, the whole thing so covered in dust that the air suddenly speckled in front of him. Mark hacked into his sleeve, breathing into his shirt and remembering how old some of this crap surely was.

Why did he want to see what Brute had brought home from the war? To share the memory? To connect in some way, at some level, that they hadn't been able to when he was young?

Someone had used it, too. Used it for something rough.

He didn't know why that struck him with morbid interest, but he wanted to find it. Finding a broken rocking horse or some meaningless detritus from their childhood was one thing, not very interesting and nothing worth hunting, but a discarded machete from World War II? That was, at least at some level, more interesting. And he wanted to wait until Brute woke up before leaving anyway, so he had the time to poke around.

He spent the better part of an hour going through boxes, a trunk filled with clothes that had to predate the twentieth century by a decade, probably a great-great-grandparent's few surviving garments; Grandma Lynn saved all sorts of odd things in the name of preserving family heritage, but she was gone now, and he had no idea what significance these things had to anyone in his family. Passing on family knowledge required engagement, the desire and ambition to care for that knowledge and pass it on. Mark guessed, with a bit of sheepish regret, that neither he nor Ann had much of that. He supposed they could sell the clothes to an antique dealer. Surely there was a market online for Victorian clothing? eBay, somewhere like that?

CHAPTER 30

Another box held nothing but Hot Wheels, loose Lego blocks, random Star Wars and M.A.S.K. action figures from when he and Ann were kids. At one time, perhaps Han Solo had been worth money with his little gun intact, but unfortunately, Mark's prized Han was an amputee that sported only one plastic arm. Mark chuckled and tossed the figure back into his cardboard heap.

He took his time perusing the oddball accumulation of things until all that remained was the antique wardrobe, standing tall at the highest point in the room. The Devil's resting place, if he was to believe Uncle Tony so many years ago—and when Mark opened it, he noticed a box that had *Alfred - KEEP* written on the side with an exclamation point. He opened the dusty flaps and peered inside.

Something stared back at him.

"Jesus!" Mark cried out, then laughed as he realized that it was the cardboard head and shoulders of Robert De Niro as Al Capone, some sort of promotional standup for *The Untouchables*, a video store promo from the '80s. It had been folded down and crushed into the box, right on top, to protect whatever was underneath. Mark lifted De Niro by the neck to discover a pile of clothes, including a Marine's hat, some letters still tucked into yellowed envelopes, and the machete, wrapped in a piece of plastic tarp, the kind you put down for painting.

What the fuck? Mark thought. He unfolded it with care, letting the plastic roll over on his palm again and again until it was uncovered completely. The blade was pockmarked with rust, the hard plastic handle cracked and missing a rivet. Along the edge was a dark, maroon-black stain that ran nearly the entire length, the unmistakable traces of dried blood.

A cunny blade. Use one of those to cut open the carcass.

Mark wrapped it back in the plastic as he'd found it, tucked it back under De Niro's cardboard bulk, and decided that he was done with plundering the attic for the day.

The last time Mark saw Brute was just before the old man passed in early April.

Tony's final appeal had failed, and Mark had decided to go see the old man in person to tell him the news. A hospice nurse was living there with him full-time, occupying Ann's old bedroom, a middle-aged woman with a quiet, almost meek demeanor and heavily sprayed '80s hair named Joanne. She smiled as Mark came in, then excused herself so he could spend some time alone with his grandpa.

"S'it hangin, kiddo?" Brute said, mustering a smile. The pain was hitting him hard, despite the drugs, and he was days away from being so medicated that one day, he simply wouldn't wake up. There was music playing from a little boom box on the end table, mostly big band and swing numbers from the '40s. *Three little words ... eight little letters...*

"Hey, Grandpa." Mark sat down where Joanne had been sitting a moment before, leaning forward with his elbows on his knees. He sighed. "It was what we thought. What they wanted."

"Mmm." The old man grunted a little under his breath, offering a slight nod, but that was all. "What

I thought, yeah. Astronauts on TV. Earlier. Going to, I think they're trying to go to, maybe Mars? Are we going to Mars?"

"Grandpa?" Mark reached out and touched the old man's knee. Brute's eyes shifted toward his grandson. "I'm sorry you're going through this. Is there anything I can do ... that Ann can do? For the pain, for anything?"

"They gotta..." Brute trailed off, losing his train of thought. "Gotta vote Madigan out." He laughed, but it came out like a dull wheeze. "November. Get him out."

Mark laughed. "We'll do what we can."

"You didn't say things like that... when we were kids, you know?" Brute pointed a bony finger at some random commercial on TV. "You just didn't talk that way, and I brought it in, you know? I brought it in the house. You don't talk about those kinda things. I should've said something, you know? About Annie? But I didn't know for sure. You have to believe that, Markie. I didn't. I brought it in. And after you guys were out there, when you came in. And your clothes. Your mom yelled at me, and I didn't know what to do. You didn't... you know we never went to Mars, right? Kennedy lied about all that."

Mark shook his head, struggling to pull out the pieces that seemed to connect. "No, you're right, Grandpa. We never went to Mars. What about Ann? What did you mean to say? I don't know what you're talking about." The old man didn't respond at first, just staring blankly past Mark. "Brute? Hey. Come on, look at me."

"You gotta invite vampires into your house, you know?" Brute tilted his head and shifted his eyes toward his grandson, as though still sizing something up just out of Mark's field of vision. "That's the funny thing. Isn't that some goddamn nonsense?"

"Sure is, yeah," Mark said, resigning himself to the tide of blather rolling from the old man's mouth. A life of deep thought, memories spanning generations, and everything ended up in a fucking soup, a liquid mess of confusion in the brain, spewing out garbage. Brute lay his head back against the seat. God, he looked old. Tears began to leak down the old man's cheeks, and Mark kneeled, putting an arm around his grandfather's shoulders. "Hey. Hey, what is it, Grandpa?"

"Just so sorry," Brute whispered, spittle clinging to his lips as he wept. "God, Jesus Christ in Heaven, we were young. We were so scared and so young, and I'm so sorry. The things we saw, the things we did."

"It was a long time ago," Mark said with soft finality. "It was a long time ago, Grandpa."

"Doesn't make it right," Brute murmured, reaching up to wipe away tears. "It's best for him, for everyone. That he's there, that Tony's there. You just can't answer the door. I love you kids, but it's best for us that he's there."

Two nights later, Brute died in his sleep.

31

It was that third visit that stuck with Mark the most now, sitting in the kitchen, smoking a cigarette, and waiting for Cory to come over. She'd sounded so excited on the phone, telling him how she wanted to make him one of her favorite recipes and how much she appreciated his wanting to meet Georgia. His hand hurt; the painkillers didn't seem to be doing jack-fucking-shit, and his body ached like he hadn't slept. He'd woken up late, smoked a little of the joint that Cory had left there from the other night in hopes that it would help him relax, but he felt agitated for no good reason that he could find. Had he dreamed about Brute dying, and something about the attic? He felt like he had those cobweb strands of dream-thought teasing him just a little, but there was nothing to grab hold of.

How old had he been when he heard about Charlie, what Charlie's dad had done to him? Was that sixth grade that summer? Seventh?

Mark felt like he was working through an unfinished conversation with himself as he stamped out the cigarette and got up, stretching, to change clothes. He'd never gotten out of the t-shirt and shorts he'd slept in, and Cory was so excited to have a date night. Her voice on the phone had sounded different, somehow. Fresh. Girlish, even. It was wonderful to hear her so happy, and he wondered to some extent where it had come from. Cory carried the weight of her concerns about Adrian, his abuse, and Georgia's future and college. All of it was there with her, even in the best moments. A guardedness, for lack of any other way to put it, that suddenly seemed to be just ... gone. Had Adrian contacted her? Better yet, had she found out that he was in jail or dead?

His phone vibrated as he slipped on a pair of jeans and a fresh t-shirt. It was a text from Ann, the first in what felt like forever.

[Ann: What the fuck, Mark?]

He hadn't heard from her in days; she wasn't kidding when she said the signal was virtually non-existent. In fact, he didn't remember what she was responding to. He scrolled up and saw the goofy picture of him wearing the costume from that first night he'd found it.

[Mark: What's wrong? I'm just dressing up for Halloween.]

[Ann: Get rid of it. Now.]

[Mark: Wtf. Why?]

CHAPTER 31

There was a knock at the door. He could see Cory's car in the driveway, and he smiled, catching a glimpse of himself in the mirror over his dresser. He ignored the throbbing in his arm and snapped off the light, hustling downstairs to answer the door.

Cory stood on the porch in a flowery dress, ready for a date. She held a grocery bag in her hand and leaned in to give him a quick kiss. Next to her stood a teenage brunette with shoulder-length hair and a thin smile, holding a purse shaped like a coffin with Jack Skellington and Sally on it.

"Hot Topic's going door-to-door now?" he said with a nod at the purse.

"Funny man," Cory grinned, "this is my daughter, Georgia. Mark, Georgia. Georgia, Mark. You signed on for dinner with all the Blevin girls tonight."

32

Despite the length of his relationship with Cory—nearly five months to the day—Mark and Georgia hadn't yet met, Cory having been reluctant to lightly let anyone into her daughter's life after everything that happened with Adrian. It was a statement on a number of levels—both to him and to Georgia—and as Cory now employed her daughter to brown some Italian sausage in a pan, Mark set to chopping vegetables for what Cory said was her grandmother's classic recipe for pasta sauce. Georgia stared into the pan, rarely looking up for more than just a weak smile at something her mother said, as Cory fluttered about cheerily. Every now and again, Mark caught a glimpse of Georgia looking casually around the room, checking out the place.

As Cory talked about a variety of things from her grandmother's pasta to the coming school year, Mark caught Georgia looking quizzically at Cory with bemused confusion, as though she wasn't used to seeing her mother this chatty, this animated. As the sauce simmered and filled the house with the rich, heady combination of garlic, rosemary, and onions, they sat around the coffee table in the living room playing UNO, and Georgia managed the occasional chuckle at some dated story about Mark and Cory in high school and how different it had been then. It all felt strangely familial as they ate at the table where Mark, Ann, Audrey, Tony, Brute, and Lynn had eaten so many holiday meals throughout his childhood. Occasionally, something seemed to catch Georgia's attention over Mark's shoulder, and he glanced out the window toward the thicket and expanse of field beyond the property, but she quickly fell back into the conversation, and when she noticed him notice her after three or four instances, she managed a tight smile and went back to eating.

"...Derenbaker?" Cory said. Mark realized that he was staring at Georgia, who now looked at her mother. "Mark?"

"Hmm?" he said, coming back into the conversation himself. "I'm sorry. What was that?"

"Do you remember Mr. Derenbaker?" Cory wound spaghetti around her fork and grinned. "American Studies?"

"Oh, god, that guy," Mark groaned, rolling his eyes at Georgia, who offered one of her first genuine smiles at his candid assessment of their former teacher. "Do you have him?"

"Yeah," Georgia replied, returning the eye roll. "Did he wipe his nose a lot on his sleeve when you guys had him?"

"He did," Mark quickly noted, eliciting laughter from both of them. "Eric Garza used to say that Derenbaker must have had a hell of a time maintaining a coke habit on a teacher's salary."

"He wasn't on coke, come on," Cory said. "He had allergies. Well, okay, that's what he said." Georgia and Mark both stared at her, on the verge of uproarious laughter, and she shrugged, finally joining them. "Okay, maybe he was."

"Allergies," Georgia scoffed. "Colombian fever, more like."

"Nice one," Mark nodded, holding out his fist for her to bump, and she did. They went on to compare notes about former and current teachers at Galesburg High School, agreeing that Mr. Ericson and Ms. Hoff were both cool while Mrs. Stone and Mr. Effers had been, and still were, a snore on all counts.

"I'm surprised that they're all still there," Cory noted. "I mean, I get that careers are long and everything, but that was thirty years ago. That they're all still there, it says something."

"Says they're stuck in Galesburg," Georgia said under her breath, but purposefully loud enough for Cory to hear.

"Okay, my globetrotting princess," Cory smiled, playfully slapping Georgia's wrist with a breadstick. "You'll be out of here soon enough. Humor me for the last year of your high school career, will you?" She reached up and turned her hand into a claw, clutching the top of Georgia's head and giving her a playful squeeze.

"You looking at any schools in the Midwest, or are you settled on the West Coast?" Mark asked, dipping his garlic bread in sauce and giving it a good swirl.

"Nah, I need some consistently sunny weather. University of Arizona, or maybe Cal Tech." Georgia looked at him thoughtfully, then glanced at her mother and back at him. "So, Mom said your uncle is in prison."

CHAPTER 32

"Georgia." Cory's humor was gone now, evaporating from her face as completely as good cheer had overtaken her just moments ago. She stared at her daughter, but Mark shrugged.

"Yeah." Mark took a bite and nodded. "He is."

"That's ... wild," Georgia said. "Triple homicide."

"Goddamn it, Georgia," Cory said, sucking the words in under her breath now. "Why would you want to—" She gave Mark a pursed smile, and her eyes pleaded for forgiveness. He winked and shook his head a little to say it was okay.

"I'm thinking of going into criminal justice," Georgia said, "and it was just ... interesting, that's all. It's fuc— it's messed up, but it's interesting."

Mark sighed and wiped his mouth with his napkin. A hard, steady wind kicked up outside, and everyone paused as it rattled against the house; for a moment, he could practically feel the October chill through the walls, his clothes, his bones. "I totally understand, Georgia. How someone could feel that way. For me, it's—" He could feel Cory's eyes on him, a sudden sorrow in her expression that suggested the celebratory tone of the night had been replaced with a dark, nameless shadow. "—you're right. It's fucked up. I don't know how to feel about it, I really don't. I feel bad, sick for the fact that it happened, but it... I don't know. Still feels like it happened to someone else's family, in a way."

Georgia nodded thoughtfully, seemingly impressed with his candor. "Have you talked to him?"

"Since he's been in?"

"Yeah."

"I have, yeah." Mark sipped his water. "I've been to see him. Once. I had to see him outside of the courtroom, you know? To see him there, to ... solidify it. In my head. That it was him."

Georgia had stopped eating now; they'd all stopped eating. Cory sat quietly with her hands in her lap, looking between them back and forth, while Georgia sat back in her chair, one elbow propped on the arm. "You didn't believe he did it?"

"Oh, no, that's not what I meant. I just had to see him in jail, you know? In the outfit, the whole thing, to really have it lock in my head, that it was real. No, I know he did it. He confessed. He never even tried to deny it. And I saw the pictures. Of the ... crime scene, I mean." Mark noticed Cory staring at him hard; she didn't know that he'd seen the pictures of the Ensinger family. It didn't matter, he supposed. He still saw those pictures in his head sometimes, though he'd done his best to push them away (*the candlestick forced home between Dara's legs, her daughter's head on the carpet*) so they didn't continue to prey on his mind more than they already did.

"Whoa. Super bad, I assume?" Georgia was sitting up in her chair now, leaning forward as though she was watching something interesting on TV, the slightest hint of an excited light in her eyes.

"That's enough," Cory said, her face grim, mouth tight, then giving way to an uncomfortable smile. "Just had dinner, you know?" Mark could see how upset she was, not at him, but at Georgia, at a night that she'd planned for, looked forward to, going a little left of center. "Can we please talk about something else, kids? For me?"

Mark smiled back at her. "Anyone for seconds? I'll tell you the story about when your mom got thrown out of the Twin-West Theater one time in high school for dropping a pickle in a lady's hair from the balcony."

Cory's laughter echoed throughout the kitchen; Georgia felt momentarily bad for bringing up the Ensinger murders, but there she was, the house in which Tony Devold had grown up and lived when he committed the crimes; she couldn't *not* ask about it. And Mark was cool. He'd rolled with her questions. It was a solid start.

She'd gone upstairs to use the bathroom, and now she stood in the hallway, listening to her mom and Mark chatting as they finished the dishes.

"Mind if I take the tour?" she called down the steps. To which Mark called back, "Be my guest. Sorry about the clutter."

The house was cozy and well-kept in spite of its age, she thought, as she poked her head into the rooms on the second floor. There was the master bedroom—probably where Mark and her mom had sex, let's be honest—and the bathroom she'd just been in. The attic was one of those old pull-string deals, and the other two bedrooms were separated by a linen closet.

The door to the second of the two small bedrooms was closed. She turned the knob and found it unlocked. *He said to take the tour*, Georgia thought, but paused before opening it. Behind the door, she could hear something: a slight, almost inaudible scraping sound, as if something was being dragged slowly across the floorboards, followed by a shuffling. Then silence.

She opened the door.

A window faced the backyard, and the sun had long since slid over the horizon; it took her a minute to adjust to what she was seeing as her eyes acclimated to the long shadows of the room against the light that spilled in from the hallway behind her. There was a twin bed neatly made with a dark blue duvet and fluffy pillows, an oak chest of drawers that stood immediately to her left, a gaudy standing lamp with dangling, plastic crystals lining the bottom of the shade, and a rocking chair in the corner of the room, upon which sat a bizarre, papier-mâché bust of some sort.

"Well, hello," she said softly; *ugly damn thing*. A head, shoulders, and partial torso, one full arm complete with a hand, and one arm that hadn't been finished. The face looked like a child had tried to draw features on the glued paper until frustration had overtaken the process and given way to slits, as if by a box cutter. "Who are you supposed to be?"

She stepped into the room and, without thinking about it, closed the door.

"What do you think?" Cory leaned against the counter, sipping her wine as Mark dried the last of the plates.

"About the sauce?" He grinned. "Oh, gold."

"Her, idiot." She shrugged and smiled, resisting the urge to close her eyes and hear his words drift through the air in the room. This was a dream. Her life with Mark had taken on the quality of a dream, a life unlived, a life rooted in the normalcy and honest, organic love she'd wanted for so long. No dating apps, no Facebook messages from old boyfriends who barely concealed

CHAPTER 32

their intentions to fuck and run. Real life. "I don't know. Us."

"She's great." Mark looped the dish towel through the fridge handle and slipped his arm around her waist. He picked up his whiskey and clinked her wine glass, wincing a little at the pain pulsing under his bandage. "I like her attitude."

"Poor baby, you gotta be more careful," Cory said, leaning over and planting a kiss on his bandage. "You could have really hurt yourself."

"I think that's what I did," Mark joked. "Nothing the modern pharmacy can't fix."

Cory sipped her wine as she stacked Tupperwares of leftovers in the fridge. "I'm sorry about the Tony talk."

"Ah, I can't blame her. You can't blame people for being curious." He sipped and sighed. "She's great. You're great."

"So we're both great?"

"*So* great." He grinned, savoring the sight of her.

She laughed, took a drink of her wine, and looked at him, really looked at him, their eyes holding.

"I love you, Cory. I ... have loved you, for so long. She—I just..." Mark trailed off, shaking his head. *Don't let the whiskey do the talking*, he thought, but that wasn't it. There was an overwhelming surge of—

"What?" Cory held his gaze, waiting. Patience. There was such patience in her, he could really think about what he wanted her to say, with no expectation, she wanted to know, wanted to get a real sense of what he wanted to say.

"I just wish that you and I—" he started, glancing up as he heard the thump of what sounded like a door. "I don't know. What if we just—"

"What is it?" Cory replied as Mark looked up at the ceiling. "What's wrong?"

"Nothing," he said, shaking it off. It was nothing—the house settling. "Come here."

"Where?"

He led her through the hallway at the bottom of the stairs to the living room, the front door. He opened the door and let it stay there, hanging open, a cool autumn breeze winding past them into the room. "Just here."

A car went by, and the trees rustled in the autumnal rustle of cool air finding its way back to the earth. "Feels nice."

"It feels safe, doesn't it?" He closed his eyes, pulling her against him, savoring the feeling of her body on his, the tangible, human sense of presence. How long, really, did one have to take in these moments? Brute and Lynn had been together for so many decades, so much time to take a night and feel the sense of connection with someone else, to pull that in, to insist in one's soul that this was the way of life, this was the intention of everything. Autumn passed through him. Everything he'd ever felt, known, struggled against, passed through him to the reality of the moment. Cory. Love. His life.

(fight)

"It does." Her voice was nearly a whisper as she leaned into him. "Mark..." She started to speak, then shook her head, and he sensed her pause, pulling her close. Somewhere outside came a soft, thrumming sound, the sound of encroaching thunder. The stereo in the living room chunk-chunked as it switched CDs, and the Rolling Stones' "Sway" stomped into the room, leveling off in its mid-tempo swagger as Jagger worked his way around a crisis of self.

CHAPTER 32

"I always thought they should have played this at prom," Mark grinned, slipping his arm around Cory's waist and moving in time to the music. "Though I'm guessing that the Stones' blues period would probably have been lost on a bunch of horny seniors."

"Likely, yeah," Cory groaned, giggling as she pressed her face into his shoulder, playing along, Mark gripping her tightly as she inhaled the scent of him, god, it felt good to be like this, the feel of her body against him, Jagger singing about losing himself in time...

"Cory," he whispered into her shoulder. *Timing, timing, timing, god, don't ruin the night with ... no.* She had to know. She *could* know. She'd be fine. *They* would be fine, but she had to know. "I want to tell you something, and I hope—I just—I need to tell you."

"What is it?" she said, her head still resting against his chest.

"When I was in my twenties, I—had a fling with this woman, and we, um, we had—"

"Geo?" Cory had broken their tryst before Mark even had time to register the sound as being behind them, and he turned to see Georgia standing at the bottom of the stairs, her body slumped under the weight of the costume. It looked almost laughable, her slight form dwarfed by the clumsy bulk of the costume, her right arm lost under its layers of paper, and the mouth, from the slit in the mouth, he saw a string of drool begin to slip through the—

"No!" Mark shouted, dashing from the door to where she stood, gripping the edges and pulling hard, pulling Georgia off balance as she staggered against the staircase, losing the fight and falling against the bannister as he yanked it up, over, throwing the thing into the kitchen, watching it hit the floor and flip, *it flipped over, landing upright, but that wasn't possible, it was—*

"Mark!" Cory yelped with surprise, quickly slipping her arm around Georgia's waist and helping her to her feet as Mark backed against the wall, staring into the kitchen, his mouth drooping in disbelief, staring, Georgia rubbing her forehead, steadying herself against the banister. "Baby, Georgia, are you okay? What is it, baby? What's wrong?"

"I'm okay," Georgia groaned, wincing as Cory tried to stroke her hair. "Stop, stop. It hurts."

"What does?" Cory stared at her daughter incredulously, then glared in confusion at Mark, who stood, immobilized, against the wall near the base of the stairs. "Mark?"

"Don't wear that," he said, the words eking out as he caught his breath. "Just... I'm sorry. I'm sorry, Georgia."

"It's okay," she said, reading Mark's face and realizing that he was afraid. "It's okay, really. I just... I was looking at the bedrooms, just taking the tour, like you said. And it was there, in a bedroom."

"Upstairs?" Mark said. "Where? Where upstairs?"

"The far bedroom," Georgia replied, openly annoyed and shrugging off Cory's motherly petting. "*Stop*. Stop, Mom. I'm okay."

"Georgia," Cory sighed, looking to Mark for anything by way of explanation. "What—why did you wear it?"

"I..." Georgia trailed off, turning to look upstairs. The attic was closed. Had it been open before? When she'd worn the costume and stepped into the hallway? Yes, it had been, absolutely. "It—it told me to."

"What?" Cory replied, stifling a confused chuckle, looking from her to Mark and back again. Mark leaned

CHAPTER 32

his head against the wall, taking deep breaths, staring past Cory to the kitchen. "What?"

"I'm sorry." Georgia stared at Mark, who finally turned to meet her gaze. His expression said it all, and she shook her head, looking at the floor as something stuck deep inside her, a sickening regret. "It told me to."

33

Mark lay stretched out on the couch with feet crossed at the ankles, hands relaxed on his stomach, sleeping peacefully while the TV flickered an old black-and-white movie to the room, a war drama of some kind. Cory didn't recognize it, but she'd never been much into old movies. She poured a glass of wine and turned the light off in the kitchen. Her phone vibrated in the back pocket of her jeans.

[Georgia: Home. Thanks, Mom, sorry about the murderino talk. And sorry about the whole costume thing. I don't really know what happened. I know that sounds crazy.]

[Cory: No worries, baby. Love you, be home in a bit, have some tea, and relax. There's a little bit of weed in my bathroom vanity if you really need it.]

[Georgia: I'm good, lol. He's a nice guy, have fun. :)]

CHAPTER 33

So much for the innocent child and protective mother, Cory thought, ending the thread with a smiley face and plugging in her phone to charge on the counter. She sipped her wine in the dark of the kitchen; it was a pinot that left her tongue feeling soft, warm. Wasn't that what happened with age? The roles reversed? Parent, child, teacher, student, all those clichés?

What the hell happened?

"It told me to wear it," Geo had said.

That made no sense. Geo wasn't easily scared or shaken; she loved crime and horror movies, was obsessed with true-crime podcast culture insofar as it had led to listeners buying into the idea of becoming armchair sleuths. The morbid fascination of the Ensinger murders and their history had played at the fringes of their lives since Cory told Geo she was seeing Mark. Cory knew that she'd likely been overprotective of Geo, no question, but her daughter hadn't felt Adrian's presence the way that Cory had, hadn't gotten a sense of his violence and cruelty. She had to keep that from happening, even if for just a while longer.

The sound of antiquated machine gun fire went off from the living room, flickering in the near darkness. Cory sat down on the couch next to Mark, relaxed into the sound of his sleep breathing and the tinny quality of the movie's dialogue. The sense of peace she'd felt that morning, the lack of anxiety, concern, fear. An absolute calm. What had happened in her sleep to make her feel that way? That feeling was replaced with a sudden, dull dread in her chest and stomach as she looked out the window at the dark street.

You were talking in your sleep about somebody being in the house. You mentioned a doctor. At Mark's, the other night, after she'd woken from… god, was it actually sleepwalking?

She had the vaguest memory of someone calling her name that night, in her sleep, and it had come from downstairs in the kitchen. But that wasn't right, either. It hadn't *called* her name. It had *said* her name, softly, no sense of urgency or concern, no cause for alarm. Just the sound of her name drifting on the air. And she did remember getting up and feeling her way through the dark into the hallway, standing at the top of the stairs for a few moments before descending like a child in the dark who was momentarily afraid to call for her mother for fear of something else breaking the silence behind her. And had the ceiling hatch to the attic been open?

Then, her name again, from the kitchen. Corene.

Not Cory, she considered. Corene. No one called her Corene.

And then at the bottom of the stairs, she came back to herself, realized fully that she'd been dreaming—and sure enough, the voice was gone. Why was she there? Yes, she'd come downstairs to the kitchen for a drink of water, careful not to wake Mark, who slept deeply next to her in a sweet, lulling rhythm.

That was when she'd seen it, in the corner of the kitchen, almost as though it didn't want to be seen. The shape. A man, crooked at the shoulders in a strange way, as though his arms were imbalanced, one longer than the other, but how could that be? The head tilted a little, unmoving, as still as a statue, except for the fingers on that long arm, opening and closing ever so slowly, flexing, wrapping into a fist, and then unfolding again.

Eat you.

CHAPTER 33

The words were in her head as suddenly as she'd heard her name from upstairs.

Take you inside.

And then there was nothing there. She squinted into the darkness, but the shape was gone, nothing but a shadow, apparently, the curtains against the wall, perhaps *(but the fingers were moving, flexing a little)*, so she poured herself a glass of water, and that's when she felt the sensation. It started at her feet, spread slowly up her calves the way a chill might in a cold room, but it was as if the chill moved in slow motion. Her thighs, her groin and hips, her stomach, over her breasts and shoulders, and Cory put a hand to her chest to feel the skin there, cool but not cold, then her face, even a tingling in her hair, and then there was nothing, as if her whole body was numb, an opioid high that slithered over her as easily as air coming through an open window.

Take your face.

When she saw the shape again, standing there between the fridge and the basement door, closer now, she forced herself to look away. It wasn't right. It had no face, or it had more than one face, as though several faces' worth of features were just mashed together, and it was hard to focus. Her eyes, numbing; how could one's eyes go numb? But they were. A sudden blankness as though her eyes had gone numb, even to the darkness in the room, the only real clarity from the moon outside. Soft, bleached rays of light across the tile floor.

Inside you.

Her hand still rested on her chest, palm pressed to her ribs just under the curve of her breasts, and she didn't start when she felt something move there. Just a flutter of movement under her fingers, something outside of her, but absolutely there. As though something had pressed its fingertips to hers. There was no panic, not really, just a feeling of inevitability, as though whatever was about to happen was entirely unavoidable, that it would happen with or without her acquiescence, and Cory felt herself getting on her knees against a growing pain in her stomach, her chest, and shoulders, a weight, as though she carried something awkward and bulbous on her back. She closed her eyes, and when she said his name out loud—Adrian—she realized that it came out wrong, because she had something in her mouth.

She spat and licked at her mouth. Blood? Coppery, but not blood, surely. It was too thick for blood. It was mud, wet but mostly tasteless, earthy, though in the moonlight of the kitchen, it did look for all the world like blood on her fingers when she put them to her mouth. She licked them clean, reaching back toward the ground (*Jesus fucking Christ, it felt so good, how could anything feel so good*) for more. The ground, yes, she was outside now, didn't remember leaving the kitchen, but here she was crouching in the mud, and this time she smeared it on her skin, her neck and face, the cold, earthy sensation coating her fingers and warm on her face. She felt light, weightless. Was she floating?

In front of her, just a few yards away, where the trees separated the field from Mark's backyard, stood the shape. The tilted man simply stood, dumbly, watching her, and as Cory opened her mouth to call out, she saw the clamoring things at its feet, the half-formed, child-sized creatures that writhed and slithered through the mud, each one wearing a human face that wasn't all there or wasn't in the right order. Eyes blinked from where mouths should be, there was a layered, vaginal gash across the face of one of them, all covered in mud.

They weren't children, not really, more like fleshy, fetal things that weren't finished *becoming*, for lack of a better word, though some of them wore actual human faces; Cory thought she even recognized one, a guy who used to hang out at Corner Connection. *A parasitic twin*, she thought dumbly, remembering a story in the *Peoria Journal Star* about a woman who'd had a baby with a parasitic twin attached: a mass of flesh, hair, and teeth that had never quite come together into an actual child. As though a baby had been digested and vomited into a messy approximation of what it had once been.

Corene. The sound of her name came out wet, sticky. Cory opened her mouth to scream, finally, but instead, she laughed, harder and harder, until the pain in her stomach and chest was from triumphant, hysterical laughter—

—and then she was in the kitchen again, on a chair, with Mark sitting in front of her. Telling her that she'd sleepwalked to the kitchen. That she'd called for a doctor, that someone had been in the house.

There had been, she thought. Something frightening. A man. But now, there was ... nothing. Nothing at all.

She remembered it all now, staring into the backyard as Mark snored to his war movie in the living room. Cory set her wineglass down on the counter and unlocked the screen door, stepping outside and closing the door quietly behind her.

The night murmured, a rustle here and there, the occasional far-off dots of light, and the distant hum of tires that signaled a truck going by on the highway a quarter mile or so beyond the cornfield. Near the thicket and patch of woods along the back of the property, Cory could see that there was a crooked cross, a stand of some kind, maybe a tomato trellis. She could see her breath; there was a deep, dry chill in the air as a flutter of activity shook through the brush. A small flock of birds settling themselves, maybe a raccoon, but Cory started, folding her arms tight against her chest as she approached the bramble entrance to the woods.

The cross was a mount of some kind, a frame for attaching something. Planters? Maybe a scarecrow, she thought, though what was there to protect here? It wasn't Mark's family's field behind the woods, and anyway, this was a solid hundred feet away, hardly effective as a deterrent for the birds. Cory's shoes squelched in the soft, wet ground around the thicket. It hadn't rained in days, and yet, the ground under her feet was a sticky mess.

"Great," she muttered, raising a foot to see the damage in the moonlight; she didn't want to get her new Vans muddy. The light shifted, and she saw the dark smears along the sides of her light blue shoes, and she paused when she noticed that the mud wasn't all dark; there were gradient smudges that looked like a lighter brown, a crimson. Cory kneeled and pressed her hand to the ground, the cold mud sucking up around her splayed fingers, and she raised her palm to the light.

It was a dark red.

She stood and looked back at the house. Was someone hurt? An animal, she suddenly thought, of course, that's what it was. *Jesus*, she thought. *Poor thing.* Maybe a rabbit or a squirrel had been injured by a dog, a coyote. It wasn't uncommon to see them this close to town.

But there was nothing, she thought, so much blood and no sign of anything across the lawn in the moonlight. Just here, where the light didn't quite reach, in this muddy little grove where the woods started. Cory looked at her legs, where she'd kneeled in the mud. Her knees were stained with that same red, as though she'd just kneeled in a pool of blood.

What in God's name..? She stepped past the wooden frame and into the little copse of trees that grew bigger and wider as it wound around the border of the field. It was dark, darker than she was prepared for, and the shapes of twisted tree branches in the scant slivers of moonlight looked grotesque, creatures with bent forms from another world. Then the breeze would skate around her, shake the limbs, and reveal them to be just trees, only trees. Cory squinted into the darkness.

Something was watching her.

About twenty feet into the patch of dense woods and thicket, something appeared to be crouching in the thicket, a shape that didn't make sense, with the slightest hint of a head coming through the ground, facing her, with glazed-out eyes devoid of pupil or color, and arms that faced the other direction, their position suggesting that something was pushing itself out of the ground, backward, with its head facing the wrong way. Cory realized her hand was shaking as she took her phone out and turned on the flashlight.

There was a broken skeleton pushing through the muddy earth. The limbs were contorted and poking out at odd angles, spotted with bits of dull, colorless flesh.

Cory turned and ran back toward the house, crashing into the wooden scarecrow stand and nearly ripping it from the ground, through the screen door, back into the kitchen, locking the door, and staring out the window.

Shaking, Cory closed her eyes and realized that she was crying; she wiped her eyes on her sleeve, hands still stained with blood, then washed her hands in water so hot she could hardly stand it, squeezing and rubbing lemon-scented dish soap into her fingers until the water went from a rich pink to clear. She looked out the window again.

There was nothing she could see, but then again, the moon had ducked behind a cloud, and it was so dark, so damn dark that nothing was really visible, nothing but—

—the door to the garage, open.

Just a few inches, but it was open enough to see a sliver of light inside. Cory paused, listening to Mark quietly snoring from the living room, the TV playing something unknown now with a low murmur of ambient noise.

"Geo?" she hissed, stepping toward the garage. "Hey, honey, did you come back?"

Nothing from inside, and she glanced at the back door as she stepped carefully toward the garage. She stopped to listen; if someone had broken in, she would have heard something. Surely, Mark would have woken up.

"Damn it," Cory muttered to herself. As if in response, there was a rustle of movement on the far side of the garage, and she froze. Her brain went back to the animal story; surely, the blood outside had been from a wounded animal. God, was she prepared to see that?

CHAPTER 33

Some possum or raccoon with a mortal injury? Would she have to kill it?

She might. She picked up a rake that leaned against the wall with some leaves still stuck to the end, carefully making her way around the car.

"Oh, for god's sake," Cory groaned, laughing at herself and putting the rake back. It was that goddamn papier-mâché costume; it had been perched on a stack of boxes and fallen onto the floor.

She stared at it. The slit mouth, the makeshift eyes that peeled back just enough so you could see out, the little bump and holes that served as a nose, the bulbous chest that suggested breasts but didn't quite go all the way. Why would anyone make such a thing?

Wait, she thought. After Georgia had found it, she thought Mark had taken it back upstairs. Did he take it here?

Cory picked it up and, without thinking, slipped it on, finding the arm and the fingers, working it onto her frame. It overtook most of her, ending past her waist, so it had to have been intended for someone taller, broader. She found herself breathing hard behind the layers of paper and tape that smelled like sweat, like ... jasmine? And then, right behind that smell, something that stunk like oil, a hot, burning stench like bacon burned to cinders in a skillet. The mirror on the workbench reflected back at her the image of someone playing dress-up, and she snickered at herself. It looked like a kid at Halloween, wearing a costume that was way too big. She took deep breaths, staring at herself. The longer she stared, the deeper her breaths, the calmer she felt. Whatever that was in the woods, it wasn't here now. Maybe it hadn't been there at all, actually. And if it was an animal, then it was nowhere near here. Hopefully, the creature didn't suffer.

Breathe.

She took a deep breath in, slowly blew it out, and again, and again. Within a minute or so, she felt her heart rate slow down, a mild loss of feeling in her fingers, and a sweeping relaxation that seemed to settle under her skin.

Breathe. Cory sat down on the stack of boxes. Was the thing on too tight? Her arms felt tingly, a little numb in some places, and her skin stung, suddenly, and in a few rapid bursts, the way she'd always heard getting a tattoo described. But the feeling was gone as quickly as it had come, and now she just felt that calm again. The absurd bulk of the thing obscured her body completely; as she stared into the mirror, she realized that, when she let her mind stop working, she no longer recognized herself.

She hadn't been to the dentist in almost two years, but the sensation of succumbing to laughing gas was what she felt now, suddenly, a weightless quality to her whole body. Not the way that people on those ridiculous psychic shows talked about the afterlife or some nonsense, she wasn't looking down on her own body, but she could only barely feel her feet or her legs, that tingly feeling settling into her nerves, her bones. It felt good, but the tattoo comparison remained apt, as there was a discomfort, not quite a pain, that went along with it.

Blood.

She felt the sudden need to cry out, and her vision was blurry for a few seconds as she shook herself out of the thing. There was a raw patch on her bicep that

CHAPTER 33

looked almost like a rug burn, but that was impossible, and she didn't have it before. She flipped the thing upside down, noticing a few light pink patches in the glue that she hadn't noticed before, either. She ran her hand along the inside, feeling nothing obvious that would have scratched her.

What the fuck? She ran her fingertips over the sensitive place on her skin. *Spider bite?*

Out of nowhere, Cory felt disoriented, unsure on her feet. She set the costume thing down on the boxes and started back around the car. She was going home. The night, the talk of Tony and the murders and whatever she saw—or thought she saw outside—was all a case of enough being enough.

She clicked off the light, and the garage was dark again; as she opened the kitchen door and started inside, her foot caught something metal that skittered across the floor with a hollow scrape. Cory kneeled and felt around for it, her fingers closing around something round, maybe oval. Smooth metal. She stepped into the kitchen and held it up in the light.

It was a belt buckle with one of those cheesecake, mud-flap designs of a cartoonishly big-breasted hitchhiker that said "NOBODY RIDES FOR FREE" in '70s looking script.

It was Adrian's.

Cory turned it over in her hand, resisting the urge to throw up. She turned it over; the dark red smudge on the back didn't look fresh, but it was blood, there was no question.

Mark, Mark, Mark, she thought over and over again.

She slipped the belt buckle in her pocket and crept through the kitchen; she didn't want him to wake up now. She wanted to go, to get out of the house, and then she was through the kitchen, into the living room, where she grabbed her coat, carefully shutting the front door behind her, letting it click into place and running, running now, to her car. She pulled out and glanced up at the house, hoping that Mark didn't see her, knowing how hard it would be for her to drive away if he did...

Mark, what did you do, what did you do, what did you do—

The shape was outlined clearly, standing behind the curtains, an imbalanced frame missing most of one arm, stock still in the flickering glow of the television.

It can't be Mark. The thing was in the garage, and Mark was asleep. It's not Mark.

It's not Mark; don't go back inside.

It's not Mark, so you should go back inside.

Then who the fuck is it?

What the fuck is it?

It was the costume—she knew this—standing, somehow, in the window, and when the curtains parted just a little, she could see Adrian's face clearly, strips of paper dangling around the circumference of his face, paper that had lost its shape. The eyes were gone, and the mouth was a ragged hole, as though someone had scooped out the inside of his head and wore his hollowed-out face as a mask. Cory could hear that voice in her head, ego or conscience or support group or whatever it should be called, her sense of self-preservation, and it said one thing over all else, a directive she followed as she accelerated down Seminary Road.

GO.

34

Ann looked out the window at the night sky beneath the steady, thrumming engine of the plane as the guy in the seat next to her snorted in his sleep. Somewhere down there was the Panama Canal, a passage from one part of the world to another. A doorway open to the unknown, offering hope and promise. Only back home in the U.S. had she found the unknown to be synonymous with dread, fear; in her experience, other parts of the world embraced—or at least accepted—the idea as inevitable, the encroaching presence of something new, something else, something undefined.

There was something to be said for not knowing things.

The attendant came down the aisle quietly, glancing from seat to seat. Ann asked for a cup of coffee, and the attendant nodded, continuing her path to the back of the plane. Ann sighed and laid her head back against the seat. Mark hadn't responded in any substantive way to her *what-the-fuck* response. Maybe it was for the best. It was too hard to explain over text; she needed to tell him in person. She'd danced around it for years, and it had strained their relationship once she'd gotten into college and found some distance from her childhood. He knew *something* had happened, but that was the extent of it. He had no idea about her, Tony, and the cast. And before that, the mask, tucked away amongst Brute's secret stash of things he'd brought home in '44.

She'd found it stuffed in an oversized Ziploc bag and wrapped in paper towels. The smell when she opened the plastic seal was unlike anything she'd experienced in her six years: a fetid, earthy smell that reminded her of how their clothes smelled after she and Mark came in from playing outside in the rain. Ann had kept it with her, unbeknownst to Grandpa B, tucked into a carrying case for her Barbie accessories. Once everyone else had gone to bed, she took it out in the privacy of her bedroom, slipped it from the bag, and flattened it out on her Strawberry Shortcake bedspread.

It was a man's face. Or at least, it *looked* like it, with little details here and there that frightened her and gave it a disturbing sense of authenticity. The flatness of the nose, for example; Ann had never considered that if you took someone's face away from their head, the nose would be *flat*. The angled eyes, the tight V of his mouth, wrinkled, and the texture of the beef jerky that her brother sometimes liked to snack on.

Thinking about it these years later, she still regretted her child's mind at the time, how she should have recognized the thing for the ghastly horror it was, something that a child should never have seen, much less touched, held, studied, or used the way she did. She remembered the way it felt, the leathery feel of the flesh, how it thinned around the eyes to a papery texture where the flesh would have met the rolling bone of the socket. It made her think of the mummy movie she and Mark had watched one Saturday afternoon when she was maybe four years old, how the withered flesh of the creature looked even in black and white. When Grandpa B said he wanted them to stay out the attic, even at that time, Ann felt that he must have had his trunk of war souvenirs in mind, the things he'd brought home from a little island in the Pacific after a botched invasion and a rescue mission that left three-quarters of his platoon dead at the hands of Japanese soldiers who'd been ready and waiting to ambush. That's where she'd found it, and she remembered holding the shorn flesh up to her face, the thought making her sick now. It wasn't the face of the devil, as he'd warned them, but it was the face of someone long dead. It was something that held its own kind of power; she could tell when she held it, though she wouldn't have been able to explain how or why. But to a curious six-year-old trying to wrap her head around the idea of her grandmother dying, it was a curiosity worth hiding away for further inspection.

The flight attendant was back, suddenly, with a small paper cup of steaming coffee. Ann sipped and stared out the window at the dark. From a plane in the middle of the night, the world below looked like one huge, endless black hole.

She remembered the night she made the cast of Grandma Lynn.

Lynn was at the end of what was to be her final round of chemotherapy, her matronly frame diminished from the aftereffects of the drugs, her broad shoulders and arms largely devoid of muscle tone, her sallow, heavy breasts sagging and clinging awkwardly to her thinning stature. Her cheeks had sunk uncomfortably into her skull, but their mother had made it a point to help their grandmother apply makeup on her good days, so she felt more human. And she slept often, sometimes suddenly, her chest barely moving at times, prompting their mother or Grandpa B to lean over and ensure that she was still breathing. It would be years before Ann learned that Grandma Lynn had insisted on dying at home.

It had been a Sunday morning, and Grandma Lynn had been watching *The Rescuers* with Ann in the "big bedroom," as she called it, her grandparents' bedroom. Ann's first-grade class had been working with paste and papier-mâché, and when she told Grandma Lynn how they used plastic Halloween masks as a frame for creating their own masks to decorate, Lynn had forced a smile to her face, dozing a little. Thinking back, Ann couldn't be sure if Grandma Lynn had actually agreed when Ann suggested that she could make a mask using her face while they watched TV. She did remember that by the time she got back in the room with the paste, paper, plastic, and the strange mask-thing she'd found in the attic, Grandma Lynn was asleep, with Bernard and Miss Bianca staging a rescue for no one.

Grandma Lynn had fallen asleep with one arm mostly under a pillow, the other stretched out flat and prone on the bedspread, and Ann quickly realized that the wig her grandmother wore to disguise her lack of hair was going to make the process difficult. Ann knew that the sick woman had been growing more and more unhappy with how much weight she was losing, particularly in her face. To make up for some of that loss, Ann carefully laid the mask she'd found in the attic over her grandmother's face, surprised at how effectively it fit over her diminishing features, almost like the plastic ones they used at school. From there, Ann watched as the two cartoon mice on TV infiltrated the bayou hideout of Madame Medusa, and she layered typing paper, newspaper, and paste, continuing over her grandmother's prostrate form down to her waist, where the blanket covered the rest of her. Ann remembered the room being cold, as Lynn was always hot from the treatments, a big box fan pulling in cool, autumn air from an open window.

At some point, she'd fallen asleep watching the movie with Lynn because she remembered her mother and Mark waking her frantically, her mother sharply admonishing her for the impromptu art project, Mark leading her back to their bedroom as their mother lifted the sticky paper frame of her grandma from the woman, who was herself just waking up and was oblivious to all that had happened. Less than two days later, Grandma Lynn passed during an afternoon nap, not unlike the one in which she was partially immortalized in paper and glue by her granddaughter.

The mask from the attic had remained inside the thing, Ann realized when she found her creation sitting on the curb outside with the weekly garbage. It had partially dried when her mother had peeled it from Lynn's skin, but in the interim, as it hardened, it had lost a little of its shape, drooping in places.

Her mother didn't even want to look at the thing, saying only, "Annie, you shouldn't have done that. That's not something we want to see," but that wasn't true, was it? She missed her grandmother, Mark missed their grandmother, everyone did! Uncle Tony had been her saving grace. He'd found her crying outside and asked what was wrong. Afterward, he'd snuck the thing from the trash pile around to the back of the house for her.

"Don't let your mom see this thing, Annie," he'd said, "or your Grandpa B, either. It'll make them sad, and they'll throw it away again."

"It makes me sad, too," Ann remembered saying, "but that doesn't mean I want to throw it away." Tony had set her on his lap then (Ann closed her eyes against the wailing baby who had suddenly awoken in first-class when she thought of that first time he'd put his hand on her six-year-old thigh) and said that she was strong to think that, that feeling sad or feeling hurt was okay.

It would be two years before he went further with those hands, and seven years before he'd actually rape her, though at the time, that wasn't how she thought of it. She trusted Tony, loved Tony, had given her virginity to him because he told her it was a safe and loving and good thing to do, that it was better for him to do it than some boy who would just use her and leave her. She'd believed him, and while she knew now—had known for many years—that Tony was a pedophile, a rapist, the worst kind of criminal ... then, he was just her uncle trying to help her prepare for adolescence.

The first time, he'd just had her touch him as he got hard, and the following years had seen the occasional tryst along those same lines, a progression of activity that culminated two days after her thirteenth birthday, her eyes closed, pressed into the pillow to keep from having to see anything or to associate anything afterward with the feeling of her uncle touching her from behind, a strange, tingling discomfort inside her. She'd opened her eyes just once, and the sight of him naked, glistening with sweat, and the smell of cheap deodorant hanging like a fog in the room felt strange—not even wrong, exactly, but not right. It was something she couldn't tell her mother, something she couldn't tell anyone, not even Mark, and she remembered even after all that time how it felt as he'd been inside her. She'd stared at the costume propped in the corner of the room as Tony had taken her. She usually kept it covered up so her mother wouldn't see that she'd gotten it back, stared at the droopy face, the ragged half smile as it watched them, a silent participant complicit in their taboo affections.

The sex had continued on and off until she was eighteen, right before she left for college. The last time had been a bizarre, drunken affair, as though Tony was intimidated, somehow, by her sudden womanhood, the distance she'd gained on a child's behavior and attitudes. They'd polished off a bottle of Boone's Farm together, and she remembered Tony getting out a Polaroid camera, taking some pictures as she posed and modeled for him, the cheap liquor giving her a heavy buzz and making her feel fun, secure in a familiar way as she prepared to move halfway across the country. He'd sat in a chair at the foot of the bed as she spread her legs for the flash of the instant camera, and at one point, she thought she remembered him wearing the costume.

It was only after she'd been away for a few months, near the end of her first semester, that it really hit her how corrupt and impossibly sick it all was. But that, in her mind, was what it was: a sickness inside Tony that he'd somehow passed on to her, in some small way. She didn't speak to Tony for many years after that, avoiding family gatherings, finding excuses to dodge any possibility of having to have a conversation with him. The next time she saw him, it was his mugshot in the newspaper, followed by a long article in *TIME* exploring the depth of depravity exhibited in the Ensinger murders and questioning—as was always the case after such an event captured national attention—the U.S.'s lack of appropriate mental health services.

God, was it her fault, in some butterfly-effect sort of way? It was tough to say, and certainly there had been something inside Tony that was wired very wrong; at the same time, had she helped to grow this thing in him, whatever it was that had allowed him to turn a family of three into a macabre display of flesh and blood?

He'd been wearing the costume—her *trophy*, as he called it after rescuing it from the trash—when he'd killed those people.

She didn't know it for a fact, but she knew. The whole time she'd been in South America, ever since Mark had texted her the picture of it and it all came back to her (not in a flash as they always said, but in little bursts that made her stomach roil and her skin cold), she'd known. Tony had worn it with her a few times, late in their time together, and when he did, he was always rougher, acting strangely as though out of his mind and body just a little. A few times, he called her by someone else's name, not realizing he'd done so until she told him after, at which point he was stunned, even embarrassed. And he'd bit her once, on the shoulder just as he came, hard enough to draw blood. He'd wrenched the costume from his body and sunk his teeth into her flesh, and Ann had cried out, pushing him off of her. Tony grinned, her blood dripping from the corner of his mouth, but when he looked down at the drops of red liquid on her breasts, slipping onto the sheets, he apologized and began to weep. Something about the thing made him different, in a bad way.

"I'm sorry, baby," he'd said, unable to even make eye contact, replete in his shame. "You give it enough of yourself, and it just becomes part of you."

She didn't know what he meant or why he'd said it, but Ann had always suspected the mask, the tanned flesh she'd entombed inside the layers of Elmer's glue and grocery ads.

They weren't a religious family, never had been, and to her knowledge, they still weren't, especially since it was only her, Mark, and their mother. She didn't really buy into the whole dark mystery of life and death, the idolatrous way in which we objectified the dead. Expensive caskets, funeral plots passed from generation to generation, names and memories spoken in reverence with a pointless, ignorant solemnity. The dead were dead, and if her time in anthropology had shown her anything, it was that. But there was also no denying the hold that the dead had on the living, for better or worse.

What if, she'd found herself considering in the days since Mark had sent the picture, there was a kind of power known only to the dead? Was it so far-fetched to consider that there was *something*, even if it wasn't anything we could relate to, identify with, explain? And how could we know? How could we even speculate?

She considered the cave drawings she'd seen during her months spent in Brazil, Bolivia. The extent to which ancient stories had been told by digging into roughly hewn rock. Stories that, for all their effort, clearly needed to be told. Images that still weren't identifiable as anything concrete in the modern world. Gods and monsters, great birds and not-quite-human forms interacting, mingling, communicating with living men and women. Stick-figure tableaus that offered their own doorways to the unknown, truths lost to centuries. Ritual costumes worn in religious ceremonies, each with its own meaning, its own symbolism. Each telling a story. Each imbued with the secrets of its wearer, if only for a moment. Costumes that led men into emotional, actionable states or patterns of behavior.

She had no idea what happened to the thing when she left for college, having only returned home a few times in her freshman year. Clearly, no one had gotten rid of it, and why would anyone see it as something to be feared, to be considered dangerous? It was paper and glue, for god's sake, a little girl's art project, but then, she'd never told anyone about the mask inside it, and certainly not about the way that Tony acted when he wore it during their time together. But what difference could those things have made, really? They added to its depravity, in her memory of it, but that was her cross to bear.

Wasn't it?

Mark, God bless him, always had a hard time with life, and he tried so hard, carried so much guilt over failures that could have happened to anyone, his failed relationships and marriage, his drifting from job to job, and then there was his daughter ... but that something about which he'd confided in her alone, though she'd encouraged him to talk to someone about it. "Contact or no contact," she'd said, "when you have a kid and that kid is suddenly no longer a part of your life, that's not nothing, Mark." She was so happy that he'd found Cory again—that they were trying to build some kind of life together, but with that thing in the house, something would happen. She was sure of it, and she felt a personal responsibility to be the one to destroy it, the thoughts of her years as Tony's lover discoloring her memories like patches of mold encroaching on wallpaper and making her feel sick, weak. Repulsive to herself, in a shameful way, though the logical part of her brain knew that it was just a misguided child's manipulation, that it was nothing she asked for or wanted. Tony was the sick one, but she thought he was always honest with her.

"I've always liked girls like you," he told her one afternoon when she was around fifteen. They were home alone, and he traced circles on her bare stomach with his finger. "It's just one of those things I have to deal with." At the time, that hadn't made sense. Now, and for many years since, she recognized it for what it was: a confession. When she'd pressed him then, he'd smile and change the subject. Now, she knew there had to be more.

Despite his predilections, Ann knew, deep down, that the costume was somehow to blame for those murders.

She'd see Tony and find out from him what had really happened at the Ensinger house. First, the prison, then Grandpa B's house to see Mark and find out what was happening, if anything

If anything.

She finished her coffee and tucked the cup into the pocket of the seat in front of her. The pilot squawked over the intercom that they were about to begin their descent into Miami.

JUNKMAN

Ann popped a piece of Trident in her mouth and chewed anxiously.

She would make everything right.

35

The sound of the television muttered behind his eyes, and he had a vague headache, probably from the wine; red wine always ended up feeling like ball bearings in his skull. Mark opened his eyes and closed them again, a few times, getting used to the room. How long had he been asleep?

"Cory?" he called into the house. Silence, save for low sounds of what seemed like *Baywatch* on TV. Those reruns were only on in the middle of the night. "Cory?"

He sat up on the couch and sighed. She'd probably gone home with Georgia after he'd fallen asleep. *Some host I am*, he thought. Mark clicked off the TV.

The murmuring sound of conversation continued from somewhere off in the house.

"Georgia? You two still here?" He got up, groaned at the annoyance of his headache, and made his way into the kitchen. The costume sat in one of the dining chairs, the one where Georgia had been sitting. Had they messed with it? It sat awkwardly upright, as though waiting to have a family meeting. Its single arm was on the table, as though it was resting.

"What are you doing so wide awake?" he muttered. Mark took a bottle of water from the fridge, swallowing most of it in three or four big gulps. God, he was thirsty; his mouth was dry, dehydrated. He sat down across from the costume.

"So how's your night?" he said out loud. The house was so quiet, so strangely quiet, that he still couldn't get used to it. He supposed he should like the silence, value the sanctity, but being honest, it felt strange, isolating. It was the quality of the air, when he thought about it. The air got heavier as you walked upstairs, and there was a—what? Humidity to it? Old houses, old construction standards. Still, a thickness in his throat, in his chest. He texted Cory.

[Mark: Hey, you make it home okay? Everything okay?]

[Cory: Home okay. Thanks]

The little text indicator showed that she was writing more, and then it stopped.

[Mark: Okay, good. Fun night, Georgia is awesome. She okay? I love you.]

He finished his water and went up to bed, brushing his teeth, washing his face, and crawling under the covers, where he browsed Reddit for a while. No response, which was unusual. Maybe she'd fallen asleep.

CHAPTER 35

Two hours later, Mark lay awake, staring at the ceiling. The brightness on his phone turned almost all the way down as he checked his texts again.

The abrupt tone of her response was odd; she was usually firing off emojis and love-bombs right and left. *Home okay. Thanks.*

Somewhere in the near distance, someone was lighting off fireworks. M80s, from the sound of it. *Fucking idiots*, he thought. God, he needed sleep. He'd been so tired of late, sleeping more and dozing off more easily than usual, though he'd often wake up feeling like he'd just worked out, adrenaline pounding through his skin. Something ebbed and flowed in his bones.

He got up, walked into the hallway, and listened. The popping of firecrackers was gone, mercifully, so he walked downstairs and drank two big glasses of water, one after the other. He was still thirsty, but it was a bit better. Mark leaned back against the counter. He was wide awake. Where the fuck was Cory? Why hadn't she woke him up before leaving? Maybe it wasn't a big deal, but it felt off.

A thump, then a metallic rattle from the upstairs hallway, followed by a muffled voice murmuring to itself, the words inaudible.

"Cory?" he called. He was getting upset, even a little angry, but the sudden disruption to everything—Cory's attitude, the fireworks outside, and now this—left something in him feeling shaken. "Cory? Babe? What are you doing up there?"

Mark reached behind him and fumbled for the utility drawer, sliding it open and pulling out the first thing that his fingers determined could be a weapon. A hammer, from when he'd been trying to hang some pictures a few weeks back. Fine. He turned and slid the drawer shut, noticing as he did that the Polaroids were gone.

Fucking hell.

That's why she's being cold, he thought. She found the damn pictures, but the pictures were clearly old, nothing recent. *Way to go, you fucking jerk-off.* Another shuffling sound from upstairs.

He stepped into the doorway, peering around the corner and up the staircase.

The hatch to the attic hung open. The rattle he'd heard was the ladder unfolding and flapping to the ground.

What the hell?

"Cory?" He craned his neck low to try to see into the dark hole of the attic, and by the time he was standing under the open hatch, his nerves had subsided. The thing wasn't in great shape. No wonder it had fallen open. He'd noticed the worn latch the last time he went up there. Probably some animal had gotten inside, knocked the damn hatch loose. "Hey. Up there. Get your scavenging ass back through the roof and outside. Last warning."

Nothing. Mark held the side of the ladder, hammer raised and ready as he took the first few steps and paused.

"Okay, fair warning. I'm gonna be eating a squirrel omelet tomorrow." He took the rest of the stairs with sudden confidence, pulling the lightbulb chain and bathing the space in a dull yellow.

There was nothing there but the usual boxes, clothes, everything he'd been sorting through. The hole Brute had repeatedly patched on the north side of the roof

CHAPTER 35

was holding, too, so nothing had gotten inside. That ruled out squirrels or raccoons.

So what, then?

After a moment, he became aware of a high-pitched hissing sound near the wardrobe.

"Oh, for Christ's sake," he muttered. An old boom box had fallen from where it had previously sat on top of the old wardrobe, and the radio had come on as a result. *That was the voice I heard. It wasn't someone in the house.* The band sat in the middle of static and some late-night talk program, two tinny voices chattering back and forth at each other. He clicked it off. After waiting a few seconds to ensure that he hadn't, in fact, missed a rogue rodent anywhere, he made his way down the rickety folding staircase again, replacing it and closing the hatch.

Back in bed, he looked at his phone. No response from Cory. He texted again.

Babe, you okay?

When there was no response after several minutes, Mark plugged his phone in to charge and left a podcast playing softly in the background to try to fall asleep to the soft sound of voices, though try as he might, it seemed to serve the opposite effect: he was wide awake and thinking. Not about Cory, but about his final conversation with Brute.

You gotta invite vampires into your house, you know?

Mark woke up in the shower.

He'd been reading some threads about Knox County history on Reddit, soldiers coming home from the war in '44 and '45 and the housing boom that followed it. Then he'd turned his phone off and lay there in the dark, until he heard the door open slowly, and the girl had come in.

He heard her enter the bedroom, though her footsteps weren't the normal rhythm one would expect, but a shuffling, dragging sound. In the thin slivers of moonlight he had to work with, Mark could see that she was misshapen, her face familiar but the features all wrong, as though the eyes didn't match the bone structure of the cheeks, the mouth uneven as if it had been molded in flesh only moments before. Without thinking, he slid over, readjusting the covers, watching as the thing pretending to be a young woman crawled into bed next to him. Her fingers were cold and sticky as she pressed herself against him. He wouldn't look, didn't want to look, but couldn't help himself, rolling over to face what was surely the product of a dream, bracing himself to wake up.

He recognized her, vaguely, as her features found something like order, rippling into place like leaves floating on water. Mark swallowed hard as she reached for him, her cold fingers slipping up his thigh toward his erection.

"Take me," she said. "Show me."

"Are you a virgin?" he'd said.

She answered by pulling him on top of her, inside her, and she moaned deeply. Lily Ensinger writhed underneath him, clutching at him, and then there was nothing.

Now, the bathroom smelled like blood, and Mark closed his eyes as the hot water pounded his skin. He pictured Cory, spreading her legs for him (and Georgia,

CHAPTER 35

that teenage pussy is all yours if you want it, brother, all yours) as he masturbated, the water fading from crimson to pink, cleaning the evidence of whatever had occurred down the drain in whispers of steam. As he turned off the water, he heard it.

The attic hatch had dropped open again.

Mark got out, wrapped a towel around his waist, and stepped into the hallway. He walked up the wooden slat-stairs, losing his towel on the way, naked, water still dripping from his body, his cock aching in spite of the fact that he'd just gotten off. Mark stood in front of the open wardrobe for a few moments, just looking at the shape of the thing: the costume, hung inside on a hook as one would hang up a coat, features pushing through the face from something underneath the layers of paper, a rotten yellow-brown color that had begun to seep through. The fingers on the single hand twitching a little the way a dog might in the throes of sleep, and the rest of the thing—the translucent, jelly-like torso and legs through which Mark could see blood vessels, masses of tissue that didn't look like anything human, a creature growing out of that paper-and-glue shell. Every now and again, a moist, lumpy tongue would poke through the slitted mouth of the mask as though wetting its lips. The outline of eyes that had begun to push through from behind into the papier-mâché face displayed closed lids.

This is where it lived for so long, Mark thought, though the thought didn't feel like his own.

"What are you?" he said quietly. He heard his voice, but he couldn't tell where it was coming from. It sounded, for just a moment, as though it had come from the thing in the wardrobe.

Playing tricks on you.
Why?
He could hear the voice as clearly as if it was someone standing next to him, but in terms of proximity, it had to have come from the kitchen. *Invited.*
Lily.
God, why did it show him Lily?

36

"Order!" the cook shouted, setting two plates adorned with greasy steakburgers and fries on the stainless-steel server's window. The server, a bored-looking redhead with a tattoo of Michael Rooker as Henry Lee Lucas on her forearm, brought the plates to Cory and Georgia's booth with a tired smile.

"Fuck yeah, cool tattoo," Georgia said. "Henry is the shit, though they took some liberties." The waitress smiled and muttered thanks as she pulled a bottle of ketchup from her apron pocket and left it with the food. "Thanks, Mom. We haven't done Steak N'Shake in a while."

"Too long," Cory agreed, shaking the ketchup bottle and pouring out a generous pool near the mound of thin, crispy fries. "Thanks for doing girls' night. I needed it."

"Derenberger still trying to get you to come over and check out his record collection?"

"Funny. No, I just..." Cory trailed off. *You what? Thought you found evidence that your boyfriend killed your ex and then saw a skeleton monster in the woods?* "I just thought it'd be nice."

"Yep." Georgia took a bite of her burger, frowned, then set it down to rearrange the pickles, taking another bite and nodding with satisfaction. "How are things with Mark?"

"Um, good," Cory said, though she didn't look up. *Things are good. Were good. Are good. Fuck.* "They're good."

The last text she'd gotten from him was just asking if she was okay, and she'd responded yes with a heart. Even that response made her feel guilty. What had she really found? Something she thought was Adrian's, but maybe not, especially since Mark had been going through decades' worth of oddities and garage sale fodder in that old place. Something she thought she'd seen outside, but they'd had wine, she'd been tired, and it had been dark.

"Really?" Georgia sounded hopeful. "That's cool. I mean, I figured they were, and dinner was tasty. He seems like a good guy."

Cory nodded. "You think so?"

"Yeah, totally." Georgia sipped her Coke and shrugged. "I mean, he seems like a good-natured dude, and he's not weirded out by any of that family stuff."

"I mean, it's not his fault. He couldn't help what happened with his uncle."

"No, that's what I mean. He doesn't mind talking about it. It's not some dramatic shit with him, you know? That whole thing is weird, he could've just been like, 'shut up and eat.'"

Cory laughed. "I've never heard him say anything like 'shut up and eat' to anyone."

"See? My point exactly." The server drifted past the booth, slowed, and kept going when she saw that the two were deep in conversation. "If he was still tight with his uncle or something, I could see that being pretty fucked up, but it sounds like they don't have any contact."

"Yeah." Cory sipped her drink. Her daughter was right, she had to admit. "That thing with that costume was weird, though."

"Sorry about that," Georgia said, shaking her head and rearranging the pickles on her burger again. "I saw it, and I … don't know."

Cory patted her arm, reaching for the salt and pepper. "It's okay."

"So, he lived there?"

"Who?"

"Tony Devold. Lived in that house?"

"He did, yeah, I mean, he grew up there, and then he lived there again as an adult, before Mark did, obviously."

"He lived there when he did it, though. The murders."

"Yeah, he did, I think. Mark and I haven't really talked a lot about that, but I think he was living there at the time."

"It doesn't freak you out to be there?" Georgia grinned. "Hooking up and whatnot?"

"Geo, come on," Cory chuckled. "No, it doesn't freak me out. It's just a house."

"A murderer's house," Geo winked.

Cory rolled her eyes and smiled at her daughter. "If he'd done it *there*, maybe that would be a different story."

Georgia chewed thoughtfully for a few seconds, then paused. "How do we know he *didn't* do anything there?"

The bones, pushing from the earth, mottled skull and pasty limbs poking through the mud—"Georgia, seriously, I've watched all that stuff on Netflix, too, but this is—"

"Hear me out. Some of the stuff that Devold said didn't make a lot of sense when they asked him about where he'd been on certain nights, things like that. Did you know that they suspected him of three other disappearances? And he couldn't account for where he'd been those nights? Said he was at home, but they couldn't prove it."

The feeling of ice water down the back of her neck returned, the sensation of dread that slipped over Cory's skin when she'd seen the belt buckle. "Where'd you hear that?"

"Reddit. There was a Knox County deputy posting on one of the true crime subs there for a while. I verified his username. It wasn't a throwaway. He was using his actual account. He said they just didn't have enough for a search warrant, or they'd have tossed that house." Georgia shrugged again, dunking a cluster of fries in Cory's ketchup. "Anyway. Mark is cool. Didn't mean to derail there. He makes you happy."

Cory sat back against the red vinyl booth, pursing her lips in a smile and nodding. "He does." *He does.* She realized she was staring at her lap when she noticed Georgia leaning in to catch her eye.

"Mom." Georgia set her burger on the plate, folded her hands, and sighed as though preparing to give a speech. "You shouldn't be afraid to commit. Everyone isn't Dad."

The urge to cry, hearing Georgia refer to Adrian as her dad—something she rarely did—hit her fast and hard, and Cory had to swallow her breath to keep the tears from coming. *Goddamn you,* she thought, *goddamn you and your smartass, bullshit scare tactics and your drugs and your violent, childish fucking garbage. Your daughter is better than you could have ever dreamed of being.* She felt the smile overtake her face, and she saw Georgia's puzzled smile in response. *We beat you. You will not beat me. I will be happy, you sorry prick.*

"I know, honey." Cory reached across the table and laced her fingers with Georgia's. "I know. I'm not. I'm really not." The server slid past again, pinning the check to the table with the ketchup bottle before moving on. "I like him a lot. I always have. And I'm really glad you like him. I really am, honey."

"I do." Georgia grabbed the check and opened her purse. "This is on me, by the way. Everyone went shit-crazy for that t-shirt I made."

"Are you sure?" Cory grinned, wiping her eyes as the lingering tears decided to roll. Georgia had printed a shirt a month or so prior that had the state of Illinois outline with an overlay of John Wayne Gacy as Pogo, adorned with a collegiate-looking logo that said *Gacy: 33, Illinois: 0.* "That was pretty sick, even for you, kid."

"Right?" Georgia grinned and raised her eyebrows. "Never underestimate the sick shit people find interesting." She slid a twenty from a pink and silver Tokidoki wallet, pinning it under her empty plate. "Let's go cruise Lake Storey Road and take some pictures. I have an idea for another shirt."

37

Mark stared at Marigold's front doors, at the paramedics rolling a gurney from inside to the ambulance parked under the circular drop-off lane right in front. A small body lay covered with a white sheet, and no one moved with any sense of urgency. Shrinking as we aged was the universe's final insult, he thought, a crude way of suggesting how insignificant we were.

He drew a deep breath in through his nostrils, out through his mouth. In ... and out. A few deep breaths, and he felt his heart slow down a little, a tingling sensation shivering through his body with each intake. The way Tony had once described cocaine was the way Mark felt now, without a single drug in his system, unless you counted the drinks last night, and those were a good twelve hours ago. Besides, those would have the opposite effect, a decrease in sensory awareness. And he felt overwhelmingly alive.

Mark watched as the medics loaded the body into the back of the ambulance. He chuckled, at first, but then it was a full-on belly laugh, so loud inside his car with the windows up, that one of the staff members standing outside and tearfully watching glanced up, aware that someone's reaction to this situation was wholly inappropriate. Mark laughed, because why not? There was nothing inside that hurt. Not the sight of a lost life, not the knowledge that someone out there would soon receive the call everyone dreads, followed by the planning, the meeting, the family members in from out of town. Nothing inside him felt painful; it was as though the core of his being was a clear pool into which a smooth, crystalline stone was being continually tossed, causing a ripple effect of pure, elegant bliss that radiated throughout his body and mind.

Something is wrong with me.

He took a deep breath, collected the Culver's bag with their two cherry Cokes, and headed inside, not meeting the eyes of those who stood gathered at the ambulance as it prepared for departure. Marigold's entryway smelled like a combination of antiseptic and lavender, and an obese Hispanic woman vacuumed the commons area as though everything was business as usual, which it was, of course, for her. He passed a small group of elderly men and women gathered around a table in the cafeteria, cups of steaming coffee before them as they chatted quietly. A couple of them acknowledged him with polite smiles as he passed. He gave a cursory knock on his mother's door before opening it.

"Alright, chicken sandwiches with extra pickles, waffle fries, and Cherry Cokes," he smiled, kissing her on top of her head and tasting cheap hairspray. "Hi, Mom."

"Hi, honey," she said, but the words came out like two indistinct moans: *huh-huhuh.* She stared blankly at the book in her lap, a photo album that Mark didn't recognize, though he knew some of the photos. There were childhood pictures of him and Ann, a family reunion downstate when he was in fifth grade (he'd spent it bored out of his mind and playing an electronic football game), pictures of his mother and Tony with Brute when they were younger. Some random shots of things that were of no meaning to Mark: a playground, a flower arrangement, a shot clearly taken from the window of a moving car.

"Something happened," he said, pointing toward the hallway. "They ... took someone out, Mom. Was it someone you knew? Are you okay?"

"Mmhmm," she said, still blank.

Circus peanuts. The Bullseyes seemed to be long gone.

He patted her hand and tried to put the bottle of Cherry Coke in her hand; she glanced up at him suddenly as if she'd just realized he was there. "Mark, honey. Thank you. I'm thirsty." She beamed as she lifted the bottle and took a long drink.

"Sure thing, I brought lunch, like I promised." He began arranging their sandwiches and fries on paper plates. "Everything been okay? I know it's only been a couple of days. Where'd you find the photo album?"

"I had this one here," she said. "Haven't looked at it in a while. Nice to look at pictures. I miss Annie."

"So do I, Mom. She'll be back before Christmas. Her project only runs until early December." He set Audrey's lunch on a TV tray in front of the recliner where she was nestled and sat down next to her, taking a big bite of his sandwich.

"I just wish I knew what happened," she said, her voice hoarse and mournful. "I just hope she didn't suffer."

"Mom, Annie's fine," he said. Reality jogged back and forth when he was at Marigold.

Why should here be any different?

Shut up.

"She's in South America working with her school, remember?" He patted her hand again. "Annie is okay, Mom. We texted the other day."

"Mmhmm," she replied, thin, shaky fingers turning the pages as she nibbled at the burned edge of a waffle fry. "This one. You were five. You hated that shirt."

Mark leaned in, saw the picture, and chuckled. "I remember that shirt, and I also remember hating it. It had a scratchy tag in the back."

"I always had to cut them out for you," Audrey replied with a smile. "And this one. That was hideous."

"Ha!" He laughed at the shot of him standing outside Sandburg Mall, wearing a long black robe reminiscent of the Grim Reaper and a monstrous latex gargoyle mask, its mouth a yawning chasm of jagged teeth and a serpentine tongue. "I loved that costume."

"Remember that girl at the record store? You went in there with that on, and she said, 'Happy Halloween, you look disgusting.'"

"Damn right. Mission accomplished."

Audrey picked up her chicken sandwich and took a bite. "We always loved Halloween."

"We did. We do," he agreed. "Remember you used to take a whole group of us out, the kids whose parents were working or didn't want to go? That must have been something to see without knowing what was going on, you shepherding all these costumed kids down the street." He sipped his Coke and glanced at the door as two staff assistants rushed down the hallway. He tapped a photo as she turned the page again. "There! That was what, fifth grade?"

"Probably," she nodded. "Annie had long hair, so, probably, fifth for you and first for her?"

"That sounds right." It was a Polaroid, the white border corralling the sight of seven or eight kids in costume, gathered in front of a big tree that marked the intersection leading to the highway, not a half mile from Brute's house where the Grinnell Park playground gave way to a subdivision of houses where they'd always had good luck trick-or-treating.

Audrey narrated as Mark studied the costumes and partial faces. "There was Isaac Brooks, Bailey Pardue, I think Jerry Roach, isn't that...?" Mark nodded or corrected as necessary while she talked her way through a shot of their costumed collective.

Mark was dressed like one of Jabba's pig guards from *Return of the Jedi*, and there was Ann, dressed as Strawberry Shortcake, with her hair in braids and exaggerated circles of rouge on her cheeks. Behind them, a shoddy but well-intentioned vampire costume, a fairy princess, a GI Joe character whose name he couldn't remember, another vote for *Star Wars* as Luke Skywalker stood on tiptoes behind a scattershot Indiana Jones who'd been forced to go with a baseball cap, though the toy bullwhip gave him some semblance of credibility.

Mark felt the taste go out of his mouth. There, in the very back, stood the unusual, almost inappropriate bulk of the costume.

"And who was that?" his mother said, tapping the thing with her finger. "That was the Barrow boy, wasn't it?"

"Charlie," Mark said, recognizing the gangly arm sticking out of the right side of the cast, and his voice came out thin, almost a whisper. "That's Charlie Barrow, Mom, yeah."

"That's right," she exclaimed, delighted. "I wonder what ever became of him?"

"I don't know," Mark murmured, unable to take his eyes off the inhuman bulk and shoddy composition of the thing. Charlie fucking Barrow under there. "Eat your lunch, Mom. We can look at the rest later."

After they'd eaten, Audrey began to drift in and out of sleep, so Mark put the photo album away and turned on the TV. Mark draped a blanket over his mother's small frame and clicked off the light, tidying the small kitchenette and writing her a note (*Back in a day or so, fresh bag of those oatmeal-raisin cookies in the right cabinet, love you, M.*) before turning the TV to a low volume and slipping out. It was mid-afternoon, but the sun was already about to call it a day, covered over with low, gray clouds. They were predicting a harsh winter, Mark thought fleetingly, which felt depressing. The pleasing sensations he'd felt throughout his body since last night had been replaced with a dull ache not unlike that of a hangover. He drove home, poured some Jameson into a cup of dark coffee, and sat at the table in silence.

How had Charlie worn the costume? Had it been *his*, after all, and somehow ended up at Brute's house when they were kids? The image of that stark, blank face and slumping shoulders was now lodged in Mark's brain like a popcorn kernel. He didn't remember Charlie wearing it until he saw that picture, of that he was certain, but now he couldn't get it out of his head.

Did Charlie remember it?

Mark got up from the kitchen table and opened the basement door. He stood in the doorway, listening.

The house made sounds. It always had. Grandma Lynn and Brute always said it was the house settling, because, of course, that's what they said. Wasn't that the excuse for any strange noise in anyone's house? The house was settling, relaxing into its age—creaks and whines in its bones. A moan of pressure on a floorboard, a temperature contraction in the wood frame of a door, a random thump in the attic like something falling over in spite of being mostly organized, a dull clank like something brushing against the water heater. The house had always made sounds.

He took the steps carefully, pausing to listen each time and measure his weight on the thick wooden boards leading to the basement, sawdust coating them like dirt engrained into pores. By the time he'd reached the bottom, he felt truly uncomfortable, as though the kitchen was a mile away, unreachable should he need to make his way back upstairs quickly. But why would he?

Mark sighed and shook off his nerves. Brute had a full woodworking shop in the basement, and a long table with a mounted circular saw sat in the center of the main room, sawdust easily an inch high at the edges and coating the floor all around it. An old cardboard box with a Quinn's Grocery logo on the side—a grinning

CHAPTER 37

fox wearing a chef's hat—sat on the floor, filled with wood scraps.

On top of the pile lay the torn Aerosmith shirt Mark had found in the brush out back.

Reluctantly, he picked it up, lifted it to his face, and smelled it. Nothing of note; the vague hint of a sweet perfume had faded, and it had none of the outdoor smell that had initially clung to it.

It smelled like oil. And jasmine.

Mark took out his cell phone and dialed Auster's number, who caught it on the first ring.

"Bill Auster."

"Bill, this is Mark Devold."

A pause. "Mark, I was actually going to call you today. Got something on that girl, Regina Marling. She, um, she did go missing, back around '91."

"Nothing more specific?"

"Unfortunately, no. She was a wild child, bad relationship with her mom. It didn't get reported as a missing persons case at the time, not properly, but it seems like she kinda went off map around then. She would have been a junior. She was at GHS with us, apparently."

"I know."

"Sorry I don't have more for you, but I thought you'd at least want some follow-up."

A deep, throbbing ache hit the inside of Mark's forehead, and he fought the urge to vomit. "I—appreciate it. Listen, did... did Dara Ensinger have cigarette burns ... in her mouth? Was she tortured?" *Better than having a stranger put a cigarette out on your tongue...*

"Jesus fucking Christ, Mark, this isn't healthy. I think you need to talk to someone, man. For real. Like, yesterday." A sigh. "On her tongue, yeah. A whole bunch of them. Listen, you okay, honestly? Do you need anything? Anyone?"

"No, I'm okay." Mark crouched at the edge of the worktable, clutching the t-shirt in his hand. Somewhere in the walls around him, the house settled. Stretched into waking.

"Seriously, I know a couple of people who can help if you need to talk to someone. No shame in it, after what you've—"

"I'm good, Bill, but thank you, really. Thank you." Mark hung up and slipped the phone into his pocket. Bill's last words hadn't really connected as Mark squinted in the dimming afternoon light that reached the basement through pocket windows.

From the storage room on the other side of the worktable, Mark saw something squinting back.

They had to be eyes, he thought, glittery and reflecting strangely in the dim light. Something low to the ground, walking on four legs like a small dog or cat, but the true shape of the thing eluded him, just shrouded enough in shadow to remain hidden.

Still crouching, Mark moved carefully toward the stairs. The thing didn't move, staring back through its glittery eyes before flopping into the maze of boxes and decades of ephemera, disappearing from view, though not before Mark saw that it bore a passing resemblance to a young woman. At least, the torso and upper body did, as the legs were nothing more than a ropy, amphibious tail and what looked like part of a third arm. An incomplete person, flopping around the basement, dragging itself around on hands.

(Incomplete, just like the costume is. No legs. It doesn't know how to make something whole.)

Fucking shut up, man. Enough with the hallucinating.

(The third Polaroid. The eyes, staring from around the misshapen male body in the foreground...)

Mark stood and ran up the stairs, his heart pounding in his chest. He reached the kitchen, rolling his shoulder into the basement door to slam it shut. As it faded back into the dark, Mark caught a fleeting glimpse of Lily Ensinger standing at the bottom of the stairs, the gaping wound in her throat yawning wide, beady eyes staring up at him, a faint smile on her bloody face as she began carefully taking the steps one-by-one, toward him. Her flesh looked vaguely liquid, amorphous as she struggled to steady herself.

"The house is settling," she giggled, but it came out like a series of wet-sounding belches from a throat no longer capable of human speech.

"Fuck off," Mark shouted, dragging the kitchen table across the room to block the basement door, lying one of the dining chairs flat on top of the table and wedging it under the doorknob. He was having a heart attack, a panic attack, an asthma attack, or all three. He groaned for air as he threw open the back door and stepped outside.

He bent forward, hands on his thighs, sucking in deep breaths of air that was pregnant with coming rain. Sitting down on the small concrete patio, Mark leaned back against the screen door and felt his lungs, his chest, go back to normal. He stared at the thick brambles at the edge of the yard, where he'd found the shirt, where he'd seen—hallucinated, he corrected himself— the thing that had tried to look like Regina Marling.

The field beyond, where the expanse of cornstalks gave way, after a half mile or so, to the highway. The drive-in was almost visible from where he sat.

On the scarecrow's frame hung the costume.

What it was, he had no idea. But he knew that, when he put that costume on, it became a part of him. He felt it under his skin, in his bones, the way it felt when a fly crawled over your hand, but everywhere, all at once, followed by the *lift*, as he thought of it, this feeling of weightless joy, the untethering of all pain and worry and concern.

But after it collected all that pain, it spat some back out, and then it was the hangover, as he'd come to think of it. The blank spots. The feeling as if something terribly wrong had happened, just beyond the grasp of his memory and cognition. Pieces of other people.

Of the people who had worn it, he considered.

God, his fucking head *hurt*.

First Dara, then Lily—

Mark choked and vomited into the muddy ground near the base of the scarecrow's cross.

He caught his breath and found his feet, using the costume to help pull himself up. He lifted the thing from the cross where it hung and slipped the thing over his head and shoulders, feeling it settle against his body. He sucked in air, his lungs suddenly infinite, sobs stifling in his throat. A heroin numbness with amphetamine clarity.

Where the fuck was Cory?

"*Dude!*"

A voice, outside the house, somewhere around the side.

CHAPTER 37

"Dude, shut the fuck up!" The voice was a deep, throaty whisper that Mark didn't recognize. "Someone's going to hear us. Stop. *Stop.*" A pause, and a rustle of bushes. "Just wait. This is the house. Just wait." A rhythmic clatter of metal.

A spray paint can.

Mark heard the aerosol hiss against muffled giggles and low voices, and he was moving across the yard, then, slowly, deliberately, his breath hot inside the costume. There were two kids, one slight and wiry, the other with broader shoulders but still pretty scrawny. The painter had a backward ball cap on his head that sported the graphic of a middle finger. The smaller of the two noticed Mark first, and he slapped the artist on his shoulder to get his attention.

"Um, fuck, dude, sorry about this, really sorry about this," the kid muttered as Mark stood, staring, motionless. "Dude, are you—you okay?" The kid with the paint can paused, brow furrowing as he sized up the situation.

"*You fucking bitch.*" Mark's voice was a muffled abstraction beneath the mask.

Paint Kid glanced at his buddy, who was visibly shaken. "You the—you the guy who lives here?"

"*I should have never married you, Cory, you lazy cunt,*" Mark growled.

"My name isn't Cory, bro." Paint Kid started to back up toward the front of the house, dropping the can in the beat-up duffel bag near his feet. On the side of the house behind him, he'd begun his train of thought in a bright orange: KILL JUNKMAN KILL!

Mark began walking slowly toward them. "*I should have killed you both a long time ago.*"

"We're outta here, dude, fuck this," the first kid said, turning to run toward Day Street as his friend skipped backward, sizing Mark up before reaching for the duffel bag full of paint cans. Mark was on him before the kid could even take a step; the kid yelped and kicked, struggling as Mark drug him by his hair toward the grove.

"What the fuck are you talking about, dude, *you crazy motherfucker*, you—" the kid's words were choked off as he was flipped onto his stomach so hard that it took the wind out of him, the man in the bizarre costume pressing a foot in his back.

"*Taste*," the man said, and the kid sucked for air, gasping, dropping his head forward to get a breath, and then he could smell it. Blood. The sharp, coppery stench of blood, right at his nostrils, as though his face was being pressed into a sea of blood. He flailed for leverage and tried to push himself up, but the soft, sticky mud gave him nothing in return, causing him to lose his balance and fumble face-first into the mud yet again before finding his feet, and then he was running, running and screaming across the yard toward his friend who was already gone.

Mark watched, slumping forward into the weight of the thing, as the boy ran down the street and away from the house.

38

Mona sagged a little in her chair, hands in her lap. She wore her favorite loose-fitting silk top with koi fish all over it and she'd done her makeup, but now she looked like someone who gotten ready for a party only to find out she had the date wrong. "Thanks for staying after. I just—I miss him."

Cory sat back in her chair and crossed her legs, trying to think of the right way to respond. "I can appreciate that, Mona. I can. You know I've been there." She paused, then leaned forward with her elbows on her knees. "I think what you miss is the idea of him, the idea of what you thought you would have with him." Mona blinked a few times, then looked up. "Yeah?"

"Probably." The older woman took a deep breath, adjusted her top, and nodded. "Probably so, I just—I want to feel good about that. The idea of that." She rubbed her hands together and reached up to wipe away angry tears. "I think about when things were—you know, when he was good, the times he was good."

"I've told you about my ex-husband, yes?" Cory got up and craned her neck to see if the hallway beyond the classroom was empty; it was the only night where there wasn't some sort of extra-curricular on campus, so it was the only real choice for the Angel Brigade to meet, but she knew the shame that often accompanied abuse, so she wanted to ensure that the progress she seemed to be making with Mona remained private, a private victory for both of them. "Piece of shit meth-head who tried to kill me? More than once?"

"Yeah," Mona said. She re-situated herself in the folding chair, tugged at her shirt, flattening it out, pulling herself together in whatever little ways she could. "Wasn't he out of state or in jail or something?"

"*Was* is the operative word there," Cory said. She refilled her travel mug from the "Sippin' Box," a twenty-cup box of light roast courtesy of the local coffee roaster downtown; the rest of the group had done good work before they'd adjourned, and there wasn't much left. She poured the last of it into a paper cup for Mona and handed it to her as Cory sat back down. "He's back. Or was." It was her turn to stare at her lap.

Nobody Rides for Free.

"He called me," she went on. "About a week ago. And he threatened me, and he trotted out all the old tricks to try and get me to see him, but ... I put him off, and now, he seems to be gone again."

"What happened to him?" Mona said softly. She sipped her coffee and squinted thoughtfully at Cory. "I mean, why would he just stop?"

"I don't know," Cory shrugged. "I really don't, but I made the decision—just the other night, actually—that

CHAPTER 38

I was done letting fear of him control me. If I let myself fill up with fear, I won't have room for strength."

Mona managed a half-smile. "That sounds like something that should be embroidered on something."

"For just $29.99, I can make that happen for you. Local pickup only." Cory smiled, and the warmth inside her made her feel like she was going to burst into tears herself. Not out of sadness, or fear, or uncertainty, but the opposite. Joy. Certainty.

She loved Mark. She was in love with Mark, whom she knew—she *knew*—wouldn't hurt someone. Couldn't possibly. There was a reason for what she saw, the buckle, and for the other things—there had to be an explanation. There was a reason for those things, and she would get it right this time; they would figure it out together.

Together.

"It's like this, Mona," she said, leaning in as though delivering a grand secret. "Life doesn't have to be a goddamn horror movie. Not forever. It can be a chick flick." She held out her mug to toast, and Mona finally smiled. *God help this woman,* Cory thought. Her husband was a fucking monster. *Give her the strength.*

Mona sat forward, toasted, and tapped her fingers against her cup. "Maybe, I don't know. Maybe sometimes it's a horror comedy?"

"Maybe," Cory grinned.

After she watched Mona drive out of the student lot and take off down Fremont Street, she texted Mark.

I'm so sorry.

She couldn't think of what else to say. What else should she say?

I'm okay. I ... got spooked, I guess. Are we okay?

Cory sighed and deleted the text. Just ... goddamn it. Just say it.

Hey, I'm sorry. I freaked out, and that's stupid, but I'm okay. I love you. I LOVE you, and I want to do this. Please, can we do this?

She hit send. Then she started the car and pulled out of the lot behind a carload of teenagers blasting hip-hop, who barely stopped at the Losey Street red light before screeching around the corner, out of sight.

Cory smiled to herself, raised her mug, and toasted herself in the rearview mirror.

39

Mark pulled the car over on the shoulder of the highway in front of the old drive-in, staring at the Barrow house in the near distance, just across the highway and behind the old Farm King Supply Outlet. He sat back in the seat. His head was pounding; Christ almighty, he hurt. He could feel his heartbeat in his throat, his pulse in his skull. His body felt like it was at war with him every day now, a constant ebb and flow, flying high and feeling great or sick to his stomach with that hangover misery baked into him.

Where the fuck was Cory? What the hell was wrong with her? Why had she just ghosted him?

Fucking bitch.

No, she's ... no. She's not a fucking bitch. Don't think that. Why would you think that?

Stop.

Mark took out his phone and dialed. The voice that answered was low and serious.

"This is Charlie."

"Charlie, it's..." he hesitated. "Mark Devold. How are you?" His voice came out more upbeat than he'd intended, which happened when he was nervous.

"Okay," Charlie conceded, and Mark could hear the shrug in his voice. "What's up, Mark?"

"Are you busy ... right now? You want to have that beer?" From where he sat in his car, he saw the lights go on in the main part of Charlie's house.

"Um, sure, yeah," Charlie replied. "You want me to—"

"I'm—just getting off work, actually, I could stop by?"

"Yeah, okay. I just got Old Style, is that cool?"

"Totally cool. Yeah, man, that's fine. Just thought we could catch up, shoot the shit, you know?"

There was a long pause on the other end of the phone, and Mark could hear what sounded like a cat mewling in the background, though the longer it went on, the less it sounded like a cat. "Yeah, that sounds good, Mark. Come on over."

Mark hung up and noticed that he had a text message, at last, from Cory.

[Cory: Hey, I'm sorry. I freaked out, and that's stupid, but I'm okay. I love you. I LOVE you, and I want to do this. Please, can we do this?]

[Mark: I love you, too. Talk to me. What the hell is going on?]

He realized that he was gripping his phone tightly, too tightly, as he sent the message. He slipped his phone into his pocket and watched Charlie's house for a few minutes. More lights came on, and Mark saw the back screen door finally open, Charlie's thin frame

CHAPTER 39

appearing through the doorway, the orange dot of a lit cigarette winking into life. Charlie stood, smoking a cigarette, staring into the distance. Mark watched him until Charlie went back inside, and then he started the car, heading toward the house.

Mark started up the driveway toward what had been the front door of the Barrows' ranch-style house, only to realize that there was no front door. A massive gray tarpaulin, the kind you'd see blocking a construction site, licked the October breeze like a swollen tongue and obscured what had been the front door and part of the living room window.

Surely that wasn't from the fire, Mark thought. Surely the house had been repaired after the fire. But the tarp wore the scuffs and pocked holes that came with age and weather, the front yard a patchwork of exposed turf, mulch, and dead grass. Parts of the roof sported holes as well, and evidence of the fire that had consumed much of the farmhouse three decades before was still there in the form of blackened beams, like an unfinished sculpture made of toothpicks. *No way. No fucking way he just ... lives here, still.*

He walked carefully up the driveway, noting the absence of any outside lights, and he was almost to the garage before he saw where the tarp (which had extended around the east side of the house) gave way to a makeshift porch, not much more than a concrete patio slab with a metal door and some pieces of roofer's tin blocking it from the elements. Mark stepped under the metal awning and knocked. After a few seconds, the door clicked open, and Charlie stood there, wearing a pair of muddy jeans and an unbuttoned flannel shirt. There were visible scars on his pale, scrawny chest, like thin pencil lines aged into his flesh. His ragged scruff of beard was as red as the thinning hair on his head, and he grinned.

"Not drinking alone for a change," he said, stepping aside so Mark could enter the house and handing him a cold beer. "Here you go. I got one in the other room."

"Thanks, Charlie," Mark replied, taking the bottle and walking inside. The smell of musky incense hung in the air. The kind of smell you only introduced to a space when you wanted to get rid of other smells.

"Welcome to paradise," Charlie grinned again, and Mark could see in his eyes that his old friend was riding a good drunk already. "What brings you out here, man? Long-lost desire to talk about shit we did in high school? Everything okay?" Charlie watched as Mark sat down on the couch, a sagging, red-plaid monstrosity with lumpy, worn-out cushions. What had once been the living room was now tarped off, destroyed by fire all those years ago, and this dining area was now pulling multiple duties. A beat-to-shit table sat behind a cheap TV cart, and there was a two-burner hot plate sitting on the edge of it with pans, dishes, and piles of silverware scattered across the rest of the table. Behind him, a plastic standing wardrobe with Charlie's work shirts and button-downs cast a shadow.

"Um, fuck, man, you know," Mark started, unsure of why he was there. "I, uh, my grandpa died."

"Big Brute." Charlie leaned on the TV, holding out his own beer bottle to clink. "Cheers to him."

CHAPTER 39

"Thank you," Mark said, tapping his bottle against Charlie's. "And I've been living at his place, clearing some stuff out, I guess, to sell. My mom and sister want to be rid of it."

Charlie nodded. "But you don't."

"I—don't know," Mark replied. "I guess I haven't thought about it. And I've been seeing Cory Blevin, and I guess things are—" He glanced down at where he'd set his phone on the cushion next to him. The screen was dark; no notifications. "Things are something, I guess. And anyway, I found some old pictures from when we were kids, Halloween and shit. I was just reminiscing."

"And then I stopped by, and you remembered old Charlie out here." Charlie clinked his bottle to Mark's again. "Cheers to that, too."

"Yeah, definitely. Cheers." Mark took a swig and sat back against the couch. The smell was getting to him, that artificial musky stink. It smelled like Spencer's, the creepy gift shop that used to be in the mall with all the joke sex toys and crude t-shirts. Mark was suddenly uncomfortable being there; maybe it was a mistake to have come. "And I saw a, I found a picture, of us, at Halloween in fifth grade, I think."

"Shit, man, you'd have to jog my ol' cells on that one."

"I was the Jabba the Hutt guard, from *Jedi*. And you were ... you wore this—" Mark wasn't sure what to call it, and Charlie didn't seem to be honing in on anything, from the puzzled look he wore. "It was like a cast. Like it went over your body? Your shoulders and face?"

Charlie nodded cautiously, studying Mark's face. Mark finished off his beer, thirsty for another. Charlie reached behind him to a cooler filled with ice and handed one over, never breaking eye contact. "I remember that, I think, now that you say it."

Mark popped the cap, drank deeply, and gave a thumbs-up. "Do you remember at all where you got that? Why you wore it?"

"Yeah, man, it was from your place. I wanna say your uncle found it in the attic. I didn't have a costume, my old man being the fuckin' prick he was, and ol' Brute let me take that for a costume, if I recall. Or maybe I just took it. Either way, yeah, it was from your place."

"You sure?"

Charlie shrugged. "I think? I know it wasn't mine. Shit, man, are you sure you're okay? You're red. You running a fever?"

"No, I don't think so," Mark said, aware of his blood, suddenly, the feeling of it inside him, the heat on his cheeks, his forehead. "No, I just... I've been trying to figure some things out, and I found the pictures, and I was just... curious. I guess."

"Fair enough, man, fair enough." Charlie slumped down into the couch next to Mark. "Hey, we all go through things. Trying to remember stuff gets harder as we get older. Fuck, don't I know it? As much I'd like to forget as anything, but I get ya. Cory Blevin, man." Charlie clinked his bottle to Mark's again. "That's good stuff. Nice work on that."

Mark chuckled. The acknowledgment felt good, though he was almost ashamed to admit it. "Thanks."

"Her ex is a real piece of shit. Tell you that."

"Yeah? You know about Adrian, huh?"

"That guy's a little notorious for being a jagoff, Mark. Not that his name has any currency beyond just a few dudes wanting to fuck him up for burning them on bets, drugs, whatever. Guy's a scam artist, does what he can to get something for nothing, and then doing all he can to pedal away from it."

"Ah, okay. I didn't know, I guess." Mark took a drink. "I haven't... I don't get out that much anymore."

"You were always a bit of a homebody, dude." Charlie laughed. "Or I just look for reasons to get out of here, I guess. Not much to come home to."

"Yeah, I wanted to ask, but I kinda hated to."

"Nah, man, don't worry about it." Charlie folded his scrawny arms against his chest and gave a big shrug. "I don't know why I stayed. I don't know why I haven't fixed the front. Time goes by, it gets a little further off. I got this, and part of the hallway, bathroom, one of the bedrooms. Probably oughta just tear the whole fuckin' thing down, truth be told."

Mark realized that Charlie was staring at him, and if he didn't know better, he felt like Charlie was almost sizing him up, the way it was when he wanted to kiss someone or open whatever door would lead you both into intimacy. "Yeah, I—I don't know, man. You know, whatever works for you."

"Yeah, I guess. I, uh, thought maybe... I don't know." Charlie finished off his beer and lowered his head. "I thought maybe you came over to talk about your uncle."

"No," Mark said. "Not much to talk about there."

"I guess not. Truth is, Mark, I didn't work with him much, and when I did, he just, I don't know. Seemed like any other swinging dick, you know? Hungover a lot, talked a lot of good-natured shit, nothing really to suggest anything, like, unusual."

"Yeah." Mark glanced around the room at the appalling conditions Charlie lived in. The house half-burned, kitchen barely functional, Christ. He regretted this. It was unsettling, and why had he wanted to come here, anyway? Mark was ready to leave when Charlie slapped his knees, stood up, and tossed his empty beer bottle into a plastic trash can near the door.

"So, hey," Charlie grinned. "Almost Halloween and shit. You want to see what I've been working on?"

"Sure," Mark said, thankful for the interruption in the odd tension that had suddenly found its way into the room between them. "I remember you were always into model cars. You had what, like two or three dozen of them?"

"When my pops decided not to break the fucking things, yeah, I did," Charlie said, motioning for Mark to follow him down the hallway. "I don't have any of those anymore, but I've been doing something else pretty cool. Lot of the local kids, they think this place is haunted, right, because of the front?"

"I mean, I get it," Mark chuckled, and Charlie responded with a barking laugh.

"Fuck, same here. So I thought I'd ramp it up this year. Funny that you mentioned that cast thing. Check this out." Charlie stepped into the bedroom and flipped on a desk light that only barely got the job done in terms of illuminating the space. Which, Mark thought, given what he saw on the bed, was probably the point.

It was a body cast, similar in stature to the one at Brute's house, but this was painted a messy brown, black, and green, and the features were childish, the product of what looked like layers of cheap model paint.

"Fuckin' Frankenstein, man!" Charlie slapped Mark's shoulder, harder than Mark expected, and he nearly dropped his beer bottle, his fingers numb, his head suddenly thick, cloudy. A Halloween decoration. Mark's relief came out in laughter; what had he been expecting Charlie to show him? Jesus Christ. Whatever was in his head these days was just too much, whatever it was. Too much, too many thoughts, about him, about Cory, about high school, about Charlie, now, and Charlie's father. And now, seeing Charlie's house this way... "How cool is that gonna be? I'm gonna paint it all up, get it ready, put it out front, and sit there making noises behind that tarp all night. Knock a few of these back, have myself a grand old fuckin' time!"

"That'll be great, man, really great," Mark said, laughing along with him now. "Maybe I'll join you."

"Fuck, yeah, man, that'd be tits. I'll double up on the spirits here if you wanna come by and spook the little rats." Charlie put his arm over Mark's shoulders, and again Mark had the sensation of intimacy, but not quite that, not quite that direct. Something deeper. A confidence. "I've been working on it like crazy. I don't sleep very well, so some nights I'm just doing shit like this." Charlie clapped Mark's shoulder again. "I got two weeks to get this thing painted. Should be enough time. You wanna try it on?"

Mark chuckled, but it came out weakly this time. "No, man, I'm good. I better be going, I just wanted to say hey." He looked for a place to set the beer bottle down, but the room had nothing in it but a dresser missing half its drawers and the twin bed, where the life-sized Frankenstein model lay like a corpse, their shadows mingling in the lamplight to cast obscene shapes across its stark frame. "But thanks, thanks for the beers and the talk. Let's do it at my place next time."

"Can do," Charlie said, taking Mark's bottle from him. "I'm gonna hit the head, but you know where the door is. I'll see you soon, man. Thanks for stopping by. Always good to break up the routine, right?"

"Right indeed," Mark nodded. The smell of sweet, heady musk and the beers, and he felt drunk, though he couldn't say why; Christ, two light beers? Charlie disappeared down the hall behind him, and Mark heard a door shut, the distant sound of piss hitting the bowl, as he made his way back into the dining room where they'd been sitting.

There was a shape huddled in the corner of the room, hidden under a knee-high pile of dirty clothes. He could see movement there, and when Mark took a step toward the clothes, the movement stopped. He paused, waiting for whatever it was to show itself, but he heard Charlie rattling around down the hall and didn't feel like being social anymore, so he showed himself out. Maybe Charlie had a cat, or maybe a fucking rodent lived in this mess. It wasn't a far-fetched thought.

As Mark backed out of the driveway, he thought he could see Charlie's shadow under the makeshift porch, watching him leave.

40

"How was Africa?" Tony rested his thick, hairy arms on the metal table, an open can of Coke Zero in front of him. His hair and beard had grown exponentially since he'd been in prison, as though he'd given up on all personal upkeep in the face of his multiple life sentences.

The change in air quality from her camp outside of Belize to a prison just outside Lake Michigan in less than twenty-four hours had given her a sore throat almost the minute she'd landed at O'Hare; the words came out rough, scratchy. Tony had barely made eye contact with her, staring down at the table blankly, but now he looked at her with a pained expression. "Hey, kiddo," he'd managed when he'd been led into the room. She couldn't help but smile a little, though it quickly went away when she saw him and thought of the articles, what she'd heard about the Ensingers, the way he'd treated her so many years ago, so many nights. She hadn't returned the greeting, presenting her blunt request instead. "I need to know everything about the trophy and what happened to you."

"South America. It was fine." Ann sat back in her chair, hands folded in her lap, still wearing her windbreaker. She'd warned herself, coming inside and signing in as a visitor, that she wouldn't allow herself to get comfortable, to even rest her arms on the table as though she was catching up with an old friend. *It might feel instinctive*, she thought, but it wouldn't be right. It wouldn't exhibit the right attitude, and attitude is all she would have in this place. It was ten in the morning, and light streamed in through the windows set in the concrete wall just inches below the ceiling—probably so the inmates couldn't break the glass, she thought—and nothing felt normal.

"Shit, yeah, sorry. That's good, I'm glad to hear it. I am glad to hear it, Annie." A guard made his way through the room, lazily sauntering between the tables. "I miss you, you know that."

There was a heavy quality to the air in the visitor's room, a claustrophobic sense of being trapped that came through in everything, from the vending machines that were chained to the wall to the guards flanking either exit and even the windows. An unopened can of Diet Sprite sat in front of her, sweating a ring onto the surface in front of her, just as she could feel her own perspiration beading at the back of her neck. Ann looked at her lap and took a deep breath. "Please, just tell me. All of it."

Tony sipped his Coke thoughtfully and relaxed into the chair. "It was animals at first. Squirrels, mostly, and rabbits. It was a test, I think. Went from one or two here and there to maybe a half dozen, some days. The

CHAPTER 40

Johnston kid down the street stopped mowing Dad's lawn altogether one weekend. Told me he was afraid the ground was poisonous or something, what with all the dead rabbits. Must've been ten or twelve of 'em."

"Was it?" Ann noticed one of the guards shift on his feet behind where Tony sat, and it made her catch her breath a little. It was impossible to feel any kind of comfort. "Poisoned?"

"Manner of speaking." He stroked a thick patch of white hair that had crept into his otherwise dark beard, the lines in his face gathering to show his age. "There was ... blood. A lot of it. Like when you and Mark were kids, remember those times you came inside and said that the ground was bleeding out there? It was like that. Like someone spilled a lot of blood or something, but they weren't hurt, that I could see. They were just *bled*. Somehow or other."

"I don't remember that." *Sounds like Ebola*, she thought. There was a village they'd spent the night in on their way to the dig site that had been ravaged by the disease a few years prior; the descriptions from some of the native residents were worse than any horror movie she'd ever seen: people bleeding from their pores, their mouths and eyes. *It was as though something had bitten a hole in their souls*, she'd translated from one of the residents. She pushed the thought away, reached to open her drink, and stopped short.

"I figured it was something they got into," Tony shrugged. "Figured they got themselves poisoned, and that was that. Hell, I don't know what would cause that. Dad put that costume thing you made out on the scarecrow post at some point after Mom died." He shook his head vehemently. "I didn't see it again for a long time, after, you know. After you went to school."

"The trophy. That's what you called it." Ann swallowed hard.

"Yeah, that—yeah. Anyway, I... I left it out there, I didn't think nothing of it. Wasn't long after all them rabbits that I found a deer and a dog. Both of 'em same way."

"Bled?"

He took a drink of his Coke and stifled a belch. "Yeah, but also eaten. I was gonna have a landscaping company out, have 'em tear up the whole back, and I brought that thing inside, I was gonna throw it away. Again." He was staring down at the table now, and Ann could see that he was looking at his reflection. He licked his lips, suddenly anxious, and shook his head. "I put it on. I don't know why, after all that time, but ... just, I put it on and... looked at things."

The way you used to look at me? she wanted to say, but she had to make sure that Mark was safe, and she couldn't get derailed by the mistakes of her own past. She couldn't have Tony shutting down or getting sidetracked.

"How'd you feel when you put it on?" she started to say his name, but she caught herself. This wasn't her uncle, not really, this was just a creature that looked like an old, damaged version of a wryly funny, troubled man who had once bought her a Barbie dream house for Christmas and then, three short years later, deflowered her in the same room. "Was it the same as before? When you wore it before? With me?"

"It was ... bad. Nauseating. Like I was breathing something, a chemical, something ... that smelled like acid, you know, where you can't breathe? And then

CHAPTER 40

good. Like, really fucking good. It was like—I don't know, have you ever smoked crystal, Annie?"

"No."

"It's this fuckin' ecstatic feeling," he explained, "just intense. It was all over my body, this ... crawly feeling that spread over me. Like a woman's fingers, all over me." Tony leaned in, elbows on the table now, his face only inches from her soda can. Ann could see it in his eyes, a desperate look as though he was still afraid of something long dead. "And I couldn't take it off. I tried. It was like it was attached to me."

She sat back, adjusting for the closeness. "Attached how, like it didn't fit right?"

"Like it was biting into me, like, to hold on." He finished his Coke and slid the can forward a few inches away from him. "And then, all of a sudden, it was fine, like I'd... I don't know. Like I'd dreamed it, just standing there. Buddy of mine on tour used to drop acid, and I tried a tab once. Everything was okay, and then like, things just jump out of their lines, the way things are shaped and the way they move and look just changes. Sometimes it's okay, and it doesn't feel wrong, exactly, but sometimes it's like something just walked out of your nightmares and decided to fuckin' hang around in your peripheral vision. That's how this was."

"So what happened? How'd you go from this thing getting you high to killing the Ensingers?"

Tony sighed and looked down at his hands, holding them up in bewilderment. "I don't know. It felt good... when I wore it. I felt like another person. I was seeing things, like, through someone else's eyes. Seeing things that didn't make sense, you know, but too specific not to be something real. Shapes. Smells, in the air, that

I don't know what the hell they were. Saltwater, jasmine, then something like a dead animal, this engine smell. Then I was upstairs, in Mark's old bedroom, with a..." He leaned in and lowered his eyes, and his voice dropped to barely a whisper. "They don't know this part, Annie. I was with a woman, and I was..." He shook his head and ran his dirty hands through his greasy hair. "I was cutting her. Cutting her all over with a big razor. Only I was watching myself do it, and there were other people there with me, watching me. We were just standing there, watching me cut this girl to pieces."

"It was Dara Ensinger." Ann's eyes were fixed on him, her mind trying desperately to entertain the possibility of his confession. "Or her daughter. You were remembering that."

He patted the table with his palm. "No. This was before that."

"You were remembering Mrs. Ensinger, Tony." She leaned forward, and she couldn't keep her voice from shaking; she'd been doing so well, but her throat was dry, the words were getting caught as they came out of her mouth. "Please tell me you were remembering her. Please tell me that. You were having a nightmare about killing Dara Ensinger and her kids."

"No, it wasn't her, Annie. It was before that." His words were even; he'd come to terms with this, and he spoke as though his life depended on what he was preparing to tell her. "It was before that, a girl named Sophie McTell. I picked her up at the Woodhull truck plaza off 74. Gave her some crystal. We were at a motel on Grand Avenue for a while, and then I was there at the house, cutting her up." He sighed, and it came out as a ragged shudder. "She's ... behind the house. There's others, too. They never found them, so far as I know. I guess you'd have heard about it."

"Grandpa B's?" Ann hissed, leaning in for the first time, casing the room with a quick glance to ensure that the guards were nowhere near them. "You crazy *fuck*, you buried her there, you—"

"I didn't have to," he said, never changing his tone, not responding to her ramping up. "The thing, that fucking costume thing just ... ate her up. I was wearing it, and I took it off, you know, to dig. And it started to ... take her. It crawled ... by itself, Annie. Through the mud, pulling itself on that one arm, and it covered her. It just ... ate the skin right off her. And it started crunching through the bones when I ran. That fucking costume thing just ate her."

Ann sat back in her chair as she noticed the guard behind Tony frown, assessing their situation. She had to keep her cool. She raised a hand, indicating that it was okay. They were fine, just two long-lost relatives catching up on family business, murders, flesh-eating monsters, that kind of thing. Nothing to get excited about. "Where is she, Tony?"

"Probably still there, or part of her, at least," he said, sitting back as he noted her shift in demeanor. "When I went back, she was gone. Like, anything I could see." He looked at his lap. "It did the same thing with the rest."

Ann's skin felt like it was lifting from her bones; she was at once light and outside of herself and anchored to the metal chair. She could barely believe the sunlight coming through the windows; somewhere, people were out there enjoying themselves, readying themselves to trick-or-treat in just a few short days, carving pumpkins, having a grand old time. She felt a million miles away from the rest of humanity. "The rest?"

Tony nodded. "There were more. Lots more. Eight, nine, I think, somewhere in there. This girl Mark went to high school with ... Gina something. There were lots of 'em." Something in his expression went gray, a sudden, fleeting darkness drifting over him as he reminisced, then looked up, as if waking from sleep. "I even buried that goddamn thing in the mud out there, just to see what it would do. It crawled out. I saw that fucking arm come out of the ground and start pulling those girls down into the mud with it. One of 'em... one of 'em was still alive. It just pulled them under the ground." He closed his eyes and took a deep breath, exhaling slowly, as though he'd just rid himself of something. "Jacko. That's its name. Jacko."

"Why Jacko?" Ann asked.

Tony's eyes got wide. "Don't know. Never asked."

"Dara Ensinger." Ann couldn't look at him now, wouldn't make eye contact again. "What happened?"

"Every time I put that thing on, I got that high, you know? That rush, deep down, I don't know how to explain it. Until ... I just didn't need to put it on anymore. I could think about doing something like that, like what I'd done with the girls, and I was outside myself. Watching. But I was watching that thing. It just came out of me, somehow. See, it's like... it's like an animal that needed a shell, and you built it a shell, Annie. That paper deal."

"Papier-mâché," she corrected.

"Yeah. Well, it's not just that. There's something else to it, I don't know what. But it lives inside that thing."

CHAPTER 40

The face, she thought. No one but her knew it was in there, buried under layers of paper and glue.

"It's like it knows what you're thinking, you know? Like, the really bad stuff you're thinking. Stuff you wouldn't even want to admit to. It knows. It knows what everyone's thinking, everyone who puts it on and wears it, even for a little bit. And it just wires you into it. See, like, everyone it takes? They're all inside it, after that. And they can come out, but they're ... not like they were. One night, I saw Sophie again. She was like this mess of skin and bones all fucked up in the wrong order, her face all eaten up like bugs had gotten to it, and her eyes were like an animal's eyes, she just kept licking her teeth with this ... tongue. I saw her again a while later, in the bathtub. She was this ... thing with all these little teeth like a... like an eel? She didn't have any legs. It takes things you understand and just fucks them all up to drive you crazy. It plays tricks on you, whatever it is. It thinks it's funny."

He swallowed hard, and the guard stepped forward. Their time was up.

"That's what happened that night, with Dara and her kids," he continued. "That thing is *hungry*, goddamn hungry, and it never gets enough. You give it enough of yourself, and it just becomes part of you, on its own. All of the people inside it... the more there are, the harder it gets to resist. And you just can't know yourself anymore. Anyway, it told me to go for Dara. I don't know why it settled on her. In my head, it just kept pushing me toward her." He stood up, nodding as the guard gestured for Tony to put his hands behind his back.

"What do you mean, it told you?"

"The voices you hear," Tony said, standing, his hands bound in cuffs. "They kept mentioning Lily, Dara's daughter, saying I should keep them in the family." The guard guided Tony toward the door, and her uncle looked over his shoulder once, the twitch of a hopeful smile playing at his mouth, distorting into a grimace as he held back tears. "I miss you, Annie. I miss you guys so much."

Ann only realized she was crying when the guard finally touched her shoulder and asked if she was ready to leave.

41

My Favorite Murder was ending as Georgia prepared to leave the library, and Elvis the cat signing off with his hilarious meow was enough to shake Georgia Blevin out of her careful scrutiny of the Register-Mail's online archive for just a second. Karen Kilgariff and Georgia Hardstark sounded like they'd be a detective team, Georgia thought, and they sort of were. She thought it was cool to share a name with such a badass podcaster who fought crime from the internet.

She had a few more little things to check back home if the internet was back up—construction down the block had forced her to the public library that afternoon to finish what had started out as an essay on the Ensinger murders for her intermediate Comp class and had grown into something more. Any kind of research, particularly for such a high-profile crime like the Ensinger murders that had seen long-term local and national coverage, had to be peeled like the layers of an onion. Her sociology teacher had told her that the previous year when she'd raised questions about the

Cleveland Torso Murders in 1935 and to what extent the Cleveland city management had screwed up the public response to the killings. Had they made the whole thing worse? Had they affected the cultural consciousness in an even more negative way? (Mr. Gunn was something of an amateur historian on Eliot Ness, which was how they'd gotten off on a tangent in the middle of a unit about Depression-era responses to poverty.)

"Every situation like the Torso murders," Mr. Gunn had said, leaning against his filing cabinet the way he always did when he prepared to wax poetic, "had multiple levels of response that all collapsed into each other. It was more complicated than just one thing or the other thing. It was a whole bunch of things, all jumbled together." It was like getting a newspaper wet: you might be able to read the words on an article, but the words on another article were going to bleed through as well, making your job that much harder.

Motherfucker, Georgia thought, looking down at the dates she'd circled in her notebook, and the pitted feeling in her stomach was part triumph, part dread at telling her mom what she'd discovered. She checked her phone. 4:30. She'd text on the way home to see if Cory was game for getting pizza so they could talk. There was no way it was a coincidence, surely. It had been hard to find what she'd been looking for; birth records weren't public in Illinois, but there were ways around that to a certain extent if all you were looking for was data.

August 30, 2002: Lillian Ensinger, born to Dara Ensinger, 28, and Mark Blake, 29.

CHAPTER 41

It lined up with what she'd found in the FamilySearch account she'd created. He'd used his middle name for the birth announcement so his family wouldn't find out.

Lily Ensinger was Mark's daughter.

42

Cory sat in her car, anxiously jogging her leg, Katy Perry on the radio. When did pop get so overproduced with all the weird vocal effects? Maybe it always was, and she didn't notice. The console clock said 4:40, so she figured she was safe to head out. Geo had texted asking if they could meet at Pizza House, that she had something to tell her.

[Cory: Just tell me you're not pregnant]

[Georgia: Definitely not that, lol. Thx, mom. Really important and too much for txt.]

Cory sighed with relief and chuckled.

[Cory: No problem, honey. Go ahead and order if you get there before I do.]

CHAPTER 42

I actually have something to talk to you about, too, kid, Cory thought. She stared at the email on her phone, the PDF.

Her leave-of-absence paperwork.

Cory felt sick to her stomach at the thought of having the conversation; if they moved, Geo would have to leave school for her senior year. She felt almost silly being so anxious. *She's your daughter, not your boss, not some judgmental internet troll.* She would understand. If she disagreed, that's where the negotiation would have to come into play. But, Cory figured, they'd cross that bridge when they had to. *If* they had to.

Mark. Adrian. The buckle she'd found at Mark's house was unmistakably Adrian's, and that was deserving of its own explanation, though she couldn't imagine how that would work. *Oh, your ex came by*, she imagined Mark saying, *and we hashed it all out. He took his pants off at one point, so that's probably how he lost the belt buckle.* Yeah, try again.

The idea that Mark did something to Adrian, though, was almost as ridiculous. Mark wasn't a violent guy, quite the opposite; by all counts, he was caring and didn't seem to want conflict of any kind, at least in his revisiting conversations with his sister about having their mother put in assisted living. But if Adrian tried something on him? Or threatened her to Mark?

This is a ridiculous conversation to have with yourself. Why don't you just ask him?

Why don't I? she thought. She could just ask if he'd seen Adrian, and surely she'd be able to hear it in his voice if a lie got caught coming out. She could just ask him.

She checked her watch. You know what? Geo would order the pizza and chill until she got there. *No time like the present, girl.*

[Cory: On my way, kiddo. Making a quick stop at Mark's.]

Cory pulled out of the driveway and made the light at the corner, opening it up a little as she hit South Seminary on the way to Mark's place. She was a big girl, for Christ's sake. She could have a conversation with him about whatever had happened, and that would be that. No more variables or uncertainty.

She adjusted the mirror and caught a glimpse of herself before looking away quickly, refusing to ask herself more questions.

As she rolled to a stop at the curb outside Mark's house, she noticed a man walking around from the side of the house. At first, she thought maybe it was a guy checking the meter, as he had a jumpsuit on, but then she saw that it was a sanitation uniform: the guy was a garbage collector. He threw her a friendly, tentative wave and smiled a little, shielding his eyes from the fading sun. One hell of a job to have in the summertime, she thought; redheads got sunburnt so fast, and this guy was a natural ginger if ever there was one. He approached the car, and she rolled down the passenger side window.

"Can I help you?" She called across the seat, sublimating her shock at the sight of the burn scars that comprised most of his face. "I don't think Mark is home, if you're looking for him."

"Yeah, he's not," the man said, now almost to the car. "Cory, right? Cory Blevin?"

"Y-yes," she replied. "Do I know you?"

"Charlie," he said, reaching the passenger side and leaning in through the open window. "Charlie Barrow? We were in the same class—"

"Oh, my god, yes, of course," she replied. "How have you been? Mark should be back later, if you were trying to find him. I was just going to leave him a note."

"It's alright, I can touch base with him later," Charlie said. He hadn't stopped staring at her, which she just now realized, his eyes fixed on her, occasionally letting them wander down her body and back up to her face. "You—um—you wouldn't be able to give me a ride home, would you? I was trying to find Mark because he was supposed to help me jump my car off. Damn battery died in my driveway. Can you believe that?"

"Oh, uh," she tried to see around him—was Mark really not home?—and couldn't see Mark's car in the driveway, or any movement or light from inside. "S-sure. Sure, I guess that's okay. Is it far?"

Charlie opened the door a little too eagerly, slid into the seat, and grinned at her a little tersely, the glossy skin pulling tight around his mouth as he pointed at the road in front of them.

"Nah. Just up the road a bit, past the drive-in." He relaxed into the passenger seat and closed his eyes. "Not far at all.

III: TRICKS

43

Eightball was asleep and snoring peacefully, an occasional snort as he repositioned himself, the only sound in the late-night silence of the block. Tony lay on his bunk, staring at the gray ceiling, thinking of Annie. It had been so good to see her. His cock agreed, pointing straight up and aching. Goddamn it. He hated it. But he closed his eyes, clenched his fist, and remembered.

He stood in front of the mirror, measuring his breathing, which felt wildly out of control, focusing on the sound, the rhythm, the sensation of his own scent inside the body cast. He stared at himself, the way it sat on his naked body, hugging his shoulders. The first time he'd put it on, it was like putting on a shell. Now it felt like armor, as though it couldn't be separated from him if it had to be. Deep, even breaths. A tantric electricity frazzled its way through his skin, his veins, his bones.

He could do anything. He could be anyone, go anywhere, but he wanted to be this. He was himself and not himself. His thoughts were his, but covered in something slick and wet, fetid and delicious, like forbidden delicacies that continued to appear in front of him, one after the other, beating hearts gift-wrapped in flesh. He devoured, again and again, their bones left to feed the earth under the cross where the shell slept. He thought of Ann, of how gracefully she took him inside her, and he knew now that he could have reached down, cut off her face, torn her to pieces, eaten her flesh and heart, and she would have had no recourse. No one could, no one would. He could devour whatever he wanted because no one had his armor.

Behind his reflection in the mirror, a faceless woman lay spread-eagle on the bed, fingers playing at her sex, a moist, wet sound that aroused him. She had no features that he could see, a faceless mass lolling on shoulders, but she smiled inside him, somehow, inside his eyes. She could take whatever he decided to give. But others could not, and that was their tough fucking luck. She didn't even seem to mind that the bed was on fire or that her flesh was melting into the sheets, running down her arms like rivulets of hot water, exposing bone.

Tony was going to take what he wanted from now on. He grinned inside the mask, but the face in the mirror, the drooping slit mouth, stayed the same. The woman on the bed smiled with no mouth and blinked with no eyes—frames cut from some place deep in the film that was clacking through his brain: rewinding, rolling, rewinding, rolling.

The woman on the bed screamed now; she pleaded for her life as he stood over the bodies of her dead children.

They were all his.

Dara, blubbering with terror as he turned to face her, would be the best one yet.

44

The door chimes tinkled brightly as a family entered the restaurant, greeted the hostess, and moved toward the back of the pizza parlor. Georgia sat back in her chair and studied the webpage on her phone, glancing up periodically to watch for Cory's car pulling into the lot across the street.

She'd been scouring 4chan and other 'sites of ill repute' as Mr. Gunn referred to them for anything she didn't yet have regarding the Ensinger case, and it appeared that her diligence had paid off. Someone with the username KillerBadger had promised to email her a link to some materials that kept getting taken down from the site for whatever reason, and Georgia anxiously bounced her leg in time with the '50s music playing on hidden speakers in the restaurant.

The server set a plate of mozzarella cheese sticks down at the table, but Georgia didn't look up from her phone. In spite of her discovery about Mark and Lily Ensinger, there were still things about the Ensinger murders themselves that didn't make sense, little details that added up to less than what they should have. First off, Tony Devold had claimed to have waited in the Ensinger's house for nearly three days, but that wasn't true. After some digging on Reddit, Georgia discovered that someone had gotten footage from a Ring doorbell camera just a few houses down, and in the video, the unmistakable figure of Tony Devold was seen creeping around the side of the house just hours before the Ensingers returned. There was no entry caught on camera before that.

Beyond that, there was the issue of Dara Ensinger's corpse. The pictures that had leaked online—while blurry in spots, scans of scans—gave the distinct impression that she'd been eaten, the edges of some wounds (sixty in total, Georgia considered, pausing to reflect on what that would even entail) bearing the same damage to flesh as that of an attack by a crocodile or similar creature, which made zero sense and ratcheted up the grotesquerie by quite a bit, in Georgia's mind. Tony had claimed to have used a machete, and that was it. The nature of the wounds, when measured against the kind of damage a machete might cause to one's flesh and bone, didn't fully reflect that conclusion.

Her email lit up, and there was the pay dirt courtesy of KillerBadger. *Hope these help*, the email read, *Viva Le Junkman!*

Whatever, dude, she thought, munching a cheese stick. The files she'd received consisted of a transcript of Tony's interrogation recorded by the arresting officer, Lt. William Auster and, almost more disturbing (though it was a sliding scale at this point), a short video clip some junior high kids skateboarding at Chadwick Park had taken, though for whatever reason, nothing had come of it. So, of course, as these things were wont to do, the video found its way to the darker corners of the Internet.

The clip was shot from the curb alongside the park, across the street from where Tony sat in his parked car: an '87 Buick hand-painted a rusty red, which Georgia found oddly creepy. He was motionless behind the wheel, and he wore the costume that she'd found at Mark's house. It was only a minute or so long, and at one point, the figure in the car reached up and gripped the wheel with both hands, revealing a tattoo of a band logo (CATACLYSM, the loopy, medieval lettering proclaimed) that had been confirmed as unique to Tony Devold.

Georgia watched the clip several times, each time looking for anything beyond the obviously unusual. If the date of the recording was correct—if everyone besides Tony was telling the truth—then his story had been largely inaccurate or fabricated. The police report also hadn't indicated having found the costume at the crime scene or at the Devold house following the murders. So that meant there were two options: either Tony had lied to the police about the timing and nature of the events—which bought him nothing since he freely admitted to the murders—or the costume was, in some inexplicable way, a part of the crime.

Put it on. She remembered that overwhelming feeling as she'd stood in the door of the bedroom where the thing sat on a chair near the bed. The sight of it in the video—off-white in spots, flat-out dirty in others, those slit-holes for the eyes, nose and mouth—made her feel a little sick as she recalled the feeling when she'd put it

CHAPTER 44

on that night: a disorienting, out-of-body feeling that both frightened her and made her feel euphoric, hungry.

The waitress arrived to refill Georgia's water glass and hustled away, waving at a couple who had entered the restaurant. Georgia texted Cory again—

[Georgia: you coming, madre?]

—before digging into the transcript of Tony's interview.

45

Galesburg Department of Public Safety
Interview Date: October 18
Interview of: Anthony Devold (AD)
Interviewed by: Lt. William Auster (WA)

WA: It is presently 17:53 hours on October 18th. In the room are myself—Lieutenant William Auster of the Galesburg Police Department—and Anthony Devold. Your first name is spelled A-N-T-H-O-N-Y, last name D-E-V-O-L-D, is that correct?

AD: It is.

WA: Your address is 344 Day Street, Galesburg, Illinois, 61401. No contact number available. Is that correct?

AD: Yes.

WA: You are *fifty-eight years of age*, correct?

CHAPTER 45

AD: Yes.

WA: You don't have a phone, Anthony?

AD: No.

WA: Thank you for clarifying. I'd like you to tell me the chronology of events that took place on October 16.

AD: When they got home to their house, you mean?

WA: Start before that. What time did you get up in the morning, all of it?

AD: I was at their house already.

WA: Yes, I'm aware of that. You woke up at the Ensinger house. You'd broken into the house two days prior, on October 14. Is that correct?

AD: Yeah, I woke up that morning at around ten in Dara's bed.

WA: The deceased, Dara Ensinger, is that correct?

AD: Yeah.

WA: How did you know where they lived, Tony? You'd been romantically involved with Dara before. Is that correct?

AD: Yeah, she worked at Dennison's Auto Parts, up front, checking people out. We'd gone out for beers, had sex a few times.

JUNKMAN

WA: *So you'd been to the house before?*

AD: *Yeah.*

WA: *So you woke up at ten, and what did you do then?*

AD: *I sat in the bed for a long time and looked out the window. I was alone.*

WA: *What were you looking at out the window?*

AD: *Nothing. I was just making sure I was alone.*

WA: *Did you think that there was someone else there?*

AD: *No, nothing like that. I wanted to be alone, and I was finally alone.*

WA: *Did you believe that you'd been followed to the house, Tony?*

AD: *No. I was just happy to be alone.*

WA: *And what did you do when you got up?*

AD: *I sat in the living room, and I waited.*

WA: *What were you waiting for?*

AD: *For Dara to come home.*

WA: Tony, I need you to be honest with me. At that point, had you already decided to take their lives? Was that something you were still mulling over?

AD: Yeah, I was gonna kill them.

WA: Why?

AD: There was something inside me that wanted to kill them.

WA: Did you also want to ... consume them? I'm asking because we found pieces of Ms. Ensinger and her two children that had been ... bitten out of them. Pieces of their bodies had been bitten off, Tony. Did you do that?

AD: Yeah.

WA: Why did you do that?

AD: Because it was hungry.

WA: What was hungry, Tony?

AD: Like I said. The thing inside me that wanted to kill.

WA: Tony, what happened then? You got up, waited in the living room, and then what?

AD: It was a long time. I made a ham sandwich and drank a bottle of iced tea they had in the refrigerator. I ate, and then they came out not too long after that.

WA: What happened when they came home? And, for clarity, this was Dara Ensinger, her daughter Lillian, and her son Dustin?

AD: Yeah.

WA: So what happened when they came home, Tony? You were in the living room?

AD: No, when I heard them outside, I went into the bedroom. They came inside. They were noisy, laughing, dropping their bags, just making a lot of noise.

WA: Then what?

AD: I waited for Dara to come into the bedroom. The kids went to their rooms—well, no, wait, one of them went to the bathroom. I heard that door shut. But Dara came into the bedroom. I was standing behind the door, and I closed it, and I held the knife to her throat and told her to be quiet.

WA: And what did she do?

AD: She got quiet. She was scared. She peed herself.

WA: You could see that she had done that?

AD: Yeah. She was wearing jeans.

WA: Then what, Tony?

AD: I tied her up. Tied her to the bed, wrists and ankles.

CHAPTER 45

WA: *Did you intend to rape her?*

AD: *At the time, I just wanted her tied down so she couldn't get away from me and make a mess of things.*

WA: *So, then what did you do?*

AD: *I opened the door. The kids were in the living room, and when they saw me, the girl, she just froze, but the boy, he came running at the door, like he was gonna come in.*

WA: *And what did you do?*

AD: *I held the knife out, and I stuck it in him as he ran forward. Like, in his side. He sorta tipped over, and as he was falling, he grabbed at me, like, trying to pull me down. I kicked him hard in the nuts, and he stopped. He started crying.*

WA: *And the girl? Was she still just frozen in the living room?*

AD: *Yeah. She was sitting on the couch, looking like she was gonna run. I told her to come to me, or I'd cut her mom's throat.*

WA: *She could've run out the door.*

AD: *That's what I was afraid she'd do.*

WA: *So you didn't want to get caught.*

AD: *Well, shit, man, why would I want to get caught?*

WA: *Okay, go on. What then?*

AD: *Then... I don't know. I told the girl to sit down, and she sat on the floor, away from the boy, kinda on the other side of me. The boy was bleeding all over. He was a mess ... all over the carpet. The girl was crying and kept leaning over to try to help him.*

WA: *Okay, then what?*

AD: *Dara was screaming and crying. She would not shut up. She was saying, "Tony, why would you do this to us? Why would you hurt us?"*

WA: *What did you say to her?*

AD: *Nothing. I didn't have any answer for that.*

WA: *And why not? Why would you want to hurt them, Tony?*

AD: *Chasing the dragon, I guess?*

WA: *You were high?*

AD: *Manner of speaking, yeah.*

WA: *What had you taken?*

AD: *Nothing, like I said, I had a sandwich and some iced tea.*

WA: *So how were you high?*

CHAPTER 45

NOTE: At this point, interviewee shook his head, smiled towards the floor. Closed eyes.

AD: Bad choice of words, I guess. The girl, she was sitting there, on the floor, her knees pulled to her chest, you know? And I was... It was just real quiet, you know? Like, they were waiting for what I was gonna do?

WA: What were you going to do? I mean, at that point, you've indicated that you'd already decided to kill them. What was going through your head?

AD: Lots of things. I kept ... seeing things. Seeing things that weren't right.

WA: What type of things?

AD: I was just, I was seeing things. I started getting scared, my stomach was sick, and I threw up.

WA: So that's your vomit at the scene, not one of the kids?

AD: Yeah, that's right. I threw up all over the floor, and then I put the thing on.

WA: Put what thing on?

AD: The costume. The Jacko, my friend, he said they'd be fun to play with, after.

WA: I don't know what you mean by a costume, Tony. We didn't find any costume at the scene. Where did you leave the costume? And can you tell me who your friend

"Jacko" is? Are you telling me that there was someone else there, at the crime scene?

AD: I didn't take it anywhere after that. I don't know. I wore it then, I'd worn it before. My friend Jacko, he... he was there, but he wasn't there. Sometimes he was, when things would get bad, when I'd have a hard time with things. He was there.

WA: Can you tell me what Jacko looks like? Where would we find this Jacko, Tony? If someone else was involved, you realize we'll need to talk to them.

AD: Um... well, I—no, I mean, I don't... I don't know.

WA: So what you're saying is that there was no one else there, Tony. Is that what you mean? That you acted alone? There was no "Jacko," right?

AD: Um... no, I mean... *pause, unintelligible* I don't...I guess so, yeah.

WA: You "guess so" what? You were alone?

AD: *long pause* Yeah.

WA: So you were wearing this costume, and then what?

AD: Then I started feeling better, feeling good, fucking, just ... good and lit as fuck, rising, fuckin' rising. I saw Annie on the bed. She looked scared. She was looking at the kids, and I felt hungry all of the sudden, so fucking hungry, like usual.

CHAPTER 45

WA: *Like usual? What do you mean?* *long pause* *Okay you saw Annie? You mean your niece Annette Devold? Is that correct?*

AD: Yeah. Dara was gone.

WA: *But Dara wasn't gone, Tony.*

AD: I know, but for a little bit, she was. I think I said I missed her, and that's when the girl got up to run.

WA: *You said that you missed Dara, or Annie?*

AD: Annie.

WA: *And that's when the girl got up to run?*

AD: She got out the door, yeah. She was screaming bloody murder, and I got my arm around her waist, swung her back around toward the bedroom. I stuck the knife in one side of her neck and threw her on the ground. Her skirt flew up, and her neck was just spitting blood. You know, like when you're hunting, and you catch something with an arrow?

WA: *And is this when you raped her?*

AD: Yeah.

WA: *To clarify, while she was bleeding out on the floor, you had sexual intercourse with Lilian Ensinger?*

AD: Yeah. The voice in my head kept saying, "keep it in the family, keep it in the family, make a dead baby, make a dead baby," and I came in her. Annie stopped screaming then—

WA: Do you mean Dara? Dara stopped screaming?

AD: Oh. Yeah, and she was just crying. I think because she was happy, you know? After I was done, the girl was real white, and I just knew it was done at that point. I grabbed back ahold of the knife and just yanked it across.

WA: So that was the moment that you cut Lillian Ensinger's throat? Is that correct?

AD: Yeah. She was gagging and choking, and I was... There was so much blood, and it was just running and splattering all over the boy. He was looking up at me and started screaming, and I just kept cutting. The more Annie cried, the more I cut, and then the girl's head just came off in my arms.

WA: You mean Dara was crying, don't you, Tony? You keep saying Annie, but that's your niece, correct?

AD: Yeah, but like I said, at the time, it was Annie. It gets what it wants, Bill. It wanted me to see Annie for some reason, being all happy, not Dara crying because I was killing her daughter.

WA: Lieutenant Auster, please, Tony.

CHAPTER 45

AD: Sure, Lieutenant, sorry. Yeah, that's when I cut her head off, and both Dara and the boy were screaming and crying. I gave the boy a kick in the ribs, and when he doubled over, I stabbed him in the back. I could see him, he was in the dirt, and there were fucking palm trees behind him, and I was in the fucking air, man.

WA: What happened then?

AD: Then it was Dara again, and she was really going at it, crying and screaming at me that I was going to hell, that I was bound to the fucking devil, that's what she said, "You're bound to the fucking devil, Tony." That's a hell of a thing to say to someone.

WA: And what did you say?

AD: I said, "Well, then, I'll make it easy for him to find me because I was tired of all this. Fucking thing lives at my house, anyway."

WA: What do you mean?

AD: The ground, man. That ground is poisoned. *pause* I need a smoke. Can we take a break?

END OF PART ONE

46

That ground is poisoned.
Georgia got off the bus and waited for it to pull away from the stop before crossing the street and starting down the block toward Mark's house. A ten-foot sign down the side of the vehicle advertised discreet HIV testing and free clinical services to those who qualified. *When you don't have time for life to slow you down!* it said, depicting a smiling African-American woman and her child reading a book together.

Her mother hadn't shown at Pizza House, texting instead...

[Cory: see you at home, xo]

...which wasn't her usual style of text-speak—but, Georgia figured, something had come up.

[Georgia: No prob, gonna run over to Amanda's place and grab my iPad charger. Probably watch a movie. Back late.]

CHAPTER 46

That would cover her for a few hours at least.

That ground is poisoned. It was a weird way to suggest a house being haunted, but she supposed that one could only crack open the riddles in a serial killer's head to a certain extent. And Tony Devold was nothing if not a serial killer, of that she was certain.

It was starting to spit rain, and for reasons she couldn't quite articulate, she didn't want anyone to see her near Mark's place; it had nothing to do with anything other than her own desire for discretion. If she found anything, then she could let her mom know. But something wasn't right about what had gone down with Tony Devold and the Ensinger murders, and the few references to a friend named "Jacko" he'd made during his questioning by police—as well as her own experience there a few nights before—had her all but convinced that something also wasn't right about that house. She wasn't sure how she'd prove it without actually talking to Tony Devold, which wasn't happening, but she was fairly certain that "Jacko" meant the costume.

Georgia sprinted the last half block or so to the driveway, then made her way around the back of the garage. She caught her breath, wiped rain from her glasses, and looked around the corner at the side of the house. From where she stood, she could see that there weren't any lights on, at least on the west side, which would have accounted for part of the living room as well as the hallway between the living room and kitchen. And anyway, if Mark was home, he wouldn't care if she stopped by, would he? She could always say the door was open, and she wanted to drop something off. She could fabricate something that wouldn't seem bizarre or suspicious.

Georgia tried the back screen door. It swung inward, the stale smell of that morning's coffee still clinging to the air, and she took a tentative step into the kitchen.

"Mark?" she called into the house. "It's Georgia Blevin. You here?" She paused, then added, "The door was open." She stepped inside and closed the door behind her.

There was another smell, something fleeting, but tangible to her senses. Mulch or wet earth. Hot oil. Had he left a burner on? No, the stove was off, and there were no dishes in the sink.

Georgia entered the hallway between the living room and the kitchen. To her right, the staircase that led to the second floor; just behind it was a small bathroom and two coat closets. In front of her was the living room, totally dark. "Mark?"

He wasn't home, surely.

Where to start, she considered, and, more importantly... what was she looking for? She had to admit to herself that she didn't know. Tony's comment about the ground being poisoned made her think of the movie with the clown doll from the '80s, the Poltergeist one. Maybe that was the title. She'd seen part of it when she was younger at a friend's sleepover, thanks to her friend's older brother, who had mistakenly assessed their readiness for such a film at eight or nine years old. It had scared the holy shit out of them all, and she'd only seen maybe fifteen minutes of it, enough to remember that it was about an Indian burial ground.

But there was nothing particularly sinister about this house, she thought to herself. Still, Tony had grown up here, then continued to live here as an adult, right up until around the killings. He was talking about something specific. The ground. But she hadn't seen anything strange in the yard. On the contrary, it seemed fairly well maintained. Muddy as hell, but well maintained.

Georgia went into the living room, reached for the window shade near the front door, and paused.

Sitting near the west window on the far side was a shape.

For a moment, she hesitated to acknowledge to herself that it was a person, because at first glance, it didn't seem to be—an amorphous mess at her peripheral vision. But now she could see that it was an unusually tall person, a man, sitting very still and upright in a chair near the windows on the east side of the living room. Surely this person had heard her calling, yet there was no indication of movement, no shifting in its still form.

"I'm sorry," she said, her voice cutting out into a raspy squeak. *You should go. Right now.* "I'm Georgia, I'm a ... friend of Mark's. Is Mark here?"

She carefully crept further into the room, until the darkness had covered her over along with everything else, and now she was just another shape, moving past the couch, toward the east windows. A person couldn't sit that still, could they? Maybe it wasn't a person at all, but—

"Oh, good fucking god," she said to no one, her legs feeling weak. It wasn't a person. It was the goddamn costume.

What was it, really? It was papier-mâché, a mishmash of paper, a little sloppy around the edges. She reached for it, grazed its surface with her fingertips.

Put it on.

What could it hurt? she thought. It was heavier than she remembered, and as she slid it over her shoulders and slipped the mask part over her head, she was immediately hit with the sensation she'd had when she put it on that first time, as though she was looking through VR goggles or something. Something outside herself. A rich, heady stink like rotting animals, maybe ocean water? And the coppery, sharp odor of blood. Then a feeling like she was floating, almost a painkiller high; she recalled the way she'd felt when she'd had her appendix removed the previous summer, the heavy doses of sledgehammer drugs; Fentanyl, maybe, or Dilaudid, she couldn't recall. Only she could move, could think, and see clearly. There had been a pair of scissors on the dresser near where it had sat in the bedroom, and she'd heard the whispered voice in her ear.

Cut.

Instead, she'd gone downstairs. Why, she didn't know, and then her mother and Mark were there, and Mark was upset, not at her, but at the costume? But that didn't make any se—

"I'm sorry," she murmured now. "I don't know why I didn't—"

Cut.

The scissors were here, now, on the sideboard next to the chair. She picked them up.

Cut.

"Okay." Her voice sounded far away in her head, and she opened the scissors, holding them up to the side of her head, the edges of the mask, digging the blade into the head-part of the thing, and there was hot, searing pain in her head, so sudden that Georgia dropped the scissors to the floor with a clatter. Jesus, was she bleeding? She reached for her face—the costume's face—and began to dig at the frayed bits of paper around the eyes, the mouth, pulling away stiff chunks of paper and dropping them to the floor. Something clicked in her brain, somewhere deep, like something snapping their fingers in her face, and she yanked the costume from her body, shoving it back into the chair where it had sat moments before.

Cut. You.

"Fuck you," she said quietly. "Get out of my head."

The thing seemed to stare back at her. For now, it looked different. The layers of glue-rigid paper she'd torn apart had given way to a dried, wrinkled-looking face that appeared to be buried inside it, and where the eyes would have been were instead ragged holes that had dried at the edges. Was it a mask? It had to be. No eyes, nothing but darkness behind the parted lips, and the material was a dark brown that gave the impression of tanned leather. It had the look of a haunted house mummy, a carnival gag, though something about it felt off. Too ... deliberate, she thought, though that felt like a strange way to consider it.

A death mask?

No.

Someone's actual face.

What the fuck? Georgia took one step closer, then stopped as she noticed that the mouth was moving. Just slightly, the way a person might when reading silently. She could see the entire chair now, and the thing ended at a torso, as it had the other night. And though she could have sworn that she'd seen legs when she entered the room, there were no legs, and the thin fingers on its one complete arm seemed to flex just a little, the way someone might stretch after sleeping too long in the same position.

"Enough of this shit," Georgia muttered, suddenly aware of how dark the room was, that behind her, all around her. The shadows shifted with occasional lightning outside, and she turned now to head back toward the kitchen, that hot oil smell stronger now, trapped in her nostrils.

As she took a step back toward the hallway, there was a thump from upstairs, just over her head. A footstep? No, it was a singular sound, accompanied by nothing else. The sound of something falling over.

You're out of your fucking mind, girl, she thought, stepping back into the hallway, *but you were not wrong. This house—this whole thing—is fucked.*

There was no hint of movement from the living room or the inhuman thing in the chair. Georgia felt as though she would vomit, breathing through her nose carefully, trying to ignore the sickening smell, her hands visibly shaking as she stepped toward the staircase. She took them carefully, cautious not to make any noise, and by the time she was halfway up, she saw the shadow on the wall. It was oddly shaped—a sloping, diagonal line that wasn't a person. She could tell that much. *Be ready to move. Fast.* The stairs curved about three-quarters of the way up, and as Georgia reached that point, she felt a cautious relief.

The rectangular, pull-string hatch leading to the attic yawned open.

Fuck. Frozen, she clutched the banister and stared into the dark hallway just five or so feet away, the open hatch with its collapsible wooden stairs like slatted teeth grinning at her. Shadows collected at the top of the hatch; there was more than one person, more than one thing, up there.

Now there was movement from downstairs, too.

Jesus Christ. It was what her P.E. teacher once referred to as the "alley trap." Ms. Brown had explained it in a special Saturday class on self-defense hosted at the high school. Lured into an alley so that the exits in front of you *and* in back of you are blocked.

It wanted me to come upstairs, Georgia thought grimly. Feeling in her jacket pocket, she came up with a pack of cinnamon breath mints and, mercifully, her pocket knife. She fished out the knife and popped it open, then took another step toward the upstairs hallway, only three stairs and roughly eight feet separating her from the entrance to the attic.

Downstairs, she heard a scratching sound, then another, then another. It followed a vague rhythm, and as she reached the top of the staircase, she stood with her back to the banister, with the attic ladder at her left, the staircase at her right. The scratching noise again, a shadow that found its way across the hallway floor from the living room, and followed, a few seconds later, by the source of the shadow.

The costume was pulling itself across the floor, reaching forward with its single arm, digging its fingertips into first carpet and then hardwood, dragging itself forward, bit by bit. Making its way toward the stairs.

Georgia's body gave up its terror, and she vomited sour bile all over the hallway floor. The attic wasn't an option, she decided, as she could hear deliberate movement over her head, something alive up there after all, beginning a slow move toward the open hatch—and so she found herself moving backward, toward a bedroom.

JUNKMAN

The costume had reached the bottom of the stairs and now paused as the scrabbling movement of something in the attic grew more urgent. It wasn't footsteps, not exactly, more of a chattery mess of noise, the way squirrels might sound. Maybe it was just rodents, stirred by whatever negative energy was in the house? No, that was her mom talking, Georgia thought, and this is not the time for that holistic, positive-energy stuff. *There's a costume with someone's fucking face in it coming after me. This is not just fucking rats.*

Georgia backed into the bedroom behind her and carefully closed the door, locking it.

She waited. There was a clock ticking somewhere in the room behind her. Throwing up had given her a head rush, which had turned into a headache that now pushed against her temples and forehead from the inside. She closed her eyes and took deep breaths in through her nose, out through her mouth. She was in what seemed like a guest room; a twin bed, dresser, and nightstand made up the bulk of the furniture as though the room had been staged for sale. There was a window, which, worst-case scenario, she could use to drop down into the yard, right where it started to slope away from the house. Realistically, she might break a leg or an ankle, but she'd be out. That was better than whatever was inside the house with her.

What the fuck was it? Nothing alive in the human sense of the word. And unless she'd lost her mind entirely between the living room and staircase—which she was confident she'd hadn't—then this house was haunted as hell.

On the other side of the bedroom door, the sound of something wet and heavy hit the upstairs hallway floor.

CHAPTER 46

Something falling from the attic hatch.

Georgia crouched on the side of the bed away from the door, trying to see under the crack. There wasn't enough light in the hallway to really see when it shifted. Georgia clutched the edge of the bedspread to steady herself, fingers digging into the wool blanket, settling into her breath. In and out. In and out. The light outside the door remained steady. Nothing. She looked down at the digital fitness band on her arm, watching the seconds pass.

Almost a full minute. Nothing.

Georgia started to get up when she realized that something lay in the bed, under the blanket.

She stood up and stepped backward, pocket knife at the ready, glancing at the door. *Six of one, half a dozen of the other.* She yanked the covers back.

It was a muddy skeleton, dressed in a pair of girl's jeans and a ragged, stained Aerosmith shirt. The skull yawned in a macabre leer toward the ceiling, and it was arranged in such a way, the spine and legs were at just the right angles to suggest that someone had been sleeping next to it. *Christ, what the fuck? What the fuck, Mark? It's not real. It's not real. It's not real. That's what Lily Ensinger had been wearing when they found her—*

Georgia screamed as the bedroom door opened, and the threshold was filled with the shadow of the mummy thing from downstairs, the tanned, withered face leering from the folds of torn paper.

"Cut," the thing said as it came around the side of the bed, and she realized that there was someone inside it now. She was not imagining the costume in motion. It walked on human legs—a man's legs—because someone was wearing the thing now, naked from the waist down, cock erect and pointing toward her, the scissors clutched tightly in the wearer's free hand.

"Please don't," Georgia pleaded, her voice weak, as pain exploded in her shoulder from the dual blades coming down hard and cutting into her, hitting bone as consciousness slipped, mercifully, away from her.

47

There was music playing, but there was no music playing. Somewhere in the house was music that seemed to phase in and out, notes and melody like a salty, rippling surf. Mark sat in silence, his breath hot against the inside of the mask, staring at the dark screen of the silent television.

Sound was a vacuum. The air outside the costume was a vacuum. He could hear only what was inside the costume. Voices in music, as though a radio was playing far away, but he was somehow attuned to every word, spoken through a tube directly into his brain.

From your lips to God's ear, as Brute would have said.
Three little words... oh, what I'd give for...
Mark stared at the floor, at the girl cowering there.
Cory.
It's not Cory.
Who?
"Please," Georgia said. "Please don't do whatever you're thinking about doing with me."

Mark stood up, towering over her, and it struck him how small she was. How fragile. She was only 5'3", slight in frame, and now she looked even smaller. Her left shoulder was a bloody wreck, two deep stab wounds a few inches apart, still seeping blood on his carpet.

"Please don't hurt me again. Mark, listen to me. This is not right. You're not right. Take that thing off, please," Georgia groaned. "I won't say anything. Just please, I'm fucking hurt. Just, let me—"

"We do what we want." The girl—she was Cory, of course she was, she looked just like Cory, but shorter and a little thinner than Cory, was her hair a different color, too?—curled into herself, pressing her face into the sleeve of her shirt, smearing blood across her chin.

Mark lifted her by her clean shoulder, just high enough to swing the costumed arm toward her, though he couldn't feel that arm at all anymore. He did feel the reverberation from the impact of his hand against her face, and her skin darkened immediately as she choked back a sob. He hit her again. The girl coughed and spat blood onto the carpet. She folded in on herself, pulling her legs to her chest, head down, fetal in her pain. She wept. There was blood dripping from her mouth, from her teeth now, a bruise blooming into life along her jawline.

He felt as though his blood was electric, supercharged, infinite.

Mark reached down with his good hand and clutched a handful of her hair, dragging her across the room, her screams carrying through the house, and when they reached the stairs, he simply pulled harder, until she was struggling to get to her feet, struggling to make the stairs without being banged against each one as her captor made his way to the second floor.

"*Please*," Georgia cried again, "I won't come back, I'll never come back, please, where's my mom, what the *fuck did you do to my mom, you piece of shit—*"

Mark's foot connected with her stomach so hard he swore he could feel her spine, and she gasped before dry-heaving all over his bare feet, rivulets of saliva hanging from her lips. He slid the costumed arm under her, then clutched her under the armpit with his free hand and picked her up, slinging her over his shoulder, as he began toting his trophy up the rickety wooden steps into the attic. She pounded her fist into his shoulder, and he grinned. He was certain that he grinned, though he was unable to even feel it under the costume.

Georgia couldn't see her captor smile under the mask as he stuffed her into the attic wardrobe, delighting at how perfectly she fit, though he noticed that her left arm, the one he'd gored with the scissors, was clumsily laid across her body, which, as he quickly discovered, kept him from latching the doors.

"People know I'm here," she wheezed. "Please, I am fucking *begging you*, just stop—"

Her screams as the bones in her elbow snapped in his hands were so loud he could hardly think, but that was quickly silenced as he closed the wardrobe, latched it, and breathed deeply. Christ, it was hard to think; the girl shrieking in agony from the wooden box, his body and arm numb, the waves and undulations of sound, music, voices, fucking Christ, enough, *enough*.

She would keep ... for a while. The air holes drilled in the side—*why were there air holes in the side? Tony, what the fuck did you do? What the fuck is happening to me? Where am I*—would give her enough oxygen to keep her going, and she'd shut the fuck up once she passed out from the pain of her broken arm.

Pain controls the body, he thought. He'd read that somewhere, an article in *National Geographic* or something. Pain response was what kept the body going.

Moments later, Mark sat in the living room again, staring at the empty space on the floor where Georgia had lain, moments before, staring into space through the eye slits in the costume. Blood on the carpet. The smell of burning. Jasmine, but fire. Oil.

Death.

And what I feel in my heart, they tell sincerely, no other words can tell it half so clearly...

Seeing her suffer felt so good, and goddamn, goddamn God almighty Christ in Heaven, he loved her so much.

48

The rain was coming down so hard that Ann had to pull the rental over at a truck stop called Sapp Bros., complete with a big, neon percolator promising hot coffee and comfort food. She sat at an old-school diner counter, nursing a cup of coffee, watching through the window for the rain to abate even a little; she was only an hour or so from Galesburg, if that. A pleasant, middle-aged redhead named Rosemary refilled her cup.

"Coming down," Rosemary said plainly, pouring herself a cup of coffee as well, clinking it against Ann's cup. "Much needed. Been dry as a desert in gosh-darned Hades around here, last few weeks."

"Is it supposed to stop any time soon?" Ann said, trying to keep the irritated edge out of her voice. Of all times. She needed to get home, Goddamn it, did she need to get home, but there was no cutting through this wall of water.

"No idea," Rosemary shrugged. She leaned on the counter with her elbows, sighing as she watched out the window. She ran her fingers along where a gold chain sat along her neckline. "Kids got me this for Mother's Day, but damn if this cheap stuff doesn't give me a rash. Sweet, though." She smiled at the thought, then frowned at Ann. "You headed far?"

"Galesburg," Ann replied.

"Be a while, probably," Rosemary sighed. "You want somethin', hon? Got some good meatloaf, got a roasted chicken plate with potatoes if you're hungry." She turned and called over her shoulder. "Ben? You got salmon back there?"

"Swimmin' upstream and ready to party," a male voice called from the rectangular kitchen window on the other side of the counter.

Rosemary turned back and smiled at Ann. "You heard the man."

"I'm okay," Ann said curtly, sipping her coffee, checking her texts again. Nothing from Mark, nothing from anyone. She'd come home to exactly what she'd feared; she was an island with no connections to anything back in the States. What she'd imagined being a liberating sense of freedom was now a claustrophobic nightmare, thanks to whatever the fuck might be transpiring at home.

Maybe nothing, she thought. *Maybe you're freaking out about absolutely nothing.* She texted her brother.

[Ann: Hey, you okay?]

"Suit yourself," Rosemary said with a cursory shrug, slowly pivoting on her heels to saunter back toward the kitchen. "Just, you said you had a long flight, thought maybe—"

"Wait," Ann said. She was starving, and the rain was relentless; she was stuck. Fuck all, but she was stuck and she might as well wait it out safely. "Wait, I'm sorry. I'm just... I'm keyed up. Yeah, let's, um, let's have that salmon."

"Ben!" Rosemary called, no more insistent than she'd been before. "Get that salmon going!"

"You want wings on that fish?" came the response from the kitchen.

Ann looked at Rosemary for guidance, and Rosemary smiled knowingly. "You want veggies on the side with that, hon?"

"Sure," Ann replied. "Yeah, sure, that sounds good."

"Make it fly, Ben!" Rosemary called to the kitchen.

"Boom shak-a-laka!" Ben replied, and the hot, sizzling sound of meat hitting an oiled grill exploded from the kitchen.

"Comin' up, hon," Rosemary winked, tapping the counter and walking away as Ann tapped into Google on her phone. Galesburg Public Safety. She hit 'call' and waited.

"Galesburg Police Department, Sally speaking," came the female voice. "To whom can I direct your call?"

"Um, I—" Ann paused. Was she being ridiculous? Was there a need for this, really, beyond her paranoia and Tony's bizarre revelations? "Is there a—is there a Lieutenant Auster on duty?"

"And whom should I say is calling?"

"Um, Ann Devold."

"Just a minute."

Ann leaned on the counter with the phone pressed against her ear. *This was nothing reasonable*, she thought. *Nothing about this situation made any—*

"Ms. Devold, this is Lieutenant Auster." He paused, and she could hear his hesitant confusion through the line. "What, uh, to what can I attribute this call?"

"Bill, it's Ann. I—is Mark okay?"

"What does that mean, Ms. Devold?" There was something happening in the background, chatter and noises, and blips of electronic devices and CBs. "I don't know where he is right now, if that's what you mean. Is everything okay?"

"No," Ann said flatly, "everything is not okay. I need you to check on the house."

Another moment of pause. "Which house?"

"Bill, I just got off a flight from South America five hours ago, and I'm exhausted, and I need you to stop being so goddamn formal with me!" Ann realized that she was shouting.

Rosemary glanced at her from the kitchen doorway, and an old man slowly making his way through a turkey melt and reading *Guns & Ammo* looked over his shoulder at her.

"Bill, I need you to go check on Mark. As soon as you can."

A radio squawk. "Why, if I can ask?"

"Because I think," she started before pausing, "I think that my brother is not in a good place. For a variety of reasons. Just see that he's okay, please?"

She heard Auster sigh, and there was a shift in the background as though he'd entered an enclosed space, maybe a car. "That's ... okay, yeah, Ann. I will. We got another call earlier, actually, about Mark."

"What about him?" Ann felt her heart racing as Rosemary appeared from the kitchen with the salmon and veggie platter, setting it down and starting into a

CHAPTER 48

spiel before Ann held her hand up to indicate a need for silence. "Why? From who? What about?"

"From a..." Bill trailed off. "...from a Georgia Blevin."

"Yeah, that, that's probably right, okay, so—"

"That's Cory Blevin's daughter," Bill said, unable to keep the concern from his voice. "I didn't get the message until just a few minutes before you—listen, Ann, do you have a number where I can call you back? We're at a pretty nasty car accident right now, and the rain is really pounding, but I'm happy to follow up, I—"

"Yeah," Ann said, reciting her phone number once, twice, then a third time, number by number as though she was teaching a kindergarten class. "Please call me back, Bill, please."

"Yeah, I will, I—gonna have to—limited resources to—sure everything is ok—" The line went dead, victim to shitty reception in general, perhaps the fault of the storm. *Goddamn, goddamn, goddamn.*

Mark was fine. She knew that, in her soul and her bones. He would be fine. He had to be fine. He had to be.

"How's that salmon, hon?" Rosemary said, appearing suddenly at the counter to watch the rain again. Ann took a small bite from the edge of the roasted fish, smiling and holding up her fork, attempting, against all else, to sublimate her fear.

"Great," Ann grimaced, reaching for her purse. "Give me the check."

49

Georgia tried to feel safe in the darkness.

There were thin reeds of light coming through what looked like air holes drilled into the wardrobe, but the doors were closed—latched with something heavy, from what she could tell—and she could think, or try to, through the pain.

Mark had thought that she was her mother. He had called her Cory. This was more than just a house with Tony Devold's bad juju. Something deeper and more inexplicable was at work. It was that costume, she was sure of that, but why, how, that was beyond her.

Georgia had figured out how to keep from moving her arm, and the flesh was fully numb now, a cumbersome slab of meat with two big holes in it; the darkness was a blessing on that front, as she couldn't see the state of the injury. The pain was unlike anything she could have imagined before, and she might lose it once she got out, so she had to learn to work through the pain. There was no telling when Mark would be back, when he would check on her or pull her from

CHAPTER 49

the antique closet just to beat her again, or worse. She had to think.

As he'd dragged her into the attic, she hadn't noticed windows as he pushed her into the wardrobe, so she couldn't count on being able to break out that way, enduring a drop from the second floor into the bushes or the yard. The issue was that she had no leverage; there seemed to be no way for her to gather the necessary strength to push against the clasp that held the wardrobe shut. Without that, she had no choice, she realized grimly, but to wait.

Unless...

Though her back and shoulder were pressed to the hardwood, somehow, Georgia heard something behind her, felt hands slipping over her shoulders. In the darkness in front of her, something began to coalesce from shadow, shades of black on black, like threads of smoke beginning to swirl together.

Her mother's face just inches from hers, grinning, eyes nothing but empty holes, that leathery mask inside the costume, pulled tight over her face.

"Cut, honey," Cory said through clenched, bleeding teeth. "The doctor is on his way."

Georgia closed her eyes as she fumbled with her pants pocket, fighting hard against the pain in her dead arm as she felt the hot breath of the thing pretending to be her mother on her cheek.

50

Mark had woken out of a dead sleep on the couch to the sound of someone upstairs, or so he thought, but of course, he'd been dreaming. There was no one in the house, and why would there be? He got up, stretched, and went into the downstairs bathroom. The bags under his eyes were like Samsonite, to borrow one of Brute's old phrases. His hand hurt like he'd punched someone. He winced, flexing his fingers; there were smears of blood all over his hands.

What the hell?

Mark washed his face—wide awake now—and watched the water go from pink to clear, his hands still throbbing, then went to the kitchen, and made a small pot of coffee before slowly making the rounds from room to room in the dark, checking all the windows. Locked, all locked, along with the doors. The clock in the hall said 3:40 a.m. He was certain he'd heard someone crying upstairs. A woman weeping. That's what had woken him up. Someone had said his name, and then the weeping, and then he was awake.

CHAPTER 50

Crossing into the hallway, Mark had barely started up the stairs when he noticed the blood. Splotches of it, leading upstairs.

"Who's up there?" he called. He breathed quietly, carefully, listening for anything that sounded off. *Fuck it, call the bluff.* "Cops are on the way."

Nothing.

Call Auster.

To do what? There would be questions, and questions required answers, and there were no answers to be had here. Mark moved up the stairs carefully, noticing that the blood trailed off the closer he got to the top. There were some smudges on the wall, but otherwise, nothing.

It had to be his blood, he considered, since there was no one else there.

No one else.

Mark went into the kitchen, where the costume sat at the kitchen table, propped up in a chair, and slumped forward a little as though the thing was drifting toward sleep. Mark sat down across from it with a cup of coffee, tracing the rim with his fingertip, letting the steam slither through his fingers. Thinking.

Sleep was off the table, for all intents and purposes; there had been times since moving to Brute's place that he'd taken sleeping pills and sat downstairs in the kitchen, in the dark, waiting to fade, tired of lying in bed and staring up at the ceiling. It felt like being in a hospital, sometimes, and he was growing to hate the bed. Maybe he would sleep in the living room for a while. The sounds of the neighborhood were still getting to him, the vacuous quality of silence, offset by the endless sounds of... well, who knew what?

The house is settling.

Mark got up, dumped his coffee in the sink, and rested his elbows on the counter. God, he was tired. He texted Cory.

[Mark: Where are you?]

Stepping out onto the back patio, Mark took a deep breath of the cool night air, closing his eyes.

Maybe living at Brute's hadn't been the best idea.

Nothing as cliched as "you can't go home again" or something like that, but maybe it had led him to—as Tony once told him—spend too much time in his own head. There was something about trying to reconcile the current version of one's self with a past version of one's self, and each time that came up, Mark found his memories cutting out on him. There were the happy ones, like holidays and late nights spent with Brute at the kitchen table talking about life, but there were also obscure, troubling motes of strangeness like the Polaroids and the minor blackouts he'd been having that led to ... well, a trail of blood up the hallway stairs. Slashing himself open in the garage. Regina, Dara, the ... things in the grove. Cory's fluctuating moods that seem to be related to her being in the house: crying with happy tears one minute, sleepwalking and spouting creepy gibberish another, then ghosting him altogether. Georgia finding the costume.

The costume.

Mark watched a lean coyote poke its head from the cornfield and look around comically before disappearing back into the stalks to pursue a skittering critter for its

CHAPTER 50

meal. There was something beyond understanding at work all around him.

Just admit it, he thought to himself. *You don't even have to say it out loud if you don't want to. But admit it.*

The house was haunted.

The costume was moving around on its own; of that, Mark was certain. What he had taken for granted as dreams the first few times was starting to feel more like a feverish, twilight reality when he slept. It watched him, on its own, standing over his bed. He could hear movement in the house, and from time to time, it sounded like the attic hatch was being opened and closed at random times throughout the night. Dreams? Surely, but at what point did a person know when those cracks between the rational world and whatever was beyond it got big enough to move through?

He'd get in the car and go to Cory's house. Fuck the whole thing. Fuck the torturous memories of his daughter Lily and what might have been, fuck Brute's house and going through all of the old family stuff—he'd let Ann tackle it when she got home from South America—fuck their checkered history, from his mother's mental illness to Tony's savage, inexplicable crimes, to the alcoholism looming over him a little longer each day.

Mark turned to walk back inside when he saw the sudden plume of flame on the horizon. Just past the drive-in, across the highway, a dot of orange light leaped into being, as though gasoline had been squirted on a distant campfire.

Charlie Barrow's backyard.

What the hell was Charlie doing starting a bonfire at 4:00 in the morning?

JUNKMAN

Maybe he should drive to Charlie's first, then head to Cory's place.

No. Something about his last encounter with Charlie, that sad ghost of a house, the whole thing had left him feeling a little less than crazy about the idea of just rolling up and checking in unannounced.

At the same time...

Mark considered cutting through the field, but he also wasn't crazy about the idea of getting lost in a cornfield. There was little to no traffic this late at night anywhere in Galesburg, much less on the outskirts, so Mark locked the back door and began moving quickly along the edge of the field, just off the shoulder of Day Street until it turned into South Seminary and wound into the country. A car went by, and Mark ducked into the looming stalks before the headlights could catch him. He wasn't sure why, but he didn't want to be seen.

51

The wind began to pitch and swirl, jerking the tarp that covered the front of Charlie's house back and forth with threatening confidence. Mark stood just behind it in the empty shell of what had once been the Barrows' living room. There was a brick wall in front of him, scorch marks all along the edges where pieces of the walls had come apart in the blaze, and the remnants of a chimney still stood in futile loyalty to the surroundings that had long abandoned it. The fire he'd seen from his own backyard was nothing more than a cylindrical blaze in a burn barrel a few yards from Charlie's makeshift back patio, but Mark could see no reason for it as he'd quickly inventoried the backyard before stepping inside. There was no sign of Charlie.

The metal door leading to Charlie's modified living space was open, and Mark stepped into the kitchen, the smell of something sharp and rotten hitting his nostrils, strong enough to make his eyes water. The couch where he'd sat and had beers with Charlie just a few nights before was piled with men's clothes, as though someone had been sorting them.

Mark stepped through the kitchen and into the hallway that led to the bedrooms and bathroom. He wasn't sure why, but he didn't want to call out, didn't want to draw attention to the fact that he was there. He paused in the open doorway of the second bedroom, where Charlie had shown him the Frankenstein decoration he was building; it was dark beyond the threshold, and from somewhere in the room came a muffled cry. Mark's eyes struggled against the near darkness, and after a moment, he reached out and clicked on the light.

"It's cool, Mark." Charlie stood in the center of the room, and his voice was even, calm, and muffled by the costume over his head. *It's impossible*, Mark thought. *It was in my kitchen just a few minutes ago. It can't be here.* Charlie was naked, the ridges of rippled, burn-scarred flesh giving away to unblemished patches of skin at random points, like a topographical map of injury. He stroked his rigid cock with violent snaps of his wrist, and Mark could see now the two human forms on the floor in front of him.

There was Adrian, bound with his wrists behind his back and gagged with what looked like a dish towel. His clothes were unnatural shades of their original colors from having been soaked in now-dried blood, and there was a ragged bite taken out of his shoulder. He was alive, weakly breathing, and occasionally given to a burst of struggle.

Next to him, hands bound in a similar fashion, gagged with an old t-shirt, was Cory.

She stopped struggling momentarily when she saw Mark, the confusion in her eyes saying everything, and

CHAPTER 51

when Adrian saw Mark, the captive's eyes grew wide, pleading, kicking his feet as though he was trying to start a motorcycle. Within seconds, Mark saw Charlie's orgasm splatter across Adrian's face and shoulder. Charlie groaned, then—there was no other word for it, Mark thought—roared from behind the costume's headpiece as Adrian weakly attempted to size up the room, his odds of escape from whatever had been set in motion here.

"Caught him creeping your place one night last week," Charlie said, his voice deep and muffled. "Happened to be there, looking for my friend here, and then it occurred to me that I might get a twofer."

"Jesus," Mark said. "At my house? He was—you were in *my house*?"

"In your garage," Charlie corrected. "But yeah, it used to be out there, ol' scarecrow on the post. You moved in, and I figured you took it inside. So I figured it wouldn't be long before you were part of things. I got tired of waiting—sorry, man, I didn't mess with anything else." He pointed at Adrian. "Well, I mean, him, but you don't give a fuck about that, I'm guessing." Charlie stepped backward, minding Adrian's periodic kicks at nothing, and put his arm around Mark's shoulder, giving him an affectionate squeeze. "Her, I knew you'd care about that. I knew you'd come back after last time, and you might as well see it."

"See what?" Mark whispered; he was going to vomit, was sure he was going to vomit, a pain in his stomach and behind his eyes, as though his body was fighting against the scene playing out in front of him. "Charlie, you have to let her go. Please."

Charlie stepped back, breathing heavily, his cock glistening with his seed, arms hanging limply at his sides. It called to mind the sight of some primordial creature emerged from a swamp or a dark cave, a being learning the contours of its own existence. "There are so many inside it now."

Mark watched as Charlie lowered himself to his hands and knees, straddling the length of Adrian's body. The paper had been torn and pulled away from the face, revealing a withered, mummified visage—the product of Brute's fight for survival in the Pacific. *Christ Jesus, this is what he meant? He actually cut off someone's face?* Charlie's body buckled and quivered, and Mark could see now how the shorn face had something behind it, as though someone was pushing putty against it to shape it, the cheeks puffing a little, the chin sharpening, something like a dog or a wolf's muzzle now pressing the mouth from the ragged, lipless slit into something slavering, laden with teeth. There was a moaning sound from inside it now, a dull expression of something like pain, the sound rising into ecstasy, euphoria, and rage. Whatever the thing was that had emerged from deep inside the costume—from Charlie, despite Mark's logical brain denying that possibility—the soldier's shorn face had stretched to accommodate the mouthful of savage-looking teeth. *Like an animal wearing a Halloween costume,* he thought dumbly.

Adrian renewed his struggle, eyes wide in horror at the sight of the dead thing moving on top of him, and then it pressed its dripping muzzle to the flesh of his stomach. He screamed into his makeshift gag, the sound so raw that it made Mark's own throat hurt a little. Blood bubbled from around Adrian's lips where they met the towel, and Mark could see the head of the thing pressing into Adrian now, tearing into him and ripping away thick, uneven chunks of flesh, patches of bone already visible. Mark dropped to his knees, open-mouthed and weeping, and even as he saw the blood rolling over his knees, wet and warm and sticky through the denim of his jeans, and even as he heard Cory's muffled shrieks next to him, he felt very far away, as if watching the scene unfold through a lens.

"It's gotta eat," Charlie explained, his voice little more than a guttural series of grunts now. "Whatever's inside that thing, it's gotta eat, and if you're good to it, and you get it fed, it'll be good to you. You ain't never shot a load like you shoot with that thing on, the things it shows you? Jesus, man." He hovered over the remnants of Adrian's corpse, staring. "The things that go through some peoples' heads... fuckin' incredible, but it's ... easy to get confused." Charlie fell back into a sitting position, wheezing a little as though what had just happened had exhausted him. He put a comforting hand on Mark's shoulder, and his voice was soft again, reassuring. "What's it shown you, man?"

"What do you mean?" Mark said, staring at Cory, whose eyes were wet and pleading.

"What's it shown you from other people? See, it takes things from the people who wear it. Painful things, things that their brains just ... want to get rid of. It collects things, as far as that goes. And then it just has those things rattling around in there until they take some kind of shape. All those bad memories, wicked shit people think about... that's what it turns 'em into. These things you see. They're real, sometimes, and sometimes not. It kinda ... spits up, you might say. Tony showed it to me, the first few times, and fuck, he was right, poor bastard. He just let it swallow him up, which I guess I understand. It gets in your head, and it shows you stuff from out of other peoples' heads that's tough to take sometimes. But, I think, sometimes it plays tricks, you know; it tries to ... amuse itself. So what's it shown you? Shit, man, it has shown me some *stuff*. Your uncle was a twisted motherfucker, dude. And your sister—damn, brother. " He reached over and clutched something from a folding chair, handing them to Mark. "These pictures, the ones your uncle Tony took of your sister? These were a nice little bonus when I found this one at your place. You knew they were fucking, right?"

Mark felt ripples in his stomach, his throat. He was going to vomit. He was folding into himself. *You spend too much time in your own head—*

"Yeah, him and Annie, you know, he was... well, the two of them were doing what they shouldn't have been... when she was young. I've seen her in there ... a lot. I think he must have worn this thing when he fucked her, 'cause I've seen her before. One night, I picked this girl up at Cherry Street, got her a little high, and brought her home. Wore that thing after she passed out, and I never even saw her, you know, during. I saw Ann. That's a complicated shit of a scenario, Mark. I'm not gonna lie, and there were others."

Others, Mark thought. *Dara Ensinger. Regina Marling. Other girls that Tony used and killed. You.*

Charlie stood up and steadied himself with his hands on his hips—a foreman sizing up a work site. "Like, one time? I saw this middle-aged lady, your typical MILF, and she was crawling around on the floor like an animal, and she was eating dead animals, like eating a dead rat? But she didn't have any feet. She was lopped off at the calves—these nasty, ragged chops, and she had these fucked-up eyes like, stuck in her face, her cheeks. I don't know what that was, but I think it might have just been something random it had to spit out. Another time, I saw dead soldiers all over the yard. Sometimes they overlap, and you get confused, like, I look at you, but maybe you're not you... you're my dad, or you're someone else. Your uncle, you know, he was wearing that the night he killed those people. I think he got confused, too. He said he used to wear it a lot, and some of the things I see... when I wear it? Definitely from your uncle, man. Some pretty weird shit, and not all of it good. He liked kids. Well, I mean." He chuckled and gave a sheepish shrug. "Not *only* kids, not for the most part, but there's kids in there, at times."

"What is... how..." Mark stared at the mess of bones and soggy, bloody meat on the floor in front of him, enough of Adrian's face still intact to be recognizable, though just barely. It had taken Adrian's cheeks, peeling them back off the bone like chicken, the skin around his mouth so his beard was only stubby patches of hair, here and there. Cory sobbed, no longer looking at Mark, though he tried so hard to get her to look at him, just to look at him, stay fixed on him, so he could change this, somehow.

"God, I hate this town." Charlie sank down onto the stained twin mattress, pants still open, cock drooping his lap as he slipped off the costume and lit a cigarette. "Everything that happened, you know, I—"

"Charlie, look," Mark offered, trying to find his words again. "I know that things were... were bad after the fire—"

The redheaded man howled with laughter, and the sound sent a bolt of memory through Mark, smoking cigarettes at the drive-in, trying to break into cars out by the old Maytag factory, Charlie's braying laugh woven into the soundtrack of those days. "Shit, man, it started before that. Fuckin' old man drunk all the time. You know that motherfucker just let my dog die? When I was five? Yeah. Just didn't fuckin' feed it. Dog took off looking for food. Pops left the door open, and Wags got hit on 67. After that, I tried to poison that motherfucker, mixed some D-Con into his scrambled eggs one time. He threw the plate at my mom instead; something got under his skin. Mission failed." Charlie snickered at his own joke. "The fire was just part of it. Fuckin' Jackie, my older brother, all the shit he did, police fuckin' hated our family, man. Whole town, everyone did. The fire... that fire just happened because that old piss-pot got scared."

"Of what?" Mark's eyes drifted from Cory to the wet mess that had been Adrian and back again. *I'll fix this*, he tried to say with his eyes.

"Of me." Charlie stood up, fastened his pants, and pointed at the costume on the floor. "Of that."

"I don't understand," Mark said. "That was... that was at our house, at Brute's house."

"Goddamn, you really don't remember? After that Halloween, after I wore the suit, the stuff I saw that night." He scratched the back of his head; his patchy red hair didn't look like it'd been washed in weeks, clumping together. "I remember lying here, on the couch, wearing that thing. And seeing sky, right? Like my house had no roof. And I was lying on the beach, I was on my couch, you understand, but I could feel sand.

CHAPTER 51

On my back. And I heard men screaming, and I felt this hot fucking pain all around my face, but that sky, man, it was cloudless and black and starry and beautiful. And I just thought, fuck this roof, fuck this house, fuck all of it. I wanted to die. Isn't that the fuckin' irony for you? I wanted to just die, and I wanted to take some motherfuckers with me.

"Old man gets home, drives his car up on the fuckin' lawn, man, on the *lawn*. Runs over some patio furniture. Comes inside, babbling about some bullshit, sees me in that costume, and says 'that's some shit costume you got there.' But you know what, Mark, and here's what's crazy. I didn't see my dad. It wasn't *him* talking shit. It was my mom. But then it was *your* mom. And my head started to hurt, fucking awful, man, and I just ... walked away. From him. I went to bed. Well." Charlie finished his cigarette and dropped it on the floor. "I didn't exactly go to bed. I fell asleep wearing that thing. Hearing voices, some of them I recognized, some of them were in different languages. Japanese or Chinese or some shit. And when I'd look around, I'd just see things ... wrong. It was my house, but it wasn't; then it was your house, the backyard, and then it was like I was underwater, only the water was like ... fluid. Like I was in the fucking womb again, you know what I mean? These blue coils, these ropy fingers clutching at me, but it was peaceful, you know? When I'd open my mouth, I'd swallow that shit, whatever I was floating in, and it had this ozone taste, but it helped me float, I guess, I was floating through it. And that's when I smelled smoke, when I was down in that hole, in my head, in that fucking costume. I woke up and went out in the living room, and my dad was crying and setting stuff on fire, lighting up furniture and whatever would take, and he just looked at me—I was still wearing that thing—and he just starts screaming at me. Just screaming, no words, just rage, like I was everything that ever went fucking sideways for him, you know? And I just sat down. On the floor. He was kicking me and screaming at me, but I didn't feel it, you know, it was like this thing was protecting me. And then he started screaming because he was on fire, too. That was a different kind of scream, brother, let me tell you.

"So, look, here's something," Charlie went on. "I had a thing for Cory, and Cory never went for me, but I'm cool with that. None of the popular girls ever really did. But goddamn, man, honestly, I'd love to get her in this mix, and you can still enjoy her that way, too." Charlie stood up, reached for something on the dresser, and held it up. A hunting knife. "Put it on for me, Mark, okay?"

"Why?"

Charlie sighed as though growing impatient. "Because it's still fuckin' hungry, Mark, and there's no one left but the three of us, alright? Put the damn thing on, or I'll have to cut you. Or her. Or fuckin' both of you, I don't know—"

"Okay, okay." Mark kneeled near where Adrian had lain moments before; Cory was close enough to touch, and God, he wanted to touch her, hold her, but he had to be smart about this, had to play this in a way that kept them safe until he could get to Charlie's knife...

"You wanna grab that for me, or do I have to do this?" Charlie said.

"Yes, Jesus Christ, man, okay," Mark said, his own impatience starting to feel as though it was coming through his pores, a bile-sick rage. Cory stared, her eyes

CHAPTER 51

wide, glistening with tears, her makeup streaking down her cheeks and forming a wet, black stain across the top of the t-shirt in her mouth. Mark reached for the costume, sticky at the edges, a rancid, meaty smell making him gag a little as he carefully slid his body inside it. *Stay with me,* Mark mouthed without sound before putting the thing over his head. *I love you. We'll be okay.* Mark struggled for a moment with the eyeholes, and then he found Cory, writhing in her bonds, whimpering desperately.

Sshh, he wanted to say, *it's going to be okay, I love you, we're going to get out of this, this isn't real, you're not real, Adrian was never here, we're going to be safe, I love you, I love you, I love you...*

He felt the tip of Charlie's knife at his back as he found a position over Cory's body. Mark trembled as Cory made eye contact with him, and just as he started to speak, he felt a hot pain radiate from the base of his spine all the way to his head, *fuck,* he could feel it in his brain, and then he couldn't see anything, just a white, hot hunger. He felt the thing's face against his begin to ripple and pulse, and then there was nothing but screams.

Mark could taste Cory's blood, her flesh, a coppery taste that filled his mouth, his throat, dripping from the thing's chin. He vomited, which was sucked back into the costume along with the gnarled, torn chunks of Cory's shoulder, forearm, the bones in her sternum, her breasts, and Mark began screaming then, until it felt like he had no air, and it could only come from inside him as a blood-soaked gasp.

After a time—how much he couldn't say—Mark opened his eyes, and stared, through the slits in the mask, at something white. A piece of Cory's skull, he realized, and he coughed, spat, forgetting that he still wore the costume as a mixture of phlegm and blood dripped along his cheek. He felt a hand on his shoulder.

That's why the ground in the grove was always so soggy. Thick with blood. That's where it fed, all these years that it hung out there on the goddamn cross. Where Tony brought it victims. That's where he fucked up, Mark thought. *He went to Dara, sought her out to hurt me, with Lily. No one knew about the ones in the grove. He could've gone on for who knew how long.*

"Go ahead and take it home, if you want," Charlie said, his voice soft and almost comforting. "It'll make sure I can find it. I'm not worried about that. It comes and goes as it pleases. You been through a lot tonight, man, and I appreciate it. Just do me a favor and leave it outside again? On the scarecrow post? It's easier for it to get to animals and stuff that way. The fuckin' headaches, when it's really hungry? Like to rip your goddamn head in half. You been getting headaches?"

"Yes," Mark croaked meekly. *I don't want to take it home; I don't want anything anymore,* Mark felt like saying, *I don't want to take it,* but that wasn't true, was it? Because he hadn't known how it needed to be fed, he just knew that high that came with wearing the thing, and the things—the horrible, forbidden things—it showed him. *Cory, fucking Christ in Heaven, Cory, baby, I'm sorry, I'm sorry, I'm so—*

Mark sobbed into the thing, and why didn't he just reach up and take it off? Why couldn't he just do that? He wobbled to his feet, still wearing the costume and watching Charlie scoop up the bones that were left on the floor, sliding them into a paper sack which he then rolled tightly. Charlie's hands—Mark's hands, too, he realized—were caked with gore, as though he'd crawled inside a dead thing. *Which,* he thought, *I guess I have.*

"These'll burn alright," Charlie nodded, then waved to Mark. "Come on."

Mark saw Charlie in front of him, but only in form, a vague shape with a voice attached, as the air between them—the air everywhere around him—was different. Mark felt like he was walking through water, shapes that didn't make sense, shapes that were nearly human but not quite, vibrated into life around him, filling the air. It had been taking little bits of him all along, he realized, and it was so much a part of his consciousness now that he couldn't trust anything he saw. Mark could taste blood in his mouth, and someone reached for him, suddenly, from the couch, from beneath the pile of clothes.

He jumped backward and shouted out loud as the hand clutched at the space where he'd been standing. The arm was thin, like stretched putty, and the fingers were thin, terribly thin, and long. Something beneath the clothes gasped for air, the arm flopping about and the fingers clenching weakly at nothing. Mark reached forward, gathered a handful of fabric in his hand, and pulled the mess of clothes away from the cushions, shouting again, as the thing underneath responded with a yawping cry. He remembered once going hunting with some cousins on his father's side, maybe nine or ten years old, and hearing the sound of a doe with an arrow in her neck, those reedy, bawling sounds that came from inside it as it fought against the inevitable. This was similar, in a way, though he could tell that this thing was trying to speak.

Which, he realized, would be impossible given that it had no discernible mouth that he could see. It was a hodgepodge mess of features set awkwardly in flesh, the way a blindfolded child might poke features into clay in an attempt to create a face. One eye was still, set too tightly in a flat ridge of skin, while the other bulged too much, creating the opposite effect, an eyeball sitting in a socket, lumps that might have been a nose, slits cut into the rest of what Mark took to be the head that more resembled gills than a mouth.

The thing was perhaps four feet tall, tapered at the waist where legs should have begun. Instead, the flesh just twisted into nothing, like a piece of caramel that had been pulled apart. There was no blood to be seen, though the flesh of the thing was discolored and bruised, distorted in spots as though it had been pulled too thin, almost translucent in places, and underneath, things were moving. Mark thought of the view of mold or bacteria under a microscope, the unrecognizable, sickening layers of hidden life in its grotesque simplicity. This was that view, but what was under the skin was teeming with rot, black chunks, like meat left in the sun.

Stretched to an abnormal length on the left side of its head was a long, white scar, the kind that might be the result of getting skimmed with hedge shears, albeit distorted in its current form.

"Tony." Mark heard his voice inside the cast, but he couldn't make the sight of this mockery into what he knew it to be, backing through the door and into the backyard, where Charlie was feeding what was left of Cory and Adrian into a burn barrel, flames licking into the air and causing Charlie's shadow to dance like some sort of misshapen creature.

Have to get this off. Have to get it off, no matter what.

It won't matter. It'll be there, in your head. It's your eyes now, your thoughts, all of it.

Cory.

Have to kill it. Have to kill it, somehow.

Mark dug his fingers into the edges of the costume, the rigid paper sticky with viscera, and winced at the pain in his shoulders, his neck; the thing was digging into his flesh, somehow, holding on.

Cory. Mark felt tears coming, but he couldn't, not yet, couldn't lose it, not yet, not—

"Ah, yeah, let me try that thing on again real quick," Charlie grinned, wrenching the costume from Mark and slipping it on as smoothly as if it was a bathrobe. As he did, Mark saw that Charlie's eyes had hemorrhaged, bloody plumes of color in his pale face that nearly matched his red hair, and there was blood in his teeth. "Oh, my god, fuck yeah. Mark, I don't want to upset you too much, buddy, but Cory is in here, and goddamn, I am gonna have that pussy…"

Charlie began to play with his flaccid cock, still dangling outside his open jeans, as Mark moved past him toward the burn barrel. "Do me a favor, buddy, and drop the rest of those bones there in the fire? Got it all ready, but you showed up just in time to have some fun with me."

"Was your dad trying to burn it?" Mark said, gathering the remaining bones near the base of the barrel.

Charlie was facing away from him now, muttering and giggling, and he stopped short when he heard Mark address him.

"When he burned the house down? Does it burn, Charlie?"

"I guess probably, yeah," Charlie said. "Ain't nothing immune to fire, you know, nothing alive. Gotta be careful. You be good to it, it'll be good to you."

"Good to know," Mark said, and if Charlie noticed the wet sensation of lighter fluid all over his back and legs, he didn't show or acknowledge it, not until Mark pushed over the burn barrel with his foot and the flame swept toward Charlie like a bright orange slash cutting the darkness. Charlie shrieked, something that sounded almost like relief—as the flames engulfed him and the costume.

Something broke inside Mark's head, a brilliant flash of light and something like a primal scream, and he felt it inside him now, as though he was carrying a child, something digging and kicking at his insides, as if writhing in concerted agony.

Mark winced against the pain, crying out now and then, but still he stood fast, clenching his fists and watching it burn, waiting until the flames licked out into nothing, the costume a blackened, misshapen shell of what it had been, along with the man underneath it.

52

His phone was ringing.

Mark forced his eyes open, sucking in a deep breath and coughing violently, as though his lungs hadn't expected to breathe again. He lay on his back, staring at the ceiling. Where the fuck was he? He sat forward and grimaced against the tightness in his stomach; he felt like he'd been in one hell of a fight, or maybe done a hundred sit-ups. Christ, he hurt all over.

Phone.

He looked around the room. The boxy little TV on the kitchen stand was turned on, humming with static. Charlie's. He was at Charlie's house.

Cory.

Fucking Christ in Heaven. His face felt puffy. The skin around his eyes was sensitive from crying. He glanced behind him, out the door, as he scanned the floor for his phone. A scorched oval in the grass about twenty feet from where he lay jogged his memory; in the middle of it lay a blackened corpse, the burn barrel still smoldering with faint, orange embers and wisps of smoke. The sun was rising and cast a dull, amaranthine glow over the grass and shadows.

Phone.

Fuck. There it was, near the couch, half-hidden under a stained blanket that reeked of mold and stale beer.

Stateville.

Mark answered, "I killed it." He waited for his uncle's response on the other end, and a few seconds went by before he heard Tony's deep, raspy voice start to speak.

"Killed what, kiddo?" Tony said quietly.

"You know," he said. "You and Ann. You fucking bastard, you and my goddamn little sister." Mark's gut spasmed suddenly, and he dry-heaved, almost dropping the phone before leaning against the couch and lifting it to his ear again. "You? And Ann? Goddamn you, goddamn you, Tony. Why would you—why—"

"I wish I had good answers for you," Tony said. His uncle's voice was soft, focused. It was unusual to hear him so lucid, perhaps because Mark never heard him speak anymore, perhaps because his uncle had spent so many years drunk or high or generally incoherent that hearing him speak normally was like listening to someone pretending to be his uncle. "I just... I don't, Mark. I'm sorry as hell for what I did to you kids. For everything I did, to everyone."

"So am I," Mark said. "But it's dead now."

"Mark, if you're—" There was a pause and some noise in the background as Tony paused, the sound of a voice over a loudspeaker. "I don't have much time, kid, but if you're talking about that thing? That costume thing that Ann made?"

"Ann?"

CHAPTER 52

"She made it, Mark, and there's something inside it that's ... just bad. It's just bad. You need to make sure you get rid of that damn thing. I don't know how to explain it, but I wouldn't be here now if it wasn't for that fucking costume."

"Sure," Mark scoffed. "Sure, you wouldn't. You fucking degenerate. You killed Regina Marling, didn't you?"

Tony sighed deeply. "And a lot of others. Yeah. Yeah, I did."

"Well, I killed *it*."

There was an exchange away from the receiver, and Tony was back. "I gotta go, Mark. But listen to me. It's like the thing dreams, and what it dreams gets spit out at you in real life. But it's not real stuff... until something is. It takes a little piece of you, and it leaves little pieces of itself behind, too. You give it enough of yourself, and it just becomes part of you. You didn't kill it if you didn't *destroy* the goddamn thing. I tried. I buried it in the goddamn cornfield, and it came back the next day."

"I—burned it." Mark cleared his throat; the smell of hot oil and jasmine had settled in his throat and irritated his sinuses. "I burned the fucker."

"Just make sure you really did," Tony said. "That's all I got. I ... just thought I should call. Do what I could. Your sister's on her way."

"What?" Mark paused, that hot taste in his throat surging. "What did you say?"

"Ann is on her way," Tony said. "For fuck's sake, be safe. Both of you, be safe, Mark."

The call dropped, and Mark slumped back against the couch. Breathing carefully. In and out. In and out.

That was where it came from. Ann had made it. Mark remembered now, a terrible sense memory; perhaps it was spawned from hearing Tony's voice, perhaps from that relentless, cloying smell of Grandma Lynn's jasmine perfume, perhaps just because the whole thing with Charlie had finally shaken it all loose. He remembered the exact afternoon she'd made the damn thing, cast it over Grandma Lynn as she'd slept, and then their mother raising hell about it, so angry at Ann for having disturbed their ailing grandmother's rest.

But why did that make it ... what it was? Lynn's cancer? *There's something inside it that's just bad.*

Mark looked around the room, seeing the decay he hadn't fully noticed before when he'd first visited Charlie. Wallpaper had started to pull away from every wall in the room, from the floor or the ceiling or both, leaving gray, mildewed patches behind it. A spotty, blackened trail of mold had begun creeping from the hot plate and kitchen area up the wall and out of sight around the corner toward the burned-out living room like a fuse. There were bloodstains on the wallpaper leading to the bedrooms, bloodstains on the carpet. Two bloody handprints just a foot or so from the floor marked the entrance to the hallway, as though someone had struggled to get away while being dragged.

Mark steadied himself as he walked down the hall, bracing a palm flat against the wall, looking into each room along the way. The house was a three-bedroom, two-bath, though one bedroom and bath had been lost to the fire in '83. The first of the two remaining bedrooms was more or less a carbon copy of the living area: clothes, dishes, mess, trash. Halfway up the opposite wall from the doorway where he stood was a wide, flat bloodstain, as though someone had been pressed against the wall and shot in the head. Or they'd been crushed, somehow, against the wall, skull cracking like an egg.

He refused to look through the door of the second bedroom.

The bathroom was a horrid affair. Mold spread in a measly pattern across the gaudy, striped wallpaper, over the shower and gathered vinyl curtain, down to the lid of the toilet and sink counter, as though someone had used a hose to spray rot across the room. The smell was unbearable, and Mark turned away as he saw that the bathtub was occupied by a human form, not entirely visible without stepping closer, which he refused to do: spindly limbs bent at strange angles, a nearly mummified hand clutching the edge of the porcelain, half submerged in mucky, dark water.

Jesus Christ, Mark thought, turning and falling to his knees, slumping against the wall and letting the tears come. For Cory, for Ann, for Tony, for, for, *for fucking fucking fuck fuck why why why why—*

He caught his breath, standing and making his way back down the hallway to the shared living room and kitchen. Beyond the doorway outside, he could see Charlie's burned skeleton kissing the ground.

Now, next to it, was the costume.

Fully intact, albeit with scorch marks around the edges.

You motherfucker.

I tried. I buried it in the goddamn cornfield, and it came back the next day.

Mark took a deep breath, closing his eyes, measuring each inhalation and subsequent exhalation. In. Out. In. Out.

Standing next to Charlie's charred, blackened corpse, his old friend's skull grinning into the dirt, Mark picked up the costume and put it on.

He took a deep breath and waited, waited for the high. It didn't come.

Mark stepped back into the house, carrying the bottle of lighter fluid that he'd dropped in the grass outside just a few hours earlier. It was still half-full, enough to do what he needed it to do.

When he'd checked his mother into Marigold, he'd had a long sit-down with one of the directors there about her condition, what to expect, and how to approach their relationship from that point forward.

"You'll need to be able to frame the idea of retracing steps," the man had said, a youngish black guy with a goatee who scratched at his stubble thoughtfully while they talked. "Part of helping those with this disease is helping them see the path, to get a sense of where they were and how they got there. That can help to provide context for those moments that are emotionally stressful."

Don't I fucking know it, Mark thought. Standing in the doorway of the house, he held the bottle away from his body, spraying the hallway, the living area, the kitchen, the blank space beyond it, everything, before reaching into his pocket and extracting his lighter. The greasy stench of the lighter fluid cut through the slits in the mask, and Mark smiled to himself, thinking of Tony, locked up forever, so stupid, so misguided and unable to take these reins, of Ann, halfway across the fucking world and clueless to everything that had happened, running from everything.

Mark felt the costume dig into his flesh with something like nails, like something about to fall over a cliff.

CHAPTER 52

It doesn't want to die, he thought. *You motherfucker, you poisoned everything. You told Tony to go for Dara and Lily. You've taken everything. Now you want to stay alive. Well, dig in, you son of a bitch. There's nothing left to take.*

He tossed the lighter onto the couch, and the flames erupted to life instantly, spreading across the clothes, the counter, the tarp that separated the room from the front of the house, which yawned across the west side of the property, unimpressed with this same show of force it had endured over thirty years ago. Mark backed into the doorway leading outside, Charlie's bones just a few paces behind him, as the fire slithered into the hallway, overtaking the walls, floor, and ceiling. Whoever found him would think he'd tried to crawl from the house. And if they didn't, there was no one to say otherwise.

Mark turned away from the blaze, walking across the field, the empty highway, toward the ditch along the cornfield that had led him to the end of his human experience the night before.

It was maybe two miles from the Barrow property to Brute's house, and it wound past the drive-in where Mark remembered all the times he and his buddies had gone out there after it shut down to drink and listen to music on that vast, empty lot that had previously been home to dozens and dozens of cars on a Friday or Saturday night. He'd seen *Creepshow* and *The Shining* there on a Halloween double feature bill right before it closed down for good in '92, and he still remembered that thing coming out of the crate, how Cory—they'd still been dating then—had turned away and put her face in his shirt as the hairy monster ate someone alive. The sound of the monster crunching bone through that tinny, mounted speaker.

Eating.

He thought of the old woman at the market that day when he'd been buying the stuff for dinner. How she'd startled at the sight of him, how she'd wept.

She knew. She knew what had already gotten inside you. She could see.

Mark grinned behind the layers of tanned flesh and paper. He felt like every step he took was on a cloud, like a cartoon character dancing through space, the high, the feeling that just, holy shit, it took away everything, it took away—

"Sir?" The voice came from the highway on his left. A car had slowed, and a middle-aged woman with blonde hair was leaning across from the driver's seat, addressing him through the open passenger window. She looked concerned. "Sir, are you okay?"

"Yes," he replied, but she couldn't see his smile, could she, not with the costume on. "Why do you ask?"

The woman narrowed her gaze and glanced down at her lap. Had she made a phone call? It was hard to tell through the mask. He couldn't even fully make out her features. "I—well, honestly, what you're wearing, um—I'm sorry. I just, you looked like—"

"What do I look like?" Mark replied.

The woman sat back in her seat and accelerated quickly, driving away from the costumed man slowly ambling through down the highway's shoulder, a distortion of a person making its way through the clammy autumn morning as the rain began to assert its dominance over the landscape.

53

Mark stood in the backyard for a long time and stared into the grove of trees and bushes, where the brambles came together into thorny fingers.

There were shapes moving there.

He could make out something vaguely resembling Adrian, and Regina Marling was there, along with Lily and her brother. And others. So many others.

Mark sat down in the grass, the bulk of the costume forcing him to lean forward.

Everything looked wrong. Colors had shifted from their correct hues and shades; the grass wasn't exactly green, and the sky wasn't exactly any color that made sense as it spat rain. There was music playing, somewhere far off, and he could hear explosions, screaming, gunfire, from what seemed like a good mile or two away. Whispers of bloodshed and horror on the breeze. He could smell garbage and flames and pussy, and something hot and tangy, like marinated meat.

The girl in the attic. Georgia.

She was still in the wardrobe.

JUNKMAN

Cory was a part of him—of it—now, so it seemed only right that Georgia should join them.

Mark clumsily got to his feet and walked toward the house. He could feel it inside him, that hunger that Charlie had talked about. He was so hungry that he felt nauseous. He locked the back door behind him and started through the kitchen, toward the stairs.

Cory stood in the doorway of the living room.

Ann stood in the doorway of the living room. Her suitcase sat a few feet behind her, and she still had her coat on.

Mark had come in through the back door, and when he came into her view, it was all she could do to not sob outright. His clothes were pocked with dirt and smears of mud, and he wore the cast she'd made, the suit for the death mask. When he saw her, he simply stopped moving, a creature made of stone.

"Mark." She tried to keep her voice from shaking. "Mark, you have to take that off."

"Can't." His voice was dull and thick, as though he'd been drinking. "Won't come off anymore, babe."

"Mark, listen to me. It's dangerous. It's why Tony did what he did. There's something… something inside it that does things—to your head, whoever wears it. It's my fault, I put it in there. I think Grandpa B brought it home from the war."

"I know." Flat; empty. His cautious stance loosened now; his shoulders slumped forward a little, a mannequin in a store window. "I miss you, baby. I need to see you."

CHAPTER 53

Ann paused. Mark wasn't talking to her; she could tell that from the tone of his voice. It was something disconnected and distant. There was a pang of something sour inside her as she realized that her brother was gone.

"I miss you, too," she noted tentatively, stepping forward. She reached for her back pocket, the folding knife there, slipping it out and flipping the blade open, her breath catching in her throat. There was something—"I need you to come outside with me, okay?" If she could get the thing off of him, she could talk to him, figure it out, reason with him. To the front porch, maybe twenty feet behind her. "I can explain everything, if you just come with me..."

Twenty feet.

You can do this.

He is not your brother.

Ann stepped forward, and Mark was on her before she could even respond. Her head snapped sideways as Mark slapped her, hard, his hand clutching her throat, pinning her to the carpet the moment she hit the ground, kicking against his thighs and crotch, gasping, her head dropping back against the carpet to look toward the door, reaching for it.

"God," Mark moaned, on top of her, and he was ripping at her jeans now, "I fucking miss you, Cory, I want you so much, I miss you, I love you, I'm sorry..."

Ann tried to scream, but it came out like a muted growl as Mark pushed her shoulders into the ground, his palm pushing against the side of her throat, and he was tearing at her pants now, pulling them open, half off now, and there was a primal rage inside her now, *no, no, no, no, no,* a sob choked off in her throat as she freed her right arm, gathering all the strength she could as she clenched her shoulder muscles and felt—

———

"Cory," Mark groveled, and he was crying now, Cory looking up at him with such sadness, the ridges under her eyes from her own tears like dull streaks of pencil lead, and she looked old, suddenly, for the first time.

Mark pressed his face into the flesh of her neck, kissing, biting—

She was in the south hallway, outside of the library, walking toward him with her best friend, Maria. Fake snakeskin boots and a black skirt, ash blonde hair pulled into a loose ponytail, bright red lipstick, laughing at something Maria said, and that smile hit him like he'd tripped over a live wire: electric, paralyzing. Then again, all these years later, outside the DMV after Brute's funeral, getting into her car, seeing her for the first time in twenty years. She was everything he'd wanted and everything he knew he'd screwed up, and if he could just have her, he'd make everything alright. Tasting her would keep him from feeling—

———

—sick, and Ann finally found her scream as she felt her brother pressing against her, attempting to have his way with her; with all her strength, she caught him under the chin with the butt of her palm. Mark's head jerked back, and she heard him choke inside the mask from the shock of the impact. She got up quickly as he stumbled backward into the hallway near the stairs, tripping over his own feet, and Ann ran, through the living room, past where Mark lay groaning on the floor, struggling to get up from the bulk of the costume. Through the kitchen, past the open basement door where she heard indistinct sounds, and out the back door into the yard.

She couldn't leave him, not with whatever was happening. Ann sucked air, hands on her knees, staring into the mess of trees and briars at the back of the property. It was the same as when Tony wore the cast all those years ago, the things he'd say, things that made sense and then suddenly didn't, grotesque suggestions as to what he would do to her ... and to other women. Kids. How it wrought strange, violent impulses from somewhere deep inside him.

And he'd eventually done it. To Dara Ensinger and her children, to the others he'd talked about during their visit, to however many more. She felt the hot taste of vomit burst from her lips and into the grass, and she sucked in the fresh air, filling her lungs again and again, her palms flat on the ground.

Somewhere behind her—inside the house—came the sound of a woman's scream.

Ann turned and began crawling, fumbling into action, back toward the house, not noticing how the shadows had begun to collect in the grove just past the tree line: eyes in the dark, shapes that hadn't quite reconciled themselves into recognizable forms.

54

Georgia coughed and spat, not realizing how much dust she'd sucked in through clenched teeth, straining and groaning against her broken arm, her free hand dropping the handful of cards onto the floor. Her bus pass, credit card, student ID; together, they'd been thick enough to slip between the doors of the wardrobe and work the latch loose from the inside. She tried to hold back the urge to cough, which made her need to cough even harder. She strained for breath, hacked into her sleeve, then wavered on her feet for a moment as pain surged through her side. She fell to the floor and fought the urge to vomit.

Was there anyone in the house? She thought she'd heard voices downstairs, but they were gone now. There had been screams, a struggle, perhaps. Something had happened.

Her arm was throbbing and swollen, and she tried to remember if, during all of her research into heinous injuries and crime epics, she'd ever learned how long one could go with a broken limb before repairing it became a moot point. At the moment, it was dead meat weighing down her shoulder, so she carefully stood while trying to balance her weight. Her feet had felt like needles when she'd gotten free of the wardrobe, and she didn't think she could walk yet. But she'd made it across the floor to a narrow window that was probably more for ventilation than anything else, too small to see much of the backyard, just a part of the lawn, the grove of snarled trees over a pond of mud that gave way to the cornfield beyond.

Someone was out there.

There was a woman, someone she didn't recognize, sitting on her knees near where the lawn met the grove. Georgia tried to knock on the window, but it was so thick with aged grime that she could barely make an audible sound in the attic itself.

And now clumsy footsteps downstairs, just below the attic hatch.

Mom, she thought, closing her eyes. *Please be my mom.*

Here goes nothing.

Georgia took a deep breath, and with everything she could, she screamed until she ran entirely out of breath. The footsteps downstairs stopped, and the woman in the yard turned, pausing before making her way back to the house.

Please, Georgia thought, and two things registered in her brain simultaneously.

One, the attic hatch had dropped open.

And two, there was a rusty machete lying between the hatch and where she kneeled.

55

Mark stared up into the darkness of the attic.
Take her face. Take her inside.

He was vaguely aware that the screen door in the kitchen had banged open and shut again, and there was a hot, growling pit in his stomach that seemed to ripple through his entire being. It was like nausea in reverse, a hunger that almost brought him to the floor. Mark clutched the wooden arms of the foldaway ladder and tried to steady himself. All of his weight felt like it was inside the cast now, and his legs felt disconnected somehow.

Ann.

He thought of her suddenly; had she been there? That wasn't right. She was still in South America. Cory had been there, but that wasn't right either.

Cory's inside. With us.

Mark moaned against the primal, surging lust for consumption in his gut. He had a moment of recollection, a sensory memory of Cory as he—or it, were they even separate entities at that moment?—had sunk its

CHAPTER 55

teeth into her throat, ripping it all the way back to her spine, her eyes gaping in disbelief at the sudden reality of her death.

Cory!

He thought he said it out loud, but he hadn't actually heard his voice. There were voices all around him, though, talking over him, a rising static of voices he recognized and others he didn't, like twenty radio stations chattering at once. He tried to say her name again, and it was as though something filled his throat, rendering him incapable of speech.

There was someone looking down at him from the attic.

There was someone standing in the hallway at the bottom of the stairs.

56

There's someone at the bottom of the ridge, Brute.
Brute lay flat on his side like a beached fish, peering at the narrow dirt path, watching the Japanese soldier who took a few tentative steps into view before slipping back into the overgrowth.

"It's him again," Hop mouthed, squatting and frozen, holding a finger to his lips as he crouched behind a massive patch of elephant ears. Brute held his position against the tropical heat that pressed against him like a physical force, and periodically, he would close his eyes for just a few seconds to focus on keeping his breathing even.

In, and out. In, and out.

The soldier had appeared alone on the path two nights before, and neither Brute nor Hop was sure why. He paced as if he was on patrol, but in the last twelve hours, he'd begun crying out over and over again, dissolving at times into quiet, uncontrollable laughter. Hop had picked up some Japanese phrases over the last few weeks, and the word that the man kept repeating had something to do with being hungry, something inside him that needed to eat.

"Maybe he's starving to death," Hop whispered. "Separated from his company?"

"Maybe," Brute agreed. The soldier walked in circles, muttering and giggling, almost out of their sight line, before resuming his endless pacing. "Maybe he just cracked up."

They watched and waited. Finally, when Hop was certain the soldier was coming no closer, he clutched the handle of his sheathed knife and gave a thumbs-up.

God, let us get home, Brute thought, and readied himself to cut across the path. Hop waved two fingers, and Brute moved fast and low, aware of every sound and movement, even the swooshing sound made by the drooping, two-foot leaves as he fell into place alongside his best friend, settling flat on the other side to catch their breath.

"What do we do?" Brute mouthed silently.

"Just wait, I guess," Hop replied. "Maybe we'll be out of here by New Year's, you think? Happy 1945 to us."

The soldier who had appeared along the path was now creeping closer, sizing up the ridge that began perhaps fifty feet along the path ahead of them and stretched out of sight, building into a rise that peaked behind them. The sandy dirt and rock had forged a kind of lip over the low vegetation where they hid, and the two young Americans drew into the shadow cast there as they heard the Japanese soldier hoist himself onto the rise. The soldier muttered to himself, his words unintelligible to the two teenage Americans, and every now and again, he'd respond to himself with a giggle, followed by something that sounded like a chant, phrases repeated over and over under his breath, barely audible through the stillness of the Pacific heat. He'd been in the area long enough for Brute to know that, eventually, the law of averages regarding their ability to stay hidden would catch up to them.

Hop slid his knife from his belt and turned, slowly, on his heels. He held out his hand, signaling for Brute to stay low, then moved ten feet or so toward the lip of earth where the ridge overhead began to slope downward. If the soldier faded to the left, Hop could—possibly, though it was a big if—make it up over the slope of ground behind him and catch him off guard.

If the soldier went right, there was almost no way he wouldn't see their position, even given the overgrown tropical plants that rippled and undulated in the dull sea breeze, and that would be that.

They waited.

The soldier's shadow began to seep across the ground, a formless shape that gradually found a human form, and it took everything Brute had to concentrate against the heat as he waited for his adversary to make a decision as to the nature of his widening patrol.

The soldier paused, then cut left as if something had caught his eye.

Hop was up and over the ridge in a flash, his blade in the man's neck, hand over the soldier's mouth, pulling him flat to the earth as dark jets of blood soaked their uniforms.

"Amanojaku, Amanojaku, Amanojaku," the soldier sputtered as Hop shifted his weight and his hand slipped from the young man's mouth.

CHAPTER 56

"Jacko, Jacko, sure," Hop admonished, and Brute considered, from his position near the bottom of the ridge, the absurdity of shushing a dead man.

"Christ," Brute hissed, "Hop, come on—"

"Stay low," Hop whispered sharply as the soldier died in his arms.

"Amanojaku," the soldier groaned, and Hop pressed his hand over the man's mouth.

"You know what that means?" Brute said quietly.

"No, don't know that one." Hop leaned into the young man's limp body, the smell of funk and sweat and the copper stench of hot blood. Brute could see that Hop was weeping as something overtook him without warning; the rage and horror at their situation rose to the surface of Brute's skin as though gasping for air. What the fuck gave anyone the right to do this? What gave any of them the right to do this—

The soldier's life gasped out of him, and as he died, his lips curled back in a grin.

Brute saw the misery in his friend's eyes turn to a primal rage, and he turned away as Hop dug his knife into the soldier's chin.

"Amanojaku, my fucking ass," Hop whispered. "Choke on it." Brute watched as Hop pushed the knife into the soldier's sneering face just above the muscle, jerking the dead man's head backward to face the sky as he cut flesh from bone.

God, Brute thought, letting the tears run down his cheeks and sizzle against his sunburned skin as he smelled the soldier's bowels go loose, Hop pulling the knife in a wide circle around the soldier's skull, the buzzing of flies and the sound of intermittent gunfire

JUNKMAN

somewhere on the island closing in on him, turning everything red. *God, please help me.*

57

God, please help me. Georgia didn't really believe in religion, but she had nothing else to lean on now as she stared down at the thing staring up at her.

It was nothing human, that was clear from a glance, and she barely gave herself the time to register the finer points of its form—the papier-mâché having pulled away to reveal that gawping, dried face of someone long dead yet somehow alive—before sitting back on her haunches, her balance coming back, her limp, heavy arm making her wince and gasp out loud; god, the pain was unreal, but she could still hold the machete by its handle with her good hand.

She had two real options: wait for it to come to her, or do whatever she could do to get out of that fucking attic.

Fuck it. Her mother wasn't coming, and the woman she'd seen outside was taking too long.

The thing started up the ladder, and Georgia crouched at the edge of the hatch, holding the machete out from her body at a right angle, locking her elbow and bracing it against her chest. If she fell fully forward and kept her arm locked, she could hit the thing head on with the blade, and hopefully, she could right her body in time to hit the ground on her good arm. If it didn't break, she might have a chance at getting down those stairs. And if she lost her good arm in the process, well... she hoped that Karen Kilgariff and Georgia Hardstark would do her story justice.

"*Hungry,*" the thing said in a voice that sounded nothing like anything she'd ever heard.

Georgia closed her eyes and let her weight shift forward as the pain in her arm took her consciousness.

58

Bill Auster stood at the edge of a cornfield on Route 41 and sighed as he watched two men lug a sheet-covered body from the ditch where a car had careened off the road and flipped over, flattening a ten-foot patch of cornstalks along with the driver.

The call from Ann Devold had unsettled him. Greatly. The call from Georgia Blevin before that had been suspect at best, but together, they painted an uncomfortable picture.

Namely, it sounded like Mark was headed down the same alcoholic path as a good half-dozen Devolds over the years. Auster hated to see it, but he'd gotten used to the way addiction ravaged its way through the countryside. It was a strange turn from what people used to expect in a small city like Galesburg: family, friends, communal scenes from holiday postcards, all that shit. Maybe it used to be that way; he'd certainly felt it as a kid, though perhaps that'd been through a distorted lens. The reality was a tragic photo negative. A steamroller of unemployment after the factories outsourced to other countries, followed by an endless, surging wave of alcoholism, cheap drugs, and a perpetual lack of upward mobility, opportunity. Mark Devold's family—along with a good half of the folks they'd graduated with, who had stayed in the area—had followed a similar pattern, though Tony's drug use and criminal activity had obviously gone above and beyond the norm. Still, sometimes erratic behavior—the kind that Mark had exhibited, by way of example—was a warning sign of, at the very least, harmful behaviors to oneself, though Auster acknowledged the slippery slope at play there.

"Mark Devold is dating my mom, Cory Blevin," Georgia had said to the dispatch unit on duty. "I don't know where she is, and I think there's something weird going on in his house." Auster had gotten her message just before the call about the accident, followed immediately by Ann getting in touch with him, and that was more than a little concerning. Hell, after everything the Devold family went through, he figured it was the least he could do to check on things for her.

"Steve," he called across the ditch to one of the officers taking notes from a woman who had narrowly missed being clipped by the ruined Honda. He checked his watch. Later than he'd thought. "I'm going to run, need to check on something for a friend. You need me here?"

"Nah," the officer called back. "Be safe, Lieutenant."

"No worries," Bill called, circling around the back of his car and sliding into the driver's seat. He started the car and felt the rush of air from the heater, which in turn gave him a chill against the cold October night. The radio filled the car with the serpentine bass line

CHAPTER 58

of Aerosmith's "Sweet Emotion" as he pulled onto the highway.

He reached for the switch for the flashers, then stopped short. No need. There was nothing to be concerned about; if anything, Mark was probably drunk and just making people worry. *Enough for a wellness check, but not enough to ruin anyone's night,* he thought. Bill sat back in the seat, singing along softly with Steven Tyler as a sign reading *Welcome to Galesburg - a Happy, Heartland Home for All!* slid past him.

59

There was a thrashing, thumping sound from upstairs, and as Ann ran back into the house and toward the hallway, she saw the girl fall from the attic as Mark cried out from under the cast, his voice dissolving into a throaty rage, and he staggered backward. The two were entangled at the top of the stairs, and there was a machete protruding from just below her brother's left shoulder, sunk in a good two inches. The girl looked at her and began crawling frantically toward the stairs, slipping and tumbling like a doll down the first few, and Ann could see that the girl's arm was broken, dangling painfully at her side. The girl screamed, sobbing in agony as the thing at the top of the stairs found its feet again, lumbering forward toward the staircase and fumbling with the machete until it had slid from the wound to clatter down the stairs.

"Mark!" Ann shouted, and the thing raised its head to gawp at her, Mark's eyes blinking in confusion from behind the leathery flesh. The girl was in the process of trying to flop down the rest of the stairs on her one good arm and her belly like a fish, and Ann waved at Mark, trying to keep his attention on her as she helped the girl to her feet.

"Ann?" The girl stared up at her. "Are you Ann?"

"Come on, come on," Ann pleaded, slipping her arm around Georgia's waist, helping her to her feet as the girl groaned in pain. "Come on, just a few more, just a few more—get down here and into the kitchen behind me!"

Ann turned back to the creature on the stairs.

Tony.

The body was unchanged, but it looked as though the thing wore the flesh of Tony's face as a Halloween mask: blank spaces where the eyes should have been, thick, ragged beard extended past the ragged jawline.

"Annie," the voice came from inside the mask as the thing made its way down the stairs with steady, lumbering intent. "Annie, is that you? What are you doing home?"

"Keep the *fuck away from* me," Ann hissed, her legs weak as the girl kneeled for a moment at Ann's side, staring in horror at the thing on the stairs. "Do you see it? My uncle Tony? Do you know what he looks like?"

"I don't see him," Georgia murmured, her voice rising in horror as tears leaked from the corners of her eyes. "It's my mom, holy shit, *no, no, it's my mom, it's wearing my mom's face—*"

"No, it isn't, no, it isn't," Ann said firmly. "It's fucking with us. Get to the kitchen and call someone, anyone, just do it!" She reached back and gave Georgia a gentle push toward the doorway. Georgia grunted against the pain in her arm, sucking in her sobs as she scrambled out of sight.

The thing reached the bottom of the stairs and stood, as if waiting for something, the wound in its shoulder leaking blood down the front of the costume. In its human hand, it held the machete.

"Yes." Ann's voice shook, and she took a deep breath. "I'm home. So are you."

"I never left," the thing replied. "Are you going to stay, Annie? So it can be like before?"

"Of course. We can be like that again," she teased, heart racing and bile pulling into her throat as the thing stepped toward her. She backed up toward the windows that lined the east wall of the dining room. "But you have to come to me..."

Ann glanced back at the curtains, which stood partially open. There had been a flash of movement outside, she was sure of it, someone moving quickly past the windows, and she realized that the front door still stood open.

A car was parked haphazardly in the driveway.

"So hungry," Mark groaned from under the costume, his voice only partially his now. "Need to eat, Annie. Need you in here with us."

It was on top of her before she could even react.

60

Whenever he dreamed about Lily, he pictured taking her to the park near L.T. Stone, his old grade school. He imagined what it might have been like to push her on the swing, to spin the merry-go-round, and he imagined what her laughter would have sounded like. He imagined what it would have sounded like when she called him Dad.

But Dara didn't like his drinking, or his family, and she had asked him to stay away from them. "It was just a night," she'd said. "It doesn't have to mean anything, and you don't have to feel guilty." And for a time, Mark believed that.

It was too late before it was too late, he'd decided after Tony had done what he'd done. Which wasn't true, of course. He knew that now, but now there was no choice at all.

I'm sorry, Lily, Mark thought. *I am so, so sorry.*

And then, standing there in front of him in the hall, Cory said she would stay. And he knew that, in spite of his guilt, in spite of the pain, everything was going to be okay.

And despite how hungry he was, Mark laughed.

61

It was on top of her before she could even react, knocking her backward, and Ann reached out to break her fall, clutching for anything she could and coming up with a handful of thick curtain. There was a wrenching sound as the rod ripped away from the wall, and the curtains fell on top of them, trapping the thing on top of her. Ann looked up at the face that stared down at her. No longer Tony, just the mask from the attic again, and she could see Mark's dead eyes behind it as he groped at her body. The lips of the skin mask began to part, as though strings were pulled from behind it, and as the dead flesh slowly grinned to reveal a mewling mouth filled with teeth, Ann swung and clutched at the thing, trying to roll it off of her.

"*Goddamn you!*" she screamed, managing to get her fingers along the edge of the mask, pressing her thumb to the paper as hard as she could and yanking backward. The dull moaning sound that had been emanating from the thing turned into a guttural wail, and its weight shifted just enough for her to catch the edge of the mask on the other side. Ann tore the flesh from the costume, the face coming off with a sound like paper tearing, and then it was Mark's face staring down at her, eyes wide in confusion and horror.

"Annie?" he said in disbelief, and she pushed away from the thing, tearing at it, dislodging its arm from the trunk, the head tearing away at the neck, dangling pathetically. Ann could see the machete just a few feet away where it had landed, and as she thrashed free of the curtain, Mark tried to get to his feet, wrestling with the clumsy bulk of the costume's remains.

Clutching the machete, Ann turned to see Mark, free of the costume now, pressed against the wall of the hallway like a child staring down at the mass of paper and glue. "It plays tricks, Annie, it plays tricks, all the things inside it—"

Ann shrieked with primal rage and brought the machete down on the remnants of the costume, swinging and chopping, bits of paper flying. *It play tricks, Annie, it play tricks, Annie, it plays tricks, Annie, it plays—*

"Ann!" The man's voice came from the kitchen, and Bill Auster stopped short of fully entering the room. "Jesus, oh, my god, Ann, what did you do, what did—"

"I killed it," she groaned, sinking onto her knees and dropping the blade on the floor with a loud clunk. "This goddamn thing, I killed it, I killed it, finally—"

"Ann," Georgia said, appearing at her side and speaking softly. "Put it down, Ann, please, okay? Put it down. It's done."

"What?" Ann looked at them both, incredulous at their concern and the horror they both wore on their faces. Georgia began to weep, and Bill stepped into the room at last, reaching for the machete, lifting it from the

CHAPTER 61

floor as gingerly as possible. "It plays tricks. You don't understand, Mark, he—Mark..." She looked around the room. The corner where Mark had been standing was empty, and only the three of them remained. "He was here, he was just here, standing over—"

"It's okay," Bill said. "It's okay, just... let's go in here, let's—I need to make a call, let's sit down. Okay? Let's have a seat and catch our breath here."

Ann looked from Bill to Georgia, then turned and looked again for Mark. Where did he go? He didn't have time to—

She looked down at the costume.

The huddled, butchered form of her brother lay in a heap, half-covered by the tangled curtains, a mess of blood and fabric.

It plays tricks.

"No," Ann wailed, and the word seemed to go on forever in her mind as she pointed at the dark, empty corner of the room. "No, no, I killed that *thing*. He was *there*. Mark was right there. *He was there!*" She dissolved into hysteria, crawling into the bloody mess of curtains and putting her arms around her brother's body, the face that was not his own staring with empty eyes toward the ceiling.

62

Bill Auster wondered at the nature of grief. He'd been inside the Devold house a few times, most recently after Tony Devold's arrest, when they'd searched the property for evidence of additional murders. Tony had alluded to having committed additional crimes, but there'd been nothing to suggest that was the case in their investigation. Of course, the media would have loved it if they'd discovered some Gacy-esque house of horrors with bodies and skeletons everywhere, but that was typical. It was easy to sensationalize something so horrible, to try to find meaning through exploitation of the most gruesome parts of ourselves. Grief was a hydra, a creature of many faces, and something not easily decoded by law, science, prayer ... any of it. You could take its head off, but it'd just grow another one to laugh at you.

Behind him, Ann Devold sat in the back of a squad car, and he'd foregone cuffs out of general respect for the family and situation. Of all things he might have witnessed that night, watching a woman hack her brother to death hadn't been on his list of possibilities. "The world deals in gravity," one of his instructors at the academy had once told him, "both as a matter of survival and matter of keeping us humble."

Thanks a lot, Auster thought. *Fuck humility.*

"What's going to happen to her?" Georgia Blevin lay on a gurney and had been sedated to combat the trauma of her broken arm. She was bruised up a bit, but she'd be okay. That was clear. "I mean... she thought... I don't know what she thought, but she didn't think it was Mark."

"Then who was it?" Auster said quietly.

"It was that thing," Georgia said simply. "That costume. It was... there was something inside it."

"Yeah," Auster agreed. "Her brother. Other than that, it was just a lot of paper all over the floor." He shook his head and looked back at the house. So much pain for one family.

"There was something inside it." There was no strength, no insistence in the statement. "Its face."

"What face?"

"The face, inside it," Georgia said, a vague concern now creeping in her voice. "The face, the thing's face."

"I don't know what you mean, we didn't find a face," Auster said as the EMT began wheeling the gurney toward the ambulance parked at the end of the driveway. "Listen, you rest, and I'll come get a statement when you're feeling up to it, okay?"

"Lieutenant?" Officer Haggerty appeared next to him with an umbrella, as it had started to drizzle. "Are we, uh, are we done here, sir?"

"Yeah," Auster sighed. "Just about. Just, uh, sit tight. With her." He marched carefully up the porch steps and into the darkened living room. The hallway where he'd found Ann attacking Mark was covered in blood, the curtains missing from the windows and on their way to the evidence room, which gave the space a stark, exposed feeling.

Upstairs, the bedrooms gave away no secrets; they were modestly kept clean. The attic hatch hung open; from what he'd gathered so far, Georgia Blevin had been hiding up there, which didn't make any sense as yet. He'd know more when he got her statement, but her arm was so badly broken that she was practically delirious, so getting her fixed up would be the first order of business.

Auster let the screen door clatter behind him as he stepped into the backyard. The landscape seemed infinite, which was the way of these houses sitting at the city limits. It was hard, in the face of days like this, not to feel isolated, to feel as though he was an island of strength unto himself, unable to keep anything from going off the rails. And wasn't that his job?

It was like anything else. We tricked ourselves into thinking we had control, and sometimes, luck found us. Other times...

Auster noticed, as he had during his previous visit just a week or so earlier, that a rickety wooden cross stood at the edge of trees along the property line. Tomato trellis? It didn't look like it, as there didn't seem to be any real evidence of a garden, or tomatoes, for that matter.

A dirty, vaguely human shape hung on the wood frame, something that looked like a big shell with one complete arm and a roundish head. A shitty scarecrow, he thought as he approached it, or an even shittier costume of some kind. It almost looked like a more complete version of what they'd found in the hallway around Mark's corpse, the chopped-up pieces of brittle plaster or papier-mâché or whatever it was, but of course, it was hard to say. Auster stood in front of it, studying it. The ragged holes in its face representing eyes and the slit mouth were unsettling, he had to admit.

A breeze rustled through the trees behind it and ripped into the cornfield beyond; somewhere far in the distance, he heard a train whistling through town. He thought of autumn and the slow fade of seasons evaporating into one another, the joys and secret terrors of childhood. Riding with Mark's uncle Tony to see Van Halen in high school. His marriage, his divorce, his job on the force, his life, all of their lives, bookended by one another in this, the hometown that, for one reason or another, they'd never left. The loves and pains they all shared. How they all kept going, in spite of all else, until one day, something finally stepped in front of you and said, "that's enough." It made him think of his grandmother's favorite Bible verse that hung on her kitchen wall over the sink. Psalm 71.

Though you have made me see troubles, many and bitter, you will restore my life again; from the depths of the earth, you will again bring me up.

"Happy Halloween," Auster muttered, tapping the scarecrow on its shoulder before turning and walking back toward the house.

Christopher Bevard is a critically-acclaimed horror author whose work has been featured in Rue Morgue, Cemetery Dance, Penny Dreadful, and Rag Shock, among others, and he is also the writer and producer of Cicatrix, a serialized horror podcast released by Sensory Eclipse Media, available wherever you get podcasts. He is an obsessive collector of E.C. Comics, his blood is made of 90% coffee and Zombie Dust pale ale, he loves spicy food, and, as we speak, he's a bit miffed that the Lament Configuration replica on his desk doesn't seem to work as advertised. He has a dog, a cat, and a wife he adores. He lives in Chicago but spends as much time as possible in New Orleans, his home away from home.

Join the mailing list, check out the author's other works, and learn more http://www.christopherbevard.com/.

BOOK CLUB QUESTIONS

(Warning: these contain spoilers!)

1. Do you think Brute is aware of the costume's influence on the family? Why or why not?

2. What do you think the "Junkman" costume symbolizes? Why?

3. How does grief manifest itself in the events of the story? In what ways do you think the characters are coping with trauma?

Discover more at
4HorsemenPublications.com

10% off using HORSEMEN10

www.ingramcontent.com/pod-product-compliance
Lightning Source LLC
LaVergne TN
LVHW041739060526
838201LV00046B/859